Seaton's Orchid

Chips Hardy

Chiselbury

For Ann and Tom

desuetude p 9

etiolated p14

In nature we never see anything isolated, but everything in connection with something else which is before it, beside it, under it and over it.

Johann Wolfgang von Goethe (attrib)

Few men realise that their life, the very essence of their character, their capabilities and their audacities, are only the expression of their belief in the safety of their surroundings.

Joseph Conrad, "An Outpost of Progress"

Chapter One

West Sussex

Even in a locality as bereft of social diversion as that surrounding Highleigh in West Sussex, an invitation to dine with Captain Ainsley Seaton at Laurel House was met with stiff resolve rather than alacrity.

As he brushed his ginger hair vigorously into submission, Dr Richardson reflected that the invitation would, in all probability, have been issued in the same spirit.

The Captain of course would be welcomed in the highest circles of the county, not to mention whatever vestiges of the smart set around Bognor had managed to come unscathed through four years on the Western Front. And having spent enough time there himself evading the Angel of Death to be invested with the Distinguished Service Order and Bar and the Legion d'Honneur, Seaton would be seen as quite a catch in the closes of Chichester too, no doubt.

All that social standing - and he's tucked away with us. The Lord giveth and the Lord setteth you down in Highleigh. Dr Richardson allowed himself a thin, knowing smile as he set down the brushes and took up his white tie; he enjoyed a reputation as the freethinker of the locality, although most of his speculative thinking was done alone, or at least silently.

He glanced over at his wife, Nancy, who was picking through her jewellery box for something the vicar's wife had not yet laid eyes on and decided once again to keep his observations to himself.

Captain Seaton kept a good table and a better cellar; the well tended gardens around Laurel House afforded delightful if formal views and entertaining walks; Foster, the Captain's phlegmatic seneschal, worked equal wonders with the kitchen garden and Nancy never failed to return home with a basket of vegetables and seasonal fruit; the gallery containing   collections of paintings and artefacts from his explorations in South Africa and latterly South America would keep legions of schoolboys quiet for hours; his wartime memorabilia were discreet, his cigars excellent, his brandy ancient and his generosity in such matters irreproachable.

Why then did one's heart sink to one's boots as one gunned the Bullnose Morris up the twisting lanes leading to Laurel House and its spruce if lonely façade?

Melancholy. That was the top and bottom of it.

"Have you ever observed the way Seaton looks at people?" Forgetting his prior resolution, he broached his theory to Nancy who as ever ignored him. "It's just like he was measuring you, reluctantly, for a shot." He was pleased with that so he pressed on, "Yes, he's like a sad sniper."

"Must you talk piffle?" complained Nancy absently. She decided on the faithful pearls. The vicar's wife may have seen them before but she certainly couldn't match them, not on this or any other occasion. She held them against her throat for inspection in the mirror and turned her head to survey herself quizzically out of the corner of a practised eye.

The doctor watched his wife at her toilette for a moment. There was a thinly disguised intensity about her preparations this evening; the papers, powders and sprays in disarray upon her dressing table, her hair newly crimped, the jade green crepe de chine draped around her thickening form all bore witness to that.

"Fresh blood!" he remembered. "Vicar's bringing that grand panjandrum down from Chichester, isn't he?"

"Dr Houghton-Copley. He holds some lay position at Lambeth Palace, if Enid is to be believed." Nancy doubted the vicar's wife would embellish the credentials of her social connections but it paid to remain prudent in such matters.

"Thank God it's not a bishop," snorted the doctor, who felt obliged to promulgate his freethinking principles even to a wife past caring. "May get a game of billiards after dinner."

"I believe he's travelled himself." Nancy turned her head to survey her pearls out of the other eye. "He and the Captain may care to swap experiences."

The doctor doubted that. He'd not had ten minutes on the subject with the Captain over the entirety of their acquaintance, a matter of five years now. It rankled slightly that all their transactions had been social; the Captain made an annual pilgrimage to a doctor resident in Harley Street, explaining that the exotic nature of the tropical illnesses he had succumbed to required nothing more than occasional but specialist consultations.

To Dr Richardson's eye, Captain Seaton was reasonably active but in indifferent health. Beri-beri would have taken its structural toll and there had been talk of bullet and shrapnel wounds. His tall frame had clearly once been lithe as a panther's but now it gave the barest hint of an incipient faltering. And a slight dragging of the left leg that the doctor congratulated himself would be imperceptible to most.

He returned to his wife and the arrival of another world traveller to Highleigh's small corner. "You don't think we're in danger of intelligent conversation, do you?"

"We may be, if you don't monopolise the evening with your fatuous attempts to entertain."

She walked over to her husband, handed him the string of pearls and turned so he could fasten the clasp about her neck. He abandoned his tie and his waspish riposte; her maid was downstairs pressing his dress trousers (they were not an extravagant household) and he felt it incumbent on him to respond in kind.

3

~~~~~

Clover Maitland kept a firm grip on the wheel of her father's decrepit Hispano-Suiza and peered intently through the midges and the dappled late afternoon sunlight as she steered the old car up the twisting lanes towards Laurel House. She had large hands, sculptor's hands some of her kindlier acquaintances had said, although Clover, in deference to her late father's eminence in the British Arts and Craft Movement, was a dedicated potter and calligraphist.

She was a large, raw-boned girl, wrapped in scarves and throws from Constantinople and beyond, capped with an outsized tam-o'-shanter in vivid, home-dyed wools and enfolded in a similarly constructed cardigan in mainly complementary hues.

Ursula had woven both hat and cardigan, so Clover would wear them at every opportunity. She would wear them until they disintegrated or until Ursula had evolved another palette of vegetable dyes based on Wiccan principles and insisted that Clover adopt her new spectrum.

Ursula, for her part, preferred to wear her furs in winter and her leathers in summer, with yards of dazzling silk and heavy jewellery in unlikely shapes and combinations. Ursula's spirit lay with the Russians, as Clover would tell anyone who showed the slightest interest. Although in the country around Highleigh few remained unaware of her Russian affinities.

Clover and Ursula had met at school, roomed in London whilst attending art school together, had tramped around the antiquities of Rome, Athens and Constantinople in each other's shadow and now occupied the converted Smithy that Clover's father had refurbished for more aesthetic pursuits, before the Spanish flu had carried him off.

4

"We're going to be bloody early again," moaned Ursula as she ducked beneath the shallow windscreen to try and ignite yet another cheroot.

The air in the cockpit of the Hispano-Suiza, already thick with hot oil, old leather and Chanel No. 5, now filled with the acrid smell of cheap Dutch tobacco. Ursula's allowance would not stretch to Sobranie and Clover refused to sponsor her friend's abuse of her lungs in this way; Ursula's cheroots thus served as a tacit if vengeful statement of Ursula's financial independence, which in fact was largely illusory.

"The vicar's bringing somebody new to talk to," said Clover, her eyes tearing at the pungent smoke. "I think he's been to China. Something to do with the church."

"I'm not sitting through lantern slides." Ursula sank back into her seat and regarded the sunlight dancing through the banked hedgerow beside her with venom. "And I am not contributing to poor heathen piccaninnies."

"Coolies," corrected Clover automatically. A generous soul in most things, she had inherited her father's pedantry and occasionally slipped unknowing into the blind intransigence of the pedagogue. "Anyway, if the Reverend Attwater is anything to go by, he'll be High Anglican not Bible Fellowships or anything like that."

"Don't suppose he'll bring any opium." Ursula gave one of her celebrated pouts to signal that her sulk was over and they both laughed uproariously.

"Why do we go, Clovy?" she said a mile or two later. "You know we won't enjoy it. Eating well done beef and watching the good Captain suffering in our presence. It's really too demanding."

"We go because we're asked, I suppose." Clover shook the conundrum away. "That's what society is, isn't it? Joining together when you'd rather not."

Clover thought about Captain Seaton. She was never

quite comfortable around him, not that he could be in any way responsible for that. He was always courteous, attentive, solicitous even, in his own quiet way but still there was such an awkward formality around their dealings together. Had she known him long enough to call him Ainsley? Although Ursula would be beastly if she did.

Clover had never been good with men. She didn't understand them and she turned into a neighing Clydesdale if in their society for too long. But Captain Seaton caused her more than the usual confusions and alarums she experienced in associating with his sex. He seemed to embody everything she assumed a man might wish for himself and yet, while he didn't seem dissatisfied with life, he didn't seem altogether pleased to be in the middle of it. When Ursula had talked about him suffering in their presence she had as usual nailed the matter, the witch.

Except that none of it made any sense. And Clover liked things to make sense.

Seaton was well travelled and accomplished, a professional soldier, a seasoned explorer and he'd done extraordinary things in the war. And he could draw. He could really draw. Even Ursula was unable to sustain the condescending smile she reserved for aspiring amateur artists, in the face of sheaf after sheaf of sketches and drawings he had reluctantly unearthed from the large mahogany plan chest in the gallery one afternoon.

Ainsley Seaton was neither aspiring nor amateur but, to Clover's great perplexity, he wasn't an artist either. He could have been, simply by picking up a pencil and taking himself and his art seriously or flippantly or any old way at all. But he wouldn't.

He'd come to tea at the Smithy once and poked through all her pots and her fonts and her own inept works in pen and ink. And you could tell by the care with which he looked at each piece, that he was assessing, appreciating and discriminating with the eye of a man who not only knows what he's looking at but can do something to match or better it. But he wouldn't do anything with it. Or anything much of anything else, really, come to that.

"I'd like to do his head in bronze," said Ursula, reading her mind as ever, "and kick it."

With that she flicked her cheroot into the tinderbox hedging and Clover steered the huge old car into the final approaches.

~~~~~

Ainsley Seaton stood at the French windows at the end of the gallery at Laurel House and watched the swallows dipping over his rolling lawn to snap up insects in the setting summer sun. He'd seen many aerial predators at work, from snake eagles in the veldt to Fokker D.VII's above the Marne, and he paid close attention to the precision turns, the mid-air taking of prey and the instinctive responses to the flight paths of fellow hunters. Their grace in flight he left to other eyes.

Turning away from the carnage, his eye caught the Witoto dart case that hung above its calabash of poisoned cotton, now desiccated and harmless, labelled and pinned to the wall that ran uninterrupted the length of the gallery. The position of the strap had changed fractionally and the case now hung at an unfamiliar angle. The change was subtle but this break in consistency troubled him. He wouldn't leave the room without redressing it.

The dart case itself was made of incised bamboo and hung from a strap made of vegetable fibre covered in some form of resin. Fairly typical of the deep forest tribes of the North-west Amazon, case, darts, strap and calabash looked to be fading in the light, like vegetal spectres against the polished West Sussex panelling. On closer inspection, Seaton saw that the fibres of the strap around the panel pin were finally rotting away. Everything rotted in the jungle. Some things took days, some weeks and some years but everything rotted in the end. The entropy was inevitable and as all embracing as the tree canopy.

He gave a small start. Entropy, canopy, he was teetering on the brink of wordplay. He adjusted the strap of the dart case to return the quiver to its original position and wondered, momentarily, about what he could apply to arrest the rot. He looked along the line of Amazonian weapons, gourds, necklaces and instruments that hung the length of the wall and knew it was futile. Everything returned to the mulch.

The hardwood sculptures and the tribal artefacts from his earlier time in South Africa, although older, stood sturdy and vibrant in their central cases. They had stood the test of time, these bright remnants of treks across the veldt, laagering around Durban, his recuperation in the Cape once he'd taken that round in his leg in Colenso and the long years of regimental service that followed it.

Surprisingly, given his experiences in France, that first wound was still a fresh memory. Sometimes he could still feel the hot impact of it. The simple, brutal fact of it, amongst the screaming confusion of battle. He could still hear the confident shouts of the Boers as his men scrabbled to drag him off a hillside their General Staff had turned into an abattoir.

If the South African campaign had been a mess, the memories of that time and the mementos he had returned with retained a clarity and a robustness, vivacity almost, that made him feel somehow awkward. As if embarrassed by the exuberance of his own youth.

The Amazonia by contrast was both entropic and miasmic. Things blurred, fell apart and sunk down. Other things overtook them, sprouting through and above them, aggressively seeking the sun until they too fell back in the futile race for space and time. And then they rotted.

He rubbed at his right thigh at these thoughts of desuetude. The muscles stiffened in the cool of evening, a daily reminder that he too was curling at the edges, heading more perceptibly every day back into the leaf mulch at the base of more vigorous trees. As if he needed reminding, he shook his head in mild exasperation. He had no need for prompts amid his permanent apprehension.

He was a tall, slim man of a once athletic build with the slight bow in the legs of the cavalryman. His regular and pleasing features, already etched with the traces of jungle fever and battle, were becoming ever more drawn. Soon he would border on the gaunt. He'd never sported a moustache and had formed the erroneous if not entirely incomprehensible impression that if he did, he'd look like a haunted card sharp. His back was beginning to stoop and his broad shoulders were a little rounded now. But, for all that, he moved with a slow and agile grace and was capable of sudden bursts of earnest vitality. It was simply his grey eyes that never altered in their calculating and sometimes wary observation.

He heard the trim footfalls of Foster's gleaming black brogues moments before his ex-sergeant doubled into the gallery, then stood on the balls of his feet, head up and alert with arms akimbo in his characteristic welterweight posture. He coughed discreetly and entirely superfluously into a battered but manicured fist to attract his Captain's attention.

"We've some early birds, Captain," he said in answer to Seaton's raised eyebrow. "Mrs Simmons was wondering whether to serve tea or fruit cup. Bit early for sherry, she reckons."

Helen Simmons was Seaton's housekeeper and Foster's inamorata, a relationship nobody acknowledged. Her husband Harry was missing presumed dead near

Ypres and, given that the German mine which detonated under his earthworks had turned over two acres of Flanders' mud in its conflagration, the presumption was a fairly safe one. However, Helen Simmons, a staunch and warm-hearted lady in her early forties, thought it only decent to offer her husband the benefit of the doubt and remained a widow in waiting. Her one concession in the matter was Foster, whom she welcomed into her bed and her affections with a similar proviso that such domestic consolation should not interfere with the balance of the household.

At the end of every evening Foster would see the household off to bed and then take the master set of keys and secure the guns, the cellars, the pantries and the gallery doors, before making his rounds outside the house to check the windows, outer doors and even the coal hole. Only when he was satisfied all was well and quiet would he walk briskly over to the tiny cottage Helen Simmons occupied behind the kitchen garden. Even then he kept off the path and stuck to the discretionary silence of the lawn.

Foster's own room on the top, servants' floor was laid out in his habitual pristine barrack room order, so it was impossible to deduce whether he was in occupation or not. Even so he sometimes spent an evening up there to buff or iron or lie on the bed smoking a Players and inspecting the Daily Sketch, for form's sake. Seaton appreciated the gesture. The maids of course were too in awe of the steward's position and too grateful for their own to say anything at all.

Helen Simmons remained Mrs Simmons to them all. Probably even between herself and Foster, Seaton was wont to think. His ex-sergeant intuitively accepted his company commander's need for quiet, unexceptional order and would do all in his power to accede to it and ensure others respected it.

"Who's jumped the gun this time?" Seaton's voice though soft had a lilt to it, and a steely edge somewhere deep below.

"Miss Maitland is parked up in the lane watching her friend finish a cheroot, sir." Foster's eyes missed nothing; it had kept them both alive some nights outside the wire. "And the vicar's wife has arrived in the dog cart."

The men exchanged the briefest of glances, too polite to comment on Mrs Attwater's arrival. They both knew that only her husband's vehement insistence that he accompany his eminent guest down from the Cathedral and directly to Laurel House could have forced her into the cart and onto the road. The vicarage horse, though placid and broken winded enough to avoid its own call-up, seemed to hold her in a constant state of alarm.

"A little cold in the summer house still, I expect." Seaton looked out across the lawns, through the swallows to the freshly painted gazebo with its trailing roses.

"Not all that comfortable, sir," opined Foster. "I'll set up in the drawing room if I may."

Seaton nodded. He waited for the man to leave.

"One more thing, sir," Foster cleared his throat. "Mrs Simmons wonders if there's anything she should know about Dr Houghton-Copley."

"I think we're all in the same situation there, Foster." Seaton sounded a little gruff. New people always involved some degree of accommodation and defining quite how much was always a precarious matter.

"In the line of his diet, sir. No special requirements, do you suppose?"

"A diplomat for the Church of England," mused Seaton, "must hold a pretty robust digestion."

"And a travelling man of course, sir," Foster added. "Mustn't forget that."

Seaton caught his own lank reflection in the French

windows as the summer light died outside. No, he thought, mustn't ever forget that. And, leaving Foster to attend to his early birds, he went upstairs to dress.

~~~~~

The Reverend Duncan Attwater kept close to his plush corner of the diocesan Rolls Royce and peered with some apprehension at the august Anglican personage who had claimed both kinship and a favour from him and now occupied the opposite corner. The bishop's private chauffeur steered their stately course towards Highleigh, removing his gloved hand from the wheel solely to sound a majestic if doleful klaxon on first sight of any bicyclist, pedestrian or carter impinging on the Episcopal delegate's view.

Gazing without much evidence of curiosity at the countryside bordering the lane, Dr Lambert Houghton-Copley was causing the Reverend Attwater all kinds of mental discomfort, from bewilderment to outright trepidation.

Firstly, Dr Houghton-Copley claimed cousinship through a sequence of great aunts that baffled him. And more surprisingly, this man – a discreet and influential dragoman of the highest ecclesiastical courts in the land – had requested a service from him that apparently only he could supply.

The importance of this service had become apparent from the moment he arrived in Chichester, as requested, to meet with Dr Houghton-Copley for the first time. He had never been so well received or courteously entertained in the Cathedral environs during his few hours waiting for Dr Houghton-Copley to be freed from a series of "irksome but inevitable" meetings with the bishop's private office. He'd experienced a totally different level of china and patisserie at tea where a canon, whose name and function the Reverend Attwood in his agitation had immediately

12

forgotten, had displayed detailed knowledge and unprecedented interest in the entirely unexceptional career that had led him to the living at Highleigh.

One of the Reverend Attwater's most consistent Christian attitudes was his equanimity towards his perennial lack of preferment within the diocese and indeed the Anglican Communion at large. He had clearly reached as far as he was going to go. Lesser men had gone further and maybe that was part of God's plan. He had accepted his lot.

What he now found almost impossible to accept was his sudden immersion in the more recherché circles of power, and his discovery that the real power to shape policy lay altogether elsewhere. In fact, it seemed that these matters worked in an entirely different and almost intangible way, where a .rarefied halation of arcane knowledge, influence and design floated through the institution seamlessly to shape the church's future action.

Sixty now, short, rotund, with a sanguine complexion especially marked on the dome of his head with its corolla of white hair, the Reverend Attwater looked very much a country parson of the Punch Magazine variety. And, indeed, he was a simple man but not an unintelligent one. Being left in a corner chair while senior functionaries fussed and fidgeted around Dr Houghton-Copley's presence in Chichester, he had begun to perceive this precious mist of powerful forces at work.

Moreover, he found that being established as the cousin of a man of mysterious and unqualified influence had endowed him with faculties and a standing he had never thought to achieve.

One of the private secretaries had forgotten himself sufficiently to presume on the Reverend Attwater's family connection with the doctor and extol the wonderful discretion of the man, the respect he engendered in the highest spheres and the feats of diplomacy and high policy he had accomplished with his customary anonymity. He thinks I'm in on all this, marvelled the Reverend Attwater, and, to his minor moral discomfort, he did nothing to disabuse the man. This tacit confirmation of his privy knowledge led to further partial confidences which, while being wholly beyond his immediate recognition, demonstrated flatly that he had been taken up in some manner by the great and the good.

The whole bizarre change of station had started with his receipt of a letter from Lambeth Palace two weeks before. This had caused him to remain standing while he opened it, so that his wife could not peer over his shoulder. Houghton-Copley introduced himself in the most cordial terms, alluding to his elevated association with Oxford University and his extra-ordinary association with the Chancellor's office at Canterbury. It then outlined the trail of great aunts and remote cousins that bestowed their mutual kinship and hinted that he would like to interview the Reverend upon a personal matter.

Both the Reverend and his wife were agreeably surprised and not a little daunted at this newfound social connection. His wife, Enid, several years his junior and of a somewhat nervous disposition, was particularly eager that Nancy Richardson should meet the cousin if at all possible, and he felt he ought to be charitable about this, given the discrepancies in both their ages and their jewel cases.

Then, one Saturday afternoon, as he was tiptoeing through a variation of a sermon for the morrow, his telephone had rung. This event, unusual in itself, was made all the more exceptional with Dr Houghton-Copley's being announced by a rather etiolated woman's voice from within the hallowed interiors of Lambeth Palace itself.

The Reverend Attwater, ever nervous of the instrument, managed to restrain himself from bellowing into the mouthpiece in his customary involuntary manner when the doctor's mellow voice gently wished him good day. Indeed, it was all he could do not to squeak when returning his compliments and hoping he might be of service.

"My dear cousin, the very thing!" Houghton-Copley sounded delighted at his acuity. "You see I wish to hold an extended interview with a parishioner of yours. Upon a matter of personal interest. A Captain Ainsley Seaton."

"He's a very private man," the Reverend Attwater had burbled before he could adjust his tone. "Inordinately so."

"But a friend?" Houghton-Copley was quietly insistent.

"I believe I could claim that."

"And it would cause you no inconvenience to introduce me?"

No inconvenience certainly, but a considerable amount of discomfort after Sunday Service the following day, when he'd drawn the good Captain aside to inveigle him into some kind of social commitment. At the memory of it, Reverend Attwater turned towards the familiar surroundings scudding past his window and blew his nose into his best paisley handkerchief, as if in some way this needless evacuation could mask the misgivings once again rising to disturb him.

The Captain had stood in the church porch with a downcast look that suggested a personal Calvary but had acquiesced after a momentary and instantly repressed grimace of pain. He shook the Reverend's hand. He would of course be delighted to meet the Reverend's eminent cousin. A traveller too, was it? He wasn't sure if he could in all honesty be of any service other than to give him dinner though. But, yes, they would make up a party, a dinner party.

15

"Mrs Simmons will enjoy that," he had said, notably excluding his own feelings on the matter.

And now, two weeks later, the Reverend Attwater peered across at the substantive but shadowy figure comfortably ensconced in his corner of the car and wondered what kind of ecclesiastical power game he had let his diffident parishioner in for.

North-west Amazon

Some five thousand miles away and long years before, Seaton sat on deck of the steam launch Guerrita and scanned the far shoreline. Beneath him the Igara Parana River ran sluggishly down to join the Amazon. Signs of life amongst the variegated and dense foliage were restricted to wisps of butterflies and the occasional lizard, no sooner glimpsed than left behind as the Guerrita plodded its way up into deep river country. But for a man with his eye, a few seconds was all that was necessary. Already that afternoon he had spotted a couple of yellows he thought he'd never be able to capture, flitting back into the shade of the trees.

He made at least two such discoveries every day, and had been on some steamer or another for the past thirty. The long haul on the Booth Line from Liverpool to Para and on to Manaos had left him relatively confident of his painting materials and resources. However, once they had delivered themselves into The Amazon Steam Navigation Company's care aboard the S.S. Carolina to make their way up to Tarapaca, each day showed how inadequately he was equipped to deal with the life around him in all its clamorous and multihued variety.

By the time they had arrived at Tarapaca, then marking the frontier between Brazil and Peru, and boarded the Guerrita, commandeered for their private purpose through some lofty interior ministry connection of the

16

expedition's leader Sir Everard Northmore, Seaton had given up trying to categorise the colours he was surprised by. Instead he determined to make the best of whatever he faced with whatever he'd brought.

He spent the heat of the day in his berth, sorting through his tubes, tubs and japanned mixing pans, trying to summon up the ingenuity he knew he'd need once he got started. He repeated his mantra that the grand old men had needed only alizarin crimson, cadmium red, cadmium yellow, cadmium lemon, French ultramarine and cobalt blue. But he also knew that none of the grand old men had taken on the rain forest.

He was, at least, still convinced that watercolour had been the right medium for the job. In the veldt, he'd been able to crate canvases, stretching frames, oils and mediums onto the regimental ox-cart and forget about them till he wished to start work. The finished canvases would dry steadily in the warm Cape air.

Here there was no chance of that. From what Northmore had told him, he'd as much chance of carrying in a grand piano as the necessary accoutrements of the painter in oils. And even if he were to succeed in setting them all up in the heart of the forest, the frames would warp, the canvases seep and run and his brushes rot.

A few feet away across the decking, Sir Everard Northmore, baronet, was digging out his pipe to reward himself with a smoke before yet another inventory check. The expedition manifests lay pinioned under a sturdy foot, though the possibility of a freak gust whipping them up and into the murky waters was remote.

Northmore took nothing for granted, though, when it came to travelling properly equipped for success. That was one of the reasons he'd brought along his amanuensis, the biologist Dr Munby, who was below in his cabin fussing with specimen jars. On their return, Northmore would deliver papers on the expedition's findings to the Royal Geographical Society, the Royal Society, the Travellers' Club and an extraordinary convention of interested parties from the senior universities. Munby would make sure he wasn't talking through his hat.

During one of Munby's few forays into after dinner conversation, Seaton had learned that this symbiotic relationship was by no means unique amongst naturalists in the academic world, and both parties seemed perfectly satisfied by it. Dr Munby gained field experience, an association with august and publicised enterprises and the freedom to pursue his own researches, which would be published as follow-ups and supports to the great man's original pronouncements. Northmore, for his part, retained his position as Society's most active patron of scientific enquiry and received the plaudits due a gifted amateur who caused regular revisions to established theories.

The busy little Lancastrian with his pale skin, large red ears and drooping lower lip would bustle around Sir Everard so attentively that some unkind tongues had suggested the biologist had been bred in the baronet's gun dog kennels. Northmore, Munby's polar opposite in appearance with his tanned and determined expression, his bristling moustache, broad shoulders and centred gait, was doubtless aware of the gibe and seemed to play lightly upon it for his private amusement.

Nonetheless, he had set Munby upon the world's stage, albeit as a side player, while the biologist was in no doubt as to his indispensability in the great man's inventory.

Quite how he, Seaton, figured on that list, he had yet to ascertain. He had met Northmore in South Africa, where the man held substantial estates, and in London, where Society inclined them to meet across a not entirely different succession of watering holes. Both men belonged to the Travellers and the In and Out. While Northmore was a fellow at the RGS, Seaton had often attended lectures there. Seaton was aware of Northmore's pedigree in natural history and exploration and, through an intermediary in one of the more select salons in Belgravia, Northmore had become aware of Seaton's exemplary military record and his somewhat incongruous but active interest in painting.

Seaton had returned to Highleigh after a long deployment in Africa with some misgivings. His incarceration under the fusty ministrations of his one surviving grandparent threatened to drive him to distraction. He'd undergone it once before on recuperating from wounds received at Colenso and it had sent him back to the Cape. Now the open-ended nature of his stay overwhelmed him. Rescue came in the shape of Northmore. Again, at the prompting of the Belgravia salon, the baronet suggested Seaton tried his "painting hand" at the exotic flora of the Amazon basin.

Seaton had spent many days in town with Northmore while the latter drew up plans for forays into one forest or another; and as many days in Highleigh wondering what the continent could yield up to him. Indeed, the days grew into months. The chief reasons for delay were periodic changes of focus from the prospective backers of each expedition. Things medicinal, minerals precious or semi-precious, vegetal foodstuffs or raw materials: everything was considered, costed, projected and re-assessed. The lines of priority were drawn and re-drawn. Time and again it seemed that some consensus had been achieved and funds were on the way, only for plans to be upended again.

In fact, over two years passed before Northmore, with the ink drying on some highly confidential commercial commissions, telegraphed Seaton to ask him if he still had a hankering to "daub in the jungle?"

Seaton's stiffening leg and imminent redeployment to India prompted him to take half pay and join the expedition he'd signed on for in spirit at Northmore's first invitation. The delay had been no bad thing as his technique with the brush had improved somewhat and his service pay along with it.

Northmore thereby gained a serviceable and self-funding artist for his expedition and Seaton the opportunity to paint and draw in an adventurous continent as yet unknown to him. Another of Northmore's symbiotic relationships, the Captain wondered?

The American contingent, Brandon Cotterill, stood in the stern in jodhpurs and leather puttees, sighting in two rifles from his extensive armoury. Wary of the upscale East Coast provisioners who'd equipped him, he'd made several previous attempts to sight in on riverside targets, but had been politely but firmly requested to desist by captain or mate, because of the number of unseen habitations and settlements that flanked the Amazon and its extension, the Issa.

"Thought this was a goddam wilderness." Cotterill would stand down with ill grace. "Every time I range in on a tree seems some aboriginal's got his family hunkered down behind it."

Cotterill was the scion of an East Coast steel magnate and an Ivy League graduate. He was also the bearer of a substantial bursary from his father which, in Northmore's eyes, made him an important team member. Not quite in the Munby league, but crucial even so.

Blond, athletic and freckled, Cotterill sustained a jaunty bearing, habitually resting his hand on the military holster housing his Colt automatic and favouring cheroots. He had not served as a soldier though, of that Seaton was pretty certain. The affair back in San Christoval had made it pretty clear.

After two days on the river, they'd been required to stop off for the Guerrita's engineer to instigate some long overdue repair. The party had found itself traipsing around the dilapidated shops, kept mainly by Chinese and Moroccan Jews – as indeed were the bulk of the smaller trading outlets along the river - picking over this and that and passing the time before returning to the launch for dinner.

They'd been enjoying a warm beer in one of the cleaner establishments when a gang of highly intoxicated rubber workers, or seringueiros, had invaded the store, rummaging through the goods and demanding a "trago", the complimentary tot of white rum usually offered to customers. When the owner pointed out quite reasonably that they had not bought anything yet, the rubber workers produced their long bladed "facas" and announced their intention of helping themselves and then toasting his dead body. One of them then knocked the owner to the ground.

Dr Munby was out in the muddy street at once, looking anxiously over his shoulder, only to see Brandon Cotterill hard on his heels, bandoliers swinging and holstered Colt still firmly in place.

Seaton and the baronet, who remained in the bar, regarded their colleagues' exit with some surprise. Then both men stood up and walked steadily over to the seringueiros. They kept about three paces between them: enough to increase their firing arc, but not so much as to be isolated from the other in close combat. Northmore produced a small Browning pistol from his canvas shoulder bag and showed it to the drunks.

The seringueiros left with as much haste as Dr Munby but with considerably more noise, scrabbling into their canoes before any bullets began to fly. Seaton helped the owner to his feet and then he and Northmore returned to their table.

"Handy little bugger," opined Northmore, holding up his Browning as the owner returned with a complimentary bottle of the undrinkable spirit. "What are you carrying?"

"Pocket watch and my pipe," replied Seaton. He made a vague gesture towards the door, through which Cotterill and Munby were now gingerly returning. "I took Mr Cotterill to be our firing party."

Northmore looked at Seaton steadily for some moments, before allowing himself a small, patrician smile. "I'm very glad you're with us, Captain."

And the affair passed off. But as the party walked back to the launch and an indifferent chicken for supper, Seaton felt somewhat more comfortable amongst them. The incident suggested he had something quiet but complete to offer the enterprise and that this had been recognised by one of the best of men.

West Sussex

A different world, thought Seaton, as he stared at the shirt studs in his hand and then up to the perplexed expression on his reflection in the wardrobe mirror. A lost world, lost even in the quality of remembrance he could bring to it. An innocent past haunted by the future he knew lay in store.

He heard the old, familiar cough and found Foster standing in the dressing room door. The man had changed into his evening dress and held a silver tray in his gloved hand. He appeared somewhat perturbed and when he started to speak, Seaton had the impression it was not for the first time.

"Everyone's here, Captain." There was an uncertain tone to his normally relaxed voice. "They're in the gallery. Have been for some time."

Seaton glanced at his watch. Where on earth had the time gone to?

The company had dispersed itself about the gallery by the time Seaton made his entrance. The Reverend Attwater, dry sherry in hand, had rejoined his wife and was stationed beside the central stand housing Seaton's trench memorabilia, listening politely to whatever opinions Dr Richardson felt obliged to propound. The doctor's wife had abandoned them and was peering at one of Seaton's landscapes of the veldt as if somehow the vision vexed her. She pecked at her sherry whilst directing an old-fashioned look at the wildebeest sniffing the air in their turn for lion, leopard or whatever else nature was sending along for their destruction.

Clover and Ursula were drinking something green, which meant they had commandeered Foster and presided over its concoction. They stood further towards the French windows, now curtained, and inconveniently close to the plan chest. Seaton hoped they wouldn't play upon the presence of a newcomer to inveigle him to unlock it. Ominously, their attention was fixed on the three-quarter profile this newcomer presented to the assembly.

The diplomatist stood at the far end of the gallery, holding his sherry glass in both hands and peering up at the furthermost Amazonian exhibit on the long wall. Seaton, although aware he had formed no particular preconception of the man, still found himself disconcerted. In his French cut frockcoat, brocaded silk waistcoat, gold watch fob and ivory silk soft shirt, Dr Houghton-Copley did not look much of a traveller. His was a pallid complexion which, with the dark shadows under his eyes, spoke of the sickroom rather that the portside out berth.

He was of medium height and build and somewhat round-shouldered. Although not quite running to fat, there was a softness about his stocky frame and a pudgy aspect to his hands. As he turned his gaze to some artefact a little further down the display, Seaton could distinguish the man's fine straw- coloured hair, tending to grey and swept back from a high forehead, fine arched eyebrows and saurian green eyes. With great deliberation Houghton-Copley unfolded a delicate pair of gold-rimmed spectacles and pulled them onto his nose. Then he leaned forward, like a quizzical kestrel, and peered shrewdly at the Witoto dart case.

Seaton at once wondered what secret it could possibly offer up to him but he shook away the thought and advanced towards the man, his hand extended.

"Dr Houghton-Copley," he said. "Good of you to come. I hope we can repay the effort."

"Nonsense, Captain!" replied his guest with professional self-effacement. "You are essential reading, I'd say. I'm lucky to have the opportunity to peruse." He favoured Seaton with a brief twinkle over his gold frames. "And I'm deeply appreciative of your hospitality."

"I understand you've travelled extensively," said Seaton, taking his sherry from Foster's tray and registering from the eye contact that he might yet talk for a few moments longer, before Mrs Simmons required them all to start eating.

Houghton-Copley brushed this aside with an expansive gesture. "Oh, here and there, you know. To some greater purpose, I dare say." He flashed the twinkle at Seaton again, a perfect replica of the previous. "Not like you, Captain. Your journeys have that personal element, don't they?"

"Most of the time I was on active service." Seaton sipped his sherry. It was warm. "Apart from the Amazon, of course. I was there in a private capacity."

"But I see in your achievements," Houghton-Copley indicated the gallery in general, "the constant presence of personal enquiry and artistic reflection."

Seaton was about to observe that his activities in no way merited any such lofty observations when Clover appeared at his elbow, with Ursula brooding behind.

"Oh, Captain Seaton is a fine artist." Clover beamed at them over the remains of her green aperitif. "Though he will allow nobody to say so."

"Which is why you will insist, I suppose," added Ursula before waving her empty glass at the hovering Foster.

"A very fine artist!" Houghton-Copley agreed wholeheartedly. "And, as I understand it, the only artist I am ever likely to meet whose work was interrupted by crocodiles electing to devour his model."

The gallery immediately fell silent. Until, eventually, the doctor's wife demurred at such sensationalism. "Dr Houghton-Copley," she protested, "I would have thought a man as widely travelled as you would have eschewed such…"

For a moment, the gallery seemed to fade away before Seaton's eyes. A smell of mouldering leaf filled his nostrils. He caught a glimpse of some ephemeral shape flitting through the tawny light that filtered down through the tree canopy and hovered around Houghton-Copley's pale face, with its glinting gold rimmed glasses. Something had emerged from the steaming forests. It was back at last.

"Caiman," he corrected in a murmur. "It was a caiman."

As the company turned to him in barely suppressed amazement, he thought he caught a wave of relief passing across Houghton-Copley's face. Like that of a traveller who has finally made it home after difficult times on the road.

Chapter Two

West Sussex

Mrs Attwater was vacillating. Her forefinger hovered uncertainly above the jellied fruits while Ursula directed a glare of such unmitigated loathing at the back of her head that Clover feared it would bore through the poor woman's skull.

"All so inviting," fretted the vicar's wife plaintively. "I never know quite what to do."

"Apricot, I think." Nancy Richardson felt no such reticence. She leaned in front of Enid Attwater and plucked out the sweetmeat in its crepe wrapping. Then she walked across to the other side of the drawing room and set it on the mantelpiece. "I can't think what's keeping Mrs Simmons," she added.

"Well, there's so much to be cleared away." Enid Attwater suspended her laboured selection to offer this up to the older woman, who even now was drawing herself up into her exemplary posture of aggrieved enquiry.

Ursula pounced. She took up the glass platter of jellied fruits and with elaborate courtesy proffered them to Clover. "Do take one, Clover," she smiled sweetly, "before they moulder."

Dinner having been consumed without incident, the women had congregated in the drawing room and left the men to their port and cigars. Laurel House was large enough to accommodate such post-prandial niceties but not large enough to offer any true privacy for the sexes to digest and reflect in. Thus, from the desultory timbre of the men's voices in the next room, the doctor's wife could deduce this separation was going to be a short if not perfunctory one.

Clearly Captain Seaton would not wish to linger over a cigar with a person prone to such solecisms as Dr

Houghton-Copley. Nancy Richardson was sure on this point. Although nobody had had the poor taste to refer to the subject at dinner, Dr Houghton-Copley had badly overstepped the mark with his crocodiles. She had taken it upon herself, despite facetious interjections from her husband, to deflect the company from the lurid nature of his revelation and onto more sociable topics, principally current productions on the West End stage and the likelihood of their transfer to regional theatres. Nancy Richardson had a yen for Titus Andronicus at Chichester but thought it unlikely, given the limited ambitions of regional audiences.

Dr Houghton-Copley had proved himself reasonably but not intrusively knowledgeable on such matters. When her husband had attempted one of his pompous perorations on George Bernard Shaw, it transpired that the diplomatist had actually met the playwright on more than one occasion; this intelligence rather overshadowed her husband's undoubted familiarity with the Irishman's work and led to their moving on to a new subject altogether. Throughout the meal, agreeable and substantial as ever, Dr Houghton-Copley had conducted his part in the general conversation with such discreet aplomb that Nancy Richardson could only wonder how he had come to unleash such a vulgar squib in the gallery before they went in to dine.

What on earth had possessed the man? She fixed Enid with her most glacial smile; Enid was, undeniably, related to him by marriage. "Your cousin seems peculiarly well informed about us all," she began.

Ursula finished her jellied gooseberry in two bites in order to riposte. "I didn't notice it in your regard, Nancy. He talked as if he hardly knew you."

"Careful dear, you'll choke," Nancy murmured solicitously without redirecting her attention from Enid.

"This business with the Captain and the crocodiles…"

"Caimans!" blurted Clover through a mouthful of sugary greengage, before she realised the awful urgency of her correction and spluttered out a "Sorry!"

Nancy Richardson watched Clover struggling to coordinate her breathing and her greengage and flashed Ursula a dry smile of vindication. She then continued her remorseless quest for clarification from the hapless Enid, who waited in polite trepidation. Ursula, on an uncharacteristically charitable impulse, passed Enid the glass platter of jellies to give the vicar's wife something to do with her hands.

"This business with the Captain and the crocodiles," the doctor's wife continued. "Are you aware how he came by that information?"

"I didn't tell him!" Enid hastened to assure her.

"But you knew?" Nancy Richardson probed surgically for any trace of culpability.

Clover gave Enid a flushed and angry look. Despite her better nature, she felt momentarily overwhelmed by the jealous notion that the vicar and his wife might have been harbouring intelligence about Captain Seaton's past. Intelligence of a highly personal nature and of which she, with her closer acquaintance and artistic affinity, had been completely unaware.

"I'm sure none of us knew," she asserted to shake the unworthy thought away. "And I'm sure that if the Captain had wished us to know, he would have talked of it."

"Yes, of course." Nancy teased out all their suspicions and left them unspoken in the close atmosphere of the drawing room.

"We know very little of him." Enid turned about herself, still holding the jellied fruits, so that she could explain to them all. "Dr Houghton-Copley I mean. I've not met him until tonight and Duncan has only talked with

28

him on the telephone once. Today was the first time he has spent any time with him." She looked at them with a plea in her eyes. "I'm sure we're as much in the dark as anybody."

"About what, exactly?" Ursula was at her most serpentine.

"I really don't know, I'm sure." There was a quiet desperation about Enid now. She set the jellies down on a side table and stepped away from them, as if hoping that they and not she would continue to command the room's attention. When she found herself still its focus, she attempted a diffident suggestion, "The caimans?"

Mrs Simmons walked into the drawing room carrying a large tray. On it were a silver coffee pot, cream jug and sugar bowl and an Adams teapot with Clover's herbal infusion. Foster used to refer to this latter as the Maitland dishwater but Ursula had ensured there was a caddy full of her herbal prescription in the Laurel House pantry (and that of the vicarage and the doctor's establishment), ever since she had prevailed on Clover to eschew coffee and renal failure, in favour of her hedgerow concoction. Ursula drank coffee of course, but her constitution was evidently more robust than her raw-boned friend's. Clover persisted with it even though it tasted peculiar and had other less seemly, though harmless, contra-indications.

"Mrs Simmons," Nancy Richardson was inclined to be gracious. "A wonderful dinner as ever."

"Thank you, ma'am." Mrs Simmons set the tray beside the cups on the monumental black wood sideboard that Seaton's grandfather had shipped back from one of his railway ventures in the Far East. "Local lamb, you know. And Foster grew everything else. I'll leave you ladies to serve yourselves, shall I?"

"We've been talking about caimans, Mrs Simmons." Nancy Richardson fussed with the coffee pot. "I don't suppose you could enlighten us?"

"I don't suppose I could, ma'am." Helen Simmons stopped by the door. Then by way of an afterthought, "But I have placed your basket outside in the porch. To the right of the door. You can't miss it."

Ursula smirked at this gentle reminder of Captain Seaton's largesse, while Enid Attwater seized her opportunity to snatch up a cup of coffee and sit herself in a corner chair out of harm's way.

Mrs Richardson gave Mrs Simmons a taut, acknowledging smile as the housekeeper left the room. "Thank you, Mrs Simmons. You are kindness personified."

She poured herself a cup of coffee as Clover and Ursula looked over towards the closed dining room door. The low tones of the men rumbled on.

"I wonder if he's telling them all about it," said Clover.

"Who is telling who about what?" replied Ursula tartly. She could smell the cigar smoke drifting under the door jamb and her exclusion was gnawing at her.

"Dr Houghton-Copley is evidently well informed about the Captain's expedition," whispered Clover in exasperation. "I imagine the Captain would be pleased to share his impressions with one who's taken such an interest."

"You've taken an unholy interest," mocked Ursula equally sotto voce. "And he's never told you a damn thing."

"That's unkind," protested Clover.

"If I were you, I'd interrogate the diplomat," responded Ursula. "Find out a damn sight more and a damn sight quicker."

Clover huffed. She only wanted to know what the Captain wished to tell her, although the possibility of there being unaccounted episodes among his Amazonian ventures piqued her curiosity and concern to almost unbearable levels.

There was an awkward cough from behind and both women turned quickly, as though to disguise some surreptitious exploit. Nancy Richardson was leafing through Tatler and Enid, seeing her thus occupied, had wandered across to them with the platter of jellies.

"Can you point out the greengage?" She smiled wanly.

~~~~~

The men were still seated at the dinner table. Ainsley Seaton passed the port. Houghton-Copley passed it on and stayed with his Benedictine. Dr Richardson replenished himself generously and the Reverend topped himself up. Seaton and the doctor had lit cigars. Houghton-Copley had produced a fine gold cigarette case containing fragrant, oval cigarettes which the Reverend Attwater had declined, notwithstanding they were from the Arch-Diocese' private stock. ("Their commission is rather as a favour to me," admitted Houghton-Copley, shyly. "His Grace does not indulge and their Lordships are pipe men in the main".) The Reverend Attwater did not smoke but indulged himself in private and wistful anticipation of the jellied fruits available to the ladies next door.

Foster ensured that the Benedictine was to hand for the diplomatist and the heavy regimental ashtrays generally distributed, before taking his leave to assist Mrs Simmons in the kitchen.

The men puffed and sipped and made themselves comfortable while Seaton pondered. The caiman attack was far from being common knowledge. As far as he could recall, and he applied himself to it, it had not been mentioned in any of Northmore's lectures, Munby's addendums, his own published account or those of the other expedition members. Munby had been killed by his own askaris in the first few months of the East African Campaign. Cotterill had slipped into Mexico upon the entrance of the United States into the Great War, contracted cholera and perished there. So it can only have been Northmore who passed the story on, though to what purpose he could not for one moment imagine. Nor could he imagine what Houghton-Copley's intended business with him was, or why after bringing up the grisly business, he had chosen to ignore it altogether.

He was determined to evade any further reminiscences; luckily this could only be construed as a fitting response to Houghton-Copley's cavalier disregard for the harshness of conditions in the rainforest. But still he felt an ominous and shapeless unease growing within him, a portent of greater dissolution, as if the jungle miasma was enfolding him once again, the smell of rot and the seeping mulch was filling his nostrils and the *piom* were even now fretting about his ears. And he knew he had very few defences against this kind of insidious apprehension, despite his all too vaunted reputation for valour in the extremis of war.

Like most men enmired in the horrors of Passchendaele, Seaton had on many occasions experienced shattering and overwhelming terror. But even as it snatched him up, he discovered that its very enormity scorched away almost all sense of self. The annihilation of personality, history, sensation and memory seemed a small price to pay, a bargain even, for the absence of preoccupation and the tormented consciousness of how things are. The present was simply no longer endurable and, contrary to the natural predicates of fear and survival, a part of him had waited gratefully for the solace and silence of death.

He'd found the abdication of identity in that moment a delicious, almost spiritual release, certainly well beyond the visceral and the intellectual. As reality conflagrated and imploded about him, he could feel himself ascending through this mortal terror towards some grand deliverance.

Once the bombardment was over, however, he was left stunned, emptied and somehow disappointed. It was as though he had been short changed, if not betrayed, by fate handing him back to the old veiled anxieties and the rest of the mess waiting for him in the land of the living.

Yet the horrors of the barrage paled beside this daily, insistent disquiet. Even though, over the years, he had somehow managed to assuage its more disruptive anxieties and mitigate its enervative power.

These days, he did not wait impatiently for the solace and silence of death, although he could never truly embrace life as a benevolent alternative. He and mortality had forged their own Armistice; though at times it was a fragile peace.

Now, through a flippant allusion to the caiman episode, Houghton-Copley had invoked in him a level of apprehension he had not been prey to since before the hard days of the Somme. The familiarity of this foreboding was almost unbearable and, as he swivelled his port glass around by its stem, he half expected the tension brooding in his mind to snap it. So he set it aside carefully and refolded his napkin, prior to engaging the doctor in some diversionary conversation.

Dr Richardson was applying himself to a dish of walnuts with the heavy pewter nutcrackers. He worked deliberately and thoroughly, without any ostensible sign of enjoyment but with every indication that he felt a professional responsibility to dispatch the nuts cleanly and efficiently. He had earlier offered one to the Reverend Attwater but, on it being declined, had focused on finishing the job alone. He looked up to see Ainsley Seaton on the point of saying something and, perhaps in the hopes of deflecting some of the attention away from his monopoly of the walnuts, he stepped in first. "So, what's all this about girls and crocodiles, Captain? You kept that under your hat."

"They're caimans in the Amazon." Seaton repeated his correction. Could they not at least settle on the precise species? "Much like the alligator. But without the bony septum between the nostrils."

"Not a close friend, I trust?" the Reverend slipped in a concerned enquiry to mask his embarrassment at a difficult subject being aired again.

The Doctor thought of an amusing riposte about whether the Reverend was referring to the caiman or the model. He wondered if it was an entirely suitable after dinner jest, though given the sophisticated nature of the company (if you discounted the Reverend Attwater), he was inclined to believe it might be. He'd just decided to risk it when Houghton-Copley, clearly in a state of some emotion, set down his glass of Benedictine to make an extraordinary statement.

"Gentlemen, I must apologise to both the Captain and yourselves for an inexcusable error on my part. An error of judgment and a gross transgression of taste. What I took to be a commonly held anecdote has proven not to be the case at all. I know that cannot in any way excuse my behaviour but may in some way mitigate it in your good opinion. Captain Seaton, with your permission, I shall make the same apologies to the ladies, once we join them."

The Captain went to make a small conciliatory gesture and an equally small speech of good-natured disavowal, when once again he was pre-empted.

"So there were no caimans," the doctor sounded disappointed. He refilled his glass. "And no girl."

Seaton breathed in, blinked away the forest light hazing down through the canopy and finally brought the past back into the present. "There was an incident, yes."

"It's a dangerous continent," said Houghton-Copley. He waved a hand, rather airily Seaton thought, at the doctor. "There are many such incidents."

"You've travelled in the region?" asked Seaton, trying to establish the man's expertise and through that his claim to authoritative information.

"Briefly. And superficially. At their Lordships' pleasure, you know." Houghton-Copley shrugged away any prospective significance of whatever task he had been commissioned to undertake.

This professional deprecation seems his constant companion, the doctor reflected as he charged his glass once again (it seemed to be coming round like a top). He subjected Houghton-Copley to be a long clinical appraisal but arrived at no conclusions, save one niggling question. If he's so unimportant why doesn't he dress like it?

"Representing his Grace amongst the savages." the Reverend Attwater beamed proudly at his new cousin. "Your vocation has led you down such wonderful pathways!"

"Just some time in Manaos and around," Houghton-Copley addressed himself directly to Seaton. "No time to venture too far into the interior. Not my remit, either."

"I suppose we'd better join the memsahibs." Dr Richardson's realisation of his own level of intoxication prompted him to consider his wife's dim view of long post prandial absences. "Or whatever they're referred to in the rainforest."

"I met precious few memsahibs," said Houghton-Copley. "And it would seem that most Europeans spending any time out there make their own domestic arrangements locally."

Dr Richardson gave Seaton a frankly admiring grin. "You are a dark horse."

"Really, Doctor! I was alluding to the rubber planters," admonished Houghton-Copley as they rose from table. "You have my assurance that nobody involved in scientific endeavours in the region would for one minute consider such a thing. Their integrity is a given."

Dr Richardson waved away such ethical considerations. In the continued absence of his wife, or perhaps because of her imminent presence, he seemed far from rebuffed. "I think it only proper to live off the land," he replied in jocular fashion and then steadied himself, before making for the door.

Houghton-Copley put a hand on Seaton's arm to detain him as the other men filed out and spoke earnestly into his ear, "My dear Captain, I am contrition itself. You must think me an insufferable bore. And we cannot permit this impression to endure."

"I assure you, Dr Houghton-Copley, that I've formed no such impression." Seaton was taken back by both the man's agitation and his persistence.

"You see, I need the benefit of your experiences in the field. On a matter of high policy." Houghton-Copley stared soberly at him and then gave a rueful grin. "Though tonight is hardly the ideal occasion for such deliberations." His look became serious again. "Or confidences."

The Captain had no intention of entertaining these confidences, whatever they entailed, but restricted himself to a polite demurral, "I'm not sure how much use I can be to you. I'm hardly a churchgoer of any regularity."

"It is your military appraisal that I'm requesting." He looked over Seaton's shoulder to see if the other men were still within earshot before continuing. "Concerning strategic matters arising from certain conditions you will have come across during your expedition."

"But it was all so long ago!"

"Your observations would be invaluable still. Never

more so."

What was this, thought Seaton, King and Country again? But what possible intelligence could he provide of service to the higher echelons of the Anglican Church? If indeed that was the institution that Houghton-Copley truly represented. Nonetheless, nothing would be gained from being perceived as recalcitrant. A desire for privacy could draw more attention than an amiable but contained interview through Houghton-Copley with the powers-that-be.

"Then I place myself at your disposal."

Houghton-Copley patted him on the arm. "Let us speak no more of these matters this evening. Though I imagine it may disappoint not a few of your guests." He consulted a gold half hunter. "I shall lodge in the Close tonight but will endeavour to spend the weekend here at Highleigh with Cousin Duncan. We may talk then at our leisure." He put a hand up firmly. "Please do not try and press your hospitality upon me in that matter, you have been too generous already. And Duncan tells me the vicarage is more than adequately furbished."

Seaton thus found himself the recipient of a polite refusal to an invitation he had no intention of making; the man was evidently gifted as a diplomatist. But as he watched Houghton-Copley stroll ahead of him and into the drawing room, he couldn't erase the memory of the expression on the man's face when he had first admitted the girl had fallen prey to the caimans over fifteen years ago. What conjecture had he confirmed? And how could that involve the Established Church?

~~~~~

The men entered the drawing room and broke formation. Seaton walked over to the coffee pot and was served with a timid smile by Enid Attwater. The doctor went towards his wife about whom he lingered uncertainly, as if in the hope of some encouraging comment. The vicar moved over to the jellied fruits but found, to his private consternation, that the greengages had all been consumed. Houghton-Copley had immediately approached Ursula and was making little fluttering motions with his hands about her head. "Miss Sweeting," he cried. "Your earrings betray you!"

There was a pause during which Ursula strove to transform her embarrassment into an affronted froideur. "I'm afraid I cannot understand you."

Clover bit her lip; this was Ursula at her most predatory. She hoped there wouldn't be a ridiculous scene to deprive her of any further opportunity to draw the Captain out on his adventures in the tropics.

"You're one of Diaghilev's closest circle, aren't you?" Houghton-Copley waggled a gently admonishing finger under Ursula's nose. "How naughty of you not to confide. And how unfortunate that our periods in the Master's presence should not have intersected."

"You know Diaghilev?" The frost melted at the very mention of Ursula's greatest hero. Clover breathed again. The evening would in all probability run its course.

"And so do you!" reproached Houghton-Copley "It is unfair of you to tease me. The Master presents jewellery of that rank to only his closest friends. Balanchine, I dare say. Karsavina certainly."

"We were in Paris at the same time," said Ursula, avoiding Clover's eye, "but we never actually met. Although I'm thoroughly immersed, no let's say saturated, in his vision." She lifted the necklace that matched her earrings up for his examination and added coyly, "I designed this jewellery myself. Which I think shows some affinity."

Houghton-Copley produced his gold spectacles again and made a close inspection. "Remarkable, Miss Sweeting!

38

This demonstrates more than mere affinity. This proclaims a communal vision. It embodies the Russian muse at her most pure."

Nancy Richardson shot her husband a searing look and he instantly forbore from making the remark she had seen forming on his lips. He smiled at her but got no reward and deduced the port might be hanging a trifle heavily about him.

"We loved Paris," enthused Clover, mainly to offset any further declarations of artistic intent and connection on Ursula's part. They had spent two weeks there, demi-pension on Clover's allowance. Ursula has suffered from a bowel disorder throughout but, somehow, it had proved a cultural epiphany for her. She had returned to Highleigh several pounds lighter and a fervent disciple of the Avant Garde. Nonetheless, Clover was determined that the Russians should not stand in the way of a closer understanding of her host's formative experiences in the rainforest.

"Who could not love Paris?" agreed Houghton-Copley, twinkling at her and clasping his hands. Dinner had clearly agreed with him, thought Ursula. He seemed so much more approachable and sensitive altogether. "Paris is one of life's great rewards."

"I've never been," said Enid, more by way of apology than complaint.

And so, despite Clover's best intentions, the talk moved to Paris with which Houghton-Copley seemed very familiar. He found it both enchanting and enlightening. The Enlightenment, though secular, had produced one of the most captivating and cultivated of capitals, he affirmed warmly, and popped a plum jelly into his mouth. Dr Richardson had cycled through as a boy with his father and recalled liniment, muscle cramps and sour wine. Seaton had been there on leave during his military service and also well before the war. For him, the town left mixed impressions. He was prevailed to talk about the museums he had visited and the art he had enjoyed, and Clover found some consolation in their mutual regard for Ingres, David and some of the wayward Impressionists. Gauguin, they both avoided.

They spent a pleasant hour in good-humoured conversation, with Foster occasionally being summoned to replenish drinks, although only Houghton-Copley, Ursula and the Reverend Attwater availed themselves. Seaton nursed a glass of tonic water, which Clover knew had something to do with his time in the tropics. Yet, having watched that topic of conversation being studiously ignored by the whole company, she had no intention of opening up that line of enquiry. It was all so exasperating for her, but she sipped at Ursula's rotten herbal infusion, even less palatable when tepid, and said nothing. Dr Richardson stuck steadfastly to his coffee and hoped that the grocery basket would provide sufficient appeasement to his wife. He was not aware, and would not be informed, of the awkwardness surrounding the basket on that particular evening and so had no way of knowing that this salvation would not be forthcoming.

When they finally took their leave and moved off towards their separate vehicles, Houghton-Copley's driver being summoned from a snooze by the kitchen fire, everyone was eager to endorse what a splendid evening it had been, although the Highleigh contingent at least left Laurel House with some sense of unfinished business. Ursula had been captivated by Houghton-Copley's tales of high art and urbane intrigue in the rarefied circles of bohemian Paris and felt the full bathos of her provincial life on his departure. She had not propounded her theories. He had not read her poetry. Yet. The word saved her evening, but left her a mite disgruntled. Clover for once did not notice her mood, which scarcely improved it. But Clover was in the same straits. She knew that she had been afforded a glimpse of something exotic and ominous in Captain Seaton's history, even though at the instigation of a chance remark by that preposterous church dandy. And yet this personal revelation remained just a tantalising intimation and nothing more.

The Reverend Attwater, now back in charge of the vicarage dog-cart, was in a similar quandary. He had learned virtually nothing about his celebrated cousin and still less about his business with the Captain. He felt that nothing had transpired that night which could possibly advance the matter. Except that, as they parted, his cousin had threatened, he checked himself, had requested to spend the weekend with them, so that he might prosecute his business with some grace and consideration for all concerned. This had disconcerted the Reverend Attwater and alarmed Enid, who now stared out into the moonlit lanes and wondered what such fine clerical gentlemen normally ate and what, at a pinch, they could be prevailed upon to make do with. Had they felt like breaking the silence on the way home and sharing their concerns, they would have discovered that for once they were of one mind. A family connection with Dr Houghton-Copley was not altogether something to be desired.

Nancy Richardson felt that in some way she had been slighted and, at the same time, that some important social undercurrent was eluding or evading her. She resented the impropriety of the diplomatist's anecdotes of Paris and its delinquent artistic community as much as she decried his allusions to unseemly deaths in the antipodes. But more than that, she felt these virtually scandalous elements were impinging on her own community and would, in some measure, affect her standing in it. Her husband, long used to her injuries and affronts, knew only that something had discommoded her severely and that he would just have to wait to find out to what precise extent.

"Everything alright, Sir?" asked Foster, as Seaton turned away from the door and his last polite farewells.

"Oh yes, everything's fine, Foster," the Captain replied. "You can lock up now. And do thank Mrs Simmons for a simply splendid table, when next you see her."

The steward bolted the heavy oaken door and took up his set of keys from the drawer of the post table, the key to which he kept upon him at all times. He watched the tall figure of the Captain make his way upstairs, and thought he looked unusually weary.

Seaton sat beside his bedroom window and allowed himself a cigarette. A Players Navy Cut. Not for him oval, Turkish blends, gold tipped or otherwise, he thought, and then shook his head at his own truculence. Why was he bothering with the man's smoking habits? Everything was not fine. Not fine at all. He knew nothing of Dr Houghton-Copley, but the man seemed to know a great deal more about him than he cared for. Any military strategist, particularly Clausewitz with his definition of the Fog of War, would have deemed such an imbalance in their intelligence as a recipe for annihilation. Mind you, Clausewitz had never operated in country you could barely hack your way through, with air that could drown you and with human interaction reduced to the poisoned dart and the shrunken head.

He stubbed out his cigarette and began to undress. Something was very wrong, he knew. But in the fog of this particular war he would have to sit tight and wait for it to attempt to overrun him.

North-west Amazon
While Esperenza's buildings would have been taken

for derelict in either Cape Town or Chichester, Seaton learned, from Northmore's briefing on the comparative luxury of the Guerrita's foredeck, that the Government's Intendencia was distinguished by a reasonably recent coat of blue paint, while the post office and combined meteorological observatory boasted a fading yellow. The Recreio Popular or sporting club was a chipped pink. And the Hotel Agosta, where they were bound, boasted an extra storey and a coat of dull grey. All of these colours were easily within his palette, though capturing the shades of grime and mouldering algae was going to be a challenge.

Esperenza's military presence comprised a company of Cholo Indians, dressed in makeshift uniforms and in boots several sizes too large. They were armed with ancient rifles which they obviously had no love for cleaning. As was common along the great river, their officers had all taken Indian concubines and these, half-naked and listless, augmented the straggling guard of honour at the end of the jetty and watched impassively as the Guerrita tied up and the expedition party disembarked.

"I've seen more life in a dead polecat," Cotterill observed of the Indian women as he adjusted his holster to a more accessible position. "Smell's about the same too."

With scant regard for local protocol, the American strode through what he took to be dockside gawpers but were, in fact, prominent citizens, their families and servants waiting to welcome the outside world. He foraged on into the tiny main square, picking his way through the mud and puddles with some distaste, as his leather puttees were smeared with a pervasive green slime almost at once. Munby had pulled on his gumboots for this occasion and processed down the gangplank to meet the reception committee with a vaguely regal air. Seaton remained with Northmore who was finalising his paperwork for the civic reception, so Munby was the first man from the party to shake hands with Ramón Suarez.

Esperenza had always been a key staging post for them. It was their gateway to the wilderness and the preordained rendezvous with their quartermaster and chief guide, Ramón Suarez. Northmore had found out about Suarez from a commercial botanist sent to investigate the feasibility of introducing rubber to the Caribbean. His mission had proved inconclusive but he had discovered a local fixer who could be relied upon; a tropical rarity, he had joked, almost as valuable in his field as a self-milking rubber tree. "Half –Spanish, part Portuguese and the rest God knows what," the botanist had informed Northmore. "But as honest as you can hope for out there. And obsessed with his own reputation."

Suarez, a thickset man of indeterminate age, with a receding hairline balanced by an elaborate moustache, stood at the end of the gangplank a few meters ahead of the local dignitaries and their party. Even though it was shaded by a wide straw hat, Seaton could see his face wore the preoccupied but determined expression peculiar to quartermaster sergeants the world over.

Suarez had not proved cheap but, by ensuring their final supplies were shipped to Esperenza and stockpiled at minimum cargo rates and with minimal pilferage, he proved himself indispensable. He had sourced everything necessary to equip a mobile workshop and service the expedition's living quarters and field laboratory, to satisfy even Munby's finicky requirements. He had been waiting there for them for some weeks, because he knew, without his presence, their supplies would melt into the terrain.

Northmore had letters to present to the chief of police and the army commander. These were one and the same man, a rotund individual perpetually the worse for drink, but with a finally tuned official dignity. Northmore was keen that his party should impress the man with their status and connections because, unless sufficiently overawed, he would undoubtedly connive in the looting of any further supplies and the misplacement of any mail.

Moreover, he would regard them as dead men until they returned to the settlement, on their way out of his region and responsibility. Peruvian and Brazilian frontier authorities were not known to volunteer assistance in times of emergency. "This isn't the Empire, let us remember," Northmore confided to Seaton having first ensured Mr Cotterill had disembarked, and was unlikely to take offence. However, local officials had a growing respect for the new commercial ministries, now the rubber boom had brought their hitherto obscure constituencies into prominence. A sheaf of government commissions and requirements under seal, and the intimation of some financial remuneration upon the expedition's conclusion, might incline the man to greater cooperation.

"If we can't frighten the bugger, we'll undertake to bribe him," Northmore summed up, bundling his elaborately sealed commissions into his canvas shoulder bag. "That way we get a fighting chance he won't cut our throats for our boots."

Their introduction to Ramón Suarez was cordial, with both parties taking stock of each other and coming away with sufficient incentive to travel in hope. Cotterill had looked about him in a commanding manner and demanded to know whether Suarez had laid in sufficient ammunition, which calibre and how many rounds, but when Northmore told Suarez, privately, that the American was a sportsman rather than a military adventurer, the guide relaxed somewhat. Munby scanned the itemised lists of hardware and timber that was waiting to be loaded aboard the Guerrita with increasing pleasure. Finally with a cry of "My hat, this chap's a ruddy miracle worker!" the ice was broken and the party broke into broad grins.

They made their way across the square to the Hotel Agosta where, they had been informed by the sergeant in charge of the welcoming party, the chief of police was waiting for them. Every day, according to Suarez, the chief abandoned the Intendencia to the depredations of mid-afternoon heat, insects and those of his subordinates not indisposed through rum or fever. Instead, he took his siesta at the hotel and discharged most of his business there.

Suarez pointed out the village church, a grubby white building to their right, indistinguishable save for a whitewashed cross set outside, at the foot of which burned a number of offertory candles. As they passed, a priest came out and stopped in the entrance to watch their passage. He was a heavyset, unshaven man, in a worn, brown cassock tied at the waist, and he subjected them to very close inspection, although he seemed to be swaying slightly.

"Fever?" asked Munby.

"Whiskey, I think," replied Suarez. "He is admired for this. Amongst the seringueiros." He smiled as he explained, "They are tough men here."

"Man's stewed?" Cotterill laughed aloud. "Well, it's his Salvation."

"Very possibly," opined Northmore as they climbed the few wooden steps and felt their way into the dark and musty interior of the hotel. There was no reception desk but a large reception area, where newcomers mingled with habitués and the hotel proprietor tried to establish their varying requirements and their abilities to pay for them. He was a hard-pressed, young man who had just inherited the place upon the death of his parents, whose small launch had upturned during one of the periodic floods.

Food and drink were walked in through a narrow door from a tin outhouse which housed the kitchen, the icebox and the slaughterhouse. There were a few battered wicker chairs spread haphazardly about the place, but the room was commanded by a large plank table. At the head of this table lay a small dead child, resting on bed of ragged linen. The tiny thing, it could have been no more than three months old, was wrapped in a white robe adorned with blue, red and yellow ribbons, and further decorated with small leaves and twigs. Around the body, they had placed numerous empty gin and whiskey bottles, each with a lighted candle set in it. These smoked abominably and Seaton could feel his eyes starting to water. Cotterill had moved back towards the open door and was now cutting off most of whatever sunlight could filter in.

Three expressionless women, heads covered by shawls, sat on stools beside the child. One of them was smoking a pipe. They stared without curiosity through the fug of the candles at the expedition party. A stream of Spanish reached them from a gruff but amused voice at the other end of the table, and they turned to discover the chief of police and his Lieutenant spooning up some kind of stew from large earthenware bowls.

"The Lieutenant says it'll be on its way to the cemetery in the morning." Suarez translated. "He also welcomes Milord to Esperenza."

Seaton and Northmore exchanged a glance on the word "Milord". Was this a reflection of some exceptional status accorded their expedition?

"And does his Excellency, the chief of police, have anything to add?" asked Northmore with what Seaton took to be an admirable quality of professional gravitas.

Suarez watched as the big man dug deeper into his stew with his spoon. He eventually concluded, "He has nothing to say. He is eating."

Munby took a quick and proficient look at the baby and then reported to the baronet. "Most likely a fever. I don't think we need be too concerned. Though I 'd not eat at the same table with it."

"Fever takes most of their young," said Suarez, offering a coin to one of the women who pocketed it without a word. "They drink. They mourn. They make another."

"Tell him the Milord will be delighted to talk with him, once he has finished his dinner," said Northmore and he turned to lead the party outside. "And have them set up a table outside, will you?"

This request caused some amazement amongst the hotel proprietor and his serving women but, true to his vocation, he had chairs and a small table dragged down the steps so that the English could eat, to his mind, in the street. This confused even those pariah dogs brave enough to flop out in the corner of the square nearest them. They stood and prowled around suspiciously, as if awaiting some trap to close.

The expedition party were served with beer, jerky and biscuits, by two elderly women who could barely contain their amusement. Everything was extortionately expensive. While he could be eating rather better for less at a chop house in Covent Garden, Seaton knew they had not been singled out for particularly outlandish overcharging. The paucity of local agriculture meant virtually all comestibles had to be shipped in, at prices which the rubber boom had quadrupled.

Finally, the chief of police arrived, with the hotel proprietor in attendance, bearing a chair for him. The chief sat down heavily, had a very large whiskey poured for him and regarded Northmore with a deadpan expression, until his Lieutenant arrived and stood to attention by his shoulder. Then he gave a small wave of command and the Lieutenant started to conduct the business at hand.

It transpired that his Excellency was conscious of the reputation and rank of the Milord and would of course offer what limited support he could. He was mindful though that a party of such experience and eminence would have provisioned itself thoroughly and so would need for nothing. He proposed to place the commissions and letters of mark in his safe in the Intendencia, where they would be best preserved, and peruse them at leisure tomorrow morning. Then, he would be best able to judge what further service he might render and what additional costs might be incurred in ensuring the smooth prosecution of their mission.

The Lieutenant talked, Suarez translated and the chief finished his whiskey. He looked at his glass in a quizzical manner until it was refilled, but did not break the flow of conversation by so much as a murmur. Seaton, Northmore and Munby received all this with expressions of the gravest attention and firm resolve. Brandon Cotterill stared over at the wild dogs. No stranger to the negotiating table in his father's firm, he knew when to keep a poker face. However, he was finding the current circumstances challenging in this regard. He could not laugh or expostulate nor could he leave the table; he rose somewhat in the Captain's estimation, as he watched the young man biting his lip.

Eventually the Lieutenant drew to a close, with a short bow. Northmore then briefly addressed the chief, again through the auspices of Suarez. The Milord had no exceptional requirements, but simply requested the assurance that all the channels of communication and supply would remain open, safe and free from interference. He had been told this was a standard protocol by the Minister of the Interior himself. And he was sure the Minister had every faith in the chief and his men's ability to confirm and maintain such an assurance.

The chief looked into his whiskey glass with a contemplative expression while Northmore continued. Naturally, upon the conclusion of a successful expedition, the Milord would wish to show his appreciation of the chief's contribution in a practical way. Of course, the more rewarding the mission, the greater their appreciation must be. But he would accord it a matter of honour that the chief shared in the fruits of their enterprise

He, in turn, fell silent and they waited for the chief's response. Would he settle for jam tomorrow? He set his glass down, nodded curtly to the Lieutenant and then rasped some phrase which sent the aide double marching into the hotel.

The Lieutenant returned with a small canvas sack which he set before Northmore. "The Milord may rely on us to safeguard his interests. In the same spirit of cooperation, may we request a small service? This would involve no inconvenience."

Seaton pulled the sack to him and looked inside. There were a few packages and letters, all addressed to various members of a Williams family. The newer were merely crinkled by the humidity but the majority were mildewed and battered. None seemed of any size or substance. "It's somebody's post."

"Mr Williams," said the chief at last. He had a musical voice, tinged with melancholy. He waved the Lieutenant on.

Mr Micah Williams had worked as a tally clerk when Esperenza had boasted a rubber depot. When his company relocated its shipping points, Mr Williams had chosen not to remove himself back to Manaos, but had defied comprehension by moving further into the forest, together with his wife and his daughter. He had established a small settlement some twelve hours upriver on the expedition's route. The Williams family kept themselves to themselves and very seldom sent down for supplies. Their uncollected mail had been slowly accumulating.

"Is he planting up there?" asked Seaton.

The Lieutenant shrugged. He didn't think so, but he thought they tried to grow corn and manioc. Mr Williams sang a great deal, he remembered. He had a very fine voice. And his wife and daughter accompanied him. The daughter was very pretty. This latter fact seemed to surprise him.

The heavyset priest walked over from his church doorway and made to enter the hotel, doubtless to officiate at some funeral rite inside. He paused in the doorway to take them all in again.

"Mr Williams!" the chief called over to him. It seemed to amuse him, as the priest ducked into the hotel with a thunderous look on his face.

The party returned to the Guerrita where they were to spend the night.

"I think we got off quite lightly there," said Munby swinging the mail sack as he walked.

Seaton wasn't so sure. Whatever they had been given he felt had been held very cheaply.

West Sussex

The owl was hooting, and a summer night's breeze rustled the grasses under her window. Helen Simmons lay back in bed and listened to Foster cleaning his teeth in her tiny bathroom. She could smell that he'd already dabbed on some of his cologne, which meant he was feeling amorous. If she were to be honest with herself, she had mixed feelings about this. A late dinner party was always a tiring business, especially as she had chosen to extend herself over the menu, given the elevation of the Captain's guest of honour. And she'd be up again at six with a full breakfast for all of them to prepare.

Still, Foster himself would be tiptoeing out before her at a quarter to. She smiled fondly at the thought of the chunky man tripping about in the dawn light like a pixie, with his trousers and boots under his arm. And a successful evening gave him such a sense of pride and purpose. It put a little spring in his step and a sparkle in his eye. It brought him to life.

"I've come over quite cosmopolitan," he'd say as he fox-trotted into her bedroom, his striped pyjamas pressed to knife edges, his hair slicked back and gleaming from the basin, and his cheeks shaved smooth, powdered and, as tonight, anointed with Trumper's gentleman's cologne.

He was a good, if straightforward, man, a kind and loyal man. It would be hard to deny him, if ever she found cause or occasion to. She'd see how she felt when he finally slipped under the covers. Unless she'd already fallen sound asleep which, clearly, would obviate the need for any decision. Foster would never be so ungallant as to wake her, however passionate his feeling for her. At the thought of his consideration, she resolved to try and stay awake, but the yawn that overwhelmed her did not bode well for Foster's love life. So, she tried conversation.

"I thought he was quite peculiar," she called out.

"Well, he certainly stirred them all up, didn't he?" Foster's voice was a little indistinct with toothbrush and paste. "Nerve of it! Dragging up caimans and then scotching it all quick as you like."

"Caimans. What about caimans?" If he was going to be in there much longer, she'd be out like a light when he got to bed.

"Captain painted somebody down there who was eaten by them, apparently. Can't think why this Houghton–Copley fellow brought it up. As he said, the bloody things are everywhere."

Warm billowing waves of sleep washed over Mrs Simmons, but she pulled herself together enough to enquire, "What did the Captain say?"

Foster bustled into the room and slipped under the

covers. "Nothing. But you could tell he didn't appreciate it. He seemed to get one of his glooms." There was a moment of silence. Then, "Your feet are like icicles."

Mrs Simmons giggled.

Chapter Three

West Sussex

The Highleigh village Post Office and grocery store was no stranger to rumour and speculation although Larry Poulter, its proprietor, did his level best to be seen not to encourage it. He and his wife, Ruth, understood the true value of being at the hub of a community's preoccupation with itself, while at no time being associated with any faction or opinion. He'd taken the shop on fifteen years previously using an annuity from his service on the railways and a small legacy belonging to his wife. Pivotal to the village's wellbeing though they undoubtedly were, the Poulters were still considered as incomers and probably always would be. This parvenu status required them to circulate any and all news of current or significant events without comment. Comment would imply they were taking too much upon themselves, and might put a strain on the cordial relations they enjoyed with Highleigh at large, personally and above all commercially.

So, Larry Poulter was careful not to trade in gossip but strove to attend its dissemination with good grace and impartiality. When Nancy Richardson's maid, Maeve, came in the very next morning after the dinner at Laurel House with stories of how some pillar of the church had outraged the Captain's guests with risqué stories of Paris, and had then accused Captain Seaton himself of painting a girl in the jungle as she was eaten by crocodiles, he had restricted his response to a sympathetic expression and the required truckle of mature cheddar.

By the following day, however, the incident with the Captain and the crocodiles had been the cause of many intense deliberations amongst Mr Poulter's customers. The vicarage housekeeper, Mrs Gibson, considered an expert as a result of her propinquity to the eminent accuser, garnered as much as she could from Enid's reticent account of the evening's conversations and then amplified this according to her experience of the vicar's wife's aversion to all things colourful and dangerous. She had gained some corroboration to these embellishments from old Mrs Jennings, who attended to Clover's and Ursula's laundry and had constructed her own version of events from snippets overheard through convenient ground floor windows at the Old Forge.

Thus, the narrative spread and developed, with each detail being hotly contested and diligently speculated over. Not that the village had much to get to grips with. Whatever wider conclusions they were inclined to draw upon the affair, there were only three constant and attested matters of fact. These were that the Captain had been painting a semi-naked woman beside a tropical river; a huge crocodile had seized her and devoured her; the Captain had failed to prevent this. None the less, the distant episode was speedily and expertly reconstructed and conclusions duly formed, so that the debate could start in earnest and the precise nature of the scandal, its ramifications and culpabilities be firmly established.

Some parties, amongst the tea and knitting circles, chose to find themselves sadly disappointed that a scion of the community and a soldier who had been decorated by the King himself, in all probability, should abandon a model, albeit barely decent and Parisian, to the ravening maw of a tropical monster. This viewpoint was roundly denounced as scurrilous by their more sentimental acquaintances and many long friendships were stretched to the limit. Old friends were railed against in private for besmirching a noble and upright man's name. In return, other old friends were accused of being blinded by foolish and romantic notions of men in general and the gloomy and reclusive Captain in particular. The man was standoffish almost to the point of disdain; unsocial behaviour like this could surprise nobody, surely?

Highleigh men were, in general, more sanguine. The Snug bar of The Tun And Pipe concluded that even the most determined rescue efforts by the Captain could never prevail once the savage instincts of the monster, further inflamed by the posture of the girl and her state of undress. At the Farmers' market in nearby Sidlesham the Captain was congratulated in his absence for persuading a woman to disrobe simply by waving a paintbrush at her, though the majority of the bidders at the auction refused to believe the story at all. After all, they reasoned, who on earth would go to the jungle to paint pictures?

Those local men who gave the story enough credence to merit further investigation, found the circumstances difficult to assess. While to a man they affirmed the Captain's exceptional courage and alacrity in any combat, nobody was sure of the speed or strength that a river monster may justly lay claim to, although the churchwarden had heard of a huge river snake that swallowed a cow whole. So the precise nature of the challenge posed by the monster to the Captain remained a mystery to them. Nor were they by any means certain of what contribution the young lady may have made to the situation. In this regard at least, the Snug bar was unanimously agreed that she would have been more likely to hinder than assist any rescue, however determined.

Having pondered at length over the issue, the neighbourhood was inclined to drop it, in the absence of any further information or developments. Positions had been established and declared and that seemed to be the end of it, although nothing much of interest or excitement had surfaced to replace it. The Snug bar was accordingly delighted to learn that one of the chief protagonists was about to reappear, and that perhaps the drama might have some further twists and turns in store for them.

The Snug bar learned this from Larry Poulter himself, and he had deduced it from Enid Attwater's behaviour on the Thursday morning, when she had entered his shop. This in itself was a rare occurrence and worthy of some speculation, but what had attracted his closest attention was the way she had fluttered about the new crab and salmon mousses he'd taken on from quality provisioners in Chichester. She'd also picked over both his sweet and savoury biscuit assortments and had scrutinised the more expensive ranges of his condiments and pickles with an equally distracted air. Finally, she'd despaired of her own explorations and confided in him that she was entertaining an eminent person at the weekend. She then asked to see whatever sophisticated foodstuffs he thought might be appreciated by the more cultivated and well-travelled persons in society. Poulter decided against venturing an opinion on the predilections of a stratum of society well above his own. Instead, he simply directed her towards the more expensive sections of his inventory.

It was thus clear to Larry Poulter, and soon after to the community at large, that the Captain's distinguished accuser was returning to Highleigh. As the tea and knitting circles duly noted, the fact that Dr Houghton-Copley was prepared to stoop to Enid's paltry hospitality indicated that there was clearly more to the matter than met the eye. Why would a man of his position not stay with the Captain at Laurel House? Was there bad blood between them? Or did the nature of his business among them require it to be prosecuted from the respectable probity of the vicarage, challenging though the conditions there might be for a man of his undoubtedly patrician background?

These questions tantalised and exasperated everyone in equal measure. After all, what was the point of evincing an interest in community affairs if crucial information was not forthcoming? How could one make a constructive contribution if such information was being withheld? It was in the spirit of just such a disinterested quest for the truth that, over a pint of mild, Larry Poulter suggested to Sam Faring, one of the more prominent dairymen of the district, that he might get a few useful indications from a considerate inquiry to Foster. Poulter knew that if Foster were to share a confidence with anybody in the district it would be with Faring.

Amongst Foster's many attributes was an aptitude for mechanical and motor repairs, acquired during his years of military service and through a perpetually adolescent love of things automotive. He derived some considerable standing in the countryside from his ready assistance with belt-driven threshing machines, recalcitrant tractors and all kinds of petrol engines now available to lighten the load of the farming man, though the lightening of this load was of course never conceded to outsiders.

Foster's competence resulted in a healthy exchange of services and payments in kind between the country around Laurel House and the household itself. But his principal satisfaction was that it had helped him prevail upon Captain Seaton to retain the Bentley – rather than opt for the Austin Tourer which the Captain felt would serve its purpose just as well. Foster's motor repairs ensured that the Bentley cost the household nothing and that he could continue to drive the sleek, racing green machine around West Sussex, as his own. His mechanical prowess also provided the gardens at Laurel House with an endless supply of manure, seedlings and straw. It also re-paned broken windows, provided the cold store with eggs, fresh lamb, pork and bacon, the pantry with cider and the fires with logs.

Sam Faring, a man of progressive temperament, cherished an ambition to set up a charabanc company to bring trippers from Chichester down to the coast at Selsea or Wittering. Mrs Faring thought little of the plan but when Sam divulged it to Foster when the latter was tinkering with the timing of the dairyman's Austin Seven, he discovered instantly that he had found a soul mate. While Mr Faring did not hold sufficient sway in his house to make the bus company a reality, he could still subscribe to the latest automotive catalogues and promotional leaflets, which he and Foster would pore over. They had an understanding. One day, possibly in a future life, they would inaugurate The Faring and Foster Bus Company. Faring's money would put it on the road and Foster's expertise would keep it there. They drank to that, regularly.

Faring told Poulter he would never break a confidence of course, but if there were some dark matter afoot and it did affect Foster's wellbeing and if it were in the power of Poulter, or some other members of the community, to help his friend in some tangible way, then he would ascertain the details and pass them on. Poulter must be content with that.

And so on Saturday morning, while Foster was wiping a proprietorial chamois over the Bentley's windscreen and headlamps and waiting for Helen Simmons to finish some business in the Post Office, Sam sauntered out of The Tun and Pipe and watched him at work.

"That church dandy's foisted himself on the vicar, I hear," he offered up to the summer breeze.

Foster had already been told, of course; nothing in the community escaped Mrs Simmons' discreet but vitally sensitive social antennae. All the same, he smiled noncommittally across the bonnet as he checked the gleam of the Bentley's marque. "Causing some commotion, is he, Sam?"

"Usual conniptions." Sam Faring shrugged

59

dismissively at the world of village gossip. Then he walked round the car so he could stand within a discreet distance of Foster, should there be anybody to hear above the house martins darting round the eaves of the village hall. "All the same. I wouldn't like to think of the Captain being discommoded. If there was anything I could do about it." He held Foster's gaze. "But you know that."

"Nothing to fret about, Sam." Foster gave him a reassuring grin. "I can't see much discommoding the Captain from that direction."

"Well, I suppose if Enid's cooking doesn't see him off, the draughts and the damp will," Sam mused, then, "Got time for a glass?"

Foster looked over at the Post Office. "Not really. I'm running Mrs Simmons over to Bognor. To look at the hats."

"What hats?"

"Whatever hats they're wearing, I should think." Like Sam Faring, Foster was not well acquainted with the vagaries of fashion.

"Nice day for a drive," opined Sam, looking up at the clear sky. "Though it'd be a whole lot nicer in a thirteen seater Maxwell."

"Now you're talking." Foster didn't rise to the defence of his beloved Bentley; this was their dream they were talking of. "Next season, maybe?"

"Next season without a doubt," replied Sam stoutly and he ducked back into the shade of The Tun and Pipe. He was pleased he had nothing to report to Larry Poulter; it saved him the problem of refusing to compromise his friendship either way.

Foster got in behind the wheel, adjusted his cap and waited for Mrs Simmons to bustle out of the Post Office and slip into the back seat. She was all businesslike when they were in the village but once they were on the coastal road, she'd tickle his neck and he'd pull up so she could get into the passenger seat beside him.

He thought idly about the vicar's house guest and what might have attracted him back to Highleigh but for the life of him he just couldn't think of anything that would do the trick. Then Helen Simmons strode purposefully out of the Post Office and he climbed out quickly to open the rear door for her. From then on, his main preoccupation was what on earth he could say that was entertaining about ladies' hats.

~~~~~

Ainsley Seaton strolled across the lawn towards the summer house, a glass of orange squash in one hand and the most recent statements of his South African mining interests in the other. He used these flimsies to wave away a persistent wasp from the top of his glass.

The sun being so strong and the day so warm he had left his jacket behind in the gallery and was wearing only ducks, an open linen shirt and deck shoes. He held his fountain pen clenched between his teeth. The thing was so ancient he knew from experience that it was positively guaranteed to leak into whatever trouser pocket he might slip it, with a particular appetite for linen and flannel. Better a mouthful of ink than one of Mrs Simmons' forbearing smiles over the laundry basket.

The sunlight was quite dazzling, picking out the formal flower beds in high relief against the uniform green of the lawn, the flowers themselves, rows of dahlias, irises and gardenias, all vibrant in this summer clarity. He pressed on towards the invitingly calm interior of the summer house, waving his financial security at the insistent approaches of the wasp and swearing lightly between his teeth.

He thought of Houghton-Copley and his imminent return to the village, with his mysterious requirements, his intimated involvement in secret affairs of State and his unprecedented interest in Northmore's Amazonian enterprise. He stopped himself there. Enterprise wasn't quite the word for a venture that had nearly killed him, what with the deprivations and the Beri-beri. And as ever there was the other business. Deeper, darker, more dislocating than any fever or indeed death could prove to be.

He wouldn't dwell on that. Houghton-Copley would be arriving at the vicarage at any time. They would meet tomorrow after Sunday Service. They would talk, within certain strict and unspoken parameters that he himself would set. The man would then go back to whatever mainstream he was predating. Nothing would change. Nothing could ever change.

He stepped briskly up into in the summer house. The sudden contrast from brilliant sunshine to deep shadow blacked out his vision momentarily and so he paused on the threshold waiting for his sight to become accustomed to the darkness. As he peered into the interior, trying to find an object to focus on, he knew she was there even before her outline had fully taken shape.

She seemed to well up out of the gloom and the dense, still air. The sharper contours appeared at first. The bony knees drawn up under the pointed chin, the tendons on the forearms clasped around them. The spiky disarray of matted blond hair, streaked with mud and what seemed to be red dye. Her features emerged gradually from these rickety fortifications. The wide green eyes, projecting fear and a kind of desperate anger, the mouth pulled back in a rictus of distaste and terror, like a smothered scream.

In the murk, her pallid skin held a translucent greenish sheen, smeared with mud that had caked to a dirty grey and streaked haphazardly with the red dye. The smell declared this latter to be some form of cloying grape syrup. He had to lean close in to ascertain this, for this smell had to fight its way through the musk of her dried sweat, the thin, flat tang of stale urine and, surprisingly, a sickly odour of warm tinned fruit and spilled milk.

Without drawing up from her crouch, she shook her head slowly from side to side, as if the horror and outrage were just too much to articulate.

Seaton swallowed heavily as his disorientated senses recreated this jungle hobgoblin. He couldn't speak because of the fountain pen in his mouth, but even as he formulated some greeting, some rueful acknowledgement of her presence, she faded into the pile of wicker garden chairs stacked uncertainly in the far corner of the room. Back then, she had both despaired of him and despised him before they had even met. What on earth could she think of him now?

Carefully, he set down his glass and his papers on the slatted floor and then went over to pick up one of the garden chairs. Sunny or not, he would work outside for the while.

~~~~~

Ursula nibbled at her pen fitfully as she struggled in the throes of literary composition. She stared out of the window for inspiration but could only see Mrs Jennings pinning up sheets and shifts on a clothesline slung across the lawn by the herb garden. She sighed, crumpled up the sheet of notepaper which bore the ornate script of her false start, and dropped it in the waste bin.

"We've not got much of the apple blossom left," observed Clover with as much restraint as she could muster. She was lying back on the pegged sofa, cutting out pictures of social events from the Illustrated News with a view to a collage at some later date. She had designed the apple blossom motif for the notepaper herself, and quietly proud of the undoubted success of her efforts, was more

63

than a little peeved by the way Ursula treated it like the scraps you used for shopping lists.

"Got to get it right," insisted Ursula. She looked down at the remaining three sheets she had appropriated. "Makes us look like cider farmers anyway."

"Ursula!" Clover threw down her scissors and glared at her friend perched at the tiny writing desk in the bay window.

"Sorry, Clovy." Ursula knew Clover was not to be trifled with on her designs. Not a battle worth winning or a niggle worth aggravating. She could sulk for days when affronted, and become quite brutal, if only in her conversation. Quite like her hectoring old despot of a father, God rest his soul. "I'm bound to get it right this time."

"I'm sure he won't find the time." Clover redirected her displeasure at Houghton-Copley; she took up the scissors again and began chopping away at a society ball in Mayfair.

"You've seen the state of Enid's carpets." Ursula's eyes narrowed as an opening phrase hovered before her. She set it down with élan before it escaped. "He won't want to spend a minute more inside that mausoleum than he has to."

"Still can't see any earthly reason why he'd want to come here, though." Clover sliced through some debutantes.

"Possibly not, dear." Ursula adopted an offhand tone whilst hunting for in the pockets of her smock for her cheroots. "But I sense his need for rather more cultivated company. We do share certain affinities, after all."

"Not your bloody Russians again." The crumpled notepaper was still pricking at Clover. "We both know you're on pretty shaky ground there."

"What can be the matter with you?" Ursula lit up and

blew cheroot smoke down her nostrils, "Not monthlies, surely?"

Clover dismissed this with a shake of the head; she was not to be deflected "You haven't met any and he's bound to know all of them. Intimately."

"The Avant Garde isn't just some address book," sniffed Ursula. "Such a bourgeois concept. We share Paris. C'est tout!"

"On the toilet all the time. Paris. All the time," Clover muttered to herself as she collected her clippings in little piles.

Ursula threw her pen down and wailed, "I can't believe you're being so beastly to me. I'm doing all this for you!"

"For me?" Clover's tone shifted from petulance to genuine perplexity.

"This is all about Captain Ainsley bloody Seaton! I know you eat, sleep and bloody breathe him." Ursula gathered herself with a perfectly executed sob. "So, I thought tea with Dr Houghton-Copley would be the perfect occasion to enquire, discreetly of course…"

"Oh, Ursula." Clover's voice quavered with remorse.

"He knows much more about the Captain than we do. And with a little finesse..." She stared tragically at Clover. "I am capable of a little finesse, you know. And I'm only ever looking after your interests, even if you do despise me."

Clover gave an anguished cry and, throwing aside her collage materials, rushed over to Ursula to enfold her in her arms. "I'm so sorry, angel! What can you think of me! I'm an ungrateful bitch! I don't deserve..."

She sobbed heavily into Ursula's hair until the latter managed to partially disengage herself. As Clover clutched at her, Ursula scribbled hasty words on the notepaper, stuffed it into a matching envelope and handed it to her red-faced friend. "Quick, Clovy, your bicycle! This must arrive at the vicarage before anyone else snaffles him!"

Clover smiled gratefully. She may not have the delicate sensibilities of her friend, but she could ride a bicycle quicker than most of the men in the village. She could now make amends.

~~~~~

Enid peered through the parlour curtains as the Episcopal Rolls drew up at the vicarage gate. She felt both overwhelmed and embarrassed by its gleaming bodywork and by the gravitas of the chauffeur as he rounded the car to open the nearside passenger door for the august personage, who stepped blinking into the light.

Dr Houghton-Copley was wearing a three-piece suit of beige linen, a pale-blue cotton shirt with what appeared to be a silk University cravat, beige calfskin shoes and a wide-brimmed straw hat which could have graced Edouard Manet. With barely a cursory glance towards Enid, hidden in her side window, he turned to supervise the unloading of a growing pile of matching luggage, in cornflower leather with all manner of straps and brass buckles. With every item that joined the well tended pile, Enid felt a little dowdier. She looked down at her Sunday dress (what would she wear tomorrow?) and felt positively shabby. The thought of exposing herself to sunlight, neighbourly observation and closeted ridicule chilled her. She gave a throaty moan of fear and exasperation, cut short by a stamp of her foot as she recalled her husband's absence.

In her moment of need, Duncan had removed himself to the safety of the vestry, busying himself or so he said with choir matters. If she wished to provoke herself, she could discern a well-worn pattern in this, but the arrival of the personage would require all her emotional strength and she knew she could not afford to give in to mute reproach, with its attendant creeping resentment.

She would have to face the difficulties alone and that meant without delay. Wadding her hankie back into her hip pocket, she dashed out of the parlour and through the side door to arrive on the vicarage front path in a cloud of dust and pebbles. She pulled up rather breathlessly and tried to gather some of her errant hair back under her tortoiseshell hairclip, although without her mirror this was a hopeless task and she gave a further little grunt of frustration.

Her sudden arrival seemed to startle Houghton-Copley momentarily but, with some aplomb, he gathered himself and, lifting his hat, gave her a brief but courtly bow. "Mrs Attwater," he called over. "I can't thank you enough for your kindness."

Enid hurried up the path to join him and they both looked at the mountain of cornflower blue luggage. "Do you have a boy?" Houghton-Copley enquired doubtfully.

"Only the choir, I'm afraid," said Enid. She tried to maintain respectful eye contact whilst leaning forward to brush the dust from her skirts. "And Duncan's using them at the moment."

Houghton-Copley looked at the chauffeur and gave him a barely perceptible nod. Then he took Enid's arm and led her back into her own home. The chauffeur picked up the first of the cases and a hatbox and walked a discreet distance behind them. His face displayed nothing; in his own solemn way he was a fearful man, only too responsive to the tacit signals of brute power.

"We're very rural here, very out of the way, not sophisticated at all. Not the way you'd know it." Enid knew she was talking too fast. "I do hope you won't find us too backward. I will do my best of course, but there's bound to be…"

Houghton-Copley held up a pink, perfectly manicured hand. "Mrs Attwater, I have tented amongst head-hunters in Papua. I assure you I shall be quite comfortable here."

As he followed her indoors, Enid sniffed at the telltale smell of the parquet floor cleaner that still hadn't dissipated since she tried to give Duncan's study some vestige of renovation. She went over what Dr Houghton-Copley had just said to her. Try as she might, she couldn't work out whether she had been reassured or roundly insulted.

At that moment she heard a bicycle bell ringing insistently on the front path, followed by an enthusiastic hammering of the door knocker and the breezy halloo of Clover Maitland through the letter box. It was clearly shaping up to be a challenging weekend.

~~~~~

Seaton sipped at his orange squash whilst the figures on his dividend statements danced across the dazzling whiteness of the paper and shimmered in half-formed, shifting shapes across the fluid of his sight. He narrowed his eyes to make sense of them, concentrating as much on fixing them to the paper as to calculate their worth and the trends in their behaviour. Try as he might, he could not bring both the figures and their value into focus, and he shook his head as much to clear his sight as to smarten up his acumen.

He'd left his straw hat on the stand in the hall and his blue glasses in the drawer of the escritoire in his dressing room, but felt inclined to fetch neither. His lassitude extended to the figures, in both their legibility and their purpose, and finally to any form of endeavour whatsoever.

He dropped the sheets beneath his chair, eased off his deck shoes and wriggled his toes in the short grass. Then, tentatively but in the partial protection of the narcotic warmth of the blazing sun, he coaxed his thoughts round to the girl.

His first sighting of her had come with its own uneasy prologue; a voyage more torpid than that of the Argonauts, perhaps, but filled with equal menace if only he'd known how to read the signs. Had he but known it, he and Northmore were sailing off the edge of the world.

North-west Amazon

The Guerrita set off from Esperenza just after daybreak with fifteen Cholo Indians sitting, cross-legged and impassive, under a makeshift tarpaulin roof on the foredeck. Suarez had recruited these with promises of regular food, tobacco to lick and a final payment of a shotgun, steel axe or cask of brandy on arrival at the expedition's projected base camp. Suarez assured Seaton that this would provide sufficient recompense for lugging Dr Munby's field laboratory and Cotterill's arsenal through entangled scrub and over backbreaking terrain.

The designated collecting ground was set at least five days' hard travelling overland, and more by water thereafter, from a landing point itself about another two days' steam upriver. The journey would be arduous with just a machete and a bag of manioc, but heavy burdens of equipment and materiel would render it near fatal to anybody not habituated to the heat and the humidity. Indeed, Suarez expected some to fall by the wayside or slip away, even though a shotgun would make each Indian a very rich man. Accordingly he had arranged for a supplementary workforce to be waiting for them at the landing point to minimise the effect of any wastage.

For some hours, they passed small clusters of dugout canoes, with male Indians in breech clouts pausing in some impenetrable conversation to watch the Guerrita's progress without comment. Some held fishing spears or nets, and once Seaton picked out two younger men with Panpipes, but if they had been playing these, they left off the moment the Guerrita's prow appeared around the densely foliaged headland, to surprise them.

Seaton only ever saw men, occasionally in ones or twos on the banks, but principally in their canoes, isolated by the stillness of the muddy water. There was never a woman, neither sight nor sound of children, nor any greeting or sign of recognition. The men stood motionless and stared. Flocks of soldados might take flight and call in alarm. Bands of small yellow haired monkeys known locally as "Frailecetos" or "Little Friars", from the black, cowl-like markings on their heads, might chatter and screech as they clambered for the higher branches. The Indians, however, remained mute and unresponsive. Until eventually they too disappeared, leaving Seaton and company to the silent disregard of nature.

All the party were intent on making the most of whatever domestic comforts the Guerrita had to offer, before their long sojourn far from the advantages of civilisation began in earnest. Munby kept to his cabin, ostensibly preparing his slides, or repacking lenses and pipettes against the violence of the overland journey. Cotterill forsook his armoury in favour of a well-thumbed copy of The Sea-Wolf, whilst strung up in a hammock in the stern. Northmore busied himself with his manifests and his journal but would often be found on a cane deck chair, reaming out his pipe and gazing sightless into the passing waters.

Seaton laid out his kit on the floor and bed of his cabin for a final inspection. He accounted for his watercolour equipment on a daily basis, from aquarelle pencils to water bottles, and he was all too aware of the limited extent of his meagre library. He turned to the neat piles of clothes, underclothes and toiletries and checked to see if any repairs or replenishments were required. He applied yet another coat of waterproofing to the seams of his poncho and to the welts, tongues and lace holes of his canvas topped jungle boots. He re-proofed his wide-brimmed hat and canvas puttees. Then he polished the leather strapping of his belts, holster and shoulder bags. He burnished the buckles and waterproofed the stitching where necessary. He checked that his linen was aired, his spare puttees, laces and shoes sealed in their oilskin packages, his personal medical kit intact and insect free, and his two watches and Naval compass in full working order.

Finally, having closed and locked the cabin door to interdict any possible conversation with Cotterill, he overhauled his Winchester rifle, his shotgun and his service Webley pistol, from firing pins to slings and lanyards. He checked his ammunition stocks and pouches for damp and misalignment. He double-checked his oils, wadding and toolkit. Suddenly he realised what he'd been in the grip of and, with an exasperated snort, locked everything back in his gun cabinet. Then he pushed this back under his bed and, throwing open the door to some semblance of fresh air, hastened on deck.

They were not going to war, they were going deep into the heart of nature, to unearth its secrets for benevolent, or at least practical, purposes and he, for one, was not going into the old routine, just because he didn't know precisely what was waiting for him beyond that eternal treeline. No doubt many challenges lay ahead, but he was there to paint watercolours and make pencil sketches, not to survive in the carnage of battle. Fear seemed somehow irrelevant and any activity attempting to dissipate or camouflage it preposterous.

He found himself alongside Northmore, who had finally got round to lighting his pipe. The baronet looked up at him through a fug of blue smoke. "Can't wait to get started, eh Captain?" he asked with irritating sagacity. "Always the same in the approaches, I find. Damn difficult to know what to do with oneself."

"We'll have enough to do in a while, I expect."

"Munby's rebuilt his lab-table at least twice." The baronet smiled broadly. "I'm not sure what young Cotterill's up to."

Seaton glanced over at the young American, whose weight shifted in the hammock as he turned over another page of Jack London. "Improving his mind?"

Northmore turned to register Cotterill's form suspended above the deck. "We'll have to ask the Williams for a tract or two for him." He turned back to enjoy his pipe. "Bound to have a few about the place, I'd say. And only too glad to hand them out."

"A missionary, you think?" Seaton reflected momentarily that wherever he'd been in the world, even on the most far-flung military forays, some Bible fellowship had invariably got there first.

"I'd say so. Reading between the lines. Fine Welsh Baptist taking his family the wrong way up the river. Mean only one thing." Northmore took his pipe from his mouth to pronounce, "The Lord's work."

"He'll be pleased to receive his post." Seaton sat down and pulled out his own pipe. "Always good to hear from home."

"Another few hours and we shall see." Northmore proffered his own tobacco pouch with little insistent jerks. "His station's the last landing point we come to before our own."

"And is ours much further on?"

The baronet rubbed an eye as his own smoke curled back into it. "Just over a day, if we don't dilly dally with the Baptists."

Cotterill spotted the Baptists' landing station first, or what remained of it. A hodgepodge of charred wooden posts emerged at odd angles from the muddy water; attached to them were the equally charred remnants of cross timbers. Some strands of wire that had not been consumed in the conflagration sprouted wildly from the twisted structure. There was a dirty diffusion in the air above the treeline on the bank. Not smoke and ash as such, but the memory of them in the stillness and the humidity.

The captain of the Guerrita anchored in mid-channel, and the expedition party gathered at the launch's rails and peered into the undergrowth. Northmore cupped his hands together and shouted in the direction of the Williams' settlement. "Mr Williams! Mr Williams!"

There came no reply, from any quarter. Not a bird went up, not a monkey chattered. The stillness was absolute. Suarez, who had arrived on deck carrying a large cutlass and with a Mauser automatic pistol stuck in his belt, shook his head sadly. "This is not a good sign, Milord. Not good at all."

Munby carried the sack containing the Williams' mail. He hefted it and looked at the others. "Well, what do we do?"

Cotterill was scanning the bank closely. "Maybe we should shout again?" He smiled apologetically, and then bellowed, "Mr Williams! Are you there, Mr Williams?"

Northmore took Seaton to one side. "You've got more experience in this kind of thing than anybody here, Captain. Can't in all conscience leave a white man to the depredations of..." he waved a hand at the bank, and then continued forcibly, "But I cannot compromise the expedition. What's your view?"

Seaton looked back at the dirty fug in the air. "If they've been raided, it was at least two days ago, I'd say. And I've never seen an aboriginal stay at the ground once he's killed and plundered. They always move away to safety. Some place to enjoy what they've taken." He looked levelly at Northmore, who understood immediately.

"They may have taken the women?"

Seaton looked at the collapsed jetty. "If you can put me ashore with a small party, I can see what's left in there. Four men, armed. One to guard our way back. We can be back in, say, fifteen or twenty minutes."

"I'm coming with you," Cotterill spoke hoarsely from just behind them. He was toting a Mannlicher carbine, twin Colts and a determined expression.

Northmore gave Seaton a weary smile. "I think that means we all are."

The Guerrita's bumboat set them down beside the jetty and its mate, carrying an ancient but ferocious looking blunderbuss, took up position at the head of the narrow, beaten track which led inland from the landing station. When Seaton questioned Suarez on his reliability, the guide replied, "He hasn't been paid yet, he'll stay till Hell freezes."

They looked a formidable crew; Cotterill and Suarez multiply armed, Seaton with his Winchester, Northmore with a shotgun, Munby carrying Seaton's revolver and the postbag he was determined to see delivered. With Suarez and Seaton leading the way, the party defiled into the forest.

"Watch at your feet, Senors," called out Suarez, as he chopped back the newly grown vegetation with his cutlass. "Wild Indian he sticks poisoned spears in the ground. Very small. Very bad."

After a few tense minutes, constrained by the narrowness of the path and the breadth of their apprehension, the party broke through into a clearing where the fate of the Williams at once became apparent. The main settlement building and both outhouses had been razed to the ground. The roofs had collapsed and most of the supporting walls had disappeared in the flames. Scattered about the ground were scraps of clothing, shards of pottery, blackened pans and fragments of shattered furniture. Almost everything had been consumed by the fire. A haze of ash, dust and something oily on the wind hung about the place.

Cotterill walked into what was once the principal room of the main building. In one corner, a section of the collapsed roof remained and seemed to be concealing something. He leant over it and called out, "There's something here." Moments later he was making for the edge of the clearing, his hand clasped over his mouth, his stomach heaving.

Suarez hacked back at the crumbling, ashy timber and revealed the corpse. The fire damage had been retarded by the fallen roof section, so they could see it was a man. He was face down, his knees tucked up beneath him and his incinerated hands clawing at the dust. The gilt buttons on his waistcoat were almost intact and the skull, though badly burned, still bore clear signs of the machete blows that had rained down upon it. Seaton and Northmore both knew they had found Mr Williams.

"I don't think wild Indians were responsible here," said Seaton, as he picked through scraps of paper trodden into the sooty residue at the base of the wall. They were remnants of printed prayers and he hoped they had provided Mr Williams with some comfort at the end.

"What makes you say that?" asked Northmore, directing Munby to see to the afflicted Cotterill.

"Smell of kerosene," replied Seaton. "Here and at the jetty. This fire's been set."

They found two women's bodies just inside the treeline behind the smaller outhouse. They had been burned beyond all facial recognition which, given their distance from the burned-out buildings, indicated they had been incinerated late in the attack. Both were naked, but Northmore scrutinised the scraps of clothing scattered about them. "I'd say this is Mrs Williams," he concluded at last from a small silver necklace welded into the torso. "But this other's a mystery. I presume it's the girl."

Munby had made his way over from Cotterill, who was now sitting in the shade, wiping his neck with a water-soaked scarf. The scientist examined the second cadaver. He studied long and hard. He picked at it with a pen knife. Eventually he stood up. "This is an old woman, Sir Everard. Look at the flattened molar there. Small, stocky. Indian for sure."

Northmore looked over at Seaton. "They must have taken the girl."

"Not far," said Suarez sadly. "As the Captain said, the men who did this are not forest Indians. They would not carry a captive off. They did this to destroy. And they will not wish to be found."

The party stood in the centre of the clearing, while Northmore made his dispositions. "We'll try and find the daughter's body. We'll bury them. And we'll deposit a written statement with the chief of police in Esperenza, on our way back. It's the best we can do."

"We could beat the perimeter, check for further outbuildings," said Seaton, as an idea struck him. "They found the kerosene store after the attack. But where are the powder stores? You wouldn't keep them all together."

Northmore shrugged. "He was a Baptist. Perhaps he didn't hold any explosives."

Munby disagreed. "Look around you, at what he's cleared. He must have had explosives."

Cotterill joined the, pale but alert. "You mean there'll be cellars somewhere?"

"I'm not sure," said Seaton. "But it's something else to look for. They may have taken her there."

They quartered and combed the area for two hours, with Northmore surreptitiously consulting his pocket watch. Suarez had brought a number of the Cholos up from the boat to dig the graves. The party knew they couldn't stay much longer.

It was one of the Cholos who found it. Once he'd learned what the white men were about, he'd laid down his spade and followed his own logic. He'd want his precious horde to be near the river, because that was always the place of escape, but not somewhere he had to dig too deep. He discovered a tiny beaten path at a right angle to the way they'd come in from the landing station. It led to two great tree trunks curled tightly about each other. Between them, a dip had been opened up over the ages by their tussling roots. And he could see by faint axe marks on the roots that someone had once cut their way in there. He went to find Suarez, who told Northmore. The baronet, busy with the interment, asked Seaton to go and look at what the Cholo thought he'd discovered.

Seaton followed the man to the dip between the huge tree roots, handed him his rifle, lowered himself under the largest lateral and found her.

Behind a narrow entrance, disguised by a curtain of leaf growth and lianas, someone had hollowed out a chamber around four feet high and eight feet deep in the compacted earth. Dynamite crates were stacked to one side and a store of jarred fruit to the other. Behind them, naked and streaked with mud and fruit syrup, in a desperate simulation of the Indians she thought were out there hunting her down, was Hestia Williams. Surrounded by her sticky sweet foodstuffs and her own excreta. A desperate pixie. An abandoned hobgoblin.

As Seaton clambered into her hiding place, she stared at him with angry haunted eyes. Too desolate to scream, too furious to show outright fear.

"It's alright," he said softly. "I'm English."

"You didn't come!" she screamed at him, beside herself with rage. "You never came!"

On this cloudless summer's day, the Reverend Attwater was perhaps the only man in the parish to be surprised at the turnout for his Sunday service. As he peered out of the vestry, he could see that his little congregation had swelled appreciably. He breathed in deeply and offered up a brief prayer that his sermon, cobbled from a minor triumph in his seminarian days, might prove strong enough to hold them and, if possible, draw some of them back next week.

He now had two challenging audiences to attend to. While most of the neighbourhood seemed to be filing into the nave and looking about them for rapidly dwindling seating space, the august personage, filled with devilled kidneys, toast and Poulter's marmalade, was installed placidly in the front pew. Dr Houghton-Copley was the more intellectually rigorous of the two, of course, but was, hopefully, a fleeting witness to his oratory. The neighbourhood, now presenting itself in such unforeseen numbers, only arrived in force for weddings and funerals, for Easter, Christmas and, if sunny, for the Harvest Festival. Sunday observance had dwindled since the Great War, in a way that the Roll of Honour on the war memorial could not fully account for.

Today, for some reason, he'd been given a sign and he hoped he could live up to it. As he checked his pocket watch, his ancient organist struck up the anthem and the Reverend Attwater went about his business.

Captain Seaton sat on his own, half way up on the south side of the central aisle. Mrs Simmons sat across from him with her friend Mrs Peters, another widow in the village, with whom she would spend the afternoon. Foster was not in attendance. He didn't make a point of it, but his observations had ceased with the regimental observances for survivors at the end of hostilities on the Western Front.

Seaton normally attended because not to go would have been construed, in a man of his local standing, as some form of social dereliction. However, he had to confess to a further motivation behind his being there today. Given Dr Houghton-Copley's presence, he knew his absence would have had a more intrusive and personal interpretation place upon it. He had come to value his privacy enough to make public appearances when required, however disagreeable. Although a few lusty hymns from the young choir and a few warm platitudes from the Reverend Attwater could not, in all conscience, be called disagreeable.

He shook his head slightly as the phrase "in all conscience" passed through his mind and looked up to see the Reverend Attwater staring back pointedly at him. He glanced at his neighbour, to see if he should be singing, but her hymnal was still clasped between her lace-gloved hands. He looked back to the Reverend in some perplexity, only to be gifted the barest nod of complicity and a small apologetic smile, before "Hills of The North, Rejoice!" was announced and they all stood up to sing praises to the Lord.

The influx of worshippers made the exodus after the service all the more confused. At his customary station in the porch, the Reverend Attwater found himself busily shaking hands with people he hadn't seen for months, if at all. It wasn't till Clover and Ursula hovered about him, Clover in a Sunday best of emerald-green, homespun tweed with a sizeable, purple beret and Ursula in a slate-blue, satin trouser suit with a short fur cape, blue toque and lace veil, that he felt amongst people he knew.

"A very thoughtful sermon, vicar," Clover offered dutifully and then, with a sudden rush, she asked, "Is the Captain inside, only we were at the back, you see?"

"He's in there fiddling with his hat." Ursula craned over a farmer's family just exiting and peered into the church. Then she too addressed the Reverend. "What time is Enid serving lunch?"

"I don't know, precisely." Attwater was flustered, not sure whether he was being pressed, rather forthrightly, for an invitation he knew he daren't make. "In about half an hour, I suppose."

"That'll do," said Ursula to Clover.

"We've invited Dr Houghton-Copley to tea," Clover explained.

"And we don't want him too drowsy," concluded Ursula, who then turned and prowled away from the porch to where it would be deemed permissible to light up. Even Ursula observed the village proprieties on Sunday; she knew old Mrs Jennings, her laundress, would draw the line and resign at the merest whiff of blasphemy.

She joined a clump of the younger men already smoking in the roadway just outside the lych-gate. Stiff with embarrassment, they proffered her a light for her cheroot and strained their necks trying not to look at her, for fear of betraying their lack of worldly experience through gawping or giggling.

Clover stayed put on the vicar's right shoulder, nodding politely but rather listlessly as each parishioner passed by to pay his respects to the clergyman. She kept peering into the darkness to locate the two protagonists of the drama she'd been hastily writing and rewriting in her mind all morning.

In this she was not alone. Most of the congregation had been swivelling their heads or craning their necks, as discreetly as circumstances would allow, for a glimpse of the main characters in the saga of the Captain and the crocodiles. While most could recognise the Captain, his accuser, in the seclusion of the front pew, was lost to all but a lucky few. And those few could gain no real impression, save that he dressed impeccably and sung in a strong, steady voice, with no apparent referral to a hymn book.

The moment Ainsley Seaton stepped into the porch and replaced his hat Clover was upon him. "My dear Captain! Terribly short notice, I know, but you will come to tea, won't you? Ursula's invited Dr Houghton-Copley and I couldn't bear it if you weren't there!"

She had surprised herself as much as she now surprised the Captain. Something in her felt ashamed that she would be party to some private conversation about this old friend. A conversation in which he couldn't defend himself. Not that she thought there'd be anything on which he would wish to defend himself, of course. But still, it wasn't right, somehow. Even if it were, supposedly, for her own benefit. Ursula could huff and puff but she'd just have to talk to that weird churchman about the Ballet Russes. They could prance around the parlour to Prokofiev for all she cared.

As this image caused her to snap out of her preoccupation, she realised that Ainsley Seaton was watching her with a somewhat strained expression. Looking down, she found she was gripping his hand powerfully with both of hers. Discovering this dramatic posture only served to redouble her efforts. "You will come, won't you? You simply must."

"But of course, Miss Maitland." He looked concerned, anxious even, Clover thought. "Please don't distress yourself."

She beamed at him with relief. "Oh, I'm not distressed, Captain Seaton. Not in the least. I knew I could count on you."

She kissed him awkwardly and quickly on the cheek, before she lost her nerve, and then hurried away to where Ursula was examining one of the new pocket cigarette lighters one of the village youths had produced. "Ursula, dear!" She gave a cheery and hopeful wave. "I've got a lovely surprise for you!"

Thinking the matter over whilst walking back to Laurel House for the cold collation Mrs Simmons would have left prepared for him in the pantry, Seaton concluded it must have been Clover's intercession that allowed Houghton-Copley to be waiting, ahead of him, in the shade of the lych-gate, as the last of the congregation passed through.

The diplomatist stepped out of the shadow, swept off his Panama and extended his hand. "My dear Captain, delighted to resume our acquaintance."

"Good afternoon, Doctor." Seaton took the proffered hand. The handshake felt firmer than it had on their first meeting. "I gather we're to meet at tea."

"Dear ladies." Houghton-Copley looked pensive. "One must always encourage the arts, don't you think?"

"I believe there was some matter you wished my opinion on?" Now that Houghton-Copley had ushered him back into the shade beneath the lych-gate, Seaton felt the shadows closing in on him. "Concerning the Amazon?"

Houghton-Copley's face lit up as if at a moment of sudden recollection. "Ah, yes! The Welsh!" He studied Seaton's nonplussed expression closely. "They were Welsh, weren't they? A cantankerous race, the men of the Chapel. And I believe as inclined to vendetta as any Sardinian. If it weren't for the rain and the demoralising passivity of their Non-conformism, I'd believe we'd find the Valleys wholly depopulated."

Seaton leaned against the cool, morbid stones of the lych-gate. "I'm afraid you have the better of me."

Houghton-Copley looked steadily at him and spoke softly, "The Williams were Welsh, were they not? Micah, Megan and Hestia?"

Seaton steadied himself. It was as he had thought. It was why she had reappeared in the summer house the day before. A mute chorus announcing the tragedy to be played out once more, only this time as a public performance. "Yes," he replied. "They were Welsh."

"Then, you know what we are dealing with here." The diplomatist looked about him to ensure there was nobody was within earshot. Then, his gaze held Seaton's as he continued, "Murder, depravity and a monstrous deception."

"I cannot help you in this," protested Seaton turning to go.

Houghton-Copley placed a hand on his arm to turn him back. "I very much think you're the only man who can."

Chapter Four

North-west Amazon

Seaton stood alongside Northmore at the Guerrita's rail and smoked his pipe, while they awaited Munby's prognosis on the girl's condition. Cotterill was on the rear deck, overhauling his arsenal in case the raiding party returned in search of further plunder. Ramón Suarez was completing their withdrawal from the Mission, accounting for every machete and shovel employed on shore. Munby was closeted with Hestia in his cabin below.

They had wrapped her in an expedition blanket and Seaton and Cotterill had attempted to carry her back towards the launch. She had clawed her way out of their arms like an uncooperative house cat, and insisted on walking the rest of the way, scowling at any attempt to assist her. When Seaton told her of her parents' death, she seemed to shrug this news off as the inevitable outcome of her time spent below ground. She seemed neither shocked nor greatly moved, but insistent on a bath and something to eat.

Seaton, like any soldier, was habituated to the presence of death and the many variants of response to it from the surviving. He had a professional's respect for sudden mortality and the privacy of those required to deal with it. His business, now, was with the living.

Northmore had clambered into Hestia's hiding place beneath the twisted trees and requisitioned the remaining stores of explosives and preserved fruit. Behind this stock pile, he'd found the torn nightdress she had wedged into the dirt during her transformation into mud-smeared forest sprite. Then, in the furthest recess, he was surprised to discover a small trunk, containing two calico dresses, a day jacket, some linen and a second nightdress, along with toilet articles, a pair of buttoned boots and some canvas shoes. Essentials that had seemingly been assembled by a mother anxious her daughter should arrive on the Golden Shore with a change of underclothes and some presentable, but not extravagant, daywear.

The trunk had been shipped on board the Guerrita, and Munby had insisted on a medical examination of the girl. She seemed more acquiescent with the little, forthright Lancastrian, and her cooperation was further ensured by a bowl of unnamed stew and some fruit, upon which she fell with an almost feral appetite.

While she ate and Munby inspected, the expedition party buried her parents' remains and those of their house servant, heaping the heaviest stones they could find upon each grave to deter the larger predators, and erecting a wooden cross at the head. Two more bodies had been behind the devastated buildings, both male Mission Indians, their corpses not incinerated but mutilated savagely. Cotterill supervised their burial himself, interring them alongside the maid and a respectful distance from the graves of their former employers.

"Damnable business," Northmore muttered. He stamped his feet on the decking in an assertive but rather directionless manner.

Seaton could see it was not simply the atrocity that was playing on the baronet's mind. Fate and a murderous band of unknowns had thrown an encumbrance in their path and Northmore was unsure how, with any ethical balance, he could dispose of it.

"Even if she is fit to travel," Seaton offered to the pensive expedition leader, "I don't think we can send her back down the river on her own. She'd be safer under those trees than she would in Esperenza."

They both looked back towards the treeline and the smuts still hovering in the oily air above it. But their minds were on the lawless depravities they'd witnessed in the river towns on the long journey from Para. Northmore shook his head and breathed hard.

"I suppose we could leave someone with her, here." Seaton considered. "Until we make our way back after the wet season."

"Out of the question," replied Northmore, as Seaton knew he would. "We can't spare a man. And we can't leave just one in case those devils return."

"Nothing for it, then."

"Of all the damned bad luck!" Northmore pulled himself up and looked apologetically at Seaton, for this seemingly callous expostulation. Seaton smiled reassuringly.

"She may know how to cook." he suggested.

"She's bound to know how to eat," said Northmore, his expedition manifests never far from his mind.

Seaton looked over to where Cotterill was reaming out one of his rifles. "He'll just have to go out for the pot more often. Somehow I can't see him raising an objection."

They were laughing at this, when Munby came up on deck and walked over, lighting up a cheroot. He stood for a moment watching the smoke float out towards the muddy shore.

"What's your opinion?" inquired Northmore, at length.

"Mr Williams spared the rod," said Munby flatly. "Knows her own mind, that young lady. Thinks she knows yours too."

"And her medical condition?" the baronet asked patiently, clearly used to Munby's method of dissertation and the price one paid for accuracy.

"Unimpaired," pronounced the biologist emphatically. "Young Hestia Williams is as strong as a horse. And eating like one." He looked at the baronet with some sympathy. "More than fit to travel."

Northmore stared into the river and then nodded. Munby looked across to Seaton with a small conspiratorial grin. "There's an aunt in Llandudno," he went on, "But no love lost there."

"It's a bloody long way to Llandudno," Northmore observed tersely. Then he consulted his pocket watch. "Tell Suarez to get a move on, will you? We've lost enough time as it is."

And with that, the expedition rejoined its itinerary, and the Guerrita's captain fired up its engines to try and regain the party's momentum.

Hestia made an appearance on deck in the early evening, wearing one of her calico dresses, her hair brushed and pinned up in some semblance of order. She walked amongst the company with a cultivated look of preoccupation and holding a glass of sugar water, from which she occasionally took sips with great concentration, as if the glass might be dashed from her hand by some sudden movement of the boat. She gave Munby, struggling against the fading light to annotate a crumpled monograph on entomological reclassifications, a slight smile hinting at an undeclared complicity. This, she followed with a cold and formal nod to Seaton, which made him feel clumsy. Cotterill, extended in his hammock again with The Sea-Wolf, she ignored completely.

Northmore was clambering with Ramón Suarez amongst the expedition stores, calculating the loads each porter would take up when they landed. If Hestia noticed them, she didn't acknowledge it.

Now that she was presentably dressed and in greater possession of herself, Seaton was hard-pressed to put an age to her. She wasn't a child any more, that much was clear. Still, to his eye, she was not quite of marriageable age, unless by the flexible standards of the outposts of Empire. Something in between, then.

She stood at the rail, swivelling gently at the waist with an easy listlessness, until Munby spotted her and went over to introduce her to the others. He took her by the elbow and ushered her over towards Seaton, who thought he detected some reluctance in her steps.

"Captain Seaton." Munby summed him up with a brisk gesture of his free hand. Then, sensing perhaps that his social skills had been a tad wanting, he added, "You're lucky he found you, I'd say."

She gave Seaton a steely look and her mouth was tight until, with a visible effort, she freed herself from whatever was constricting her. Could it be some adolescent reaction to the solecism of her previous nakedness, the Captain wondered, which accounted for this froideur? He was inclined to think not. The whole party had been witness to that and she seemed at peace with them, or at least in a posture of armed neutrality. For some reason, she had it hard with him. Perhaps she found in him some unacceptable representation of the intrusive adult world. His had been the first presence underground. He had been the prime invader of her private nightmare and her sanctuary.

He had also been the herald of her parents' mortality and her own helpless dependence in a capricious and unkind world. It would be hard for a young girl, in such circumstances, to distinguish between the harbinger and the terrible news he brought. Perhaps time would lighten this darkness between them.

Hestia proffered a hand stiffly and, as he shook it, she said, "It seems I'm to thank you, Captain. Though quite what for, I'm not at all sure."

Munby and Seaton exchanged a look at this, while Seaton replied as gently as he might, "We are all deeply sorry about the death of your parents, Hestia. This must be a very difficult time."

The girl pursed her lips as though considering the validity of this statement, and then spoke to Munby. "Are we to walk very far tomorrow?"

"Daylight hours." Munby's tone avoided any invitation to complaint or observation. Hestia appeared to feel the need for neither but simply nodded, pursed her lips again and walked back to the rail to continue her aimless half turns.

"She must still be in shock," Seaton hazarded. "A loss like that…"

"If you want my private opinion," said Munby, "I don't believe that young lady's in the grip of any great loss. Repressed or otherwise."

Seaton thought about the mortalities and bereavements he'd witnessed throughout his active soldiering and his various recuperations from it. "If she's not, that would make her an exceptional personality, Doctor."

"I'm afraid so," the biologist concurred. He considered for a moment, before continuing hesitantly, "I'm not prone to flights of fancy, Seaton."

"I can see that," smiled Seaton, wondering of what emotive revelation this was the forerunner.

Munby lowered his voice as if the observation were an awkward, almost indelicate one. "When I first examined her, with the affair fresh upon her, the deaths, the destruction, the end of her home, she evinced nothing less than a sense of release and liberation."

"She'd been in that pit for days, man," Seaton argued.

"I'm telling you," Munby stated categorically. "It isn't that pit she thinks she's escaped from."

Northmore and Suarez emerged from the bulk of the stores and the baronet announced his wish that the party retire early for the night. They were to arrive at their disembarkation point before dawn and it was his intention to go ashore at first light, appoint the order and loading of the expeditionary column and depart for the interior immediately.

Munby put his cabin at Hestia's disposal but Cotterill then announced his intention of sleeping on deck, to savour the a few hours of tropical breeze. Accordingly, the girl put herself to bed amongst the American's bandoliers and foraging equipment, while Munby retired to enjoy a final night between thin cotton sheets, in his narrow berth.

Seaton snuffed his cabin light and lay back to stare up into his mosquito net. Shapes shifted beneath its apex, as the pale moonlight seeped in through his cabin window. The Williams family had provided an unforeseen complication but he knew such happenstances were all too frequent on the campaign trail, and he tried to clear his mind of them. The girl herself could not present any significant interference. Cotterill should be able to provide her with whatever companionship she might require; he was the closest in age to her of them all.

He lay back and listened to the jungle night, the stillness punctuated by the rustling of leaves, the shifting of lianas and the susurration of weeds at the water's edge. As the noises blended and the clouds merged in the heights of his mosquito net, Seaton felt his mind wandering over to the opportunities and awakenings, unarticulated but keenly felt, that he knew awaited him in the mass of primal forest he would enter as the dawn broke.

His was, in part, a voyage of personal expansion. As if, through painting in the deep forest, he might discover how he saw the world and thereby what it meant to him. Furthermore, he might move on to grasp a way of dealing with the things he could not understand. Far from the open challenges of the veldt, the adrenal confusions of battle, even the delicate choreographies of West Sussex society, he might finally apprehend the ability to live with uncertainties, mysteries, doubts, without any irritable reaching after fact and reason. Negative Capability, what would that make of him? He chortled quietly at the thought of what Munby would make of a cavalry officer, on half pay, silently conferring with Keats, the night before he was going to cut his way into thousands of square miles of hostile tropical thicket.

He awoke to the churning of the engines as the Guerrita turned itself around, prior to berthing at their jumping off place. The moment they were safely unloaded into the boundless forest, the launch would be returning to more secure, or less ominous, surroundings.

The expedition party assembled on deck and peered into the mist-shrouded bank. Makeshift shelters had been thrown up around the landing station, a meeting point for stragglers and derelicts and ex-Mission Indians passing through from one tract to another. A further body of porters awaited them by the landing station here, delighting the expedition party. There were twenty-three in all, if you counted the three women but excluded the baby one of them was suckling. Northmore having completed his head count from the guard rail and clapped Munby on the shoulder.

"Capital! With the men we've brought up, we've got more than a full working party, Munby. What a fellow that Suarez is!"

"Got the luck of the devil, that bugger," replied Munby, but his eyes were shining with relief. Transportation of provisions and equipment was the most precarious element within all of the expedition's tenuous logistics. Suarez had arranged that a sufficient workforce was at the right place at the right time. Given the habitual inconstancy of the region, this was nothing short of miraculous. There would be no agonising choices between foodstuff and scientific equipment to be made. No prioritising of experiments and research projects. No risky downgrading of medicinal supplies or ammunition. They could take it all in.

That included Cotterill's photographic equipment, which he suddenly produced, with a shy pride, now that he could see there'd be bodies enough to carry it into the depths of the unknown. It consisted of a Graflex camera with a high-speed shutter that Cotterill announced to Seaton was for "capturing jaguars and such", a large-scale plate camera with several dozen plates and a quantity of print paper. Cotterill said he had decided to make his prints on site rather than risk carrying the plates back out again.

Seaton was taken with the young American's freshly disclosed enthusiasm, and just a little put out. While he had hoped to be the artist of record for the Northmore enterprise, in a somewhat anachronistic way, it had only been a half-formed aspiration. The young American would be capturing what he saw, while he was going to attempt to capture what he felt. There'd surely be room for both mediums, and rewards from each. Still, he wondered why Cotterill not mentioned photography before, but confined himself to, "Well, this is a surprise."

Cotterill disclosed an inherited canniness, "I didn't want Sir Everard to choose them over the guns, Captain. If we ran out of backs to carry in." He shrugged. "He's a scientist. A great scientist. But our priorities might diverge on that."

While they watched Cotterill assemble his small photographic section for disembarkation, the baronet grinned at Seaton. "I'd seen the crate, of course. Just thought it was more firepower."

The forest was slowly coming into relief as the early morning sun began to burn off the mist. Suarez supervised the crew of the Guerrita and the Cholo Indians, as they unloaded the stores in a premeditated configuration along the shore. Foodstuffs, medicines, scientific equipment, workshop and building materials, armaments and personal effects were all marked out with an allocated number of porters to each section and load. Meanwhile, Northmore presided over a final breakfast on the aft deck.

Hestia had arrived at the table, dressed and ready to go. Her feet were encased in light canvas shoes, tied on with cotton puttees that disappeared beneath the hem of her calico dress, which was now hitched up a foot or so above the ground. She had a scarf knotted about her neck and had provided herself with a sturdy walking cane and a gunny sack, in which she kept her immediate personal requirements. She had evidently traversed the forest on foot before, at least in some measure. No doubt when Mr Williams was constructing his Baptist haven down river. She sat in silence, nibbling at the cornbread and eggs set before her. Some of her reserve had faded with the advent of a new day, and she smiled prettily while passing the salt to Sir Everard, but otherwise kept her own counsel.

Suarez joined them at last and Munby pressed him to eat. Northmore unfolded his map for the final briefing while the quartermaster replenished himself with sliced ham, eggs and coffee. As ever, when he felt a speech seemed to be required, Northmore rose to the occasion. His logistical briefing was accompanied by a brief reiteration of the purpose of the expedition and a slightly longer peroration on what was so auspicious about the arena and the tasks he had chosen for them.

They were to proceed north on a set bearing. Naturally this would mean certain diversions and adjustments but, if they maintained this bearing for a week at most, they would come upon the southernmost tributary of the Kahuanari River, which itself flowed eventually into the Japura. They would then follow this tributary down

93

stream in a north-westerly direction, rafting where possible, till it merged with another and both flowed a further thirty or so miles into the main Kahuanari itself. The meeting of the tributaries and the accorded diversity of flora and fauna made this an ideal collection ground. It was isolated by distance and by the relative impenetrability of the terrain. It was diverse. Above all, it was virgin. Many years ago, a French adventurer, on a vague commission from the Peruvian Government, had mapped the general area with equal vagueness but the close terrain remained uncharted. Crucial to their purpose, the light of science had never shone there. The land around it was invested principally by the relatively peaceable Okaina and Nonuya tribes. Coming upon the collection ground by this circuitous route meant less risk of encountering the more warlike Boro and Menime, who preyed upon each other in the areas around the Kahuanari as it flowed east, and along the Japura River that ran on the northern parallel to the Issa Parana they had just negotiated.

"An extra two day's hard walking perhaps, gentlemen," he concluded as he folded the map away. "But the trek will be more comfortable in other aspects."

Seaton saw a ghost of a smile cross Hestia's lips. Whether it was at the baronet's assessment of the exceptional nature of the collection ground, or the dangers attendant on their reaching it, she was clearly not disposed to say. It was a knowing smile, the Captain thought, but she was keeping the knowledge to herself.

The column was larger than that normally considered feasible for traversing such difficult terrain. The baronet had deliberated long and hard about whether to split the party in two, with a day's interval between them, so the latter unit could make use of the camp sites the first unit had vacated, before both parties assembled beside the Kahuanari to build the rafts. However, control of the loads,

94

and the imperative of a swift, coordinated approach, dictated they would stay together. A few nights cramped camping would be a small price to pay for arriving on site with all the scientific supplies safe and in order. Accordingly, the column was to be divided into sections with a cutting and scouting party at its head, which would be replaced regularly, at intervals dependent on the difficulty of the terrain. The expedition's provisions would follow immediately behind, followed by the armaments and medical supplies. The bulkier items for the workshop and the delicate scientific equipment would then form the last section of the column proper. This would allow the bearers of the latter to take advantage of a well trodden path, and afford them full warning of any obstacles or perilous situations on the route ahead. An armed rearguard would ensure that nobody and no equipment fell by the wayside, as well as assuring their security from attack from behind, a favoured method of ambush throughout the continent. Each section would remain in full sight of the section behind it, and runners would connect the head and the rear parties at intervals of no more than half an hour.

Ramón Suarez would remain in the van to supervise the cutting and, with Northmore, would be responsible for the navigation. At the outset, Cotterill would advance with the provisions, Munby with the scientific equipment and Seaton, with his service experience, was ideally suited to bring up the rear. When Cotterill seemed about to protest at his station with the cookpots, Northmore assured them all that once their progress was regularised, their posts would be rotated. He himself would range the column, to ensure the parts were functioning as an effective whole. Any modifications would be made on the march.

He then produced a several monogrammed silver whistles which, with some solemnity, he handed out. On hearing one blast, each man would ensure that his section stopped immediately. On two blasts, they would resume. On three blasts they would halt the men and make their way immediately either up or down the column to see what was afoot.

At his request they all checked their whistles with vigorous and protracted blasts. Hestia burst into peals of laughter at this and when Cotterill lent her his to blow, was unable to pucker her lips without being convulsed again.

"They may prove life savers, Miss Williams." Northmore was determined his whistles, commissioned at his private expense from Harrods, should not be undervalued; but then when she managed a breathless peep at last, he joined in the applause with them all.

Twenty minutes later they were assembled on the bank, watching the Guerrita drawing out into mid-stream. The launch had departed with almost unseemly haste the moment the gangplank had been stowed, as if impatient to disassociate itself with such a reckless enterprise. Its Captain gave a final wave and an uninflected shout of "Va con dios!"

As soon as they stepped off the gangplank, Munby had handed them each a small glass stoppered flask, with a peremptory, "This is your quinine water. It's up to you now. The dispensary is closed."

And with that admonition, each turned to find the section of baggage and men he would be responsible for.

"Gentlemen." Cotterill's voice, unusually diffident, floated over to them. Seaton turned to see the young man standing there with his Graflex camera at the ready. "If I could ask you to group together for a moment." He coloured slightly and then addressed Hestia, who was standing off to one side, poking absently in the dirt with her cane. "You too, Miss. If you'd be so kind."

So, breakfasted but still slightly bemused, Seaton peered into Cotterill's lens in the early light, surrounded by the expedition party. Hestia had at once positioned herself at the edge of the group, but had been shepherded to the front in accordance with her sex and her age. Wayward strands of her blond hair were brushing against his chin. He tried to ignore this with parade ground discipline, yet was all too aware of the faintest suggestion of personal vanity.

After what seemed an eternity, Cotterill announced himself satisfied and they broke up. He called out to them, by way of apology, "This way we'll have proof we arrived."

Before he walked off to locate his personal equipment, rifle bearer and contingent responsibilities, Seaton mused that they'd first have to get out alive for any such proof to be delivered.

West Sussex

Seaton cut idly with his Malacca at the more prominent cat's ears standing proud amongst the stitchwort, ox-eyed daisies and tufted vetch that jostled with the grasses along the footpath to one side of Sam Faring's meadowland. A brown meadow butterfly was chasing an orange female along the peak of the hedgerow, in which the linnets were nesting again. In five minutes he'd be at the stile entering onto the lane, and in five after that he'd be at the Old Forge.

The sun was still high and strong and he almost regretted forsaking his soft shirt for the formal aspect he intended to present to the diplomatist during Clover's tea. He had retained the suit he'd worn to church, a charcoal grey three piece, but had affixed a cut yellow rose to his buttonhole, in recognition of the lighter social aspect of the call he'd been coerced into making.

He'd searched out Foster, who was attempting one of Mrs Simmons' puzzle pages in a deckchair in the kitchen garden at Laurel House, and had made the exceptional request that he be picked up at the Old Forge no later than five o'clock. Sunday afternoons were traditionally a rest period for the entire household and this requirement was out of keeping with common practice. Yet Foster had given a ready assurance that he'd be there, and that he'd enjoy some respite from these infernal conundrums.

Now, with arrangements for a strategic withdrawal in place, all he had to do was complete his plan for the campaign. This was simplicity itself and easy to hold to, once committed. He would not engage, not so much as a skirmish, not even so much as a feint. He could not permit this high functionary, however well connected, to interfere with ghosts so carefully laid to rest. He would neither refute nor suggest. He would remain hors de combat. The Williams were long dead, God rest their unquiet souls, and he would not be party to this specious exhumation, with its questionable associations of subterfuge, political stratagems and now murder.

He would listen. He would strive to be agreeable and, if possible, diverting, but he would dispense nothing more than general conversation. If the diplomatist possessed half the competences that his reputation precursed, he would understand that there was no more to be drawn from the situation and take up his researches, if such they truly were, in some other arena.

Seaton felt the familiar twinge in his knee as he climbed over the stile; God alone knew how he'd mount a hunter these days. Although he had to concede the likelihood was remote. He brushed the pollen and seeds from his trousers, straightened his tie, adjusted the set of his buttonhole and then strolled up the lane. The ancient hedge leading up to the front wall of the Old Forge was covered by high-banked honeysuckle that wafted out its soft fragrance into the hazy afternoon. It would smell ever sweeter in the twilight, by which time he would be safely home. Behind the Old Forge he could hear the newly-fledged rooks cawing as they circled high above the rookery.

As he followed the lane round to the carved stone gateway, he saw a dapper figure walking briskly ahead of him, taking a number of prim steps to his own off-centred marching gait. He picked out the wide-brimmed hat, the yellow gloves and a flash of light blue leather in the hand as the figure turned into the Old Forge yard. The diplomatist was ahead of him again.

Seaton slowed his progress and then halted. He breathed in the honeysuckle and let the cries of the young rooks carry his mind skyward. He'd allow the man to settle at Clover's hearth before he made his entrance.

Ursula had changed from her church clothes and now sported a vividly floral tea-gown and a large bandana of abstract design tied, gypsy fashion, about her head. This, she had set off with a profusion of amber and jet beads, and was now inserting one of her cheroots into an amber cigarette holder.

Clover sighed to herself as she finished arranging the cake stand to its best advantage, on the low octagonal table set in the middle of the room. She thought Ursula's costume inclined more to absinthe and sugared almonds, as Ursula herself had intimated with the subtly disdainful look she had given the tea service. This after they'd both gone to Mr Poulter's store to select the marble cake and iced fancies now on display. Mrs Jennings had offered a rock cake but neither of them had thought it was quite the thing for a man of the diplomatist's rarefied tastes and experience. In the absence of the Green Fairy, it was to be Darjeeling and marble cake, with a fondant or two to toy with besides.

Mrs Jennings had sent along her grand daughter, Lettie, to provide some semblance of household. The captain would know of Lettie's temporary status but Clover felt she could rely on his discretion in this matter. In her Sunday dress and borrowed starched apron, Lettie was now watching the large kettle boiling on the stove in the tiny kitchen, sniffing slightly and praying she would not drop anything. Sir Austin Maitland had, of course, designed the tea service and even though Lettie was unaware of its provenance, the huge teapot still looked like a year's wages to her. Clover shared much of her apprehension but had decided to leave the teapot's wellbeing in the hands of fate. The diplomatist would be habituated to the presence of servants, and nobody wanted him discommoded, particularly when an easy and free conversation at tea was of paramount importance.

Ursula leafed through some records by the gramophone. "Shall we have music, Clovy?" she asked, but then reflected, "He'll feel more discursive if he thinks he is determining the mood, of course."

"We can always offer some after," suggested Clover and with a nod of agreement, Ursula set down the records and went to adopt a languid pose in the bay window, which commanded a view of the front path.

"He's here!" she said, so sharply that Clover felt obliged to steady the cake stand.

Indeed Houghton-Copley's arrival, albeit minutely anticipated, set both their pulses racing. Ursula sat down on the little chair beside the gramophone to compose herself. Clover looked in on Lettie, which she hoped might forestall any potential catastrophe, and then walked swiftly up to the main door to wait for the man to knock.

Scarcely had the impacts of the brass knocker, forged into a rugged likeness of the Lion of Judah, finished echoing about her ears, than the door was open and the diplomatist was framed in the doorway. Houghton-Copley removed his wide straw hat and dabbed at his overheated brow with a voluminous and finely scented handkerchief. He stood in the threshold, flushed and breathing hard, despite the cool linen suit and silk shirt that he'd changed into for the occasion. Then, having gathered himself, looked about him as if entranced.

"The heart's blood of English arts and crafts," he pronounced, with an airy wave at Clover's father's interior, preserved by her with a curator's zeal despite frequent incursions from Ursula's eclectic predilections. For a moment his rapt appraisal was arrested by several yards of purple crepe interwoven with lime green satin, draped over Sir Austin Maitland's hand wrought and 'improved' farm implements that hung along the vestibule wall. Swiftly shaking any reservation away, he produced a sigh of deep satisfaction and advanced, beaming broadly, into the main living area.

"Ladies, dear ladies. I see about me the perfect twinning of aesthetics and diligence. Craftsmanship is too meagre a word to celebrate this inspired flourishing of the spiritual within the pragmatic." He sat down a shade too quickly on an unforgiving armchair, but recovered to observe, "What a pleasure it must be to spend your days in the midst of so strong and so devout a design for living."

Clover looked across at Ursula for assistance here. Both of them felt her father's presence keenly about the place, and it was an uneasy relationship at best. Sir Austin's rigorous design principles held them in thrall from beyond the grave. His was a robust simplicity, tinged with various lush transcendentalisms (He had bequeathed a small volume of mystic hymns to the nation, which awaited an English composer of sufficient folkloric credentials.) and it brooked no deviation from the path. The Old Forge was his shrine, as visionary, sculptor, joiner, stone mason and mystic jack-of-all-trades. Clover and Ursula felt they were its handmaidens. They didn't exactly live in it.

Ursula might toss the occasional brickbat with some Turkish cushions here and there, the intimation of joss sticks throughout, a largely decorative samovar over by the gramophone, but, in this, she was merely trying to soften the austere and unyielding prospect of formalism and functionalism that Sir Austin had decreed should frame their remaining years. Her heart may have been in Paris, but she slept in one of his severe, hardwood bed-frames, decorated with reliefs of spring sowing and harvests, a renovated medievalism on the passage of time.

For Clover, her surroundings were a constant reminder of her obligation to carry on the Maitland tradition of progressive artistic discipline and her complete inability to live up to the standards set by her father on his demise. The more he was vaunted, the more she felt she would be found wanting. She had tried to prove herself exceptional as a calligrapher, as a potter and as a watercolourist. She had discovered early on that she was merely ordinary. In the normal course of events, she might have been inclined to find that quite agreeable, but her father's shade would not permit such laxity. So she elected for her position as curator, as somewhat the lesser of the evils thrust upon her.

"We try and make it home," she replied, when she saw that nothing would be forthcoming from Ursula. Then she noticed that Houghton-Copley had brought a small blue leather portfolio with him, which he had slipped discreetly to one side of the arm chair.

She may have peeked fractionally longer than good manners dictate, for at once Houghton-Copley waved the portfolio in the air. "Delights. Surprises. Small fragments of wonder," he admitted merrily, but then held up a mock admonitory finger. "But first the cup that cheers."

Clover bustled out to bring in the Maitland teapot and its attendant hot water jug. Lettie was relegated, to her intense relief, to ferrying in a range of sandwiches, from Poulter's new salmon mousse to Faring's ham and mustard to home-grown cucumber. Houghton-Copley took up his napkin with relish, just as the Lion of Judah hammered out again and Ainsley Seaton, swiftly divested of hat and Malacca, was ushered into the feast.

He glanced up at the large wooden clock on the mantel; etched with medieval players, mummers and tumblers, it showed the time to be a quarter to four. Still, he felt he was some way behind the proceedings.

"I'm dreadfully sorry," he said. "I appear to be late."

"You're not late at all, Captain," Houghton-Copley replied for his hostess. "But you are quite forbidding. Do sit down, my dear fellow."

The Captain did as he was so affably bid. Ursula handed him a plate and surrounded him with sandwiches. Clover poured out tea and dispensed milk and sugar to request. Houghton-Copley expressed great appreciation of the salmon mousse but demurred at another round, preferring instead to move straight on to the marble cake, which he ate with a hand cupped under his chin to protect his waistcoat. Seaton stuck with his Faring's ham, although he'd finished a salad of the same not an hour before. Conversation had so far been slight and of an entirely practical nature and he thought there was every chance of the occasion passing off without incident. He would simply draw Houghton-Copley aside as they left and reiterate his inability to be of further assistance, in a manner from which the other would further conclude that no more social interaction would be forthcoming.

"I have something here I believe might be of interest to you, Captain," said Houghton-Copley, once he had assured himself that no vestige of marble cake besmirched his suiting. "It has already piqued Miss Maitland's curiosity no end, has it not?"

103

Clover waved a dissenting hand. "You're teasing me," she protested.

"All shall be revealed," replied the diplomatist gaily. He drew the blue leather portfolio onto his knees, opened it swiftly and produced a yellowing sheet of stiff paper, about ten inches long and eight inches wide, which he handed across to the Captain. "Voila! A fond memory returned to its owner, I think."

"It's a photograph!" announced Clover, hoping to prevent Ursula from pushing her aside in order to see.

Seaton looked down and saw Munby, Northmore, Hestia and himself clustered on the riverbank staring out of an Amazonian early morning. Their pale gazes had travelled across fifteen years and along an all but inconceivable sequence of connections, coincidences and unknown interventions, to surface here at Clover's tea .

"Where did you get this?" he murmured.

"One simply has friends." Houghton-Copley demurely swatted the provenance away. "Doesn't the Captain look resolute, ladies?"

Clover took it from the Captain's hand. "They all look perfectly intrepid."

"Even the girl," Ursula commented shortly.

"That's Hestia Williams," explained Houghton-Copley. "A waif the Captain rescued from the depredation of renegades. Don't deny it, Captain." He'd seen Seaton straighten in his chair and moved quickly to cut off any interruption. "Parents both dead, home destroyed, a missionaries' daughter. And the captain found her terrorised in a secret place beneath some trees."

Both women looked at Seaton in some surprise. They'd hoped for some relatively exotic disclosures and now were apparently being presented with a storybook adventure. Clover felt the focus on Hestia Williams to be a little too protracted, though. "And who are the others?"

Again, Houghton-Copley seized the response. "The man beside the Captain, with the large ears, is the late Reginald Munby, quite an eminent natural scientist in his time." He affected to look to Seaton for some form of confirmation but chose not to wait for it. "The large man with the moustache is Sir Everard Northmore, expedition leader and an old acquaintance of mine."

"From where?" asked Seaton, as casually as he could.

"Here and there." The diplomatist sat back with a complacent grin. "Oxford, Westminster, Lambeth. You know how it is."

Clover and Ursula looked duly impressed. Ursula produced a cheroot but Houghton-Copley proffered his bespoke gold tips, and she accepted with alacrity. As an oval it was a difficult fit with the amber cigarette holder, so she swiftly dispensed with the accessory and sat back too, blowing coils of blue smoke at the ceiling. "What it must be to have so many friends in high places," she said.

He's not merely displaying his connections, thought Seaton. He's setting out his store of knowledge. Intimating at repositories of facts he has not yet placed in plain sight. But there are some things he can't know. Because they are unfathomable and thus beyond any prying eye, however expert or persistent.

"Tedious in the main, but invaluable on occasion." Houghton-Copley confided chiefly to Ursula, affording her a glimpse of the wearisome nature of lofty social connection. Then he produced his twinkle again as his hands slipped back into the portfolio. "For without them I should never have been able to reunite the Captain with these."

He scattered a number of pencil sketches on the octagon table and, at once, Clover knew even she had undervalued the quality of Seaton's eye and hand. And very probably the core qualities of the man himself.

105

"Incomparable!" cried Houghton-Copley. "How would you possibly have allowed such things to moulder away unappreciated?"

"I had no idea they were in existence." Seaton spoke softly, as he fumbled with the nearest. "I thought I'd seen all the collated material when I produced the monograph for the RGS."

"Oh, they'd sequestered a fair bit of material out of the archives. As they usually do," said Houghton-Copley carelessly, picking up a study and handing it to Ursula to peruse. "I had a little rummage through, and lo and behold!"

"You've written a book!" Clover was amazed at Seaton's hitherto unknown accomplishment before the drawing in her hand claimed her full attention.

It was a pencil sketch of a small naked Indian girl squatting in the act of micturation. She was accompanied by her even younger brother, in a similar state of nature, who was steadying himself with a stubby hand on the top of her head. He was chewing his finger. She looked out at the artist with an expression of utter complacency.

"I didn't notice that she was in fact…until she…That is, until I saw," Seaton waved a hand awkwardly over the sketch as if to erase it, "she was engaged in an act of nature."

"It has a magical purity, captain," Houghton-Copley enthused. "You have captured the forces and functions of nature in one small child."

"And her brother," added Clover. "Look how he chews his finger. With all the wild world about him."

Clover passed her picture to Ursula and received the one she had been looking at in turn. Another small girl sat on her haunches, poking a stick into an ants' nest with an expression of dogged concentration, against a hatched background of lowering scrub. The pencil had captured the child's absorption in a private and purposeless task so well that Clover was reminded of her own isolated and desperate drives in her pre-school years.

"My God," said Ursula quietly, as the squatting child looked up her with mesmerising passivity. She breathed in, gathered herself and studied the drawing again, to feel herself once more entranced by the innocent yet somehow empty stare.

After that, they took up the remaining drawings in a flurry, passing them around, returning to favourites, while Seaton sat motionless in their midst, pinned down by their appreciation. Two girls fixing a basket to the back of a third. Another husking corn. Four girls in an aimless and solemn embrace, their bodies decorated in swirling patterns. Yet another of a boy holding a blowpipe. A wild childhood in a desolate place, ameliorated only by routine and family obligations and, without exception, the same quiescent acceptance.

"They're beautiful," said Clover.

"All dead now, I should think." Seaton gave her a regretful grin.

Clover felt a sadness pulse through her to see a man so divorced from his gifts. How could anybody become that separated from their own powers of observation, compassion and creative reflection?

"What I find so exceptional is this blend of innocence and sensuousness," said Houghton-Copley examining the sketch of the four girls embracing at arms length. "One sees the anatomical facts, rendered with almost scientific precision, down to the slightest cleft. But in all these children, slight though the lines may be, effortless the forms and planes, we feel their essential femininity welling up. About to burst into flow."

Clover looked back at the little girl poking the stick in the ant hill. "I think you go too far. This is innocence.

Innocence and nothing more."

"Oh, come now," Houghton-Copley beamed congenially. "You are Sir Austin Maitland's daughter. Surely you have an affinity with those who blend the innocent with the sensuous? Look at his sketches for the Magdalene. And those for the Dancing Crusade. How different were they from these?"

"He drew me on a number of occasions in my childhood, it's true." said Clover. Ursula stared hard across at her. "But never poking a stick in an anthill."

"You *were* his model, then!" Houghton-Copley contemplated Clover fondly. Seaton recognised the flickering trace of relief that played across his mouth, as if he had achieved some secret and uncertain purpose of his own. "Of course, Sir Austin would always work with the finest natural materials to hand."

"They were friezes of a religious nature," said Clover tightly. "Frankly I didn't know what we were doing. I just had to stay still and not fidget until he told me I could go."

"They were delicate portraits of spiritual grace and physical endowment. A new form for the English nude."

"Actually I kept my drawers on," Clover replied, feeling the blood spreading up her neck. "It was a damn sight colder in the barn than it would be along the Amazon."

"I was Ruth amongst the wheat sheaves, for a while," interrupted Ursula, and Clover shot her a look that seemed to blend alarm and gratitude. "During the school holiday. Oh, and I was going to be Guinevere but I got something bronchial."

"So I filled in till she stopped coughing."

"And we are all the luckier for it, ladies. The innocence of childhood occasioning timeless and profound works of art." The diplomatist smiled benevolently at Seaton. "We are in your debt."

Seaton shuffled embarrassed in his chair. He felt the floor rock beneath him, redolent of the heaving decks of the steamer home from Para in his bygone, fever-soaked days. Too many impressions, memories and reflections were forcing themselves upon him. Unbidden, unannounced and profoundly unsettling. Then, suddenly, a ratchety scraping accompanied by a doleful clanking filled the room. Sir Austin Maitland's mantel clock was tolling the hour.

Seaton rose to his feet as slowly as he could. "Good Lord. That time already? I'm afraid I really must go." He walked over to the bay window. Mercifully, Foster was parked outside the main gates. "Thank you so much for a thoroughly," he searched for the words, "entertaining and substantial tea. I feel quite replete."

Clover gathered up his drawings and placed them in a pasteboard folio with her apple design on the front. She handed it to him shyly. "You'll want these."

He didn't look convinced, but took them with a courteous nod and walked to the door. As he got there, the diplomatist raised himself from the sofa and called out, "Might I trouble you for a lift to the vicarage, Captain? We could talk on the way."

Seaton looked at the girls standing in their tea dresses, smiling at him. He looked at the cake stand, at Sir Austin Maitland's hand-carved clock, at the draped farm implements and felt himself at the mercy of the most cultivated ambush he had ever encountered. After the usual valedictory proprieties, he ushered the diplomatist out of the Old Forge and over to his waiting Bentley.

"Wasn't very forthcoming about that girl, was he?" said Ursula, encompassing both Seaton and Houghton-Copley in this accusation as she gathered up the tea cups and set them on a tray. "And we forgot to ask about the damn caimans."

Clover finished off the last fondant. "Still, we saw those wonderful drawings."

"Yes." Ursula widened her eyes momentarily at the intensity of the experience. "Quite extraordinary. But what on earth was he doing out there?"

"Excuse me, miss." They both turned at this querulous note from Lettie.

Lettie was standing behind the sofa, with a tea plate in one hand and one of Seaton's drawings in the other. Staring at them aquiver with shock and suppressed misgivings, she held out the drawing of the micturating child. "I think the captain left this behind."

Chapter Five

West Sussex

Houghton-Copley had insisted on taking a rear seat of the Bentley, and was holding his hat firmly in place against the vagaries of any sudden summer breeze. Foster was intuitively putting his foot down, discreetly enough not to occasion comment, but with enough vigour to ensure they'd arrive at the vicarage without a moment's dalliance on the road. Seaton could sense the man's tactful haste and appreciated it. He looked down at Clover's portfolio with the apple motif and a chill passed through him, an icy memento of the fever that convulsed him a short time after he had first made the drawings it contained.

"Charming girls," Houghton-Copley called out across the seat back to the Captain, above the noise of the motor and the hedgerows flashing by. "The father was a curiosity in the grand old style, of course."

"You knew him?" This was more by way of a challenge than a polite inquiry.

"Never met him. Not in the flesh." Houghton-Copley seemed to find the expression amusing. He beamed at a hawthorn bush that missed his nose by inches as Foster declutched into the vicarage lane.

"But you seemed to have formed an opinion."

"He bedevilled my tutor at Oxford with all kinds of bizarre requests for theological precedents and biblical interpretations. The physical nature of epiphany. Polygamy amongst the ancients, vide Solomon's wives. The sacred vitality of the Patriarch, vide the sacrifice of Isaac. Even the reproductive powers of the Holy Spirit. Quite unsettled the old boy. So he came to rely on his scholars to answer some of the letters. The ones he didn't burn, that is."

Seaton stared ahead without comment. He felt there was something distasteful about Houghton-Copley's

111

disclosure of Sir Austin's enquiries and the proclivities they implied. It was as if, in some unwholesome way, Houghton-Copley was trespassing inside the Old Forge and asking him to view areas of Clover Maitland's family history that he had neither right nor wish to view.

"A muscular Christian. Passionate and vigorous," the diplomatist concluded. "No time for the Episcopacy, of course. We were the lean kine in his view. Lean and ill favoured, as Genesis has it. So our paths never really crossed again."

Foster drew up outside the vicarage, pulled on the handbrake and sat with the great engine idling. Houghton-Copley climbed out and came round to Seaton's passenger door. "You have to help me," he said simply. "Surely, now you've seen that Sir Everard Northmore…"

"I cannot be of any help to you, Doctor," said Seaton evenly; he looked directly into the man's green eyes, flecked with the sun low in the field behind them.

"How can you know?" replied the diplomatist with quiet urgency. He sounded almost plaintive. Then as if to counteract this, he asked with advocate's probing acuity, "Or should I ask what it is you know that says you cannot be of help to me?"

"I know nothing," said Seaton flatly. "And I regret that is the end of the matter."

Houghton-Copley gave him an earnest and amiable smile as he moved to open the passenger door. "You are a decent and upright man, Captain Seaton. I beg you, give me but five minutes here in the vicarage, with the vicar present if you will, and I know you will actively wish to offer that help you believe is not yours to give. You cannot refuse me that, surely?"

There was a moment of stillness between them, with only the caws of the rookery drifting down into the village and the murmur of bumble bees lately returning to their nests. Seaton could sense Foster's bulk behind him, could feel the power of the idling motor ready to speed him away. He looked at the diplomatist, standing now with hat in one hand and his empty blue portfolio in the other and he knew, as sure as the rooks would call and the bees bumble their way home, he could not break the natural cycle in Highleigh that afternoon. He could not turn away.

He climbed out of the Bentley, left his hat and cane along with the portfolio in the rear seat and followed the diplomatist down the vicarage path. Foster switched the engine off. His eyes followed the Captain like a hawk's.

Houghton-Copley pushed open the front door of the vicarage, without even a token regard for the bell-pull, and they were at once within the dingy closeness of the hallway. Mrs Gibson appeared in some surprise at the kitchen door down along the passage, holding a large ceramic bowl and a drying cloth, but Houghton-Copley waved her silently away. Almost at once Enid opened the door to the small drawing room and made to step out. She was holding a book from a postal library and Seaton thought he saw something by Lawrence. She peered out at them with a startled and rather perplexed expression, the afternoon light in the room behind her throwing her figure into a supple and ephemeral silhouette. Houghton-Copley took her by one shoulder. "I only have him for five minutes, my dear, otherwise we would dawdle," he said, and gently turned her back into the room. She looked over her shoulder at Seaton with an expression that betokened some unvoiced request coupled with a mute apology, and then she was gone.

"I have to take you into my particular confidence, Captain," Houghton-Copley threw this over his shoulder as the passed the drawing room and made for the vicar's study.

He pushed open the door in a peremptory fashion but

the study proved to be not much lighter than the hallway. The Reverend Attwater was seated at his desk pouring over piles of paper. He stood at once with a tentative smile before throwing out both hands. "Gentlemen, you are most welcome but you catch me at my Parish subscriptions."

"Yes, yes, Duncan, carry on." Houghton-Copley sank into one of the armchairs that flanked a small and empty fireplace and gestured Seaton to the other. "We won't interfere with your deliberations. We merely require you to observe, as it were. Like the recording angel." He looked directly at the older man. "If you would oblige."

"Delighted, delighted," said the Reverend Attwater uncertainly, before he made a dash for the tantalus on a heavy mahogany side table. "A sherry perhaps?"

Both men declined and so the vicar did as he was bid and sat down to wrestle with the promissory notes his flock had made to the upkeep of their church and its various Christian commitments. Houghton-Copley watched him with a governess's stern approbation before unbuttoning his jacket, pulling on his gold spectacles and leaning forward in his chair in a forthright manner to give Seaton his full attention.

"You know I have visited the Amazon region. I may now tell you I went there on a commission that was closely involved with your own experiences there. And I need your clarification on certain events. For reasons of State." He flicked a hand irritably at the Reverend Attwater, who had jumped to his feet at this and was endeavouring to collect his papers and leave the room. "Oh do sit down, Duncan. We won't be disturbing you."

Seaton smiled at the vicar as if to confirm that they were both out of their depth here and also to mask the alarm that this sudden and particular confidence had produced in him.

"Their Graces charged me to look into the

unfortunate missionary situation." He looked up as if to confirm this meant something to Seaton, and then explained further. "There'd been a number of incidents in Columbia, you probably know. And Bolivia. Missions destroyed, land torched or sold off. And not a few fatalities. Bible societies in the main, of course. And North American to boot."

"Poor, poor people," sighed the Reverend Attwater setting down his subscription lists and nodding sadly to himself.

Houghton-Copley ignored him, produced his cigarette case and, after offering it to Seaton who demurred, lit a cigarette. "Still, their Lordships were becoming decidedly unsettled." He tossed his spent match into the vicar's wicker wastepaper basket and surveyed his cousin for a moment, before directing his gaze back to Seaton. "Between us. There were signs of Roman involvement."

"Impossible!" cried Attwater. He stared open mouthed at the diplomatist. "I simply cannot believe it!"

"We all have our faith tested at some time," Houghton-Copley commented tersely and then continued to address himself solely to Seaton. "Not at any elevated level. Not overtly anyway. Not a trace of purple in the underbrush. A red hat, possibly, in Manaos refusing to countenance vague rumours about such misdemeanours. In all probability a few illiterate local priests handing out the kerosene and the machetes. But enough to trouble their Lordships. The Oxford Movement has not quite drawn the teeth of the Church Militant." He watched his cousin bridle at this casual reference to Anglo-Catholicism and it seemed to afford him a small degree of pleasure.

Seaton remembered the taciturn cleric in Esperenza, his surly and aggressive demeanour. Then he recalled the way the police chief had goaded the man with the Williams' name. Surely it was farfetched to suppose that he might have instigated some punitive raid by the drunken faithful that the police chief was aware of? In any case, such circumstantial remnants of memory could not be accounted as reliable intelligence. Moreover, what purpose could such intelligence possibly serve?

"And what would their Lordships do if you provided them with proof?" he asked.

"Concessions, Captain, concessions." For the first time Seaton could see the kind of world Houghton-Copley operated in and some of the qualities required to be so capable within it. "Our main thrust as you know has been in China, the South Seas, Southern Africa. Spheres of influence we would prefer remained untampered with. A discreet understanding reached with Rome on unfortunate events in Latin America," he paused to ensure Seaton understood precisely what was in the balance, "might occasion a more flexible response to our expansion in other areas."

"You intend to trade on murder!" Attwater gasped at the realisation and then looked anxiously at Houghton-Copley to see if he had, in some ill-defined way, damned himself.

"The Church is built on sacrifice." Houghton-Copley gave him a reptilian stare. "I'm sure you need no reminding of that." He turned back to Seaton. "So you can see it is on a matter of Church and State policy that I ask your assistance."

"You want to know if I saw signs of any Catholic involvement in the destruction of the Williams' mission." It sounded so simple now he said it.

"In part, yes." Houghton-Copley smiled at him. The Reverend Attwater, seeing this evidence of good humour, returned quickly to his lists. He shuffled and reshuffled his papers and scribbled hasty calculations, in the hope his diligence would deflect any suspicion that he might be unsound on matters of Church high policy.

"It was all so long ago."

"But never so pertinent as it is today."

"Could not Sir Everard furnish you with the expedition journal? All the relevant facts would be in it." He looked down at his hands; they were steady. "I can't see what would necessitate your seeking me out to corroborate."

"Sir Everard had very little to offer on the matter. He was reminded that you had scented kerosene on the charred buildings and the mortal remains. He thought you would be more qualified to venture a forensic opinion on how the engagement might have gone. Simply from your experiences during the South African conflict. You must have come across the aftermath of similar massacres?"

Seaton nodded. "I said what I saw at the time. An organised party of men had attacked the settlement, overrun it and fired it, once they had dragged off whatever they could and had murdered the inhabitants."

Houghton-Copley seemed to think this over. Then he stood and leaned towards the fireplace and dropped his cigarette into the empty grate. "He told me that you developed quite a close relationship with Hestia Williams. The only surviving witness."

Seaton held up his hands in a gesture of ignorance and mild contrition and then let them drop into his lap. The Reverend Attwater crossed out some of his calculations and tried once more. He huffed a little in perturbation at the behaviour of the totals to date.

"But you were the first white man to find her." The diplomatist persisted. "Might not she have told you something? While the experience was still fresh upon her?"

"She wasn't well disposed towards me at the outset. She relaxed somewhat later. I think she confided most of her story to Munby that night."

117

"Alas, Munby is no longer with us." Houghton-Copley took off his gold spectacles, closed his eyes and pinched the bridge of his nose. He seemed momentarily exhausted. "And as things turned out, it was you who spent quite some time alone with her. I must ask you, Captain, what did Hestia Williams confide in you as your relationship became more, as you put it, relaxed?"

North-west Amazon

Seaton, Northmore and Ramón Suarez held one last consultation on expedition security before they started to cut their way inland. The party far exceeded the norm for navigating rough terrain, numbering thirty-eight Indians and, now, six whites. Their biggest challenges would be maintaining momentum and providing food. Given the terrain, neither would be easily overcome; wild game was never easy to capture on the trail, despite Cotterill's ambitions, and the standard 'Indian file' method of traversing the forest would be in the main denied them. They would have to cut channels wider than was usual or risk splitting the band into two files which, with some of the load they were transporting, would be impracticable, if not impossible.

Thankfully, they would not be bringing the workshop materials out again. These would be left to moulder on their departure at the end of the dry season, possibly to be resurrected in any future investigations of the area. The main body of the porters could be discharged once they had safely arrived at the collection ground. But for the moment, they would have to push the unwieldy unit through thick forest and feed it as best they could.

One thing would improve on the journey. The deeper they went into to the wilderness, the less likely their bearers would be to mutiny or desert. They had ferried in outlanders precisely for this reason; their porters were no more at home here than they were, and possibly in greater mortal danger from the indigenous tribes. Nonetheless, Indians were known to fade away, inexplicably, in even the most hostile regions and Ramón Suarez therefore provided Seaton with two of the men he had known long enough down river to consider trustworthy. With these stewards, Seaton was to ensure everybody kept in column formation, resuscitate stragglers and intervene, if necessary, should any of the porters attempt to disrupt or abscond. Suarez retained one trustee with him as an additional overseer to the cutting parties and allocated another, despite the baronet's protests, as a personal guard to the head of the expedition.

Northmore pulled out his pocket watch. "We've got around nine hours before it rains," he said and, with that, the second phase of the Northmore incursion commenced.

It took time for the cutting section to progress far enough for the party to be able to take up their burdens and file in to the hinterland. Seaton could see Hestia listening to Cotterill as he waited for his section's turn to move off. She was smiling politely at each verbal sally but when he had to pick up his knapsack and rifle and follow his men into the thicket, she moved back down the remainder of the column to hover near Munby, poking yet again in the mud with her stick.

If this disappointed Cotterill he had no real chance to display it, but plunged in after the food and medical supplies, his rifle at port, his eyes peeled for wildlife or intruders. Munby was wearing stout boots and leather puttees and Hestia said something to him about them. He shrugged at this and they both stood silently and looked into the river, while those at the head of the workshop section strained to manoeuvre the more unwieldy of the harnessed baggage through the narrow entrance hacked into the bush. After the most cumbersome units had disappeared, the scientific section picked up its fragile particulars and set off.

Seaton waited to see if Hestia would now come down to him but, instead, she walked briskly away, to enter the jungle alongside the foremost porter and a good six men ahead of Munby. This seemed in keeping with her aloof disposition towards him and he was prepared to dismiss it in favour of his rearguard responsibilities, when just before the entanglement swallowed her, she halted, as if on a sudden remembrance, turned sharply and gave him a vigorous wave of acknowledgement, accompanied by a warm if formal smile.

He raised his hand to return her salute but she had already disappeared into the forest, leaving him to ponder whether her change in demeanour indicated a change of heart or just contrariness, pure and simple. However, he had work to do. Munby had followed his bearers into the jungle and Seaton found himself the last of the section leaders on the river bank.

He looked over at the slow moving Igara Parana, at the appreciable distance across to its far bank and at the steadily diminishing Guerrita. This sense of space would have to last him for days to come, he reminded himself, and he breathed in deeply, inhaling the expanse of pale morning light as much as the misty air. Then, with a brief nod of command to his armed company, he led them into an unforeseeable future.

Even for a traveller as experienced as himself, the monotonous regularity of the entanglement surprised him and bore down upon him as the day grew long. The party progressed on a tortuously winding, narrow path, with damp mulch underfoot where it didn't actually merge into swamp or narrow riverlet, in dingy light and with underbrush forcing itself back upon them every step of the way. Even though more than forty humans, most of them heavily laden, had passed through it before him, cutting as much of a swathe as their personal resources would allow, Seaton could feel nature was already trying to close back in around him.

They were enfolded in silence too, except for the sporadic calling of frogs, occasioned by no clear stimulus and all the more unsettling for their random outbursts. Things went noiseless in the jungle, the better to evade their predators and surprise their prey; even a call of alarm could bring something deadlier down upon them from some unpredicted approach, and so was eschewed except for moments of unbearable jeopardy.

All around was soundless and sombre, as if all light, all life and colour had climbed up into the tree canopy. Indeed, if he craned his neck up from the twisting alley of dense foliage he was negotiating, he could make out patches of azure sky. High in the canopy, the sunlight caught on blossoms, mauve, yellow and dazzling reds, forty feet and more above him, with the flickering shapes of butterflies, and other insects, attending them.

Everything climbed; birds, insects, animals and the vegetation itself. Everything climbed to escape from the sodden earth, and up to the sun. Creepers climbed upon each other, parasites intertwining up towards the light and the space. Light and space that Seaton could only peer at, while his party groped their way along seeping water tracks, around collapsed and jagged trees, over leaf and mud filled gullies. And so they progressed, tripped by lianas, clutched at by thorn bushes, slashed at by branches anxious to re-entangle themselves above the rotting leaves and fungi that composted constantly to feed the trees towering above them.

Nothing stayed dry, and eventually nothing he owned started out dry to become wet. In the wet season, it rained torrentially and continuously; in the dry season, it rained without fail daily from two till five in the morning, from four till six in the evening and intermittently besides, at which the appellation became tinged with irony. The sopping state of his clothes, the chafing and the chapping, the slick on his skin, the film in his eyes, the sodden and slippery surfaces of the wet wood beneath his feet or at his elbows, and the clammy leaves and fronds that invariably draped over him, sapped the spirit. With a horizon in these dank environs reduced to a few feet in front and behind, and a matter of some inches to each side, his mind was in danger of feeling as constricted as his breathing. If it weren't for the breezes set up along even the lower labyrinths of the forest floor by continuous evaporation, he felt he would have poached.

Of course, it was simply a matter of developing the necessary outlook and routine to make the most of it. He was after all a professional soldier; going where he was sent, adapting quickly and performing well in difficult conditions were the mainstays of his vocation. There was a satisfaction to that, a sense of personal honour in circumstances endured and put to good account. The very same philosophy applied here. He had been commissioned to paint in the jungle; the jungle operated on its own terms so he would adapt freely to those. However, there was one major departure in that he was here in his capacity as an artist. So, while he would comport himself on the terms laid down by the terrain, he would paint on his terms alone. He had the artist's overriding responsibility to put his feelings down in colour and line, regardless of rain, Indians or insects.

He would have the most trouble in disregarding the insects. It wasn't their varying shapes and sizes or their often alarming aspects and painful stings. It wasn't even the fear of agony, death or paralysis many of these tiny creatures could wreak with their poison or their burrowing eggs, the dangers of which Munby had meticulously outlined. The chief obstacle to his sense of perspective, where insects were concerned, was their sheer number and ubiquity.

Where birdlife was scarce, mankind scarcer and animal life unseen and silent, insects were everywhere. Butterflies flitted in the high thermals above, where moths would venture at nightfall. Termites processed in battalions from tall mud structures up to fourteen feet high, wasps and bees surged from huge black nests suspended above the path like coagulated chandeliers. Myriad species of ants plagued the paths in some areas, turning even the bushes into pulsating sculptures of busy and venomous marauders, piled layer upon scrabbling layer in their ineluctable mechanics of survival. Insects teemed under the smallest leaf; they colonised the falling spikes of palm trees. They dropped from flowering boughs high up in the canopy above; they did secret work under the rotting leaves below. They fed variously on fruits, leaves, spoors, decay, each other and man, if so presented. Injudicious brushing against an overhanging branch would cause a shower of ticks to fall upon one, down one's shirt collar, up one's sleeve, onto one's shoes, each working its way in sightless haste towards the haven of warm, sweat-slicked skin, in which to burrow. Insects hung in the air; they infested every surface, vegetal or animal; they skimmed on water, secreted themselves beneath floating matter or scavenged blindly in the slimy beds of streams. They were almost as pervasive as the forest air, and considerably more vigorous and alive.

Now and then he would come upon some lizard frozen half way up a trunk, sleek with this profusion of food but alert to the multiple and grievous risks to life about it; Seaton fancied there could never be enough lizards or frogs, birds, tapirs or spiny anteaters to make even the slightest impression in this entomological tumult.

There had been periodic halts to progress, due to some unseen difficulty ahead, when Seaton and his men would come across the tail end of Munby's workshop and science group, squatting and staring dispassionately into the ground. These interruptions lasted for a few minutes at most, before the column started off again, and the Indians hauled themselves to their feet, shouldered their burdens and trudged on. At none of these halts had Seaton seen Hestia, or indeed Munby, by now somewhere at the head of their section. Perhaps Hestia had relented on the eager American and moved further up the column to join Cotterill.

Only once was there a whistle blast and immediately Seaton's riflemen, Callard and Bowser, had defiled alongside the track, according to his hasty riverside instructions, and taken up sentinel positions, peering into the leaf wall over the barrels of their rifles. Seaton, while anxious to immerse himself in the life of the indigents, found himself incapable of pronouncing the men's Quechan names and, for the sake of clarity under fire, had rechristened them after the toffees shipped out by well meaning matrons to his troop during the African War. Callard, the elder and sturdier of the two, carried Seaton's Winchester as well as the Mannlicher rifle he expected to own, once his employment with the expedition was over. He had spent some time with the Peruvian militia in an undisclosed capacity and was, thankfully, used to following some series of military manoeuvres. Bowser, his younger colleague, had a startled but determined expression and was fiercely loyal to the older man, whom Seaton took to be either an elder relative or a chief. Both had accepted their nomenclature with the same alacrity as they had taken possession of their rifles, and both seemed intent on keeping what was, to them, a privileged position alongside

Seaton at the rear. Ramón Suarez was clearly a fine judge of men.

When the two blasts of the all-clear sounded, the column moved off again and Seaton motioned his men to rejoin the track. According to standing orders he would receive a report within thirty minutes, but when neither the baronet nor any intelligence was forthcoming, it was clear to him that conditions further up had rendered those arrangements impractical. Nonetheless, the lack of word would only add to his feeling of constriction and isolation.

When the baronet did eventually materialise, he had undergone a major transformation. Gone were the bulky bush jacket, thick trousers and heavy boots and, in their place, he was sporting a pair of baggy, and bespattered, cotton pyjamas, canvas-topped boots and a large towel around his neck. With a shotgun slung over his shoulder, a cutlass in his hand and a soft felt hat jammed down over his sweating red face, he looked more like a pirate than a fellow of the Royal Geographical Society.

"Sorry to keep you, Seaton, but it's hot and wet work up there. Suarez is sticking to the bearing where we can, but there are some infernal nooks and crannies between us and our overnight site. No time for chat." He must have caught some element of Seaton's mute surprise at his appearance. "Want to ditch your heavy togs till we're at the collection ground. Like a blasted Hamam at the front of the column. And watch your boots. Munby turned his ankle on something, which is why we blew the whistle. Got him strapped up and in his rubbers now."

They walked on in silence for a while, and the baronet seemed to expand with the relatively relaxed posture of following a trail already cut. He rummaged in his haversack and produced a leather-covered flask. "Absolutely frowned upon in all reputable exploration journals," he announced, as he swigged heavily from it and passed it over, "but they didn't have to listen to Munby carping when I bound up his ankle. Girl was no better. Said she'd warned him."

Seaton took a short pull of the brandy and realised quite how dry his throat had been, despite the dense humidity enwrapping him. The spirit produced a peculiar warmth within the sapping heat, a sharp soporific if such a thing were possible, and he decided to forego any more before nightfall. He handed it back to the baronet who returned it to the haversack, tucking his cutlass under an arm as he buckled the bag shut. That done, he squared his shoulders and took the bull by the horns.

"Look, old man I know I said we'd rotate, but it's damn tricky. Munby's hobbling along like Long John Silver. I've got to keep up with Suarez because there's a decision to be made every fork of every blasted streambed. And Cotterill, well he's keen but he's unseasoned." He breathed out shortly, trying to find the words to form what he thought might be an unwelcome sentiment. "And it's too damn important, guarding our backs, watching for strays, you know..."

"I'm more than happy to stay here," said Seaton equably. If isolation were to be his lot, he would at least be free from the hurly burly of cutting a swathe through primeval swamp, and then forcing bulky crates through it.

Northmore gave him a beam of relief and a slap on the shoulder. "Good man. Knew I could count on you." He quickened his pace to regain his position at the expedition's head, but called back, "Would you like me to send the Williams' girl back to you? Bit of company might pass the time."

"We'll manage," Seaton shouted in reply as he indicated Callard and Bowser either side of him, rifles at port. Northmore gave a short barking laugh before striding away, with a flourish of his cutlass, and disappearing from sight.

On they trekked, hour after meandering hour, picking their way through uneven ground with sudden hillocks and tumbling gulleys, all coated with uniformly entangled brush, pierced by endless trees and roofed by the dripping leaf canopy. Until they came upon an area fringed by giant hardwoods where there had been some primeval disturbance, for here was a smattering of collapsed trees, their shattered boughs interlaced with those of others they had torn down with them. The jagged, vegetal landscape was coated with lichen and strangled with thorn, and there were treacherous pools of algae-covered water between the ancient tree skeletons. It was here, as he picked his way around the safer perimeter in the tramped mud track of his precursors, that Seaton next came upon Hestia.

She was standing off to one side of the track, down a small leaf-strewn gulley, over which a collapsed tree was scrabbling up towards the light. An Indian woman was attending her, or Munby would not have passed by without chivvying her on. She was scooping up water from a tiny stream, all but hidden by the leaf carpet, and was trying to cast it on Hestia's feet. With a shrill cry more of desolation than anger, Hestia pushed the woman away. Then standing immobile, fingers sunk into her unpinned hair, she made a low keening sound.

Seaton handed Callard his Winchester and went down into the gulley to investigate, holding onto a splintered trunk of a tree to keep his balance. At once his hand seemed to catch fire and he looked down to see it was coated with small red, stinging ants. Walking over to Hestia, wincing and cursing under his breath as he tried to shake them off, he saw cohorts of ants straddling the gulley, spreading out in raiding columns, surging to and fro with demonic energy. The Indian woman had stepped back at his approach, and was standing ankle deep in a pool beside the climb up to the track; she stood stock still, impassive and yet watchful, her hands at her sides.

The gulley floor seemed alive with fire ants. Stepping gingerly across the heaving ground, he traced one of the principal lines of attack, with an uneasy fascination, over the leaf mould to Hestia's canvas shoes and puttees. Ants were climbing up her legs, clinging to the hem of her dress and foraging up both the inside and the outside of her skirts. It was this pitiless assault that the Indian woman had been trying so vainly to wash away. The girl looked at him, her hands entangled in her unruly hair. Her eyes were filled with tears but, though he knew from his throbbing hand that the pain of the bites must have been excruciating, she forced out some determined yet noncommittal smile. She was shaking and speechless with the rapacity of the onslaught, but still she wouldn't acknowledge it; she simply faced him with this tearful grin.

"Come on, Hestia." He tried to pull her away but she shrugged off his hand and stood still. Her hands now bunched into fists at her sides, the ants now navigating her waistband. Eventually, she could not repress a gasp of pain.

"You must come with me at once," he said, quietly but urgently, hoping this cry betokened some weakening of her resistance to him. "We cannot stay here."

Ants crawling up his own puttees and he slapped at them with his scarf. Then, remembering the Indian woman, he splashed water upon them, slowing the approach. He looked up at Hestia from these scrabbling defences. Her eyes were steaming with tears now.

"I didn't die," she said quietly but earnestly, as if that explained everything. "I didn't die."

Now, at last, she had said something he could understand, voicing the hapless guilt of the survivor; once accepted, there is no price one can pay to expunge it. He'd seen it in sieges, in defences and in attacks, even in cholera

128

wards. Walking out of danger with the dead about you meant coming to an understanding with them, a compact to continue walking the earth denied them.

"I didn't die," she insisted.

"That was their greatest wish. You were their child." She just shook her head, so he persevered. "I am a soldier. Many good men have died so that I could be here, talking to you today. They have given me life. Am I to throw it in their faces?"

Her brow furrowed and she was shaking as though mortally cold. He kept on. "Your parents planned for you to escape when they could not. They will be looking down right now at peace, because you are alive. Is this really the way you'd choose to repay them?"

He had nothing more to say, so he simply stood and watched her, slapping the occasional ant from his hands. Hestia stared searchingly at him, suspicion flickering in her eyes until their narrowing merged into a slight frown of concentration. Then she looked up at the tiny patches of blue trapped between the swaying boughs of the high canopy. A breeze had grown up, as it always did at this time of day. Soon it would be still and then, after a moment of calm, the deluge would fall. She searched in the canopy for a while more, and then returned her gaze to Seaton. She winced as yet another battery of tiny bites tore into her. Then, she held out her hand.

He pulled her out of the gulley, back down the track and over to another pool which fed a burgeoning colony of palms, out to conquer the fallen hardwood myrmidons. The Indian woman waded in with her to help her divest herself of dress and puttees and Seaton led Callard and Bowser further down the track, so they should be unsighted. The riflemen examined his hand with scant interest and, after a moment or two, Bowser wandered off. Seaton wondered if prurience or curiosity hadn't got the better of the startled-looking, young man, but the Indian soon returned with a bunch of dark green leaves that he chewed vigorously before rubbing them all over Seaton's affected hand. The pain relief, though partial, was immediate and the swelling ceased almost upon the moment.

With that abatement came the chastening realisation that he had forgotten to blow his whistle on first discovering Hestia's plight amongst the ravening ants. This dereliction of security procedures hit him like a hammer blow, and he was grabbing at his jacket pockets to locate Northmore's silver siren when Hestia appeared on the path, restored to a semblance of composure though sopping about the legs. She had wrapped her scarf about her head and the Indian woman, who still accompanied her, had found her walking cane and returned it. She stood erect again, a hand on one hip and the other resting on the cane, held out to one side like a staff of office. With this noble posture, the gathering of her skirts around her legs and her large turban, she bore a marked resemblance to an Eastern potentate in some child's tales of the Orient. Clearly the mortification on the ant hill, and the confidences then exchanged, were very much a thing of the past.

"Thank you, Captain." She had assumed a caliph's courtly manner. "I am quite fit to continue now."

Seaton disregarded her patrician manner and led them all swiftly along in the expedition's footprints, hoping to regain his correct defensive position before any encroachment could be made on the main party. Hestia and the Indian woman scurried along to match his pace, while Callard and Bowser maintained their rearguard positions in a steady lope.

In the event, a porter had lost purchase on one of Munby's larger propagation trays, navigating a submerged tree-trunk bridge across a sluggish brook, and the party had halted while the naturalist mourned its loss. The destruction of the sheet of glass was most keenly felt and its large shards were being retrieved and repacked for possible service later. Seaton rejoined the party and Hestia, still with her Nabob aspect, left him with a brief smile, to move up into her more familiar position at the head of the temporarily stalled workshop and science section.

With that it began to rain. Fat drops, discernible individually to start with, hammered down through the foliage, to flatten against the mulch or dive into the mud. They fell like glistening plumb lines, tracking the straightest route from heaven to sodden earth, diverted into ricochets by only the staunchest resistance from bough or leaf cluster. They fell so heavily that a direct hit on the cranium resounded and stunned, and Seaton wondered if Hestia's exotic turban was simply the result of a rather pedestrian premonition, based on past experience of forest weather. If so, she hadn't shared it, but then again she would presumably expect seasoned explorers to have, if not greater knowledge than her of local conditions, at least a rudimentary awareness of tropical storms. He pulled his forage hat from his haversack, unfolded it and pulled it over his head. It softened the impacts marginally.

Munby looked up and swore softly. "Too bloody early and too bloody heavy!"

The period and space between drops grew ever smaller, though the impacts still retained their astonishing force, and the rainstorm began in earnest. Northmore hustled his way back through the squatting Indians, with his bodyguard in hot pursuit, to where Munby was gingerly removing broken glass from the stream. "We need to get a move on," he called over to the naturalist, maintaining a respectable distance between them while hopping from foot to foot like an impatient bear. "The next stop will be it for today, and we need to be further on, if we want to make the tributary in five days."

Munby gave Seaton a jaundiced look, his arms elbow deep in the stream "Wasn't it going to be a week, Captain? When we first wandered into this maze."

Seaton gave him a sympathetic grin. He was used to the variable aspirations of General Staffs and the ensuing route marches and counter-marches; itineraries, priorities and objectives all changed upon the hour under the guise of a flexible response to fast evolving strategic situations. He'd ridden, marched and fought through many a night as a result of flexible responses. "We were going to remain flexible, if you recall?"

Munby cautiously produced a large shard of glass from the streambed; as it surfaced, it snapped in his hands and he looked sternly at the separated pieces. "Pity our damn glass won't," he said, but carefully packed the pieces away anyway.

For the next hour they fought both the forest and the torrential rain, inching their way through ever more dense undergrowth, towards their projected overnight camp. Conversation, if indeed anybody had been so inclined, was impossible as a result of both the noise of the downpour and the exertion required to move through it, while keeping their footing and a firm grip on their various drenched loads.

Then as the light began to fade, Suarez and Northmore pulled up on some rising ground where a tree had given up its struggle many years before, possibly scythed down by lightning, to form a small clearing. This had been repopulated by palms, which provided a multi-arched roof structure to deflect some of the driving rain, and abutted a convergence of two rivulets which afforded some cooking and washing facilities. Aware of the fatigue and the hunger gnawing at the party and the debilitating effect of overextending on the first day of a march, the baronet deemed it the right place to stand everyone down.

The entire party set to work erecting two basic wooden structures, to stretch tarpaulins across and hang their hammocks within. Young palm trees and saplings were co-opted into the configuration, giving the whole a higgledy-piggledy outline, but it served to keep out most of the rain, and cover both the cooking areas and, most importantly, the sleeping areas. These shelters were enhanced with freshly woven palm matting and a judicious nail or two; Suarez was parsimonious in the extreme about these and supervised the hammering in of each, to ensure their easy extraction in the morning.

As the Cholos built a smoky fire to prepare their cassava and a thin vegetable stew, Cotterill dragged on a poncho, selected one of his smaller bore rifles and went out with Bowser and Suarez's pointman. To everyone's surprise, including by his own admission the American's, he returned with two agouti, a close cousin of the capybara, with a preference for deep forest life. These rabbit-like creatures, skinned and jointed by the hunter himself, were added to the stew being prepared for the white members of the party. Callard returned from a silent excursion of his own having dug out some sort of iguana, which he offered to Seaton but, on his request, took it off to the Indian cookpot.

The Indians were mystified by separate provisioning fires. Among their own people, even if a number of cookpots were being used, any Indian would dip into any stew, provided its owner was present, and the making of cassava bread was communal. Suarez explained they had concluded white people required special ingredients toxic to Indians and so prepared their food in different bowls. As the evening meal progressed, they restricted their curiosity to a few casual glances, not wishing to cause offence or indeed attract any of the tocsins they believed to be integral to the white party's culinary preparations and related dining rituals.

Hestia's hammock had been strung up between the two centremost poles of the white party's Tambo, with Suarez and Northmore set between her and the forest wall on one side and Seaton and then Cotterill on the other. Once they had eaten, she had retired, leaving the men to smoke and assess the day's progress around the embers of their cooking fire. Two kerosene lamps flickered above them, attracting an astounding variety of night flyers. In the Indian Tambo they had eschewed lanterns and the majority of them had already settled down for the night. A few vague shapes could be seen moving about in the dying light of their own fires.

The rain was falling steadily, but after the demonic force at the height of the storm, the men barely registered it. The all-pervasive damp brought a chill to the evening, and Seaton had pulled on a sweater cadged, on the man's strong recommendation, from the purser of the Booth Line steamer from Liverpool. When he finally retired he would climb into dry trousers and socks, and change back into his wet ones for the morning's trek. One got soaked so quickly, that starting off wet made scarcely any difference, whereas coddled beneath an army blanket in dry socks would be an almost blissful, if temporary, reprieve.

Cotterill looked over to where Hestia's hammock was swinging gently in the darkness. "I think the girl shaped up pretty well today, don't you?"

Northmore's expression showed he hadn't given it much thought, while Munby squinted over at her berth. "Kept up with the hard going alright," he conceded, and then he turned to face Seaton. "But she dropped out late in the day, didn't she? You brought her up, Captain."

Northmore looked over at him, and spoke between

drawing a match into his pipe. "Anything we should know about? Keep an eye on, you know?"

Seaton could see Hestia's pain filled eyes as she stood her ground, the ants burrowing and biting beneath her clothes. "A temporary indisposition," he replied at last. "Female business. Nothing of any real concern."

At the notion of this female business, the men returned hurriedly to their smoking, their contemplation of the rain and the last dregs of coffee which Northmore had generously spliced with his brandy. Seaton stood up to retire, wondering why he hadn't confided in them about Hestia's hysterical episode. Possibly it was because her misplaced and desperate guilt seemed too delicate a topic to bring out before these various men of action. Then again, he was a man of action too and he was capable of appreciating her distress. So why was he caching this experience away from plain sight?

As he walked across to his hammock to take his dry clothes from his baggage stacked beneath it, he could hear some light but shapeless whispering coming from Hestia's recumbent form. Opening and searching the bag containing his clothes as quietly as possible, he focused on this noise until it developed shape and progression and became not a sequence of words, contemplative or casual, but a recognisable melody, hushed but true, blending into the night breeze and the incessant rhythm of the rain. Hestia, in the dark heart of the forest, bereft of family and familiar surroundings, journeying into an unpredictable future in the company of strangers was singing herself softly to sleep.

"In the good old summer time,
In the good old summer time,
Strolling thru' a shady lane
With your baby mine.

You hold her hand and she holds yours,
And that's a very good sign
That she's your tootsie wootsie
In the good, old summer time."

West Sussex

The vicarage study clock chimed the quarter hour and the Reverend Attwater ascended jerkily from his desk in a flurry of papers. "Forgive me, gentlemen," he cried. "Evensong! I had all but forgotten."

This wasn't entirely true. All the while Attwater had stayed pinned in his position of ecclesiastical witness, he had been fretting about the advent of his choral evensong. Normally his best supported service, he wondered if the turnout for parish communion earlier in the day would deplete attendance, with many of his flock feeling they had already made sufficient observance of the Sabbath and opting to stay at home with the wireless and the Savoy Orpheans. Still, whatever the number of the faithful, his choir would be assembled and rudderless and even now his stalwarts would be seeking out their pews. Finally, he could take it no more, and with this pretence of forgetfulness, a courtesy he felt he owed his guests, he made his excuses and bustled out of the room. Seaton rose too from his seat and looked down upon the diplomatist. "I shall endeavour to recall anything I think may be of interest to you from that period, Dr Houghton-Copley. Though, at the outset, I must repeat that nothing comes to mind."

Houghton Copley looked up at him with a grim smile. "Oh, it will, Captain. Of that I have no doubt. And I am happy to return here at any time to hear it."

"You will travel from London on such a slight eventuality?" Seaton's eyebrows rose in incredulity that he should occasion such an interruption in the man's schedules and itineraries.

"I shall be in Chichester for the foreseeable future," replied the diplomatist. "Much remains to be done. And, as I averred before, your testimony alone is of such significance as to more than warrant time spent in," he made a rather disparaging gesture with his left hand, "cathedral environs."

He escorted Seaton to the door, neither Mrs Gibson nor Enid Attwater being in evidence, and showed him out. Foster started the Bentley's motor on the first glimpse of the Captain stepping into the evening sunlight, and within a few moments they were making their way back to Laurel House. Both men remained silent but looked about them with an easygoing regard for the familiar countryside, as if imbued with a tacit determination to shake off a minor but discordant interference with their normal Sunday routine.

Seaton kept a firm hold of Clover's portfolio containing his revenant sketches and, in all probability, that frozen moment beside the Igara Parana, captured by a long dead young American to defeat the passages of time and the obfuscation of history. His past had never deserted him completely, he would never permit it, but it had shifted shape and receded into shadowy coexistence with what he was now prepared to accept as a present. The little Indian girl poking the ant hill and that cluster of dawn faces, staring into a lens with formal expectancy, had returned to bring that collusion to an end. What saving grace might be available to him remained to be seen.

Houghton-Copley closed the vicarage door, walked down the passage to Enid's small drawing room and opened the door. Enid was sat by the window, still immersed in her library book, bent over it in the pale light, her head hunched into her thin shoulders and her knees pressed together as she read avidly. She looked up with a start as Houghton-Copley's shadow fell across the page and went to stand up, but he waved her back into her seat with both fluttering hands.

"Lawrence, is it? How intense the man is." He reached out to take the book from her and scanned it with fond acquaintance, before asking with an affability that could not quite disguise a penetrating interest, "Tell me, Enid, how does he affect you?"

Chapter Six

West Sussex

Dr Richardson washed his hands at the tiny sink in his surgery and watched through the lace curtains as Mrs Faring fussed with the catch of his front gate. Having finally mastered it, she wandered off towards the village with a healthy supposition that her rheumatism was going to be ameliorated by the tincture he had provided, yet again. It was a clinical fact that her rheumatism would be considerably more ameliorated had she spent some money on getting a girl in to black her stoves and red lead her doorsteps, but this would not take place. Richardson, having dispensed with his receptionist as the number of prosperous patients and the fees he could charge the remainder both diminished, understood only too well economies occasioned by tight domestic budgets. Yet as far as he could ascertain, nothing of the kind applied in the Faring household; Faring was a farmer and was sitting on pots of the stuff. As long as he was, Richardson would load up his wife with embrocation and a highly distilled opiate and send in his account for an old-fashioned sum, which Sam Faring invariably settled well within term.

The doctor's problems had all started with the march of progress, much though he espoused it in public. Modern developments in transportation and communication meant the country was growing ever smaller and the well healed becoming ever more mobile. These days they sought medical opinions in Chichester or in London, were they fit enough to travel. It was only in emergencies or unsociable hours that the telephone he had installed, at pernicious expense, was grudgingly called. Even then, he dared not charge a substantial fee for fear of offending and missing out on the next haphazard consultation. He was gradually being reduced to the status of a village quack. His was getting dangerously near a practice for artisans and domestics, while those patients he retained of what Nancy described as 'our sort of people' presumed on their long acquaintance to leave bills unpaid for months, even at the modest discount he felt obligated to offer.

Not everyone was so parsimonious. Captain Seaton engaged his services for both his housekeeper, Mrs Simmons, and his steward, Foster, and although their needs had been scant and infrequent, the Captain had always paid on time whatever sum had been accounted. But the Captain wouldn't deign to call himself and that still exasperated him. Not for the financial aspect, he wanted to be clear about that. He was not obsessed with money; it was merely useful as a palliative for a wife with a position to uphold. It was more that the Captain's position in Highleigh meant his presence on the patient list would in some way ratify his own. It would remind the right quarters that they had a physician of consequence amongst them, a physician people of their class could ill afford to ignore.

He was hauling on his tweed jacket when he observed his wife walking up the path with the expression she adopted for a display of restrained but definitive vindication, mingled with the modest avowal of superior wisdom. Something in the world had proved her right, once again, and while she was resolved to be magnanimous about this, she saw no reason to be unnecessarily reserved.

It was one of her better moods, and Dr Richardson thought he might essay a small sherry before lunch on the strength of it; accordingly, he contrived to be in the hallway walking towards the decanters in the drawing room with an affable grin as his wife entered the house. She looked straight at him but called out, "Maeve!"

"Yes, miss?" Maeve stuck her head out of the kitchen door; a smell of chops and cabbage followed her into the hall.

"A word," said Nancy Richardson and, ushering Maeve back into the kitchen, she shut the door behind them. Dr Richardson carried on to the sherry regardless; when she was in this conspiratorial mode, his wife would scarcely notice his small indulgence.

As the chops broiled and the cabbage bubbled, Nancy Richardson had what she had heard in the village, bruited apparently by Mrs Gibson to Mrs Poulter and originating from Mrs Jennings' Lettie, confirmed by Maeve. Maeve was Lettie's closest friend, confidante, dancing partner at village entertainments and chaperone at the cinema in Chichester once a month. If Maeve corroborated Lettie's account of something, it could be taken as the Gospel truth. And so it was in Nancy Richardson's kitchen, every nuance and detail of it.

She then walked briskly out of the kitchen and entered the drawing room at the moment Dr Richardson was refilling his schooner with the Christmas Amontillado. He had been right about her absorption; she did not raise the customary eyebrow at his aperitif. Instead, she informed him with calm authority that the church diplomat about whom she had harboured grave doubts, for which she had been vilified in her own home, had in fact spent his Sunday afternoon disseminating indecent pictures at the Old Forge, and it appeared the Captain had actually produced them. She gave her husband a short and condescending smile of triumph, and then walked back out to supervise the mashing of the lunchtime potatoes.

The sherry did not turn to ashes in the doctor's mouth, but the sinking feeling in the pit of his stomach did little to add to his pleasure in it. His wife was talking nonsense again, in concert with the village grapevine, and he would have to endure it and the concomitant indignation at his failure to endorse the truth of it, despite incontrovertible proof. He had no strong feelings about indecent art. Indeed, to his faint regret, he had never come across any, except for some fanciful pornographic daguerreotypes passed about at medical school. Beyond that, he had been exposed to the human body for too long to harbour any libidinous notions about it and doubted very much that he could mount any spirited engagement in them, even if the opportunity presented itself. Yet perhaps because of the paucity of his intellectual and physical familiarity with such celebrations of the flesh, he felt himself well qualified to judge that no man as disappointed in himself and in life as Captain Seaton could possibly have created something with that colour and vivacity. He sat down in a mood that wandered between the fatalistic and the melancholic and awaited the tolling of the lunch gong and further inevitable disclosures.

The Indian drawings were abroad in Highleigh and, as ever with such controversial local topics, they were met with a widely divergent response. In the Snug of the Tun and Pipe they were broached and then dismissed as small beer, compared to the naked model and the river monster. Simply more queer stuff from folk who had too much time on their hands and suffered from an unhealthy lack of exercise. Hard work, penury and family obligations gave few opportunities for such tomfoolery and even less for philosophising about it. There was even some doubt as to the drawings' existence. Lettie was known throughout the locality for being not all that bright, and had only escaped the soubriquet "Poor" Lettie because her elder sister Maude had claimed the prefix by right, through her performance at the village school many years before. The phrase 'ten pence in the shilling' was often employed in connection with Lettie and, despite protestations from her grandmother Mrs Jennings as to its veracity, her evidence was widely deemed to be contentious. Only in those circles where it served to ratify conclusions previously reached about the principals, Captain Seaton and Houghton-Copley, during the great debate on the demi-mondaine and the crocodiles, was Lettie's testimony given any real credit.

Not a few in the village were mystified as to why an artist should waste time and charcoal rendering "a little native girl doing her business" as Lettie had reported. Others declared that the artistic imagination clearly knew no bounds, which was precisely why it had no place in well-regulated society. Some enquired about the photograph but, as Lettie was incapable of satisfying their curiosity as to its subject, were inclined to pass over the matter altogether. There were too many questions attached to it. How had the drawings come into the possession of the churchman? Did not his possession of the same indicate the material was thoroughly respectable? Miss Maitland and her companion Miss Sweeting, though somewhat eccentric it had to be allowed, would never have been party to anything less than respectable; her father would turn in his grave, God bless him, such a strong Christian soul.

When Mrs Gibson alerted Enid to this disreputable episode, she was herself surprised by the vociferous manner in which the vicar's wife dismissed the possibility of prurient activity and asserted the prime responsibility of artists to be unflinching in their representation of human behaviour. Mrs Gibson had not found it easy to report on Lettie's experience at the Old Forge, without implying that Dr Houghton-Copley, a figure of evident moral consequence, would personally condone such offensive studies and she had done her best to be sensitive in her apportioning of censure. Now she was astounded to be confronted by strong words on art and responsibility, when she had expected a sad acknowledgement of the decadent and wayward thinking of a once well reputed member of the Parish. She retired to her kitchen in mute condemnation. What on earth had got into the woman? Was that any way to talk in a vicarage?

While a chorus of disapproval and concern was elaborating its harmonic structure as far away as Sidlesham and several good houses in Wittering, Sam Faring was speaking for a large male contingent of the farming community, when he told Larry Poulter, "Drawing some kiddie doing a widdle doesn't make him Beelzebub. There's a bloody statue of one in Brussels. They sell postcards."

Opinion remained vociferously and indulgently divided, but as discussions and speculations continued in drawing rooms, taprooms and parlours, a miasma of impropriety was settling around Laurel House. The reclusive war hero now had really too many unanswered questions about him for popular taste, whatever its shade of opinion on the matter at hand. Even his staunchest supporters in the area had to allow that conundrums associated with the Captain were of a questionable nature.

~~~~~

Seaton himself sat in the gallery at Laurel House, wrestling with an altogether more pragmatic problem. The drawings that Houghton-Copley had unearthed had been made on identical paper to those studies of Indian life and artefacts which, with his watercolour studies of Amazonian flora and fauna, he kept in his plan chests and displayed on request. Yet even now, he could not truly recognise them, nor summon up the circumstances surrounding their creation. He had laid them alongside some of his catalogued works on top of the cabinet containing his decorations, and tried to fuse the two strands into some state of recollection. True, he had recalled his embarrassment on discovering the child he was sketching was engaged in a private function, but that was only on sight of the drawing at the Old Forge. That brief illumination had faded immediately, and the absence of that particular drawing from Clover's portfolio only added to its chimerical aspect.

He took up the riverbank photograph and stared at it. It, too, was fading away, but the sight of Hestia's blonde hair all but obscuring the bottom of his face, brought back the sensation of those stands brushing his lips and nostrils, keeping him on the brink of a sneeze or a jerk of the head. With that sudden apprehension came the smell of the river mud, the throaty rasp of the Guerrita's engines and, to his surprise, a faint taste of quinine water, but no accurate representation of his state of mind at the time, apart from some indistinct unease. Although, that impression may just have been the present breaking from tradition by bleeding into the past.

Houghton-Copley's insinuations about some sequestered archive had unsettled the Captain deeply. He had no way of knowing what had survived the trek out of the jungle, it had to be allowed; his febrile condition at the end of the mission had prevented any conscious collating and ordering of his personal effects. But clearly some drawings, and perhaps other effects, remained of which he had been completely unaware. Could the baronet have removed items from the expedition archives without informing other members of the party? He assumed that Cotterill and Munby had remained in ignorance, but then how was he to be sure? Both were dead

One day towards the end of his recuperation from jungle fever and its related nervous prostration, Northmore had arrived at Laurel House with two trunks of papers, artworks and the artefacts that now adorned the gallery walls, to enjoin him to complete the illustrated monograph commissioned at the start of the venture. Then, he had had every reason to believe he had taken possession of the entirety of his notes and sketches. The larger paintings remained the property of Northmore, but the notes and sketches were his. The baronet had even assisted in unpacking and collating the material, and had left the following day with a cheerful admonition for the Captain to get right at it, because he had everything necessary to the business. Northmore had made no mention of any documentation, diagrams, sketches, photographs or personal memoranda being held back from the public gaze. The expedition's ulterior purpose, and its accordingly circumspect relationship with the Imperial Institute, might well have occasioned some such precaution but, as one made privy to such intelligence, he would have expected to have been informed. Yet the baronet had remained silent on the matter.

It was quite possible, though, that Houghton-Copley had fabricated the existence of such an archive for some deception essential to his own esoteric purposes. And yet, if there were no confidential records, from where had Houghton-Copley extracted the drawings that were clearly his own work, and of which he had such devastatingly partial knowledge? And where had he found the photograph that, by rights, should have been with Cotterill's effects? He was clearly in no position to ask, without entangling himself in a net the diplomatist had so painstakingly and yet so evidently laid out to trap him. Yet, what possible motivation could the man have? His unfathomable matters of Empire and Church policy could not be served surely, by the indiscriminate broadcast of private papers?

There was nothing for it; he would have to require some clarification on the putative archive from Northmore himself. This new enigma afforded greater cause for anxiety than any spectres his inquiries might conjure up from the murk, some of whom would be old familiars. He would have to talk to Northmore; that much was clear. He was owed some explanation of the privileged nature of Houghton-Copley's information and what had occasioned the baronet to part with it.

He walked over to the writing desk, tucked away behind a potted palm and beneath a landscape of a blazing day on the veldt. He had written his monograph at it, but now it was used only for infrequent and obligatory correspondence. He rummaged around in a drawer to search out some telegram blanks, wondering which of Northmore's several addresses he should send to. When he finally unearthed the slips, he decided on the scattergun approach.

They hadn't been in contact since the war but Seaton had heard Northmore had lost a son in France, Royal Flying Corps by all accounts, and that he had not taken up his pioneering activity again with the Armistice. Some lectures, some steering committees, RGS electioneering and a great many club dinners seemed to be the sum of the man's existence. After the war it seemed a lot of active men had withdrawn into an exhausted stasis, more than could be explained by simple physical fatigue; the vitality of the survivors had perhaps been swamped by the carnage they had so narrowly escaped.

He wrote the same message four times, 'Request meeting soonest opportunity Seaton', and addressed it to Northmore's country seat in Hampshire, his apartment in Charles Street, the Travellers' Club and the Imperial Institute, where he understood the baronet's exceptional services had retained him a pigeon hole. Then he called in Foster and asked him to send them off from the post office in Bognor. Foster took the slips without query; both men knew that Bognor was the sensible option now. There'd be enough talk in the village as it was.

Seaton returned to the drawings and gazed at them once again. Although he knew he had painstakingly recorded what he'd seen, sensitively enough to reflect some personal engagement with the strange new life thriving around him, these scraps of paper offered up only a chasm of difference between the man standing there now and the observer taking his first steps into the true, pulsating core of nature.

North-west Amazon

Seaton watched the men on the raft ahead struggling to bank it in the mud and thicket just above the convergence of the Kahuanari with its western most tributary. The waters were choppy, moving far more quickly than the waters they had been negotiating on this eastern arm throughout the day. The men on his own raft were poling furiously to divert their progress from midstream into the western bank and in behind their sister craft. Behind him, the crew on the third raft was starting up similar, hectic manoeuvres. Many on the platform ahead were grabbing at overhanging boughs to pull themselves in, while their fellows drove deep into the mud from the stern to force themselves up onto the narrow bank. He could see Northmore at the crouch, clamping his hat on his head with one hand and directing operations with the other, as the raft bobbed and jolted.

They had fallen upon the river on the fifth day, but a few hours after Northmore's final revised projection. At the sight of so much running water, Seaton could feel his chest expand and his heart pound. He drew river air deep into his lungs as if he were on an Alpine peak, and a giddy elation ran up his spine. They all looked about them with broad grins on their faces. Cotterill threw his hat in the air, Suarez and Munby shook hands vigorously, and Northmore planted both feet wide apart on the bank, hands on his hips, and surveyed the Kahuanari with an almost proprietorial air. Even Hestia danced a little private jig at the waterside and then dipped down to cup her hands and splash water about her face.

The Indians made a great play of churning up the shallows with sticks to deter all but insect predators and the entire party then waded into bathe. The Indian women joined the men as a matter of course but Hestia, possibly with as much regard for the party's sensibilities as her own, wandered slightly up river to wash both herself and her clothes in privacy. The party were laughing and light-hearted; even Munby who, with much theatrical business, raised a great lather of shaving cream on his face to the delight of several of the younger Cholos.

The monotony, grinding effort and apprehension of the past hard miles were all dissolved in the space, the light and the bustle and flow of the water course. Their progress had been a uniformly dull one, further muted by the gloomy realisation that Cotterill's haul of agouti on the first evening had been extraordinarily felicitous and that, with the optional exception of frogs and lizards, nothing fresh would be enlivening the evening stew before whatever they might snare at the riverside, once they came upon it. Occasionally, as hour plodded after hour, Suarez and Northmore would halt for yet another earnest consultation about the compass, their sequence of deviations, and corrections already made and necessary again to accommodate the implacable might of forest giants and their attendant thorn. Everyone knew it was all too easy to become inextricably lost in the wilderness, and that made the explosion of relief at the river's edge all the more intense.

On the morning of the third day, Munby had left the camp to perform his ablutions and had come across a rusty cache of tins and three disintegrating, mould-streaked blankets carefully stacked at the foot of a tree, in a small clearing of its own. Seaton, Cotterill and Northmore had returned with him to comb the area, but there was no other indication of the owner, the party he belonged with or their eventual outcome, save a sheet of notepaper tacked into the trunk at eye level. It had borne a message in ink, but the rain had washed it away and time had faded and curled the paper, still waiting to deliver precise instructions to its unknown dedicated recipient. They could make out neither the language nor the sentiments, but left the whole arrangement as they found it, in memory of those unfortunates who had passed that way before, only to perish so far from home.

Raft construction started immediately everyone was bathed and refreshed. Having located a cluster of balsa, they cut twenty-foot lengths of the soft, lightwood and formed them into three platforms, each with three crosspieces of strong, flexible shrub. These, they bound with thick resilient 'tamshi' fibres and secured with ropes to the bank. The afternoon rains arrived during the last stages of this work and, rather than risk their provisions in the torrent and the half light, Northmore decided to camp there for the night and load and board in the dawn, regardless of whatever downpour may greet them.

In fact, apart from the perennial mist, things went very smoothly the following morning with not one case lost into the water. Northmore and Suarez took charge of the pilot raft. Seaton and Munby brought up the larger part of the scientific baggage in the second, having more opportunity to sight obstacles and, hopefully, more time to avoid them. And Cotterill took possession of the third, with Hestia and the stores.

The drift downriver was leisurely compared to the rigours of the forest; they were able to cook, eat and doze on route, without retarding their progress, occasionally being called upon to navigate some tangle of deadwood in the river or pole away from some encroaching mud bank.

Then, at the sighting of their landing ground before the conjoining of the rivers, all idle speculations ceased and they were plunged into a flurry of activity. Within fifteen minutes, all three rafts were jammed into the bank and secured, three riflemen were holding a picket line a few yards into the scrub and the stores were being steadily unloaded. Everybody had a part to play; even Hestia fetched and carried, as the supplies were once again organised into their convoy sections.

"Right," said Northmore, once he had gathered the founder members together. "We know where we are. Time to find out who else is here."

Cotterill looked up to the wall of trees that fringed the river. "Are we supposed to go in and get them, or are they going to come out and get us?"

Suarez formed probing parties to beat the bank for the Indian paths, recent or abandoned, that would undoubtedly be there. The promontory formed by the confluence of rivers concentrated wildlife and plant types, and provided ready access to whatever fish stocks and turtle were to be had. This made them attractive to Indian settlement, despite the abundance of piom, and the fact that tribal enemies would almost invariably arrive by water to attack them. There would be a trade-off between hunger and security and somewhere, perhaps as much as half a mile inland, masked by intersecting paths, blind alleys and thorn patches, there would be a site or sites of previous tribal settlements and perhaps even a current settlement.

Northmore had set down their position. If there were Indians in the area, hopefully Nonuya or Okaina rather than the warlike Boro or Witoto, they would seek to settle within a discreet distance beside them, study their habits, particularly with regard to their plantation work, and hopefully employ them, in as far as forest Indians could ever be reliably prevailed upon. If the Indians proved hostile, they would try to suppress whatever attacks were made and hope to force them to withdraw, until they might be pacified through the gifts the party had brought for the purpose. Suarez thought outright hostilities highly unlikely. If the Indians had no wish to deal with them, they would simply fade away into the forest, leaving a burned tribal house and a prickly carpet of poisoned spikes along its entrance paths.

Should the probing parties prove unsuccessful, they would wait for some sort of contact at dawn, when the Indians came down to bathe, although in some tribes, the women would bathe throughout the day. Northmore and Suarez were convinced, however, that the best way to avoid the Indians disappearing altogether would be to come upon their camp, with gifts and evident peaceable intentions.

Cotterill offered to lead a probe, but was politely reassigned to guarding their stores and supervising the assembly of a temporary riverside shelter. As Hestia was there, hovering around the cooking fire, he didn't appear much put out. Soon, they'd arranged a kitchen area and converted one of the rafts into a lido, where they sat, he reading his novel and she washing and drying a change of clothes. Northmore was disinclined to take part himself in any patrol himself, as he said to Seaton, "Best left to the beagles. You and I wouldn't spot anything even if we were standing on it."

Seaton felt differently. He had to accompany, Suarez and his men in this work, not simply to reconnoitre but to acclimatise himself to moving about in the forest where other, unseen, human beings were present. The journey up from the Igara Parana had been a forced march through a labyrinth, in pursuit of a bearing offset by topography. Here, there was a different relationship between him and the terrain. He was no longer traversing it; he was, in the most benevolent sense he could muster, occupying it. He had to be fully equipped and aware in the territory he intended to make his temporary home, and he knew the only way to ensure that was front line experience.

Northmore waved him off with Suarez's party and, with two of the Cholos leading the way, they picked their way inland. Distinguishing between underbrush and camouflage seemed to be a sixth sense with the Cholos who disregarded certain hard packed areas to clamber over a fallen tree trunk and scout away in a totally different direction. They were attuned to the need to hide; they mirrored it in their hearts and in some way were moving alongside the hidden ones. Seaton could only be carried along by this movement, a passenger in the hands of their intuition and their experience. He tried to settle into a kind of blind faith, despite the fact that every second he had to remain keenly alert, scouring the brush for habitually concealed observers, with their blowpipes, their arrows and their poison.

And so it was that in the middle of their searching, double guessing, doubling back and searching again, two male forest Indians, appeared in the thicket in front of him barely five feet away. Both were naked, apart from a strip of bark cloth around the loins, and one wore a necklace of what might have been human teeth, being too short to be the jaguar teeth favoured by the chiefs. Its owner, the more fearsome of the two, carried two throwing javelins made of chonta wood in his left hand, poisoned palm spines affixed to their points. Both held short hardwood clubs.

Seaton's first impression was of deer discovered in some ferny Highland glen, alert and still, their eyes seeking out the future as much as the meaning of what confronted them. Suarez moved gently past him to the point position, saying in a calm voice, "I think we have Okaina here."

The quartermaster produced a small canvas bag from

153

his haversack, held it high in the air, said something in a guttural voice and placed it on the track in front of him. He then stepped back, reversing into Seaton and easing him back down the path a further pace or two. The two Okaina men looked down at the canvas gift impassively. Then they turned and slowly walked away.

They didn't look back but Suarez silently indicated that he, Seaton and their scouts should follow. Nobody spoke, sensing perhaps that a sound would fragment the fragile nature of the encounter. After a few minutes of silent procession, Suarez leaned in to whisper in Seaton's ear. "They may be taking us to village. They may be going hunting. We have to wait to see."

"Did you say Okaina?" Seaton was rifling through his memory to remember what Northmore had told him about tribal affiliations and propensity for warfare. There were considerably more Boro and Witoto than anybody else. The smaller tribes formed a buffer zone between their territories. The Boro, Okaina and Resigero were no friends, though Boro might marry Resigero. They were united in their detestation of the Witoto. The Andoke would fight with anybody, as would the Okaina, though they did trade. The Okaina and the Nonuya were neighbours and in similar straits, but made no attempt to trade at all. Warfare was based on fear; trade and cooperation were almost unknown. It was worse than the Balkans.

"Is a Witoto word. Means capybara," Suarez whispered. "They are also called Dukaiya but most people call them Okaina."

"What do they call themselves?" Seaton thought people might be reluctant to call themselves after a guinea pig.

"They don't. Nobody has names. Only what they are called." Suarez shrugged.

154

They followed the waif-like figures through forest that grew ever more gloomy, meandering with no clear purpose, until Seaton began to suspect they were actually being led away from any settlement or, indeed, any recognisable trekking point. He partly expected the Okaina to disappear as suddenly as they had arrived, leaving his party hopelessly lost, to starve in impenetrable thicket, with food and friends but a few hours walk away in an undiscoverable direction. This fear grew steadily and he was on the point of voicing it to Suarez, when they suddenly emerged into the full light of a large clearing.

In front of them was the Okaina's Maloka, a large house some thirty feet high and almost twice that in diameter, thatched and ridge-roofed like a gigantic hayrick, and standing proud in the open. There were no visible windows, the palm leaf and bamboo thatch reaching almost to the ground, with the last three feet being made of a closely set palisade, lined with matting He could see a tiny section of thatched palm leaves, some three feet by two, had been set aside and indicated where the only door was. No smoke emerged although, as Suarez had told him, their fires were kept alight continually.

In front of the Maloka, stamped into the earth, was the large dancing ground which with their unsighted plantations completed the community. If the Maloka was devoid of any sign of fire, the whole place was motionless and devoid of any human presence. Nor were there any dogs. Perhaps there was nothing to feed them on. After his experiences in Africa, it was a peculiarly depopulated place, devoid even of artefacts or rubbish.

The Okaina sentinels ducked in through the tiny doorway and left them to their own devices. Not one word or sign had been exchanged.

"Some of the men will still be out hunting. Some of the women will still be at the plantations." Suarez looked around the clearing, then pointed in the opposite direction to the where they had entered. "They are maybe some way through there." He thought a little more. "Those men were not wearing war colours."

"We ought to introduce ourselves," said Seaton. "Don't you think?"

Suarez squared his shoulders, told the Cholos to wait outside with their rifles cocked, and then led Seaton inside. In the hot, smoky darkness they could sense the presence of people before they could see them. Gradually, Seaton could pick out what looked like a smoke-filled circus tent, supported by four great poles, with a great many smaller posts and cross beams, all adroitly lashed together. There were children playing in a clear central area with family cooking fires spreading out from around it, slow moving human shapes clustered around them. The chief's larger section, for his extended family, occupied the far end beside what Seaton could just make out in the gloom as another tiny entrance.

Stepping between the enervated Indians, Seaton could distinguish each family's living space by the hammocks hanging around their fire in a roughly triangular formation, with the male taking pride of place. Mats were strewn with no great pattern, but people seemed to store their possessions in the rafters above each family area. Rifles slung on their shoulders, Suarez and Seaton advanced in a semi-crouch and picked their way through to where they hoped the chief, or some members of the village council, might be found.

They found a torpid but muscular man, wearing a necklace of jaguar's teeth, lying in a hammock, while a woman sat on the earth beneath him and suckled a baby boy. Two other women were ferreting around in the rafters, arranging their woven cassava squeezer for imminent use. Off to one side, a much older man was supine in his own hammock, dipping a stick into his tobacco pot, one leg dangling.

Suarez pulled out his little canvas gift bag again, and laid it on the ground. This time he added to it a small folding fruit knife, which he opened to show the blade. The breastfeeding woman picked these up, without comment, and handed it up to the man Seaton supposed to be the chief. The chief didn't look at the objects. Instead, an erratic, guttural conversation sputtered out between him and Suarez. Seaton could see Suarez was trying to work his way through to some dialect acceptable to both of them, but it was a haphazard and one-sided conversation at best. After a minute or two, the chief seemed to lose interest and Suarez turned to report.

"He wants to know if we are Peruvian. I said no. He asks if we plant rubber. I said no."

"Did you tell him we are English?" Seaton thought this might distance the Northmore enterprise from the excesses for which plantation owners, and especially the Peruvians, were notorious.

"He will not know what that is," replied Suarez. "But we can go now."

They turned to pick their way back to the main entrance and left, to the complete indifference of the chief and his family and only the mildest curiosity of the children playing in the middle of the house.

It was dark when they found their way back to the river camp and they were met with some cordiality, which both disguised and dissipated the apprehension their prolonged absence had caused. Northmore immediately took Suarez aside for a report, while Seaton sank down at the dinner table and slaked his thirst with lemon water. Hestia, who had brought the jug and beaker, was not content with this unspoken release of tension. Her whisper managed to be both sharp and reproachful. "What on earth have you been doing, Captain? They were getting concerned for you."

Northmore came over with Suarez and joined them. "A small Okaina tribe, then. Sixty souls or so?" Suarez nodded. "We'll build alongside, a respectable distance from their settlement, but close enough to make our presence felt."

"Safe, do you think?" asked Munby. If he had any trepidation it was buried under a tone of strict scientific neutrality.

Northmore adopted a grave expression as looked across the table at Seaton and the Captain felt his role within the expedition move, once again, from artist to military advisor. "You've seen the settlement, Captain. What's your view on our security?"

Seaton ran through the layout of the Maloka and its grounds in military terms, but the jungle obscured any lines of communications, firing positions, observations posts and fields of fire. "We are a strong force currently and we should be quite capable of building a suitably defensible camp," he said finally. "Though I would hope by the time our carriers depart, relations with the Okaina will be such that we won't need to defend ourselves."

"And if we have to?" Cotterill lit a cigarette and offered the pack around, even to Hestia, who shook her head in some mild vexation.

"We could fight our way to the river," replied Seaton. "But after that?"

"They only ambush, At night," said Suarez. "But they won't do it to us."

Hestia stood up suddenly and walked off down to the water's edge. She stood there, hugging her arms and doing her little aimless twirls about the waist. The men looked awkwardly at each other. With the exception of Cotterill, they had all been involved in some battle or another, but at that moment she seemed the authority in the suffering and jeopardy that warfare invariably brought with it.

Northmore dispelled all such introspection with a thump on the table. "It will not happen to us. And we shall establish ourselves on that site tomorrow. Without fail."

The following morning Suarez led them back to the Okaina village and, having settled on a site nestling in a palmed area due south of it, they beat a separate path back to the river. This separate access, designed to demonstrate the unobtrusive nature of the expedition, would discreetly provide an additional line of withdrawal. In fact, both paths became thriving thoroughfares, as the Cholos ferried in the construction tools and materials for the job ahead.

First, they erected a basic Tambo style structure, with sloping roof and a flat earth floor, for shelter while they built more durable structures, based on Seringueiros' dwellings, raised on piles, with exterior and interior palm walls. Northmore and Munby had drawn up a simple projected expedition village over long hours at the RGS and to their delight it seemed most of the plan would be realised. Hestia's arrival had occasioned some slight modification, to the extent that an additional cubicle would be required for her in the "main house", but this was easily incorporated.

Then began a furious business of chopping, logging, sawing and hammering, with twenty and more men clambering over heaps of timbers and cut trees, lashing sections together with hemp and liana based rope, and prising nails from Suarez's treasure trove for critical junctions. Men hauled the skeletons of the houses into the jungle sky and tethered them with creepers. Other men were building sections of thatching, weaving matting, lashing and nailing sections of wooden flooring. Suarez kept them on schedule with early starts and constant application throughout the day. During the afternoon rains, they sheltered and worked on the matting, the flooring and fixings. Once the deluge had receded, they would set to on the house frames again, stopping at last light to return to the river and eat. Steadily, from amongst all this antlike activity, the semblance of a tiny settlement emerged.

The Okaina ignored this discreet but frenetic colonisation in the trees. They rose before dawn to stir their fires, went down to the river at dawn to bathe and then filtered off to their separate, unhurried activities in the plantations, the forest or the river.

Northmore's camp was drawn up into three buildings. The main residence comprised of five identical rooms and one larger one, opening onto a wide and covered veranda, all under a ridge-backed thatched roof. The whole was supported on piles, with a central stairway leading from the veranda down the five or so feet to the packed earth beneath. Each of the smaller rooms served as a bedroom and the larger room as laboratory and specimen room. Washing facilities were in an outhouse behind the structure, with a divided cubicle for Hestia. Further storage areas were demarked beneath the raised wooden floor, where the powder magazine had been dug, and a false pile set on top of it.

The Big Tambo, as it was known, was completed first and the scientific and medical supplies stored, at last, in safety. Frames for the camp beds were finally unpacked, mosquito nets and rudimentary furniture set out and, with an engaging parody of civic pride, Northmore presented each member with the lodging to be his or her home for the months to come.

Cotterill's room was at the far end of the veranda, next to that came Seaton's, then Hestia's, then Munby's and finally Northmore's, beside the jungle laboratory and library he had spent so many years to accomplish. They stood on the veranda, much like passengers embarking on an ocean liner, introducing themselves to each other for the duration, with a mixture of formality and anticipation.

"It's basic, but it's sound, my dear," Northmore told Hestia, almost apologetically. She had, after all, been deprived of her home to be brought to a small room, with a bed, a mosquito net, a bucket and a tiny chest of drawers, once intended for herb specimens.

She walked into her room with her small trunk and set it down in a corner. "And it's mine?" she asked. "To do as I like?"

"Entirely, Miss Williams," replied the baronet, somewhat perplexed at the question. "Nobody will intrude on you here."

She surprised him with a wide, warm smile and moved around the room, running her hands over the walls and humming to herself. After a while she said, "I'm going to make it beautiful." and with that she seemed to forget he was there. He moved out awkwardly onto the veranda again, where Suarez was supervising the lifting of laboratory glassware up the front steps.

"Can we put a lock or a bolt on that door?" he asked the quartermaster, pointing to the woven screen entrance to Hestia's room.

Suarez considered for a moment. "On the inside or the outside, Sir?"

Within two days, they'd finished off the secondary house that consisted of Suarez's quarters, a workshop, a food storeroom and a dining and convening area. This was lower to the ground but had a gallery overlooking the cooking pit that lay between it and the third structure, which housed the remaining carriers and the remainder of the supplies and unused building materials. This last was more rudimentary still, simply because the Cholo workforce saw no need to expend energy on comforts they neither valued nor understood. They were happy enough with a well-established roof and places to hang their hammocks.

With the settlement finally completed and routine maintenance set in place, Northmore and Suarez discharged the bulk of the carriers. These, on inquiring of the Okaina about Boro presence to the north and receiving no sound intelligence but plenty of alarming conjecture, discarded the easier option of rafting out down the Kahuanari to the rubber settlements along the Japura River. Instead, to the expedition's astonishment, they opted to return the way they had come, cutting their way to a place opposite the site of the raft building, crossing by canoe and taking up their old path back to the Igara Parana. They would not be persuaded otherwise; their terror of Boro savagery and that of the Menimehe, who lived along the north side of the Japura, brooked no argument

There were no farewells, not even to those whose cooking fires they had shared, although this lack of courtesy seemed to affect neither party. The women left with them, leaving only the men Suarez had commissioned in Esperenza. Callard had proved so reliable that Suarez had signed him on for the duration of the "collection". His protégé Bowser had been discharged, but decided to stay on with his mentor. He would not be paid and did not seem to expect it, but when Seaton made sure he would be fed with the rest, both he and Callard showed more than a flicker of emotion. The older man held the boy's hand for a moment, then dropped it and sat down to clean the bolt action on the Mannlicher rifle that was now his personal property.

"Right, gentlemen," Northmore addressed them, as the departing carriers filed into the forest. "Now we can begin work in earnest."

With that, the Northmore expedition set out to advance the course of natural science, while alongside it the Okaina kept to their monotonous daily routine, indifferent to the great works being attempted beside and about them. The divergence of pace, impetus and direction between the two parties was almost as great as the distance between their geographical origins.

The Indian day followed its course alongside the nature around it and possibly with even less variation. True, there was hard work to be done, simply to survive. Although crammed with species and deluged with fresh water, the forest did not offer up its bounty like some Sunday school rendition of the Garden of Eden. There was endless work for the women, cultivating the maize, pineapples and manioc in the families' plantations, tending the fires, cleaning and cooking about the tribal house and looking after their babies by the way. For the men there was difficult terrain to be negotiated, scarce game to be hunted or trapped, fish to be caught, foods like wild honey to be gathered, and all of it to be carried back. Tribal enemies had to be scouted for, fended off or attacked. Yet all these things were done with a lassitude and disinterested automatism that verged on torpor.

Coca was chewed to help get things done and tobacco licked to recover and repose, but Seaton detected there was no real interest in daily events and not much curiosity about the activities of others. Apart from moments when something so surprising turned up in an expedition member's hand, or in their behaviour, that some degree of inquisitiveness was engendered, time passed with an indolence that rendered it occasionally static.

In but a few days this somnolence affected even the most directed and motivated members of the expedition party; it exasperated and palliated by turn. Munby railed against Okaina promises of assistance that never came to anything and the fragmentary nature of their information about the location and properties of trees and shrubs or the habitats of birds, mammals and insects. He decried the Indians' effortless disregard for timescales set outside dawn, dusk and meals. Nevertheless, he told Seaton he often been astounded, upon pulling out his pocket watch, to discover he'd lost an hour or two without being in slightest way aware of his employment during the course of it. As when he spent an hour around an energetic termites' nest, when he'd only intended a brief investigation to update his notes of the day before.

Seaton had experienced exactly the same thing, possibly with greater personal discomposure. Apart from some general involvement in expedition matters, he was his own taskmaster. He felt this appreciable freedom came with an equally appreciable responsibility to spend his time gainfully. It disturbed him when his pocket watch became a witness to the same kind of truancy that Munby had described. This was not simply because his timekeeping was in some insidious way being encroached upon. These subtle and all too frequent dislocations of time itself meant his timepiece lost its associated reliability. It was no longer the sole arbiter of process and progress.

Progress was, of course, the ultimate purpose and driving force behind the expedition, and local conditions could not be allowed to divert it. Northmore drew up rosters and quotas, and the completion of tasks regulated the day. Each man knew, intuitively, that if all their timepieces foundered, their calendar would eventually drift away and, like the Okaina, they would come to rely on daylight, rain and heat to put their self-appointed tasks into some kind perspective, and give their purposes a sense of ending. They tended their watches in the same way the Okaina tended their fires. Neither could afford to let their most precious possession peter out. The Indian had no means of making fire, and their wet climate permitted no natural conflagrations. Embers were as precious as life. The expedition had no power to restart the European passage of time. They only had matches.

Early that morning, Munby and Northmore had trekked off beyond the plantation ground, to search for deviations in moss growth on cinchona trees, should they have the good fortune to find any cinchona trees, which had so far proved elusive. Cotterill had gone to scout the western tributary bank for capybara. Bowser had reported some Okaina rumour about a jaguar prowling the grounds at the furthest point of the forested promontory, trapping its prey between the walls of water and its murderous teeth. The jaguar had played on the young American's mind and so he was off to see whether some bait could be trapped or, if necessary, killed and left out for the cat to fall upon. He'd taken Bowser with him in the somewhat totemic conviction that the man who had picked up the rumour from the Okaina would prove the fittest instrument for tracking the animal down. Bowser, proud of his new status as a jaguar hunter, saw possibilities for the beast everywhere.

Munby had opined that if they did establish that a jaguar was in the vicinity, the enclosed nature of the terrain would provide unprecedented opportunity to study its foraging habits, and possibly even its mating behaviour. Cotterill had nodded along silently to this, but Seaton didn't give too much for the cat's chances if it stalked into the American's sights.

Hestia had kept to her room, absorbed in what she termed her "homely touches", weaving mats out of rushes and grasses she'd found on the more accessible paths, strewing them across her small floor space or pinning them to her wall. Seaton thought she would have had to have been exceptionally charming to Suarez to secure some of his precious nails. The mats were set in place, considered in

165

fine detail, adjudged in need of improvement, taken up, or down, altered and reorganised; the process seemed endless and, he supposed, provided some comfort in its domestic orderliness. Seaton spent the morning on the veranda of the Tambo and made sketches of sections of tree bark Munby had brought in the day before and in which the Lancastrian seemed particularly interested.

They met to lunch on some dried fish and fresh fruit, taking this on the Tambo gallery rather than in the tabled section attached to the cooking area. He asked the girl if she would like to accompany him to the Indian settlement after the rains but, although appreciative, she was unable to find the time. Her decorations were but partially resolved. He felt her some of her restlessness of spirit was being tidied away, even if not swept up altogether.

At the Maloka, he found a larger number of Okaina on the dancing ground than was usual for the time of day. The women were painting the girl children for a dance planned for the night and the men and elder boys being in the forest, fishing or lazing in their hammocks, these delicate preparations could continue unobserved. While Okaina men wore a breech clout they never removed in the presence of others, Okaina women went naked as a matter of course, and the scene called to mind Matisse and his three bathers. The colours were fauvist too, he thought. Half gourds of dye, principally red, yellow and a bluish black, were scattered on the ground. The girls stood placidly beside them while their mothers dipped sticks into the dye pots and drew complicated if crude patterns up their legs to above waist height and, on occasion, right up to the breastbone. These outlines they then filled in with colour, requiring the girls to turn and turn about, with short clucks of command.

Seaton sat down and rummaged in his satchel for sketchbook and charcoal. With the desultory progress being made, the number of the children and the variations in complexity and design, he could make studies without hurry and without any particular aim in mind. The seriousness of the children, their immobility beneath the stick and the dyes now flecking the ground at their feet, would have been inconceivable in a European setting. In all the days he had been there he had yet to hear a child cry. The seaside bedlam of Bognor and Brighton washed before his eyes, the throngs at Crystal Palace, at Ascot, at Henley. He conjured up symphonic variations on the bustle and the brouhaha of English mothers and their young, the spinning of hoops and tops, the perennial changes of clothing, the losing of gloves, pandemonium at sports matches, trains back to school and Christmas entertainments. Compared with this, the silence of Okaina babies appeared to reflect an awful profundity; their silence was their inheritance, a watchfulness of generations.

He was working on a sketch of a particularly stolid child having a wild sequence of zigzags inscribed on its sturdy thighs, when he felt a presence behind him. Two of the girls, now fully decorated in vivid yellow and red motifs, stood silently behind him and gazed down at the charcoal lines with which he had summoned up their sister in his book. He held the book out for them to see but they shied away in sudden alarm. Fearing he may have committed some solecism, he quickly walked over to the mother whose daughter he had just sketched, and held out the book to her. She was crouching at the girl's feet, about to plaster sections of her design with the red dye, a fibrous and sticky compound from some local root.

She looked at the drawing uncomprehendingly. Seaton smiled in what he hoped would be taken as a calm and friendly manner, and then pointed from the drawing to the girl repeatedly. Eventually the woman arrived at some conclusion. Without a word, she handed him the dye stick, rose to her feet and stood back. The girl, with no change of expression, turned and presented her person for him.

He found himself the object of everyone's attention, and some whispered conversation. His next steps were lost to him; he might cause as much offence by walking away as he could by daubing the girl. She herself offered no clue to the protocols involved. Then one of the other girls said something to her mother and they went on with her preparations for the dance, the woman dipping her hand in the red dye and smearing it into a ziggurat raising up from the small of the child's back to her shoulder blades. Seaton's model looked round at this and then turned back to Seaton. While she didn't make any remonstrance to her own mother or anybody else, something in her posture made him feel he was letting her down in an already awkward situation. With a sigh, he dipped the stick in the red dye and set to work, hoping this was the way most likely to repair the disruption he had wrought.

The girl looked at him with solemn eyes and a pursed mouth that indicated some kind of concentration, the stance Hestia took when called upon to concern herself with difficult subjects. A warm mud smell came from her, and her fleshed dimpled and flattened under the pressure of the stick as he tried to spread the dye on her leg. The dye itself was surprisingly resistant, and he remembered, with a throbbing in his temples and surge of warmth to his throat, that the women used their hands to apply it as evenly as the material would permit. This, he had no intention of doing and he realised, almost in despair, that he had ensnared himself in a situation that was both acutely uncomfortable and in breach of all anthropological practice. He tried desperately to avoid looking at, or indeed even registering, her pubic region, around which her mother's pattern had been ingeniously entwined, and signalled with his free hand for her turn around, so he might apply some paint to a relatively inoffensive portion of her back. With whatever self possession remaining to him, he determined to demonstrate some minimal but courteous engagement in the decoration process before making good his escape. To his consternation she stayed stolidly where she was for a brief moment, incommunicado, and then moved docilely a step further towards him.

He put a hand up to her upper arm and gently turned her to face away from him. Her mother had constructed a lattice work from the backs of her knees to the nape of her neck. Gratefully he applied himself to some of the figures between her shoulder blades. She adjusted her posture a little and, mindful of ruining her pattern by painting over a line, such a nursery admonition, he kept his hand on her arm to steady the both of them. After a while he looked up to see if everyone around him were sufficiently occupied for him to make a discreet withdrawal and, instead, saw Hestia observing his efforts from a few paces away. She was standing motionless under the makeshift parasol Munby had constructed for her out of strips of lawn and some split cane, from the depths of the workshop supplies.

Once again he felt the flush raging up into his face and a sudden pounding of his heart. He couldn't find words or expression to alleviate the moment, so he gave her a civil and hopefully purposeful nod and returned to the last section of the pattern he had set himself to complete.

Something in Hestia's expression lingered with him, something more unsettling than the gaffe he had committed amongst the Okaina womenfolk and their daughters. She had displayed no disapproval, no shock nor yet incomprehension. What he found most disturbing was that she had been looking at him as if he had been merely shearing a sheep.

West Sussex

"They must have been dancing," said Ursula in quiet realisation. She was sitting, busy with her ballet scrapbook, in her usual place in the bay window at the Old Forge. She had strewn the table with pictures and sketches, sets and costumes by Leon Bakst, Benois and Goncharova, by Miro and Matisse, by De Chirico and Picasso. She often pored over this effusion of colour and design. She felt imbued by the movement, the sublime technique and lofty abandon at which the Ballets Russes excelled. In a way, it was her dressing up box, lending her a sense of escape and a transcendence she had never really found in the adult world. Today, as she looked at all the sensuous colouring and line offered as an oblation to radical musical gods, she suddenly made the connection. "Yes," she said, happy in the conclusion. "They were dancing."

Clover was barely listening. She'd come back from the village in poor spirits after a battery of insinuations and gentle probing about her tea party with the Captain and Houghton-Copley. Why on earth had the wretched man brought those drawing here? They'd upset the Captain desperately, she could see that, and they'd turned the village into a whirlpool of malicious suggestion.

She'd hidden the drawing he'd left behind in a drawer beneath some remnant wools of her mother's, but she had no idea what she was going to do with it. Beautiful, elusive and yet so dangerous through the misconceptions of others, it could only do harm once it was taken out again. She tried not to see it, but the little girl's eyes stared up at her and her little brother looked so lost and the delicacy of the line caused her stomach to contract.

"Those Indian girls the Captain drew, Clovy. We thought they were hugging each other." Ursula held up a postcard depicting the poster for Satie's Relche, a sylph

170

pranced gaily in the air, her body kissed with polka dots. She smiled fondly at it. "But they were dancing. They'd been painted to dance."

Clover looked into the face of the little girl she'd hidden in the drawer; untouched by anything, just getting on with what she had to do, her innocence caught for ever by the Captain's charcoal. She was her mirror image, identical yet opposite. She could smell her father's hair oil, feel the chill air of the barn as she stood goose pimpled before him, feel the warm, brusque, impatient hands take hold of her and mould her into the positions he wanted.

"How wild and wonderful," said Ursula softly.

Chapter Seven

West Sussex

Among Mrs Simmons' many accomplishments was a fine apple pie with flaky pastry and succulent apple, lightly spiced with cinnamon and nutmeg and sprinkled with brown sugar. She baked once a week and the aroma alone reminded Foster of all the things he dreamed of during those chaotic, mud encrusted, blood spattered years in the trenches. It was the second, most tangible home comfort he could think of; the first also being provided by Mrs Simmons, but with a natural delicacy he passed over that till a more appropriate occasion. Instead, he concentrated on pouring thick cream onto his portion from the ridiculously tiny Georgian silver cream jug that Captain Seaton had inherited from a great aunt and bequeathed to the kitchen shelves, in favour of a more serviceable porcelain model. Mrs Simmons liked the tiny creamer because it reminded her of a long-gone age of grace and crinolines. So Foster persevered with it, obliging to the last.

"He's going up to town tomorrow," he said, surreptitiously wiping the spout of the little vessel and licking his finger, before forking away at Mrs Simmons' pie.

"Will you be driving up?" asked Mrs Simmons. She set down two cups of tea on the table and then settled herself down to watch him enjoying himself.

"Just to Chichester," he looked guiltily at her because he was talking with his mouth full, but a desire both to eat and to inform ran neck and neck with him. She affected not to notice. "He's taking the train."

She stood up and wiped her hands on a kitchen cloth. "Will he need a bag packing?"

"Not likely." Foster sipped his tea. "He's having lunch with Sir Everard Northmore. I just brought him the

172

telegram. Lunch at the Travellers', it says. He won't want to stay up there. Can't stand the place any more."

"Makes you wonder why he goes at all," Helen Simmons sat back to enjoy her tea. "Couldn't he invite the man down here?

"Think he's had enough of visitors for the time being." Foster put on his most engaging grin. "Don't suppose you could spare another slice of that pie?"

Pall Mall, London

Foster had set him down at Chichester Station in time for the ten minutes past ten up train to Victoria. While, as he noticed from the timetable, this would mean stopping at Barnham, Arundel, Pulborough, Horsham, Sutton and West Croydon before getting into Victoria around two hours later, the previous through train would have him into London Bridge over an hour earlier, with nothing to do save avoid old acquaintances. Reasoning that he'd rather be in transit than in town, he'd opted for the slower train and an uninterrupted view of Southern England moving steadily past on a bright summer's day, with the meadows alive with buttercups, the pink flash of tall stands of foxgloves on the woodsides, the sway of the cornfields and the new fruit swells on the beech trees. He'd brought along the Times for when this summer profusion ceased to hold sway, and his leaky fountain pen for when the crossword won out over the Thunderer's opinions on the day's events. Despite all these precautions, he knew he'd have to complete his preparations for his conversation with Northmore, even though he'd been in the gallery to the small hours, smoking his way through to what he hoped would be clarity in the matter.

Finding a cab at Victoria Station proved rather easier than the Times' crossword's obdurate fourteen down, which had confounded him since Sutton, and he found himself skirting Horseguards' Parade almost before he had time to experience any trepidation about the interview ahead.

Northmore was waiting for him. As Seaton arrived, the baronet got to his feet and stood with an air of mildly confused forbearance, like a bull elephant in its last ponderous moments amongst the mahogany and brass furnishings which, with the cast of the Bassae Frieze, so characterized the agreeable interior of the Travellers' Club library. Seeing him thus, Seaton felt the rush of years, both as the painful remembrance of things past, but also as a visceral realisation of the true interval between them and the present. Northmore had retained his moustaches though these, like his thinning hair, were now silvery white. His face managed to look both ruddy and subsiding. His long and bony hands protruded from the sleeves of a lounge suit that seemed to hang off his once powerful frame. His imposing figure had become somehow insubstantial, as if the spirit had been drawn from it.

"Ainsley!" Even his voice, Seaton noted, was somewhat hollow now. "Good Lord, man, you're almost as cadaverous as I am."

He shook the Captain's hand firmly, for all his gaunt aspect, and then sat back into his leather armchair, waving to Seaton to sit across from him. He had had two large whisky and sodas served on the small table set between them and had clearly made major inroads into his own. "We can go in presently," he said, referring to the Coffee Room in which they were due to lunch. "Can't hear myself think for all those buggers chomping away. Now, what's the problem and why the mad scramble?"

Seaton sat back in his chair, ignored the whisky and soda and addressed himself to the conversational gambits he had rehearsed the night before. Yet in some way Northmore's incipient decrepitude rendered his planned and measured perorations both slick and unseemly to him. He found himself at a loss and, accordingly, said the first thing he felt he could decently and honestly contribute to their reunion. "I was sorry to hear about your boy."

Northmore looked over towards the oak wood fireplace and possibly further away. "Thank you," he said quietly, and then continued in this abstracted mode. "Beggars belief, doesn't it? An entire continent slaughtering its children. Your deep forest man will put away the sickly, the deformed, even the younger of twins perhaps. But whole healthy children? And so very many? Can you envisage the Witoto or the Okaina scything down a generation?"

He turned back to Seaton, with a small, self-conscious smile, and let his hands drop into his lap. Seaton decided to drink the whisky and soda after all; the man's open demoralisation was unnerving. "A man called Houghton-Copley turned up the other day," he began, feeling his way towards the accommodation he needed so badly.

"Oh him," Northmore snorted dismissively, reaching for his glass. "Rum bugger. Well connected, though. Always whispering in somebody's ear."

"He brought me some of my drawings," continued Seaton carefully, "and I had really no memory of them…"

"You were in a bad way," interrupted the baronet. He took a mouthful of whisky and soda. "When we came back. You were a very sick man."

"He mentioned a secret archive. Expedition papers. Sequestered material was the way he put it." Seaton was in the final approaches now, upwind and with barely a footfall. The bull elephant appeared indifferent or impervious. "He said you'd given him access."

Northmore sighed deeply and shook his head from side to side, in world-weary acknowledgment of some unspoken but evidently foreseen conclusion. Seaton could almost see the sun glinting on his shattered tusks. "It was a complete, bloody mess wasn't it, Ainsley? The whole damn thing was a disaster."

North-west Amazon

External conditions soon dictated scientific activities be conducted in a timetable closely akin to the Okaina's own daily routine; Munby and Northmore would rise at dawn and spend at least two hours on ornithological pursuits, before the heat of the day quieted most wildlife and human activity. Cotterill would often accompany them in this, albeit under a strict firearms embargo. The young American proved a keen and ingenious student, demonstrating the fieldsman's characteristic fascination with those species he would later choose to hunt, despatch and collect. Northmore, with his pedigree in land and game management, understood this ambivalence instinctively but Munby, whose interests in fauna were scientific and absolute, harboured grave reservations about the young American's motivations and indeed his mental makeup. He thought the meticulous interest Cotterill took in the siting of nests, the rearing of young and protection of territorial rights, to be somewhat grisly in view of the lack of compunction with which he could despatch the selfsame species to either the cookpot or the taxidermist. He could not equate his specimens with Cotterill's trophies, which he viewed as the fruits of wanton, vainglorious destruction. Northmore's calm and engaging presence seemed to act in unspoken arbitration

They would assemble on the gallery at first light, foregoing all thought of breakfast, and then process along the jungle paths together. Munby would be loaded down with his field glasses, his net, his egg box, his collection bag, insect boxes, thongs, pouches and pin cushions to retain whatever specimens they chanced upon along the way, for

176

while their sole business at that time of day would be birds and more birds, who could tell what opportunity the teeming complexity of the environment would place in the assiduous collector's path? Munby's appetite for species, their aspects, habits, proclivities and comparable behaviour was as voracious as that he ascribed to Cotterill, and he would gather in whatever was set before him, collating on the move. Cotterill, while less hungry for the fruits of categorisation, would be similarly laden, to assist the Lancastrian in his endeavours, with the addition of a double-barrelled shotgun over his shoulder for strictly defensive purposes as he would earnestly affirm each morning. Northmore, lightly equipped with pruning shears, note books and specimen bag, would lead them into the forest as the sun slowly burned off the morning mist.

Seaton would hear their assembly in the early hours, which was invariably all but speechless but with many heavy footfalls and some repetitive activity in and out of the laboratory, selecting equipment to take with them, punctuated by the ineffectual repression of Suarez's smoker's morning cough. Sound travelled easily through the Tambo and as his eyes were still focusing on the enlivening world outside his mosquito netting, Seaton could assess the determination of the party and its makeup; while that impression was forming, he would make his decision about whether to roust out and accompany them. He was no stranger to early morning stand-to's, but found that in these circumstances the decision as to whether or not to join the party came from a wholly novel set of criteria. He would allow himself to surmise what might be the most profitable subject for him to paint or draw that day. He waited simply for the call, whether it came from life around the Maloka, the eddies of the river where the turtles concealed themselves, the clouding of butterflies behind the plantation, or the extended and strange leaves of some plant glimpsed the day before. And then, overcoming a lifetime's reservation about acting on impulse, he wagered on his instinct.

Sometimes he would jump through his netting, drag on his clothes and haversack and join the party tramping silently down the Tambo steps. A pause for some water by the cooking area, both for immediate consumption and the filling of water bottles, and the men would be off. All this was accomplished with a simple nod of greeting and often his first words of conversation would be a good fifteen minutes from the moment he had stepped out of his room. Nobody felt the lack of it or any implied discourtesy; they felt, as one, that it was a marvellous way to get to grips with determined activity on a tropical day.

Sometimes he would listen to them tramp away and then drift back into sleep, preferring to take a leisurely breakfast and prepare his mind and his materials for the day's work ahead, over some coffee, fruit and cassava bread. On rare instances he heard the muffled interrogations of Hestia, as she tried to shrug off sleep and follow the bird watchers, notionally in the hope of the sight of some vibrant plumage or little chicks to cradle, and his instinctive inclinations would apparently change. On those mornings, he'd find himself clumping down the Tambo steps behind her, pulling on his forage hat and returning a grin that the early hour always imbued with a conspiratorial air, confirming their shared place in the wake of the experts. Hestia's affections were somehow unconstrained by the early hour, as if the warmth of her bed still in some emotional way enfolded her. This early morning, silent proximity seemed to alleviate the awkwardness between them, and it appeared that she felt the easier for it too.

Ornithological forays fell into two categories. They would either sweep the river banks and clearings, like the

Indian plantations, where birds could fly easily in and out of the treeline, or they would target some cluster of trees and clamber up towards the canopy, the flowering fruits and the safer access to shelter and food that these heights provided. Cotterill proved especially agile in this regard, something he attributed to childhood holidays in New Hampshire, and, with Bowser, would scale great heights to secure rope ladders or construct temporary platforms for Munby, a diffident climber at best, to perch precariously on. The Lancastrian gave no indication of his vertiginous feelings and indeed his intense commitment to close surveillance, and the accuracy of the notes he scribbled in his field book, must have saved him from many a queasy moment.

After two hours of such activities they would return to the Tambo for breakfast, putting the specimens away in the jars and cases built up in specimen room, and setting out those which required more investigation upon the working surfaces of the laboratory area. Then they would all gather at the tables around the cooking area, the Cholos at one table and the principals at the other, to debate the morning's progress with equal dedication. The Cholos were affected more by the diversity and number of the specimens gathered than by the quality. They were also inclined to view the process of spotting, identifying and categorising a species as something of a failure compared with netting it for dissection or display. Cotterill went to some lengths to disassociate himself with this body of thought, seeking to dispel Munby's impression of him as some kind of indiscriminate slaughterer. He was at pains not to jeopardise the one hunting trophy that possessed him body and soul, that of the black jaguar. The cat was his Holy Grail and he ruminated upon it in private, never once allowing his aspiration time in the open for Munby to pounce upon. When he could restrain himself no longer, and being sure to be out of Munby's earshot, he would describe the jaguar's prowess and its grace to Hestia with a passion that verged on the poetic. She would in turn ask him why, if the animal so captivated him, he should want to see its head on his wall. When he fell silent at this reproof, she had a natural sensitivity to frame the question as some kind of affectionate teasing, and his pleasure at being chosen for this coquetry would undo the pain at having his appetites so clinically portrayed for him.

When Seaton heard her chafe the American, it was a comforting indication that the horrors of the powder store at the Mission were in some measure behind her. Her wellbeing occupied him more than he would have wished to concede. Indeed, the memory of her anguish in the maelstrom of the fire ants' nest pressed itself upon him intermittently, while he worked amongst the leaf forms and shadows, sketching out the nuances of nature, as it either prevailed over its many challenges or was consumed by them. He could summon up her pain, something both physical and spiritual, in minute detail and this surprised him, for he had seen a great deal of distress and torment in his life. Why he should separate out this particular instance was beyond him, although the realisation that he had followed a profession which thrived in the proximity of pain, confusion and misery was a startling development. However, if he found himself dwelling on such introspections, he only had to pull himself up, ward off the nearest stinging fly, feel the sweat tricking down his spine and the throbbing of his temples as the humidity and the heat pounded upon them, and he was back beside the Kahuanari.

The rest of the day, till the rains came, was given over to entomology. Munby was of the firm opinion that the time leading up to the greatest heat of the day offered the greatest opportunities for insects, although Seaton regarded this as a matter of degree. He couldn't plant his travelling easel, or yet set a brush down, without disturbing some multi-legged or winged thing and sending it scurrying about its business. Northmore had gridded a map of the surrounding area to systematise their search in terms of habitat and conditions. For three consecutive days, the party spanned the western tributary, crossing by canoe, to investigate the distinction between species that these natural boundaries inevitably produced. The results were startling and Munby's scribbles and diagrams covered the specimen room walls with sightings, variations and projections of parallel development.

Hestia expressed a fondness for the hues of the more extravagant beetles, and between them they had, as act of accidental kindness, founded a separate collection on her behalf. Everybody kept an eye out for something vivid and new for her, on top of their commitments with the expedition's business. Munby himself was an active patron. He had brought back something with a carapace that would have caused wonder in the Forbidden City, and pinned it for her so that she might display it on the wall of her room. After that, the perfectionist in him drove him on to surpass its beauty and aspect. Luckily the forest provided ample opportunities, from coruscating butterflies to tiny bejewelled frogs, although Munby was here constrained to diverge from accepted field practice. Now, when he discovered some tiny and flamboyant arachnid, he would find himself searching round for a pair, in order to avoid any tension between his scientific priorities and Hestia's pleasure in his largesse. He would not be overly swayed by the latter but, even so, was reluctant to relinquish any experience of it, should nature prove bountiful enough.

Hestia was flowering along with her room. Her demeanour changed subtly once she was in occupation and she received visitors, even on the most mundane of business, with good humour and courtesy. Seaton wondered if she had been permitted such pride of ownership and design over her own surroundings before. Perhaps, Micah Williams, taken up with hymn singing and celebrations of the Word in the deep forest, had not had much regard for such feminine occupations.

Cotterill supported Hestia's collection with his usual robust commitment but was tacitly thought to have exceeded the bounds of their small aesthetic diversion, when he arrived at her door with a large and freshly excavated turtle shell. This had to be left outside, for the insects to finish their cleaning activity. It exhaled warm, rotting river air about the gallery, where Northmore was wont to sit and read of an evening. Realising that even pipe tobacco would not alleviate the atmosphere, the baronet knocked at Hestia's door with a request that he might remove her objet trouvée to a more hygienic distance, prior to it's being waxed and incorporated into her furnishings. Hestia, who had appropriated the Oxford Book of English Verse, the knapsack version on India paper, from Seaton's depleted library and was cultivating a poetic mien, was gracious in her acquiescence and Northmore took the thing away. It then became his responsibility to check on its progress, and he ended up waxing it himself and taking no little pride in its finished appearance.

Hestia reciprocated by insisting on taking sole responsibility for writing up the expedition's specimen records, labels and observations in her own copybook script. She had a firm, but delicate, hand and each afternoon, during the rains, she would sit down to her task at the specimen room table, beside the dissection bench, and translate each individual's handwriting into a uniform whole. When he saw her sitting with the specimen cages dangling about her, suspended on twine smeared with bitter vegetable oil to deter insects, beneath inverted

182

copper bowls to impede rats and mice, Seaton was reminded of Tenniel's Alice. Munby, whose scrawl baffled even him on occasion, was especially appreciative of her diligence.

Seaton had parted readily with his Oxford Book of English Verse one lunchtime when Hestia had seemed particularly listless and he wished to be away, to complete his colour sketch of a particularly ornate *Gustavia augusta*, whose large pink and white flowers lit up a wall of thicket on a waterway at the far side of the Indian plantations. His sporadic attendance on the insect foraging parties meant that he had little occasion to present Hestia with anything else, though she did not mention it and indeed it would have been an awkward transaction. He had provided her with an escape from the earth, and somehow that exempted the two of them from more superficial and frankly agreeable things. They now held to this unspoken yet sombre compact as a mark of mute respect, yet he sensed some equally unvoiced reproach in her meticulous courtesy. She would break off from twitting Cotterill, or listening with patient affection to one of Munby's discourses on minute discrepancies in recorded plant behaviour, to enquire after Seaton's wellbeing as if he were some kind of bedridden but forbidding great aunt.

Once, he'd found himself sketching an outline of her at breakfast, holding up her coffee cup and laughing at some sally of Cotterill's, and when the rest of the party had gone off to prepare for the next sortie, he had presented it to her. He was surprised at his own diffidence; it was only a doodle after all, something to set beside the shells and the butterflies. Her reaction had been equally awkward, almost to the point of embarrassment. She gave him a rushed smile and left briskly to return it to her room, returning almost upon the instant to finish her coffee and leave the moment behind. It was as if there were something indelicate in his setting down an observation of her, an intimacy that did not sit easily with her, and he was inclined to believe that she actually found it disturbing.

The expedition party comported themselves, in the main, with that benign civility the British adopt when required to sustain each other's company at close quarters for extended periods of time. Even Cotterill tempered his youthful athleticism, confining it to his solo forays with Bowser in search of the black cat or other game. Northmore oscillated between the avuncular and the distractedly academic. Munby was at pains to reduce his natural asperity. Seaton found his natural reserve gently steered toward the sociable, and Hestia sang.

Seaton would be set down in the bush, debating the suitability of gouache over watercolour to capture the elusive display of purple bronze and lemon flowers of an ancient *clusia*, when he would hear the strains of '*Meet Me In St Louis, Louis.*' wafting towards him, as Hestia came in search of some diversion. This diversion normally entailed asking him what he was doing, imparting some snippet of information about the occupations of the other principals, waiting in vain for some undefined recreation, and then moving off suddenly while singing *"In the Shade of the Old Apple Tree."* or *"Shine On Harvest Moon.".* Her repertoire, she told Seaton, had been provided by a Mr Kettering, who had worked for the rubber company with her father and had subscribed to all the latest sheet music publishers, even though his long ordered player-piano had repeatedly failed to appear. When the depot closed, Mr Kettering had returned to Manaos taking his music with him, but not before supervising Hestia in the performance of her favourite pieces. There were about ten of these and, as she was reluctant to wear them all out, she concentrated on her favourite three or four. The parakeets, macaws and other calling birds seemed equable with this reduced programme and, after a while, the expedition principals became so accustomed to the tunes that they barely registered them. What the Okaina made of them, she had yet to find out.

Face to face in any inescapable encounter, the Okaina remained reticent and lethargic, as if the merest animation might put them in thrall to the beings they were doggedly determined to live without. They held frequent tribal dances, with no regard for the visitors. The men, in their feathers, colours and beads with their dancing poles, their flutes and monkey skin drums, and the women, sometimes corseted with feathers and beads but otherwise naked and elaborately painted, entwined in separate circles singing and chanting for hour upon hour. The torches flickered, as the kashiri spirit flowed from the gourds of men already heroic in their coca consumption, while the women became intoxicated simply by the rhythms and the occasion. The intricate, gentle but sexually charged mockery of their refrains rotated and turned upon each and all of them. With the same absolute disregard, they held their tribal councils, deliberating on imponderables over their tobacco pots, and handing down irrevocable judgments on matters from the ill luck occasioned by the malevolence of rival tribes to the dispersal of widows amongst their own.

The expedition, in their turn, tended to steer clear of contact. Northmore and Munby, whilst professionally curious about the indigenes' behaviour and folklore, had prioritised their botanical, ornithological and entomological programmes, and could not spare time to devote to the study of their neighbours. Cotterill, after a brief fascination, was wholly taken up with his black cat, Hestia's collection and providing Munby with the physical support he deemed the man needed. Hestia kept to her own paths; following the incident of discovering Seaton painting the child, she had avoided the Maloka altogether.

Seaton had been struck by the essential apartness of indigenous populations, wherever he had served. Here, the Okaina seemed to embody this separation in its most extreme and dislocated form. Their diffidence played upon his own and he restricted his advances to casual sketches of whatever Okaina life presented itself. Or he might try to recall the details of surprising artefacts he had glimpsed, which he would then conjure up in the gallery during the rains, while Hestia was busy with her calligraphy in the specimen room.

In the wake of these spur-of-the-moment impressions and conjured approximations, he was soon to discover something that separated out his art in the forest from any work he had hitherto produced. What had been a painstaking and on occasion laborious process in South Africa and England had become in some way both precise and yet free flowing. When he looked at his work, he saw in it a more sympathetic rendering of his environment, compared with the respectful recording of it that had characterised his previous efforts. Perhaps he was personally involved now, although he was less conscious of the process itself. Just as the time itself seemed to fade away in these environs, so did his awareness of the concerted effort and concentration he normally put into his work. Yet the results he had to admit, and Northmore had enthusiastically attested, were beautiful, detailed, observant and alive. It was as if nature were at last coming out to meet him, or there was such a plenitude of natural forces around him, that they could not help but suffuse onto his paper through his own brushwork. He felt, in this channelling of hidden affinities, that there was a degree of unconscious creation in his work now. With all these mysteries and uncertainties, he conjectured idly, if Keats were to show up with his Negative Capability he might now be able to give as good as he got.

At the time Seaton was enjoying his new freedom from technical restraint, Cotterill was finally able to corner the black jaguar and shoot it. The American returned to the Tambo with the animal slung on a pole, carried by two Cholos, including an exultant Bowser, but with the embarrassed demeanour of a dog caught worrying a dead pigeon in the hallway. Munby became incandescent with rage, declaring that unique scientific opportunities had been eradicated by Cotterill's irresponsible and brutish proclivities.

"Why didn't you net it, you idiot?" he yelled down from the Tambo gallery as the beast lay in the dust by the steps. It looked small and utterly graceless now; hardly a suitable antagonist for one of Cotterill's much cherished feats of derring-do.

"Put a net on him, you old booby?" Cotterill was equally incensed by this deeply insensitive appraisal of a hunter's skill. "He'd take your arm off at the shoulder."

"We've lost incalculable data. All for juvenile posturing!" Munby was, for once, eloquent in his time of scientific deprivation. "Only a trigger happy imbecile would destroy evidence on that scale."

"Oh!" Cotterill laughed with heavy emphasis as he pointed with scorn towards the specimen room. "I'm to lose an arm so this old ghoul can get his scalpel under the thing's ribs and smear its innards all over his notebooks in there."

"Gentlemen," Northmore strode into view and stood magisterially at the top of the Tambo steps. "There are many roads to Rome."

This intercession baffled both parties into an aggrieved silence. Hestia came out of her room to look at the dead jaguar, which was now attracting attention from the ever-present flies. She saw Seaton walking out of the bush behind the cooking area, painting knapsack over his shoulder, travelling easel in his hand.

"Another portrait for you, Captain," she called over and, as he arrived to look down at Cotterill's contested trophy, she added the corollary, "Or would you prefer to work from life?"

Northmore guffawed. Cotterill and Munby stared red-faced at the ground as Seaton stepped over the jaguar and moved up the steps to his room. "Perhaps a photograph might be better," he said, disengaging himself from any controversy.

"Can it still be a portrait when it's dead?" asked Hestia as she accompanied him to the door of his room, and the question appeared a serious one.

He thought for a moment of the death mask of Nelson, and, for some reason, Michelangelo's Pieta. "Only if it's a very important person."

They looked at each having enjoyed a profound, if rather feckless, speculation and each gave a little grin. She popped her head up to whisper in his ear, "Expect you'd rather paint Brandon, now that he's huffing and puffing!"

With that, she disappeared into her room. Munby and Cotterill, directed by Northmore and determined not to address or look at each other, lifted the predator's corpse into the specimen room and onto the dissecting table, to be wrangled over at a later date. Seaton put away his equipment carefully and sat on his bed. He felt quite uplifted by this latest interchange with Hestia; harmless and transitory, its mild flirtatiousness and whispered confidences connected him with a light-hearted sociability that he had seldom had time or confidence to entertain.

The next day he was sitting beside the Kahuanari, not so far from the morning bathing space, where a *bromeliad* flourished on the bankside, from whose amphora-shaped leaves emerged inflorescences of a delicate coral colour, which danced across the placid river surface. The waters were always calm in this tiny inlet, protected from the main channel by a submerged tree that was, over the years, transforming itself into a moss covered island and a microcosm of the thousands of square miles about it. The view was a good one and he'd sketched out a general context, before setting out his colour pans, intent on some studies of the delicate complexity of the leaf clusters, set amongst all the wild rampaging of the surroundings.

As he traced the minute veins of the leaves, which replicated in meticulous detail the tangle of the surrounding lianas, which was itself echoed in the striations of the bark of entangled trees, he was suddenly overwhelmed by a ringing in his ears, accompanied by an acrid tang in his nostrils and an airy sensation behind his forehead. It was becoming insufferably hot. His spine trickled with sweat and his balance was challenged in spurts of queasy vertigo. The ringing transformed into an insistent hissing and, as the space behind his forehead expanded violently, his focus was sucked into the leaf skeleton which then merged into some green and dank wholeness. His diminishing rationality could register it was in the grip of something completely beyond its power, and his last response was terror, before the green totality enveloped him and in that totality he was expunged.

From a dimension that was completely beyond him, came urgent, repetitive sounds and, once aware that he had registered this, he turned his attention from the murky depths.

"Captain! Captain!" The sounds finally coalesced into words, anxiously spoken.

The voice had no provenance and its otherness was fearful. It belonged to somewhere of which he had no conception, but when he listened to it, he faced the true terror of not knowing where he was or what he was doing. He shrank from such powerlessness, such disembodied alienation, back into a reawakened awareness and found he was looking up into the wide-eyed, anxious face of Hestia Williams. For an instant he experienced in acute detail the moment he was wounded at Colenso, the insupportable physicality of his injury and the instability of his return to consciousness as the battle raged about him. A moment later he was back beside the Kahuanari, flat out on the track with Hestia kneeling by his side.

"Captain!" Her hand was placed lightly on his chest, too scared to shake, too anxious to withdraw.

"I'm alright," he murmured, but how could he be?

As she helped him to his feet, he glanced anxiously at his trousers but fortunately, unlike at his wounding of Colenso, he had remained continent. He offered up a small prayer to the gods of propriety, as he leaned on Hestia's shoulder and got his bearings. He could feel the tension in her as she stared up at him. "I thought you were dead." she said.

"Sorry if I alarmed you," he tried to smile, but his words came slower than he'd anticipated. "I'm quite alright now."

He turned from her to make sure his equipment and materials were all still in place; if his colour pans went in the water, half his purpose there was lost. Luckily he'd pitched back away from the easel and all the japanned accoutrements were intact around it. At the act of turning, though, the storm in his ears raged and his interior gyroscope once again began to fail; he sat down rapidly on a hummock and put his hands to his temple to still the winds.

"You're not alright!" It came as an almost tearful accusation, until she steadied herself. Then, while he sat willing himself back to competence, she took up all his pans, brushes and jars and packed them into his haversack, with an instinctive expertise. "I'm getting you to bed.

190

Doctor Munby will be back soon. He can look at you."

Seaton raised his head to contradict her, but his vision swam and the ferrous tang swept through his mouth and up to his nostrils. He yearned for the warm nurture of the jungle loam but some perennial soldierly pride would not permit him to lie down feebly at the feet of this bustling girl. Instead, he allowed her to raise him up and place his travelling easel in his right hand, to use as a walking stick. He also allowed her to drape his left arm around her shoulders and to guide him back along the path. She had hung his haversack across her chest to her left side, to counterbalance his weight, but still had to jut her hip into him to support him in their slow progress back to the Tambo.

After fifty paces, the remnants of his soldierly pride had vanished beneath the physical challenges of getting back to their base without blacking out again. Indeed, the possibility of his life ending as a sequence of recurring avalanches into unconsciousness became agonizingly real. Her body was warm and supple against him, but this presence was a great deal more than physical; some other life force reached out to his embattled soul. In this heightened state he could sense deep, undeclared aspects of her were being transmitted to him. She stretched out her legs determinedly and forced her shoulder up under his armpit, to take the strain of both him and the art bag at her side. He could feel her joints moving with fluidity, the locking on of muscle as she balanced and rebalanced, and the expanding of her chest as she breathed heavily with the exertion. This muscularity was tempered by a tender sensitivity in the way she adjusted her weight on her hip to accommodate his staggering footfalls, by the firm but considerate grip of her arm about his waist, and her constant scanning of the track ahead for any obstacle that might threaten their progress. And the little song she

191

hummed all the while, neither music hall nor hymn, but a gentle, jaunty incantation to smooth the way.

He could feel her concern for him, layered over by social obligation, but compassionate and unconditional nonetheless. It flooded into him, staving off the darkness, the waves of nausea, and the vertiginous loss of self that racked him. This young woman was holding him upright and taking him to some safe haven because he was worth doing it for and she wished to. He felt the urgent working of her muscles against his. He smelled the sweat in her hair, felt her breath on his neck as she turned to check on him, and the heat rising up from beneath her clothes as they struggled on. This connection in compassion, physical and implicit, was all that guided him from the swoon of the riverside, over the tortuous pathway, back to the hope of oblivion in crumpled but clean sheets.

The steps up to the Tambo were their final station of the Cross. Seaton felt sure he would pitch beneath the piles, and equally sure that such a posture would be perfectly agreeable, compared to the pains that gravity was inflicting on him. Their resolve was not to be so tested because the cook and Bowser, busy preparing dinner in the kitchen, came running out to assist. They replaced Hestia as Seaton's crutches and she lead the unsteady trio into Seaton's room, and had the Cholos sit him on his bed. Then she despatched them, the cook for some lemon water and Bowser to see if Doctor Munby was on point of returning, and knelt at Seaton's feet to unlace his shoes.

Feeling more intimate assistance was imminent, he gestured to say he could manage, but she read this, correctly, as an urgent request to lie down and helped him sprawl back on his bed, shoeless but still clothed. She leaned over to manhandle him into a position where his head could fall onto the pillow and, once again, he felt the warm contact of her, the breath of her body rising up through her collar, the brushing of his breast by hers. As he closed his eyes on her close, dextrous ministrations, a new smell replaced the metallic fug he had carried home with him, for she brought with her the warm mud smell of the Indian girls at their dance, with just the hint of summer hay. The scent soon receded, and he searched out for it, desperately trying to recoup its loss and retain his bridge to life as it is lived, but the vertigo struck him down, and he became a thing of shadows again.

His world became a succession of erratic but fervid impressions, their sequencing superseding all passage of time. Daylight dazzled him and then plunged into an oily darkness, which was not dispelled whether his eyes were open or not. He was, from time to time, aware of some opalescence hovering above him, and once he put a hand out to connect to it and felt the familiar touch of mosquito netting.

Sometimes his orientation was not quite so comforting, as when he felt the arctic tundra about him and shivered at the chill and the immensity of the space. At other times, the air would come crowding in on him; garbled voices, at once both loud and interrogative, would suddenly fade into murmurs. He was aware of raging thirsts and a pounding pulse beat that threatened to fragment him, both of which arrived without warning and waned into velvet numbness with equal mystery. He was aware of exhaustion and of struggle and resolved to hold on; he had to find out what he was involved in and whether he would prevail.

Then, with no more warning than the arrival of his thirsts and palpitations, Northmore, Munby and Cotterill appeared at the foot of his bed, silent, motionless, with all the daunting aspect of the Court of Appeals. He stared blankly back at them, wondering what misdemeanour had occasioned this steely disapproval, when suddenly

Northmore's face broke into a relieved grin.

"Bugger's back with us!" he chortled and clapped Munby on the back.

"You've been out with a fever. Five days," explained Munby as he came over and examined Seaton closely, taking his pulse, checking beneath his eyelids. He gave a grudging nod of satisfaction. "Some blasted ague. Not malaria. You may also be carrying some incipient Beriberi. But I'm pretty sure it's jungle fever."

"Welcome back to the living, Captain," said Cotterill in his purest Yankee tones. "Thought we'd lost you. Had us all fooled, I guess."

"You can thank God for Munby and Warburg's tincture," added Northmore. "And the Williams girl who pumped it into you day in, day out."

"Five days!" Seaton was astounded. He shook his head slightly and there was the sound of distant drums, while his focus swam but then rectified itself almost immediately.

"It's likely to recur. Little bouts of it. Before you throw it off completely," said Munby, filling a glass with water and handing it to him. Then he looked at him with troubled eyes. "It may recur on you when you get back, too. I have no way of knowing."

Hestia appeared in the doorway, carrying a folded towel. She moved in purposefully, her dress clean, her hair shining, then gave a little start as she became aware that Seaton was conscious. Quickly, she smoothed her dress and gave him a little flash of her eyes and a small smile, before standing demurely at Northmore's shoulder. Her gesture had the flavour of their conspiratorial greetings in the early entomological mornings and Seaton felt his heart warmed by it.

"Feel fit enough to talk?" asked Northmore. He glanced at Munby who shrugged.

"I think so." Seaton felt bound to say so. The conflict

between urgency and decorum was written on Northmore's face.

Northmore turned to the others who filed out. Cotterill ushered Hestia before him and she managed a last look over her shoulder, before the American closed the door behind them. It all seemed very formal. The baronet pulled a chair close and sat down.

"We've been waiting on you." He waved away Seaton's intended apology. "We need to go further incountry. As soon as we can. I had hoped you'd be part of the core party, but you're too unfit to travel."

He looked at Seaton's face, saw the disappointment mingled with the confusion in it, and continued in a softer voice, "The truth is, Captain, this venture has always had, shall we say, a sealed commission built into it. You know our ostensible purpose. Categorise the fauna and flora of the deep forest. Along with a roving brief for any new medicinal shrubs we might finagle past the authorities and home." He pulled out a large handkerchief and held it in his lap. "Our more private duty was handed to me by the Imperial Institute at the private behest of," he coughed into the handkerchief and put it away, "the Chief of the General Staff. You may well divine why a man of your military background was so essential to me."

"This is a military mission?" Seaton was rocked by this revelation.

"Not exactly." Northmore looked less comfortable by the minute. He produced his handkerchief again and mopped his brow. "Munby and I have been required to perform certain experiments. On cinchona and coca plants. To create high yield strains we might...er...introduce into colonial production."

"Don't we already...?" Seaton strove to remember He was surprised at how quickly his faculties, though not precise, were returning to the fray.

"Barely adequate. Nothing like what the Dutch are producing in Java." Northmore straightened his shoulders. "Cotterill's father is financing the procedure. Has major pharmaceutical interests in North American and Europe. And wishes to expand those interests in our favour. So we need to get cracking."

"What on earth has this to do with the Chief of the General Staff?" It was a simple economic matter. Confidential, certainly, and the Foreign and Colonial Office might perhaps be involved. But the military? Seaton couldn't work it out at all, although again he had to admit his powers of reason weren't entirely on top form.

"I can't tell you, Captain", sighed Northmore. "But I can tell you that Ramón Suarez has located the siting of previous coca plantations back up the western tributary. A favoured area with the indigents, I'm told. And there are reports of healthy cinchona in the vicinity. Sounds an ideal testing ground and we need to move onto it at once. We need decent propagation periods, before the rains come."

Seaton tried to sit up and shake off the frustration and the disappointment, but his elbows couldn't stand the weight. The baronet effected not to notice and Seaton was grateful for the courtesy.

"Can't be helped, old man," consoled Northmore. "That fever practically carried you off. Munby'll just have to do his own pencil studies and Cotterill will have to learn to act like a soldier at last."

He stood up and went to the door. "We'll leave you with Miss Williams and a couple of the Cholos to cook and whatnot. And Callard, if you like. Yes, he'll stand to as a firing party until you get your breath back, won't he?" A thought struck him. "Probably a good thing to have some semblance of a camp here. Though who'd be watching in this wilderness…" he smiled at the implausibility. "We'll aim to leave tomorrow and I'll send back to you in a month. Perhaps if both parties are going well, you can join us then."

Northmore left him with that optimistic sentiment, closing the door carefully. Seaton leaned back against his pillow and registered the details of his room. There was a reassurance in the fixity of the objects and the evenness of the light. Sounds that before his illness he would have considered merely ambient, flooded in from outside, attesting the bustling reality that he was rejoining.

With this reorientation, came the realisation that he was to be marooned beside the Okaina for weeks and possibly months, with only Hestia for company. However, his recuperative state spared him a full appreciation of this. He was clearly very weak and knew, from the experience of recuperating from his wound, that he needed to progress in gentle steps or risk a sudden decline. His first ambition would be to make it onto the gallery and sit in the sun. After that, he'd see what life in the deep forest held in store for him.

Pall Mall, London

Northmore maintained a discreet silence until the Club waiter had wheeled the cheeseboard away; the Coffee Room had emptied and only he and Seaton remained. The baronet spooned ruminatively at his stilton, before setting the implement down and taking a steadying pull on his schooner of port. He was staring into the damask, waiting for a decision to settle upon him. Once it had taken, he looked up with a greater fixity of purpose than he had shown in the library before lunch and in the Coffee Room throughout it.

"The coming war was pressing hard on everyone back then, Ainsley," he said as if by way of mitigation. "The Admiralty was nosing out submarines and armour plating from here to Vladivostok. The Imperial General Staff was crawling all over the damn globe counting howitzers, trajectories, shell bursts. The Imperial Institute was tasked with logistics. Gun cotton, bandages, it all had to be grown, you know. And grown on our territory. Territory we could keep hold of. We had our duty to do. Do you see?"

"You told me something of the Institute commission before you went up country, Sir Everard," Seaton reminded him quickly. He needed to convert any retrospective apologia into an inventory of, and access to, the expedition's sequestered archive. "That's what perplexes me about Houghton-Copley. I can't imagine why the Institute would countenance a church functionary of even his eminence," this he made sound questionable, "having access to their private instructions and records on the matter."

Northmore appeared not to have heard the suggestion. "They had a good idea of the extent of the casualties even then." A spasm of disgust crossed his features before he took another palliative sip of port. "Not the devastating and unholy totals to which we finally succumbed. But they'd calculated the carnage. From bayonets to fevers. Cool as you like."

"Trying to produce a stronger yield of quinine and cocaine was a laudable thing to do, sir. Whatever the pretext. Any advance would have been invaluable."

"Oh yes," Northmore observed drily. "Our mission was deemed an essential precursor to the successful commencement of hostilities. If we succeeded, we would be better able to drug the maimed and wounded, and send men deeper into malarial swamps. To be killed by men rather than mosquitoes."

Seaton watched the old man connect his part in these bellicose projections to the death of his only son in the oil-splattered skies on some rain-soaked Bethune morning. He felt honour bound to suggest that the secret game had been worth the candle. "Think of the suffering you might have alleviated."

Northmore's eyes flashed at him in a sudden fury and he whispered vehemently across the table. "Might! That's the word, Captain Seaton. We might have. But we didn't. We failed dismally." Then, very deliberately, he picked up his napkin and wiped his mouth with it. All signs of chagrin disappeared with the gesture and he continued in a tightly measured but more courteous tone of voice. "Couldn't make it work. Cinchona or Coca. Munby drove himself frantic. We became desperate men. When you were...." He waved a hand trying in some way to both articulate and mitigate Seaton's prostration, several days hard day's travel away. He smiled sadly at Seaton across the table. "We could have used you, you know. If just to make up the numbers as we watched every experiment turn back into mulch or kindling."

"Perhaps, if you had involved me earlier," Seaton suggested, as tactfully as and as coolly as he could manage, "I might have helped in some way."

Northmore threw up his hands, "Hated to keep you in the dark, Ainsley. Absolutely loathed doing it. But Horseguards decreed. Only Munby and latterly Cotterill to be appraised till we got on site. RGS didn't have a clue. Probably still don't." He looked earnestly at him. "I told you as soon as it was possible. You're a military man. You understand, surely?"

"And Houghton-Copley?"

Northmore looked perplexed, "What bloody use is some High Church intelligencer to an enterprise like that?" He snorted with derision. "What am I saying ? Hardly an enterprise. A bloody disaster. An irreversible sequence of setbacks and reverses, adversities and calamities, false hopes and consistent bloody bad luck. Like so many of the War Ministry's special projects. Months of humbug and interference back home, petering out into misfortune and defeat in the field. You were better off out of it, in many ways."

Both men looked at each other. Neither believed that, but it served to divert them from so many implicit derelictions. Northmore expanded his account, seemingly to allow Seaton some sense of advantage in his disassociation from the project. "Nothing went according to plan up there. When we found the plants, we couldn't find the soil. None of the tricks the Indians taught us worked. When we got a hybrid to look promising, we were deluged out. Or the blight arrived or some other pestiferous onslaught from damn Mother Nature. The seedlings rotted in the propagation trays. The cuttings never took. Not even with the procedures we'd worked on in Kew. Abject failure. The jungle was not going to give up its power for transplantation."

"You never even got to publish the experimentation?" Seaton offered supportively. Was that how Houghton-Copley had involved himself with the affair?

"Christ, no! Stuck in the Institute basement with all the other Imperial skeletons." Northmore spooned at his stilton again, clearly in search of some consolation. "In the end we could see it was no use. It was never going to be any use. Cotterill decided to take his father's money off to some other venture. Building Zeppelins, I dare say. When we finally made our way back, we found you, in your extremis. And then I brought the whole shambles home."

"And Houghton-Copley is aware of all this?"

Northmore looked mystified once more "Why on earth should he be?"

Seaton decided not to mention the matters of Church and State that Houghton-Copley had cited as the reasons for his investigation, but returned to subject of the archive with a dogged determination. "He told me he'd been through everything you'd held back from the expedition's public documentation. Sir Everard, will you tell me what that private archive contains?"

Northmore frowned deeply as he looked over at the Captain, struggling, it appeared, to understand him. "And you came up to town for this?" he said at last.

"Yes," Seaton admitted, simply. He was at the old man's disposition now.

Northmore stood up, taking his schooner of port with him. "Well, you'd better see for yourself. It's in a box room here. What there is of it."

Ten minutes later they were following a Club servant up the winding back stairs to the attics. They paused while the porter unlocked the final doorway to the roof storage, and Northmore turned to Seaton with one last caution, "Are you sure you wouldn't be better off leaving all this undisturbed?"

"I'm sure I would be," replied Seaton, "but that course is now denied me."

The porter retraced his steps downstairs and the baronet stood back, to let Seaton enter the room where the mementos of his past had lain in quarantine for so long, and added a final caveat, "Remember, Ainsley, you were a very sick man."

There was a large and battered trunk in one cramped corner; a curling luggage label affixed to a side handle had Northmore's name scribbled across it. Somehow Seaton had envisaged the archive to be a grander affair; glass fronted cabinets or an installation much like the one he had in the gallery at Laurel House, but more austere and grandiose. He crouched down at the front of the old trunk.

"The place took more out of you than you thought." A note of concern was creeping into Northmore's voice as he handed Seaton the key. "When I was gathering up your effects on the Kahuanari I failed to notice certain drawings," he coughed, "and colour works too. They only showed up when we were doing the reconciliations back in the Institute."

Seaton placed the key in the lock, but was surprised to find the trunk had been left open. The elder man appeared not to notice, as he ran a hand through his thinning hair, sipped his port and continued.

"I sequestered certain drawings I considered unseemly. Detrimental to your character. And the reputation of the expedition." He glanced apologetically at Seaton. "I couldn't allow them to affect future funding. Not hard on the failure of our central purpose."

Seaton looked up at him. Was this the dancing girl sketches he was talking about? Northmore had a distant respect for the arts and a fairly good general knowledge of them. How could he think them unseemly? Northmore set his empty schooner on an adjacent pile of suitcases and planted his hands in his trouser pockets. He seemed to feel more comfortable in that way.

"Well, it's happened to chaps before, hasn't it? Wouldn't be a whorehouse in India if it didn't." He made his final case for the defence. "I didn't think you'd want it known."

"I have absolutely no recollection of this, Sir Everard." Seaton wondered how much of his past remained for him to be reacquainted with and what other phantoms remained, to reinforce those who already tormented him.

"There's some kind of notebook too," Northmore concluded his confession. "Not so much a diary but jottings. I didn't read it all. A couple of pages were enough..." he faltered, "but it was all in much the same agitated vein. You must have been beside yourself, man."

Seaton felt a shudder of foreboding run through him. What on earth could Northmore have been saving him from? What inner workings were too depraved to be acknowledged to their owner? He swallowed hard and opened the lid of the trunk. Then he pulled aside a faded hessian blanket to find that it was empty.

"God Almighty!" Northmore gasped and he set both hands on Seaton's shoulders to steady himself. "That churchified devil must have made off with them!"

Chapter Eight

West Sussex

Five ancient apple trees made up Dr Richardson's orchard at the far end of the modest patch of land, principally turned over to unsettled roses and lawn, at the back of his house in the village. Small, gnarled and tentative in their fruit bearing, these trees nonetheless provided a welcome screen from scrutiny from the drawing room windows, where Nancy Richardson would sit in the early evenings to listen to the wireless before the lighter and more superficial music programmes came on. That evening Dr Richardson was crouching beneath the grey and twisted boughs of one of the trees furthest from the house, balancing on an equally ancient set of wooden steps, more for form's sake than any thing else, and peering at what he took to be an altogether novel type of blight that had decided to compete with him for an apple crop in the fruit bowl atop the waiting room table. The air was cool in the shade, welcome after a particularly warm day, and he had pulled on his garden duster, with some secateurs pitched into a pocket for wholly decorative purposes. He scraped with his fingernail at the dry brownish crust forming on a small hard green apple, which was holding on for grim death in front of him, and wondered if he would take this up himself or ask Faring to send a man down to spray, or whatever they did.

This pastoral idyll was interrupted when he heard the sharp tones of Nancy's voice, loud enough to indicate she was standing on the paving outside the French windows and had been separated from her improving concert by some unforeseen domestic obligation. Not only had her cultural appreciation been interrupted but it was quite likely that she had been forced to repeat herself, which never did much for her demeanour, and it was a truant joy to stand in the dusty shadows and know it was in his power to delay her further, even if only for a few seconds.

"Are you there?" she said irritably, and he knew for certain she was addressing him, both from her tone and by the fact she had not called him by name. She never did. If she were calling Maeve, she would use that appellation, but his remained just an exasperated or disappointed aspirant.

"Are you there, Colin?" he amended softly to the apple, before replying equally sotto voce. "Yes, my love. What can I do for you?"

He stooped under the outer boughs and emerged from the orchard, waving his secateurs in what he took to be an engaging fashion. When he was sure he was clear enough of the blighting leaves, he stood to his full height and called out with infuriating affability, "Hello dear!"

She waved this away with disdain. "Captain Seaton has been at the telephone. Perhaps you would attend to your calls?"

He sped across the grass towards her, cramming his secateurs away as he came, too excited to protect himself from her opprobrium. "What did he want?"

"He wanted to consult you this evening," Nancy replied curtly, turning back into the drawing room. "I told him to come at seven."

Richardson followed her in, pulling off his duster and making for the back pantry to hang it up. He ignored her pointed glance at his garden shoes as they crossed the drawing room carpet. This was a turning point in the history of his practice and he had no time for vexatious household trifles. "Coming round to us now, is he?" he said with a blend of optimism and triumph. However fleeting this moment would be, he intended to make the most of it.

Nancy settled back into her armchair and reached over to increase the volume on the wireless set but, just before doing so, she acknowledged to herself the responsibilities that came with a lifetime's partnership to a husband she could, when required, read like a children's book. "Tomorrow's shirt is in the airing cupboard." She awarded him a small knowing smile. "I'm sure if you return it there after your consultation, it will be no worse for an hour's wear."

He returned her an open smile of gratitude. She was alright, in her way, when one found oneself in a tight corner, he thought. Priggish, self-absorbed but made fundamentally of the right stuff. "I'm obliged, Nancy," he said and rushed upstairs, humming some half-forgotten ditty, to wash, shave, change and prepare to discharge his professional duties.

~~~~~

Enid Attwater walked along the lane back to the village, a posy of unidentified hedge flowers in one hand and her straw hat in the other. Although it was still warm, a light evening breeze coursed between the high grasses banked on the verges, and she could feel its breath on the nape of her neck, where her hair was matting in the damp. It traced out, in a cool frisson, the moisture running the length her backbone and outlined the film of sweat coating the inside of her thighs. She was wearing an airy, floral, cotton frock that swung about her legs, but a five-mile hike through the country on a hot June day had left her perspiring freely.

She'd heard the church bells an hour before and knew that Duncan was now at work; some men went down mines, some men tilled the soil, others amassed wealth in bourses and commercial agencies, still more sweated out in factories. Men built ships, automobiles and power stations. Men threw railways across hostile continents. Duncan went into his church and chipped away at Highleigh's souls. And came home worn out by it all.

She'd been too far away to turn back and join him for their customary tea prior to parish evensong. Not that Duncan would have minded terribly; he'd probably take it in his study, obliging Mrs Gibson to set a separate tray for him. Today they'd been spared the presence of whatever parish coven had decided it was their day to call and complain about local affairs, and tea was a purely domestic affair. The formal teas were, for Enid, a succession of mini-tribunals in which, implicitly, she would be found wanting. Highleigh itself could descend into Sodom and Gomorrah and the parish covens would not turn a hair; it would be much as they expected and indeed had foretold in their many social convocations. But, if for once Duncan were to be seen with a badly ironed handkerchief, the Devil would be proclaimed loose, the rites of exorcism would be called for and contumely heaped upon her. Indeed, when she had first arrived in the village, she had spent evenings with a flat iron, improving on Mrs Gibson's casual efforts to evade any such eventuality.

The malevolent scrutiny of the parish covens used to make her sick with anxiety and her awareness of that anxiety had frightened her even further into her own shell. Never a particularly forceful person, she now felt herself falling into a pit beneath everybody's expectation and each tremulous attempt to climb out resulted only in greater diminution. How strange then that finally, and upon no particular stimulus she could recall, some small spark of selfhood should have rekindled inside her. Some tiny light that refused to be smothered by the heavy vicarage curtains, the dark and ancient furnishings, the damp of the carpets, the melancholy calm of the bed sheets and the baleful glares of the Highleigh women, whose position as ministering angels to Duncan she had somehow usurped by becoming his wife. Onward Christian ladies, she laughed out loud and gave her straw hat a little flourish. Guilty of spiritual adultery, every last one. Slipping in as close as they could to Duncan's vocation, tinkering with his ministry, arranging his flowers, polishing his altar-ware and loitering wistfully around the vestry as he strove to reclaim the parish for the forces of righteousness, before hot milk at ten and then bed socks and deep, noisy sleep.

She was aware that her anxiety had defined her, given her shape, purpose and easily identifiably characteristics for the Highleigh communion to register and reaffirm. She could see that she had been, both for herself and for the parish at large, timid Enid the little church mouse that the vicar suffered so charitably. While she wasn't sure if she'd been born timid, she knew that she had embraced the hesitant personality that everybody acknowledged to be hers. Now, to her surprise and some consternation, she felt it didn't really suit her any more. She didn't know quite what was what, but she knew something had changed irrevocably within her. Her sense of discomfort was now less due to anxiety and guilt and more due to some sense of constraint or, rather, to the awareness of farther horizons.

The subscription library had in some measure opened her eyes to this new perspective, although she had read widely as a girl and her father, an assistant head teacher in a school not far from Duncan's family home, had encouraged her in this. She had read Dickens and Eliot and Austen and even Dostoyevsky but, the truth is, she had forgotten them. Perhaps she had only read them out of duty. Perhaps married life had simply tidied them away.

Through the subscription library she had found Flaubert and Lawrence and Zola and the rest. They intruded into the vicarage and asked indelicate questions; they pulled back the curtains and let in disconcerting light. She had wanted to tell that to the odious Houghton-Copley, with his insinuations, but couldn't risk the effect of his weighty condescension on her newly arrived sense of self-determination. Still, it wasn't just her reading habits that caused her to cast aside Mrs Gibson's teatime assortment and work herself up into a delirium of heat, sweat, dazzling sunshine, heady grassy scents and blissful solitude all on a hot summer's day. A delirium so delicious she felt she could have walked all the way to Wittering and thrown herself into the sea, to feel the cool waves buffet and invigorate her for the walk back.

It was only when she looked down and saw the fragile state of her sandals, that she had to call a halt and return to the fold, the prodigal daughter with sweaty legs and a bunch of hedge flowers the names of which, to her regret, were unknown to her. Lawrence would have known their names. Lawrence would have sported hob-nailed hiking boots. He would also have been insufferably pompous about it all, in a mannish sort of way, doing his Swedish exercises on the beach before diving in to execute a formal breast stroke.

She heard the sound of a motor approaching from behind her and frowned; the final Chichester bound bus of the afternoon was surely long gone. She refused to turn round, on the grounds that she didn't wish to be thought of as some gawking bumpkin, and also on the fairly reasonable assumption that if her neck was anything to go by, her hair would be plastered about her face, her cheeks would be glowing red and she must look like a farmer's wife, just out of the fields after a hard day. She upped her pace and kept walking purposefully along, swinging her hat with patrician nonchalance and ignoring, with Spartan discipline, a sharp little stone that had insinuated itself into her left sandal.

The motor came to a halt beside her and, as she glanced sideways to see who was peopling this intrusion, she came face to face with an attentive and rather pale Ainsley Seaton. The Captain's face was so close to hers he must surely feel the heat rising off her, and possibly hear the rivulets of sweat running down inside her shift. All noble thoughts of self-determination and personal development faded away in the heat haze, the smell of hot oil and the rumble of the engine; she stared at him like a vole breaking cover directly into the path of a dog fox. Oh my God, she thought, what now? What am I overwhelmed with now?

She clapped her hat over her head to hide her dishevelled hair and reduce the gleam of her burning cheeks. Then she nodded distractedly and tried to turn away and walk on, if only to escape the dreadful awkwardness of the situation, but Captain Seaton was already stepping out of the passenger door and raising his hat to her. She could hear phrases like "Mrs Attwater, you must allow me ...", "Far too hot." and "No trouble at all." And without knowing quite how, she was sitting in the front seat of the Bentley, next to Foster, hanging on to her hat as a revitalising wind rushed through and around her and restored her to some social coherence.

Even so, it was some time before she felt able to turn back to the Captain and engage in civil conversation. She had decided the surprising burst of heat would be a suitably anodyne topic but before she could hazard something of the sort, she noticed that the Captain looked far from well. His eyes had lost their customary wary and alert fixity, his mouth was drawn and he seemed more than usually distracted. It appeared an effort to him simply to address himself to her, although he pulled himself into the requisite courtesies and leaned forward to hear what she might have to say.

"You don't look at all well, Captain." Her concern usurped any social proprieties. "Are you quite sure you should be out?"

He acquiesced with a small wave of his hand and smiled shyly. "A touch of fever, I believe, Mrs Attwater. Nothing to concern yourself with."

"But you must go home at once!" she protested. "I can walk from here, easily!"

"Oh, we're used to these recurrences, aren't we, Foster?" Seaton handed the conversation over gently and adroitly.

Foster spared her a reassuring glance from the road ahead. "We're taking the Captain into the Doctor's, miss. Once we've dropped you off. So you see, you're on our way."

"To Dr Richardson?" Her surprise was out before she could suppress it and for a moment she longed to be her old, retiring self. She turned back to the Captain to retrieve the situation. "He's a very good man I believe. Medically. Duncan thinks very highly of him."

None of that had come out the way she'd intended, so she finished with an apologetic smile and turned to face the road. Foster gave her another comforting look, which made her feel all of twelve years old. "Been very good with me, too, Miss. We have high hopes."

With that they drove in silence to the vicarage, where Enid proffered her thanks and her wishes for the Captain's swift recovery, both heartfelt, climbed out of the Bentley and walked up the front path, ignoring Mrs Gibson's presence behind the drawing room lace curtains.

The Captain stayed in the back seat as Foster drove

off in the direction of the surgery.

~~~~~

Seaton stood buttoning his shirt while Dr Richardson sat at his desk ruminating over the notes he had just taken. Here was a puzzle alright, though not one calling for the usual detective work he employed with the hypochondriacs and complainants that peopled the majority of his consultations. Captain Ainsley Seaton was definitely unwell. His pulse was irregular, his blood pressure higher than might have been expected and, by the man's own account, he was finding his balance impaired and himself prone to fits of extraordinary lassitude, possibly on the verge of blackout. All this with breathlessness and a concomitant loss of concentration. So far so straightforward, except that the patient claimed it to be the familiar symptoms of a recurrence of a fever and its attendant dose of Beri- beri, contracted all those years ago in the rainforests of the Amazon.

Dr Richardson did not like to be seen getting up and consulting a volume from the impressive row of medical reference books atop his poison cupboard. However, from his limited knowledge of fevers and agues and his quotidian familiarity with the nervous prostrations simulated by his women patients of a certain age, he was more inclined to diagnose stress than yellow fever. In fact, he would have bet his consultation fee on it. The man was suffering from many of the attested symptoms of extreme anxiety and appeared to be fighting against some kind of collapse

Dr Richardson scribbled a few meaningless addenda to his notes, to give himself more time for consideration; how on earth was he to tell a war hero, a man who'd won damn near every medal going for valour in combat, that he was suffering from an anxiety disorder? Nonetheless he had to, before Seaton was overwhelmed by escalating

212

panic attacks.

"I can't find any evidence of fever, Captain," he said outright, hoping years of a reasonable bedside manner would come to his assistance as he went along. "Blood pressure's more than I'd like, pulse is a little racy, but nothing really to cause concern. This feeling of swooning is what interests me most."

Seaton had put on his jacket and sat down to face the doctor across his desk; he was very pale. Dr Richardson continued picking his way to an acceptable disclosure. "It seems to me that you're feeling the effects of some abnormal internal strain. Our nervous systems sometimes overload, you know."

Seaton gave a look of mild disbelief. "Fever, I can understand, doctor but nervous strain?" He followed this with a short and not altogether convincing laugh. "There was enough to worry us in Flanders, you know, and I never felt like this."

Dr Richardson had, for the moment, forgotten Seaton's place on the social register and his desirability on the patients' list; he now saw him simply as a man of action unable to countenance the possibility that his mental workings could lay him low, and in real danger because of it. He stuck gently to his guns. "Is there something preying on your mind, though?"

"Not unduly," answered Seaton, though he wasn't clear whether this was a lie or simply wishful thinking. He remembered the tenebrous and clammy desperation that had enmired him in the box room of the Travellers' Club. Northmore had sat down heavily on the emptied expedition trunk and sought out some explanation for Houghton-Copley's behaviour and, in doing so, only added to the uncertainties, mysteries and nagging doubts that now plagued Seaton and had rendered his homeward train journey a queasy, semi-conscious

213

nightmare. Keats be damned. Keats was long dead, his Negative Capability insufficient defence against the consumption that devoured him.

"He said it was a matter of State," the baronet had at last confessed, completely at a loss. "Told me he was entrusted with an enterprise of the very highest confidentiality and importance. Matters of great weight, he said. He'd been through the expedition's archives in the RGS. Said he believed there might be something amongst your private papers to show you were an unsuspecting witness to some great calamity. I said he should contact you straightaway. Your discretion was guaranteed." He shook his head at the speed of his own capitulation. "But he said his mission was of such delicacy that he would not trouble you unless it was absolutely necessary. A brief examination of your papers would be enough to establish whether to involve you or eliminate you from the matter."

"What matter?" Seaton kept his voice low and calm to belie the rising panic clutching at his throat and buzzing in his temples. "And what led him to include me in it?"

"He was not empowered to tell me more than that." There was some asperity in Northmore's voice now; he was clearly put out by the palpable deception the churchman had subjected him to. "What could I do, Ainsley? The man's known at the Palace."

And I'm not, reflected Seaton and he could feel an uncharacteristic bitterness creeping into his perceptions. His exclusion from the innermost purposes of an expedition that had so nearly killed him was not the whole of it. Though when he thought of the extended and laborious preparations that he had been party to, he was astounded at how much had been kept hidden from him. He had been of sufficient social standing to be hurled into

214

the prospect of certain and futile death every day for three years on the Western Front, at the head of the dependent and the doomed, but was deemed not of sufficient probity to be privy to the back door dissembling in the grand offices and chanceries that had fostered the carnage. For generations the families of Northmore and Houghton-Copley had belonged to the governing class and he would always be subordinate to their covert protocols and dynastic precedents. Theirs was one of the hazier connections of Church and State, but it was none the less substantial for that. Northmore would not have hesitated in opening his secret archive to Houghton-Copley, whatever the implications for a fellow expedition member; there were no such secrets between the great and the good, certainly none that might jeopardise their continued position. What had kept Seaton from the true purpose behind his Amazonian experiences would, by its very nature, conjoin to destroy him in his respite from them. It was the natural order of things.

"I didn't feel comfortable about the business, even then. So I left him to it." Northmore coloured at the memory. He drew ferociously on his cigar and then shook his head with incomprehension at the sequel. "But when he came back to the library, he told me he needn't trouble you after all. And we might as well draw a veil over the matter." He looked contritely over at Seaton. "But he hasn't, has he?"

"No, he hasn't," replied Seaton through a constricted throat. In the normal course of events, Northmore's contrition would have affected him and he would have told the old man it was both unmerited and necessary, trying to put his mind at rest. But he now had more pressing concerns. He wanted to know what had brought Houghton-Copley down upon him, what tracking mechanisms he was employing and what motivations were driving this relentless deception. Above all, he wanted to know exactly what the man knew.

As he stood up to offer the baronet his hand and leave, he thought he was going to pass out. The insidious metallic tang flooded up through his throat and his nostrils, a ghastly queasiness churned within him and the familiar hissing erupted in his ears. He struggled for his self possession, and it may have been the baronet's anxious and sorrowful expression that helped him regain it. He needed to be alone, to work out what threat there was upon him. For that he needed to leave the sad, old man to his port and cigars.

"You're not letting all this nonsense in the village get to you, I hope?" Dr Richardson's bluff and cheery enquiry drew Seaton back from Northmore's regrets. "Highleigh folk are like sheep, only in my view not quite so well dressed."

"I'm not quite with you," observed Seaton politely.

I can see that plainly, thought the doctor, but he pressed on with his raillery. He had to establish some bridge to the Captain's disquiet. "They gossip about anything outside the improprieties behind their own lace curtains. It never lasts. They have the attentive capacities of goldfish."

Goldfish, sheep, how many more metaphors am I going to throw at the bugger before he opens up? Richardson pinched the bridge of his nose.

Seaton smiled wanly at him, while Northmore's parting speculation on Houghton echoed in his ears. "He couldn't be involved in anything improper, surely? He has a reputation to consider." At this, the Captain had pleaded an early train and headed off. The baronet had added contours, rivers and place names to maps across the globe, and yet whole swathes of humanity evidently remained virgin territory to him.

He now focused on the doctor sitting across this desk from him, noting that his professional smile barely concealed an air of nervous inquiry. Richardson's raw-boned hands toyed listlessly with a fountain pen and a frown flickered across the broad brow, beneath his shock of red hair, with almost mechanical regularity.

"I'm not one to bother much with the village grapevine," the Captain offered, and was pleased to see the doctor relax back in his battered leather chair. "If I do feature in it, I'm sure it's something outlandish, erroneous and above all transitory."

Dr Richardson stood up suddenly and, pulling a tiny key from his waistcoat pocket, proceeded to unlock his poison cupboard. His fingers traced across the rows of tiny bottles within until he selected a small blue hexagonal one. "I'm going to give you some chloral, chloral hydrate. It should help you sleep and dispel these dizzy spells." He held up a hand to forestall any protests. "I know, I know, you're sleepy enough as it is, but believe me this will alleviate that." He wrote out laborious instructions on a label, checked the legibility and then wrapped it around the little bottle. "You take it in drops, a small amount in the morning and mid day and a larger dose after dinner. I've written the details on the label, but I think it's better you hand the whole thing over to Foster, or Mrs Simmons, and let them take care of it."

"I think I'm perfectly capable of self- medication." Seaton took the bottle as courteously as he could. Did the man think he'd taken leave of his senses?

"You'll feel rested, renewed and, above all, very relaxed," explained the doctor. "Some people become so relaxed they forget whether they have dosed themselves." He looked steadily at the Captain. "And this has proved fatal in the past."

"So, it's kill or cure, then?" Seaton laughed as he put

the little blue bottle in his jacket pocket.

"I rarely kill my patients," replied the doctor, accompanying Seaton to the front door "And never before they've settled my account."

"Thank you, doctor, you've been most reassuring." Seaton shook Dr Richardson's hand. The man, for all his freethinking bombast, was seeped in human sympathy. According to his lights, both professional and personal, he'd provided understanding, judgment and support in an ever more dangerous world. "I only wish I'd consulted you earlier."

Dr Richardson waved this away magnanimously; he would savour his gratification over a small celebratory sherry, Nancy's wireless programmes permitting. He walked Seaton to the front gate, where Foster was already starting up the Bentley. "I'll pop over in the morning to see how you're getting along."

Seaton turned to assure him it was not necessary but the doctor was resolute. "I insist, Captain. Call it a professional responsibility. The chloral, you see. I would not feel comfortable otherwise."

He waved Seaton off and then walked back down his path, hands in pockets and whistling a half-remembered jig. He was now appreciated amongst the better element. And he'd not done a bad job of calming the man and setting him on the road to a little breathing space, if not true balance. Provided he let Mrs Simmons dole out the drops, he looked set for recovery.

"What was it?" Nancy was on him the moment he'd closed the front door behind him. He started, and then walked with measured poise into the drawing room.

"Nervous exhaustion, I suspect," he called over his shoulder as he made for the sherry decanter.

"You suspect!" Nancy snorted derisively. "Don't you know?"

"I cannot discuss my patients," he replied stiffly. Her habitual slight on his competence weighed even more heavily after the Captain's grateful appreciation. "But I'm satisfied with my diagnosis, thank you."

"Piffle." Nancy shook her head at his obstinate ignorance. "I'll tell you what he's suffering from."

"Enlighten me, do," he said, with an acid tone he knew he'd be taught to regret later.

"Debauchery and guilt," Nancy pronounced these self-evident truths as if talking to a half-wit. Then she left the room.

Dr Richardson sank another schooner of sherry. He felt he'd earned it.

~~~~~

The moment they'd arrived back at Laurel House, Seaton handed over his bottle of chloral hydrate to Mrs Simmons without a qualm; he had more serious matters to occupy his time. He went into the gallery, poured himself a large scotch and soda and stared out of the French windows, waiting for the swallows and commencing his strategic review. Houghton-Copley was in possession of a number of his private papers, drawings and, God forbid, a journal. These were all items Northmore had adjudged would be scandalous to the public view and yet the diplomatist had made no mention of them. He had simply made off with them, in manner showing complete disregard for the consequences of later discovery. Was he that confident that nobody would challenge his role in their disappearance?

He needed the return of those papers. He needed to ascertain what Houghton-Copley wanted with them, and why he had chosen to pursue him in this insidious manner. Despite his dislocating lapses of memory, he was sure his possessions could play no part in any political machinations the preposterous man might be enmeshed in. The threat was un-defined and surreal, in a way that only added to its terrifying aspect, and he had to bring it into the cold light of reason without provoking any escalation. He mustn't provide the man with any further cause for meddling in matters best left buried in the primal mulch of a tropical river bank, in the days before the Great Powers had ripped the innocence from the world, and he had consigned his own future to inexorable desolation.

North-west Amazon

Late in the morning, two days after Northmore had led his party down to the canoes and crossed the western tributary, Seaton made his first unassisted visit to the outhouse and, having completed a restorative toilet, walked carefully round to the dining area outside Tambo 2. He sat at one of the tables and looked cautiously at his surroundings. After the extraordinary experiences of the last week he had rather expected, against all reason, some dramatic transformation in the daily routine. Yet everything appeared to be continuing as usual.

Nonetheless, he felt imbued with a sense of discovery, an intensification of observation that rendered the familiar new and somehow in high relief. The rustling and secret flexings of the trees, the sporadic calling of the birds and the crackle of the kitchen fire had a crystal clarity, each sound separated from the other and yet in concert with it. The smells of the mulch, the ripening fruit, the rain-sodden trees with their fantastic blooms and the hazy odour of heat-soaked earth drove the last vestiges of fever reek from his nostrils, each smell attuned differently within a warm and golden spectrum of scent. As for the colours all about him, he felt this little bout was going to do wonders for his selection and mixing and, hopefully, his pictures. He wondered if absinthe had done the same job for all those French fellows, and then chuckled as he realised he was indulging in his first careless speculation since Lord knows when. The teetering balance of life and death was no longer his all-consuming calculation.

The cook, normally a taciturn individual, gave him a crumpled smile of welcome and hastened off to bring him a cup of coffee. Seaton rummaged around in his haversack and fetched out his pipe and tobacco. Back in business, he thought. A trifle winded and unsteady but making very creditable progress. He filled the pipe, clamped it in his teeth and returned to the haversack for his matches.

"Don't you dare." Hestia plucked the pipe from his mouth. She was doing her level best to look irate. "Dr Munby says at least a week. He'd have a fit if he saw you lighting this up now."

Seaton reached out for his pipe with as much dignity as he could muster. "Then it's a good thing he's days away, isn't it?"

She held it close and squinted at him. "You're not relapsing on me, Captain. I've had enough of cleaning out your bedpans!"

At this unanswerable sally, the cook set a cup of coffee before him and withdrew to a safe distance, to chop up yams, bananas and pineapple for some exotic salad in celebration of the soldier's return. Hestia propped an elbow on the table, rested her chin in her hand and watched him minutely, as if a man drinking coffee were of unparalleled scientific interest. Seaton noticed she had rearranged her wardrobe during his illness. It wasn't a matter of dress number one or dress number two any more. She'd evidently adapted one of them into a full skirt, which she now wore with a camisole that had the sleeves removed, and her canvas shoes.

Evidently, jungle life had not been kind to the garments and she was responding to conditions and climate as best she could.

He sipped his coffee; it tasted of life to be lived and of the warm secrets of natural growth. Callard passed through the kitchen area, an axe over one shoulder and his precious Mannlicher rifle over the other. He set both down carefully against the wall and hastened over to Seaton's table where he hovered. Eventually, he rumbled out something that sounded part Spanish and part Quechan and was evidently heartfelt.

"He says he's pleased to see the lord back to life." Hestia translated.

Seaton exchanged a grave nod with the Cholo, who then picked up his rifle and axe and moved off. He finished his coffee and galvanised himself. "Right, I think I'll make for the river with my pastels."

"I'm going that way." Hestia stood at once and then, amended quickly, "Unless you'd really rather I didn't?"

After her week's work in the sickroom, how could he possibly mind? And so, with Hestia disguising her nursemaid attentions with a rousing chorus of "Shine on, shine on, harvest moon!", they retraced their steps towards the river and the *bromeliad* with the amphora shaped leaves.

"How on earth did you carry me back from here?" he asked, as they clambered down to the little inlet where he had collapsed. "I really can't thank you enough."

She received this without comment, but sat down with a grin and watched him haul out his pastels from his haversack, to make some sketches of the *bromeliad*, which thankfully was still in place and as delicately decorative as ever. She hummed away to herself for a while, shading her eyes to survey the opposite river bank, and slowly became her usual fidgety self, until she offered, "I can bring your paints down for you, if you like."

He thanked her but he wouldn't go further than pastels today, easing himself in, so to speak. In truth, he was unsure quite how competent he'd be following the fever. A few quick pastel sketches might show if he retained his new lightness of touch or not. If not, he faced the dreadful prospect of trying to pull himself out of his own way all over again.

Hestia's face clouded momentarily as this pretext for moving off was denied her. Seaton swiftly assured her that he felt much his old self and was certainly not going to pitch headlong into the river and, while glad of her company naturally, would not for the world detain from her own activities. They could meet, perhaps, for dinner and share the fruits of their day?

This seemed to satisfy her for she stood up, rapidly, dusted herself off and then strode off back in the direction of the Tambo. She turned before disappearing from view to call back, "I shall bring you something at tea. To keep your strength up."

For a good while he was lost in the process of drawing and then, taking his cue from a sudden flurry of macaws across the river, he pulled himself up to review his work. To his great relief, he could see at once that that he and nature were getting along just fine. If anything, there was a bolder almost savage feeling to the robust simplicity of his line. He hadn't lost his newly attained and intuitive expression. It had come for him once again. The flowers seemed to open themselves before him, to draw him into some fertile, urgent activity beside the Kahuanari, which flowed by on its own imperative, unfathomable purposes He looked around to show Hestia but she, of course, was long gone.

Their subsequent perambulations followed the same routine without fail and without reflection. Seaton would announce his intentions over breakfast and Hestia would nonchalantly accompany him to his starting point for the day. She invariably gave the impression that she had something to do elsewhere, but was happy to contribute her time and company to make his task a little easier. She would go along with him on whatever endeavour he had set himself, see him safely established and then flit away, to return sporadically under the guise of looking after his comforts and interests.

In between such spurts of service, he immersed himself in his surroundings and when she paused for breath and settled for a while, they both started, indirectly, to introduce themselves. Hestia would arrive with a sudden burst of interrogation, seek to outflank any equivalent probing on Seaton's part and then launch into some piecemeal reminiscence, all the more affecting for its blithe candour. Seaton built a patchwork history of the girl with the patience of the intelligence specialist. It was slow work, until she finally gave him what he thought was at the heart of it.

One morning he was sitting in the Okaina plantation, sketching the women hoe around the burned remnants of cleared vegetation, with the peculiar wedge-shaped stakes that seemed to serve for every agricultural purpose. Hestia sat down abruptly beside him and together they surveyed the steady hard graft of the women, some carrying babies, as they rooted about the manioc crop. Of what Hestia saw he had no notion, but what he saw was an unequal struggle of human muscle against entropy.

In his first days at the settlement, Seaton had written up a report for his monogram on how the Okaina women cultivated manioc, plantains and mangoes, paw paws, bananas and pineapples, pumpkins and sweet potatoes, alongside essential supplies of coca and tobacco.

However, it was now apparent that the term cultivation implied far too much control. His illness had brought him some visceral affinity with the anarchic power of the reproduction around him; debility had amplified his impression of a blind regeneration of enormous and irresistible power. The Okaina women, far from cultivating, were battling to retard the rate at which the jungle would overrun the clearing their menfolk had burned and dug out for them. They were scrabbling at a tidal wave of growth and trying to divert and channel some for their own purposes. The moment they stopped, they would be overwhelmed. Their struggle was hopeless, beautiful, muscular and somehow sensuous. He took up his pencil again.

Seaton concentrated on the rounded shoulders and swinging breasts of a woman pulling at an enormous pumpkin, somehow entangled in an exposed root system. He tried to capture the tensile strength in her arms and thighs as she hauled on it. Another came to join her, squatting beside the giant, knees out wide, her sex exposed without thought in the mechanics of the lift. Their industrious nakedness held more animism for him than any of the classic nudes he'd trudged docilely around, in tours of antiquities back in Europe. Here was art you could smell, the nude with a sweat-slick all its own; he didn't think even Matisse had managed this, though he was sure the man would have breathed it in, had he been sitting beside him now. The immediacy of the women's bodies had some inner glow, in which animal spirits limbered and swayed, uninflected, the pure embodiment of corporeal appetites. He thought of the *bromeliad*, by the river, offering itself to him in primal need, a passion uninterrupted by mind or soul. Flowers, forest, women, pineapples, even the macaws above, all seemed interconnected. There was something in the light, perhaps, something fecund.

"Were you always a soldier?" Hestia's investigations invariably started without warning, pretext or association.

"I seem to remember spending some time as a small boy," replied Seaton, keeping his eye on the women struggling to extricate the pumpkin, his pencil busy.

"What did you do then?"

"School. Hobbies. The general beastliness of small boys." The Okaina women secured the pumpkin and set it to one side; they wiped the earth from their hands onto their thighs and moved back towards the others still busy amongst the manioc.

"No!" she huffed with mock exasperation. "What did you do after?"

"My father was an engineer. Built railways. So I went into the army." It seemed such a muted act of rebellion now.

"A hussar!" she scoffed in a grand dame's voice. "Very lah-di-dah!"

She evidently knew all this already, thought Seaton. Munby had probably filled in his military pedigree, though God alone knew why. "It doesn't feel very lah-di-dah when people are shooting at you."

"I was twelve when we came here," she dodged the ramifications of his reply. "For the rubber. Dad thought he'd make a great success of the rubber. And go back and buy a big farm in Caernarfon."

"Dairy or sheep?" He watched the women line up to clear some earth around the tobacco plants. They wouldn't be permitted to smoke it, a tribal taboo on their sex, but, as with the coca, it was they who planted it, nurtured it, and cut it.

"Don't think it really mattered," Hestia admitted. "He never got near one. He wasn't cruel enough for the rubber. Oh, he tried to be. Tried his very best." She caught her breath and continued in a wistful vein. "He was forever trying his best. Never quite found the knack of it." Then, she brightened. "We had a nice house though, for a while. And servants. And people calling. And parties sometimes."

"And Mr Kettering, with his player-piano."

She was pleased he had shown sufficient interest to remember, and favoured him with a further confidence. "I wanted to stay at home, in Caernarfon. Glynis Watkins stayed back with her auntie, and she was just eleven. Only she ran away to Swansea later and was consumed with sin!"

"I've been to Swansea," said Seaton, "and I don't believe it's possible."

"Well, Glynis managed it," Hestia giggled, and then lay back and played the sybarite. "Can you imagine being consumed with sin? What do you think it feels like?"

Seaton studies his sketches for a while, the Okaina women sweating beneath his fingers. "About the same as being bitten to pieces by tiger ants."

She sat up at this, pulled a strand of hair off her face impatiently and continued her story. "Then the rubber kicked him out and he went and found God. Mam and me wanted to go home, really. But dad brought us up here to save souls. Souls in Caernarfon weren't good enough, I suppose."

She stood up suddenly and brushed the earth, ants and twigs from her frock. "I'm going to get Callard to take me into the forest, to find some honey."

Seaton shaded his eyes from the sun as he looked up at her. "Don't drag him out too far."

She didn't resist this paterfamilias stance but wheedled as sweetly as she might, "Why don't you ever go anywhere? We're always stuck round here."

"When I'm back on form we'll go after another

jaguar," he said carelessly, searching for his pencil sharpener in the lees of his haversack.

"Only to look at, mind," she called out as she strode away. "The other one's still stinking up the specimen room."

He hadn't ventured far in his convalescence at all; he stayed close to the tambos, the Maloka, the plantation and the river bank, running like a branch line train along the familiar tracks, taking pleasure in the stability of his bearings, which in some measure offset a growing and uneasy awareness of nature's riotous tendencies. After his hallucinatory isolation in the throes of fever, he'd come to value even the surrogate sense of community that observation of the Okaina's daily routine offered him. As if this constrained regimen might hold the key to surviving the torment and dislocation he knew to be waiting for him inside, either by relapse or simply a hypersensitivity to this remote and hostile environment.

Constrained or not, he'd accomplished a great deal more within this familiar ground, both artistically and personally, than he would have believed possible before his illness. He'd certainly established some sort of presence in Okaina community life, if only as an object of fascination amongst the Indian children, who now followed him solemnly, at some remove. Working on his South African experiences, he'd rooted round the kitchen stores and discovered some sugar packets the rain had penetrated. These he handed out in twists to any who dared approach, which shortly meant all of them. A provisional relationship being thus established, he stationed himself on the dancing ground and painted them; this, in time, drew their mothers and one or two of the younger men; these he sketched, leaving several sheets on the ground, for them to view at leisure.

The following day, he collected some old jars and

empty tins, went to the dancing ground and made a formal presentation of them to one of the chief's many dependant women. She, in turn, brought out the number one wife from the Maloka and a short interchange ensued, with Callard as translator and major domo. The jars and tins were received with suitable gravitas, a drink of kawana, a floury and insipid favourite made from some pear-shaped fruit, was proffered and thus he became an acknowledged presence in the Okaina's vision; they registered him at last.

What the Okaina made of his and Hestia's ad hoc re-enactment of Genesis, he could only speculate. All communication to date had been led, delicately, by him. If a man or woman showed a willingness to talk, whether amongst the plantains, or fishing by the river or simply sitting around the dancing ground, Seaton would probe for words and phrases in Okaina, a branch of the Witoto language as Northmore had told him, using sign language and Callard and a mixture of painstaking effort and trial and error. He told Hestia he was aiming to construct a lexicon, but his aversion to isolation was so fresh in his mind than he felt any transaction with people would build up his defences against its return.

Hestia, if not fluent, had a wide command of Spanish and some basic words of Quechan. Callard, somewhat to Seaton's shame, was fluent in Spanish, Quechan and Witoto, and was picking up English phrases faster than Seaton could absorb the Okaina. For himself, the only exchanges in which he could freely engage were as an artist with nature itself. Nature addressed him directly in a way which, to his growing discomfort, was becoming consistently and explicitly sensual. He had never considered himself a voluptuary, even in the commonplace amatory activities of a single officer's garrison life, but observing how nature now presented itself to him, he realised it was Pan rather than Apollo that was being called to deep within him.

It had been a gradual and subtle subversion of reason by instinct, accelerated no doubt by the hallucinatory paroxysms of his recent fever, but he felt he could trace some personal development along with it. He had already absorbed, as a physical and then intellectual experience, the primacy of regeneration across all forms of forest life. His march up from the Igara Parana had confronted him with the perpetual and irresistible drive to survive and reproduce, endemic from the larger carnivores to the fungal spores on the slides under Munby's microscope. Munby had also furnished him with a forthright appreciation of the mechanics of attraction and pollination in plants, shrubs and trees.

Yet this had been superseded by an occult awareness of the powers beneath, in which he was presented with whole new layers of allusions and associations. He would be painting amongst the riverside trees, picking out the pale-yellow bracts of *Heliconia acuminate* and, in their hazy and glowing colour swathe, the fluttering skirts of a mulatto whore who had once entertained him in Cape Town's better house of assignation, would quiver before him in the breeze. The tiny, pink and cream, gaping mouths of the orchid, *Catesetum discolor*, spoke to him of urgent and expert intimacies; so intricately indelicate were they, that he had looked around him to see if anyone else, principally Hestia, had been party to these erotic confidences. If these were the artist's uncertainties, mysteries and doubts, they were a lot more red-blooded than he really felt at ease with, and he fancied Keats would have fled at the earliest opportunity. Yet, as an artist he had a responsibility to express his responses, however unanticipated. None of his drawings need be deemed prurient, but neither would he seek to hide the primal drives operating in his subject matter.

That afternoon he moved off from the cultivators in the plantation and walked down towards the watercourse, simply to prove that he could extend whatever boundaries he had set for himself, at least within the requirements of recuperation. He discovered a narrow, freshly made track, which he hoped might indicate tapir rather than caiman, and broke through to a black water inlet teeming with plants.

At first, the entrance down to the inlet was so narrow and the plant growth so profuse that, as he pressed forward, his face was almost buried in flowers and he had to step back for fear some spider or snake might fall upon him. Then, as he worked his way further down the path, he found himself enveloped by an expansive *Philodendron brevispathum*.

He was close enough to see every fold and nook of the pink and white spotted spathes of this delicate but agile climber. Its smooth, firm petals enfolded the sleek and engorged anthers in a way that was both private and explicit. Russet hairs swayed alert and aroused on its stems. Beside it, a *Scuticaria steelii* with complex and playful yellow flowers dappled with reds, exuded a wonderful and delicate perfume, but it was the *Philodendron* that captivated him. With its leaves flung out like expressive hands, the delicate creamy flesh flecked with blood spots and the tremulous russet hairs on its elegant, slender limbs, it seemed both passionate and fragile.

He unpacked his watercolour pans, his bottles and brushes and set to work, daubing details, flower clusters, patterns and impressions. Then, feeling that he had gained some familiarity with it, he teased out a cluster of its flowers into the light breaking through the canopy onto the path, in order to attempt a complete painting. He had been working on this for some time, with an intensity of focus that strained the tendons in his neck and upper back, when something intruded into his composition with a powerful and intimidating disregard for the magical relationship between his eye and the plant. A large, armoured centipede broke its way out of one of the tighter folds and stood rearing on its hind quarters for a full minute, teasing the air with all its front legs. Having registered its protest at its scented haven being summarily shifted out into the pathway, it prowled with menacing ease across to the next flower-head and thrust its way down inside.

He looked down at his painting and, with a shiver, realised that even as he had been observing the creature, he had painted it. It squatted on the flower- head in his picture with the same carapaced malevolence that had infected the air around it. Hurriedly, he collected his materials and equipment, packed it all away and pushed his way through the flower curtain and back out to the wider spaces. He told himself it was time he rested, but something else was driving him away.

When he reached the dancing ground there seemed to be a kind of rehearsal in progress. A group of young Okaina women stood in close file. One hand resting on the shoulder of the girl in front, they were chanting and swaying and dancing down the ground. The dance step involved a high prancing flexion of the right thigh up against the body followed by a full extension of the leg, repeated twice, before the foot was stamped down hard and the process repeated with the left. This they then reversed with a narrower pace, so the line was always advancing, despite taking these little retrograde steps. The motion was feline and regal, supple and with a solid discipline in the rhythm. Having progressed some appointed distance, the women stopped on the beat and turned with the precision of guardsmen on parade. Their hands found the shoulder ahead of them once more, and they processed back the way they had come, swaying and pacing while repeating the same refrain over and over.

The scene was mesmeric and charming, graceful and savage. These were the young women of the clan, black eyed and full lipped, their hair shining from the river, their breasts still firm, their pot bellies as yet unchanged by childbirth. The traces of previous dancing decorations shadowed their thighs, and they danced with a gravity that conferred on each of them a solemn beauty. There were seven of them in all and Hestia had taken her place at number four.

She kept to the beat and sustained the same sinuous flexibility of movement, despite the encumbrance of her long calico skirt, which billowed up each time she raised her knee high prior to stamping into the dust. She frowned with concentration, but kept her body swaying and her head bobbing in concert with the others. Then, some atavistic instinct must have taken over and she let herself be carried along by the communal endeavour and the refrain. She looked back over her shoulder to the girl behind and seemed reassured by the nod she received, gave her a broad grin and then returned conscientiously to the measure.

Seaton stood in the shade of the Maloka and watched. As the dust swirled and the song pulsated up to the empty sky above, there seemed no difference between Hestia and her indigenous sisters. They fused into a timeless feminine incantation. The dust and sweat on the Okaina legs merged with Hestia's form, outlined against the constrictions of her skirt. Her breasts bobbed and jutted beneath the cambric like theirs, her hair danced about her brow like theirs, her face was a little more flushed, perhaps, and her eyes distinctly brighter, but her feet were as naked, dusty and sure in their stride. Six thousand miles and two millennia of Christianity may have separated them, but not on that afternoon at the dancing ground.

She spotted him soon enough and threw him out a casual grin, in part confidential, in part challenging, before turning back into herself and the protective union of her dance coterie. Seaton left his pencils and pastels in his haversack. Somehow, he could not draw this. He could not bring himself to intrude upon her privacy, but he could not take his eyes from it either. Hestia was being transformed subtly into a woman rather than a required acquaintance, while she sung her wild and ancient song. With a discreet and, he suspected, unregistered wave, he turned and made his way back to Tambo 2 for some tea.

He was sitting on the gallery, leafing warily through the folio of his morning's work with the *Philodendron*, when she appeared, panting and sweat soaked, carrying her shoes in her hand. She belatedly returned his wave from the Maloka, then skipped up the steps and sank into the canvas chair beside him. Having caught her breath and pulled free some strands of hair that were plastered across her cheeks, she said, "Well, what do you think?"

He smiled across at her, placing a masking hand across the image of the centipede invading the *Philodendron*'s delicate inner folds. He knew it to be a desecration of natural beauty, a reptilian violation of secret places, and he prayed she wouldn't wish to see it. "I think you could do with a bath."

Hestia laughed softly, and stretched. He could see the tiny blonde hairs on her forearms as distinctly as he had traced their equivalent on the stems of the *Philodendron*, both trapping the tiny spores floating in the afternoon light. And as she stretched her arms out and above her head, he watched the rivulets of perspiration form an infinitesimal labyrinth that ran down from her collar bone and across the exposed area of her breasts, before disappearing beneath the damp restrictions of her camisole. He felt a warning jolt of the dizziness he so dreaded and a light hissing in his ears, the ominous precursor of helpless vertigo. It could not be coming back so soon, surely? He would not, could not, allow it.

"They do it for days, you know," she shook her head in quiet wonder. "I don't know how."

"A form of natural intoxication, I believe." His preoccupation with this fresh onset of giddiness made him sound like a schoolmaster, prim and unyielding.

She stood up, extended her lower lip to blow some cooling air up across her face, with a somewhat simian expression, and then plucked at the calico skirt, clinging to her legs. "Course, they're not wearing all this," she said, and went into her room to prepare for her bath.

"Shall I check your feet?" he called out, as he spirited the centipede painting back into its portfolio. Casting off her shoes like that in close proximity to the Maloka would have made her an ideal target for all kinds of jiggers, mites and worm. Screw worms, hook worms, ringworm, the parasites were legion; a daily pitfall, though usually avoided if you were careful about what you brushed against or stood on, and what protective covering you arranged for yourself. A barefoot dancing girl might prove altogether too enticing to the tiny creatures, some of whom were equipped to wait patiently for weeks for an accommodating host to burrow into. A needle and kerosene was sometimes the only way to remove them, if you could spot them early enough.

"Yes, please," she called out from her room and then walked out onto the gallery, clad in a sheet, her towel in one hand and her remaining dress in the other. "That'll be a lovely way to spend an evening, won't it?" She smiled impishly, and then off she went to bathe.

~~~~~

It was a great occasion. The air was heavy with the night scent of orchids, fragrant perfumes, cigar smoke and expensive liqueurs. He was in dress uniform, standing alongside the society swells but, as ever, not quite feeling at home. That feeling of displacement changed abruptly, though, when Hestia waltzed past him, with that confidential but challenging smile, her hair sweat-slicked about her face. She was naked except for kid button boots, protecting her feet. The dazzling lights of the huge chandeliers in the ballroom glimmered in the sheen on her skin and outlined the rivulets of sweat on her thighs. The light hairs on her forearms stood erect, as she was cooled by the fans of society women, who looked on with voluptuous interest. She stamped down her feet and swayed away to the insistent rhythm, laughing with delight. He was surprised to see that she had followed the Okaina custom and depilated, and that the little pink mouth of her sex was fully reflected on the glistening dance floor. He tried to follow its reflection, but her haunches turned away from him and stole it from his sight. He stretched out his hand, hungrily seeking those little pink petals with the flecks upon them.

Seaton jerked awake in blind panic and struggled through the smothering embrace of his mosquito net, to light his acetylene lamp. He sucked in air, as the blood pounded in his temples, and tried to bring himself back to some sense of the particular. Outside, something scrabbled four-footed along the gallery, leaped to the packed earth below and slipped into the treeline.

236

Chapter Nine

West Sussex

"Sleep alright?" Dr Richardson dropped Seaton's wrist and put away his pocket watch. The man's pulse was slow and measured. The chloral was doing its job; if he'd taken it. Otherwise, it was yet another mystery. "You seem on altogether a more even keel this morning."

"Mrs Simmons has been dosing me," replied the Captain. "So there really was no need for you to turn out, you know."

"Missed her vocation, that one." Richardson returned to his seat.

"Thankfully," agreed Seaton. He leaned forward to offer the doctor a cigarette; a habit acquired, he told himself, in the Somme. "Though it is to you, I must attribute such an unprecedented recovery."

The French windows of the gallery opened onto a small terrace, still shaded at that time of the morning, and Seaton had received the doctor there. They sat in large wicker armchairs, a pot of tea between them on a small oriental table. Redolent of Simla, the doctor thought; Seaton's family had been hanging around far-flung corners of the globe for generations, governing and occasionally educating the natives, and carrying back exotic mementoes, furniture and other booty. The doctor was no stranger to such accoutrements. His practice had once had a substantial weighting of ex-Indian army men, all of whom had been laid low in some fashion by the life. Most suffered from digestive or liver problems, not of necessity caused by years of curry, flyblown tiffin, dehydration and the indifferent hygiene prevalent in their postings, but mainly through alcohol, chota pegs then, Madeira or port now. Over the years, Dr Richardson had attempted to arrest the course of their bilious decline, on occasion sharing a consoling glass or two in their erstwhile trophy rooms, without the irony impinging for more than a moment upon his consciousness. They were all hard-used men of the world, after all; with onerous pasts and indifferent futures.

Laurel House made a refreshing change. The looting of Seaton's forbears had been judicious and tasteful and from a number of continents. This wasn't the remittance men's compensation for decades of homesickness and cultural confusion. This was an appreciative commemoration of travel, endeavour and achievement. Yet, the man sat ill at ease amongst it all, his courteous melancholy dramatized intermittently by recurring and, to the doctor's mind, self-induced fever.

"While I'm sure the symptoms will cease to present in time," Richardson began, judiciously feeling his way around a topic he knew the Captain would prefer he did not broach, "I'm convinced their cause is remedied by more direct and less chemical means."

Seaton was looking at him with the patience of a saint, he thought, although he detected the merest hint of a hunted expression in the tightening of the lines in the corner of the Captain's eyes, and in the uncharacteristic and rather directionless smile he was proffering at these deliberations. The man was locked in with something behind that stoic expression, something attritional, relentless and sinister. Richardson pressed on.

"Over the years, Captain, I've seen a number of patients, older men and spinsters mostly, who will dwell on a thing until it makes them ill. Many, having nothing really substantial to dwell on, will create one. An imagined threat, a dark foreboding, some presumed family susceptibility. Any precedent that can be built into just cause for a decline. In my experience, most of them do it, in a topsy turvy way, to complain about the way life treats them, or the lack of attention the world pays them. That's why we call them 'complaints', after all. They're complaining about the world, or their lack of headway in it. Their lack of experiences and success in the past. Their lack of opportunities in the future. They make themselves ill because of an uncaring world and, as the world shows no interest, they can happily sustain their debility." He paused, sipped his tea and then set the cup down, with short outward breath of determination. "I would say, Captain that you have little in common with such people."

"Being neither an old man nor a spinster," Seaton shook his head and managed a wry smile to supplant his stoic and sociable one.

"Having nothing to complain about," corrected the doctor. "But you present very similarly. Oh, I don't mean the indulgent declines enjoyed by most women of a certain age from here to Selsea. Yours, I believe to be a different kind of fever. I suppose it's what the Romantics used to refer to as a brain fever. Shelley's a prime example, of course. Although, I'd say it's caused by thinking too deeply about nothing much for far too long."

Seaton stood suddenly, smiled to excuse the abruptness of his move but spoke formally, nonetheless. "Dr Richardson I'm most grateful to you for restoring me to my sleep and normal routine. But none of what you say bears any resemblance to my situation. Now, if you'll excuse me, I have many matters to attend to."

Richardson sighed deeply as he got up from his chair and looked round for his bag. "I do hope I haven't offended you, Captain. I have spoken not only as your doctor, which would permit me such professional concern, but also I hope as a friend." He found his bag and picked it up, then abandoned his precise and professional demeanour and spoke with outright, pained consternation. "If you keep yourself stuffed up in here, and inside that head of yours, you'll go under, man. I've seen it before. Please, make an effort to get out and about. Into the community, society, the world at large. Not for their sakes, but just to get out of your own company."

"Do you think my own company would be that demoralising?" Seaton smiled.

"If it's anything like mine is to me sometimes, it'll be agonising," replied the doctor. There was a small and awkward silence and then, realising he may have stepped over a threshold he hadn't even seen, he added, "I'm convinced isolation is a major factor in what afflicts you."

Seaton looked at Richardson with what seemed a quiet and ready sympathy, "And what exactly would you prescribe for that?"

"Well, as soon as you're able, I'd suggest travel, provided there was some social contact to it. I don't suppose the Cote d'Azur, Monaco...?" He read the Captain's expression. "Perhaps not. But some positive change of scene. A new set of experiences. A new set of problems, for all that. In the meantime, I'd try and expand your social calendar. You surely have friends in London, you could look up?" Again, he tried to read the Captain's response; this time the view was more opaque. "In any event, you ought to cut a swathe through Highleigh. Force a blast of fresh air through all the lace curtains. Look, there's a Bring and Buy Sale at the Church Hall on Thursday afternoon. Some fete for the restoration of Old Attwater, not sure quite what, but no doubt something in desperate need of renovation. Stupid bugger wouldn't hold it on Saturday, in case we got swamped by trippers and his precious lawns were churned up by the hoi polloi. But there's hoop-la and tombola and the Boy Scouts will light fires and tie knots and the Women's Institute will be selling pickled this and

that, shrunken heads with beetroot in all probability." He
saw the Captain was laughing now, and rallied himself
along, "And there's a sale of work; local produce, arts,
crafts and grand culture. Miss Maitland will have donated
something calligraphic and her friend will wear heavy
jewellery and criticise. You should be in the middle of it,
Captain. Teach the buggers what for." He snapped his
fingers, inspired. "Why don't you donate one of your
drawings for sale? That'll confound the lot of them."

"I couldn't possibly consider it. The bloody things
are best kept out of sight." Seaton sat back down in his
chair and reached for the cigarettes. The doctor sat back
too, at this tacit invitation, declining the proffered packet,
to pursue his quarry.

"You couldn't, Captain. But I bloody well could.
Hand one over." He held out a bony hand, with a wolfish
grin. "Something exotic to frighten the verger's wife."

The Captain stared hard at him, lit a cigarette and
drew the tobacco deep into his lungs. He shook the match
out with one hand and squinted thoughtfully through the
smoke. The physician's complete disregard for the
pomposities of village life obviously flourished when he
was allowed to air it, which the Captain judged wasn't
very often. And, in truth, there was something
refreshingly untrammelled about it; an almost youthful
irresponsibility; it held something of the optimistic energy
of cadets in the officer's mess, before the Great War
brought them to more mature considerations.

"It'll be unutterably ghastly!" Richardson concluded
his appeal. "You've simply got to come."

Seaton stood again and, shaking his head and
smiling at his own compliance, he led the doctor into the
gallery and over to the plans chest.

"What do you think?" he asked as he pulled out the
drawer housing the Amazonian sketches. "Something in

241

colour or some plain pencil work? There's a rather nice Epidendrum. Orchid, of course."

"Got anything with a man-eating spider?" Richardson caught himself up. He didn't want to undo his work through flippancy. "Perhaps, some village study. The simple splendour of savage life. Take the mystery out of it all."

The Captain carefully produced a sheet from the drawer and studied it gravely, "Well, there's this."

The doctor moved over to look. It was a study of several adult male Okaina, some practically up to their waists in river water, spread out in a semi-circle to close up a small inlet, while aiming below the surface in front of them with bows and long arrows. There was a concentration, a motionless but muscular focus about them, as they sighted into the waters.

"Shooting at fish!" cried the doctor. "The very thing."

North-west Amazon

Three of the Okaina men were wading up through the river, smacking at the surface with branches and sticks. Behind them, two more trod warily, with javelin at the ready in one hand and a further four in the other, scanning the waters over the shoulders of their branch-wielding colleagues. Beating the water, the party moved steadily towards a small inlet with high, grassy banks. They had chosen this time of day, and their position in the river, so that the sun cast their shadows behind them. It also meant that the bowmen on the banks of the inlet cast no shadow either. In any case, these stood motionless as herons, their arrows, indeed their whole muscular attention, fixed upon the waters directly beneath them. For the fish they expected to be arriving there, there would be no tell-tale sign, no alarm and, thereby, no escape. Two other men stood waist deep on either side of the inlet's mouth, their bowstrings taut and the tips of their long and poisoned arrows almost touching the dark water.

Hestia stood on the opposite bank to Seaton, both hands to her mouth as she gnawed, excitedly, at her knuckles. Occasionally she would dart a complicit glance at the Captain, who was raking the Okaina men with his own concentrated gaze, his pencil busy as he set down their flexed, predatory outlines.

Seaton and Hestia were paid up spectators. The gift of used jars and bottles Seaton had made to the chief's wife had resulted in a desultory trading, over which the expedition's cook reluctantly presided. This worthy eked out a parsimonious ration of empty tins and other domestic debris, in return for fishing hooks made from palm spines, small, dead lizards and other tributes, left on the tables in front of Tambo 2, almost as act of coincidental generosity

One morning Seaton found Callard and the cook bartering with an Okaina man over the trade of a tarnished table fork for a pirarucu, a large fish, although this specimen by no means as large as the monsters often to be found in these waters. He had requested to accompany a fishing expedition, with the promise of an equally tarnished spoon in payment. This promissory note had been extended by one more such spoon and a handful of Cotterill's spent cartridges, for which the intended use remained unclear.

Two days later, Seaton had been wakened by Callard in the early hours and taken out to receive a delegation of silent fishermen, at the foot of the gallery steps, who had come to take him with them on their foraging party. He noted the chunto-wood bows, the javelins and the quivers of arrows; clearly this was to be a special occasion, a display of the prowess in fishing for which the Okaina were renowned. Their standard method was to poison, normally with juice from the barbasco plant which, when sprinkled on the river surface, caused fish in the area to asphyxiate, without apparent adverse effect on anybody consuming them later. This, together with netting and the ingenious use of palm spine and chunto-wood hooks, formed their almost daily occupation. However, their foremost prowess and greatest diversion were in hunting and shooting fish through the waterline. Their vision and coordination were reputed to be uncanny, and Seaton felt a degree of elation at the thought of witnessing this at first sight.

Despite the early hour, Hestia had materialised, fully dressed and prepared, while Seaton was filling his water bottle prior to their departure. No objection to this was forthcoming from the foraging party, and the Okaina lead them off into the forest. Callard brought up the rear, his Mannlicher slung over his shoulder, a noisome cheroot already smouldering between his lips.

Seaton had been at pains to include Hestia in his more outgoing activities. He'd cast her, in his mind, as an agreeable if juvenile companion in need of whatever instruction he might summon up and a measured amount of emotional support. He was keenly aware this portrait was principally an instrument to distance her from the introversion to which he found himself increasingly prone. An introspection that was often heralded by recall of her naked appearance in his dream, or her sensual performance on the dancing ground, and at which familiar prompts he could find himself groaning out loud. So, he determined to restrict their relationship to genial but correct and active adventuring, which would stave off any flirtatiousness on her part, whether actual or conjured up by his rather heated imagination. The jungle may be a huge mechanism of procreation, death and regeneration but they were there purely for educational purposes. Hestia, for her part, had shown no overt appreciation of such mature reflections, but simply carried on regardless.

She was now staring at him wide-eyed over her clenched hands, as the Okaina beaters neared the mouth of the inlet. One of the bow-wielding statues on the bank beside her made some hushed sound, and a little shudder of anticipation ran through her shoulders. Seaton felt the familiar taut apprehension that had marked the beginning every action he had ever fought in. He steeled himself, as then, to keep his wits about him and record his impressions succinctly.

The beaters had just reached the mouth of the inlet and the javelin men were stealthily passing in front of them, when the bowmen loosed their arrows. The sudden concerted attack, the snap of the bows and the instant hissing passage of the long arrows beneath the waters, drew a muffled scream of surprise from Hestia, who although she must have expected the moment of slaughter, was still taken unawares by the abrupt and decisive force of it. Scarcely had her scream reached the tree tops than the Okaina gave vent to their own cries of triumph, as the arrows protruded through the water skin, bobbing and swaying with their heavy burdens dying beneath. Two men jumped in to assist the javelin men lift out the catch onto the bank.

Hestia fell to her hands and knees and peered into the choppy brown water, as Seaton gained the edge of the other bank; they exchanged a quick grin of affirmation, at the privilege of being present and at the dynamic power of the moment around them. At once, a greater turmoil rose up from the silt in a flurry of dirty bubbles and shifting mud. The transfixing arrows swayed crazily. The

Okaina in the water darted back uncertainly, and one cried out and fell heavily against the bank, plunging his hands beneath the waters to some unseen wound in his leg. The bowmen in the river notched another arrow and aimed at the muddy confusion, trying to pick out whatever was mounting such a wild assault from the mulch. The men from the bank, pulled frantically at the wavering arrows, hauling up dead and bleeding fish and unloading them onto the bank like so many sodden sandbags. Hestia was buffeted by a large and slime covered tambaqui, which she dragged behind her, before holding out her arms to the wounded man, now sprawled against the bank, his blood staining the earthy waters at his waist.

There was a volley of false sightings, commands and counter commands, as the javelin men tried to range in on the marauder, loosing three darts into the mud, between the tangle of bodies trying to scramble to safety. Seaton and the bowman beside him managed to haul the wounded man up onto the bank. He had a deep track gouged out of the fleshy part of his calf though, with its coating of slime and the free bleeding, it was impossible to tell if it were a bite or a slash by some tail or fin.

Hestia's outstretched hands had been filled with some kind of gaping catfish, winding its body, in a sturdy and mystified way, about the arrow that spitted it lengthwise. She sat with this expiring beast in her lap and stared, mesmerised, into the churning waters. Horror and exaltation seemed to vie within her for pride of place. "What is it?" she cried at last.

The threshing continued unabated, until finally, as the remaining Okaina managed to clamber onto the bank, a length of brown, armoured tail broke the surface amongst the bubbling filth in the reeds. In the space of a heartbeat, it had slashed savagely from side to side before withdrawing with equal speed through the foam and into the roiling mud of the inlet shallows.

"I think it's a caiman," Seaton shouted across to her, using his scarf as a tourniquet for the Okaina, who sat and stared fatalistically at the gash in his leg, blood now puddling around his foot. "We must have struck an entrance to its nest."

Callard stepped in front of him and unslung the Mannlicher. He shouted out something short and pithy to the Okaina, who all stepped back from the bank, in some apprehension, and then fired several shots into the area in which the beast had finally let itself be seen. Hestia cried out again, as the bullets fizzed into the water, and covered her ears, smearing her hair with fish scales, slime and blood.

Everybody peered into the inlet waters, which gradually returned to their normal placid disposition. Eventually, with a little prompting, the younger of the javelin men slipped charily back into the water, to retrieve the darts still protruding through the surface. He climbed back out immediately, and joined his older companion on the bank above where it was thought lay the monster's lair. They probed with sudden and urgent thrusts of their javelins down into the water, fearful of provoking the beast, yet imbued with the hunter's determination to finish the kill. The beast itself had, according to a whispered aside from Callard in Seaton's ear, grown considerably bigger since the only sighting. When he'd seen the tail, he'd calculated the beast to be small and young, but now, in its menacing absence it had been elevated by the Okaina into a full grown, vengeful female, the most ferocious of the species.

Youngster or Leviathan, the caiman never resurfaced, and so, bearing their catch and with the wounded bowman hobbling behind on a makeshift crutch, they returned to the village to celebrate this brush with a monster. Seaton and Hestia declined with extended courtesy the offer of a drink of kawana or a parcel of coca, and made their way back to the Tambo, Hestia to wash off the detritus of the hunt and Seaton to work up his sketches and notes of the skirmish.

Later that afternoon, she brought him a cup of coffee onto the veranda and watched him smoke a cheroot, while they rehearsed the events of the day. Somehow this exploit, despite the injury to the fisherman, had put a healthy cast on their relationship. Not quite the talk of field sports and hunt balls he'd envisage as their social equivalent back in England, perhaps, but nonetheless he felt a physical tension lift from between them. They had witnessed savages wrestling with nature in full cry and, thereby, had reaffirmed their true position as civilised observers. They belonged to a more measured world, and had experienced the gulf between it and life in the forest around them. He felt he could now regard the palpating rhythms infecting some of his drawings as aberrations, and put any suspicious and improper allusions to Hestia from his mind. They were both safely buttoned up again.

That said, in the days that followed, he would still find himself stranded along some track, absorbed by an unholy quietus, as the light filtered down on him from the cathedral heights of the canopy. Time would, once again, stand still and his senses, straining beyond the murky aggregate of moist fug, dull sounds and miasmal outlines, seemed to gorge themselves on the perpetual cycle of savage life churning inexorably about him. His nostrils would cloy with the scents of the profusion of orchids, plunging from the tree tops in overblown cascades. He would register, in tormenting detail, the constant creaking of the trees as they settled and realigned; the rustle and seep of the mulch beneath them, as insects and tiny mammals scuttled through in their frantic occupations; the shape-shifting and pattern-forming that consolidated or receded, depending on the vagaries of the ever-changing light, and the tantalising breezes, coming from nowhere and similarly destined, to play upon his skin and give temporary lie to the perpetual, enervating humidity. This deluge of sensation would paralyse him, as if the only true reality was to be had in stillness, in the microscopic space between one sensory impression shifting into another.

Still, despite the minor variances in his overall recovery, he was confident that the time spent waiting for Northmore to return could be spent productively, in preparing himself to rejoin the expedition in a significant role. In the interim, and as a supplementary concern, he was pleased with the way his relationship with the girl was shaping up. Although, it had to be said that the business with the howler monkeys was something of a setback

The enterprise had started out promisingly enough, with he and Hestia being taken up the eastern tributary by dugout canoe with members of the previous fishing party, ostensibly to watch the poisoning and netting process but, in truth, to break from the inner constraints the familiar walkways had placed on them. They basked in the space, the horizons and the river breezes. Hestia sung away to herself contentedly and squinted through the morning sunlight as the river widened and the shores receded.

The party were in three canoes, Hestia and Seaton in the first and Callard in the rear, chewing on yet another cheroot, his rifle between his knees. Seaton had brought his own Winchester with him, following the pandemonium on the last trip, and restricted himself to a sketching block and a pencil. The Okaina poled and paddled with effortless ease, looking for water conditions that presaged the presence of shoals of fish, with configurations of river bank that would make an enclosed poisoning feasible. Every so often, one of them would give vent to a series of roaring and whooping calls, to no apparent purpose. Initially, this was disconcerting, but after a half hour on the water, Seaton concluded it to be simply some kind of propitiatory call to the river gods. After a few giggles when one of her songs was interrupted in such a mournful fashion, Hestia seemed not to notice it at all.

Then an answering call floated back from the nearest bank, and the day changed altogether. The Okaina's heads came up and, paddling furiously, they made instantly for a narrow playa on that shore and beached the dugouts, all thoughts of fishing forgotten. Three produced bows with arrows from the bottom of their canoes and, with much whooping, they tore off into the forest, craning their necks to peer up into the treetops.

Callard dashed over to Seaton and Hestia, left stranded by the riverside, and urged them to follow the Okaina. "They hear monkey"!" he cried. "No more fish. Hunt monkey now!"

Hestia threw Seaton an apprehensive look, but he caught up her elbow and pulled her along with them. "We'll need to stick close," he said. "No knowing where they'll get to, without us to chivvy them back."

After a short and breathless sprint through the labyrinthine tracks leading back from the river, the foremost Okaina gave a triumphant yell and pointed into the tree canopy where a troop of howlers were clambering frantically. At once all the Okaina set up a caterwauling and shrieking, causing the bewildered, frantic monkeys to screech and call back. A madcap race ensued with the howlers scampering, terrified, through the high branches, while the Okaina, howling like banshees, tracked them below and tried to steer them, as far as the forest tracks would permit, into a sparsely leafed section, where they could get a good shot at them. Seaton kept up as far as he could, the sudden turns and leaps more reminiscent of the rugby field than any military or hunting pursuit he had known. Callard seemed to anticipate every change of the direction the monkey troop made, his eyes constantly roaming the canopy, his Mannlicher in both hands, his stance perfectly balanced at all times.

"Leave them alone!" Hestia yelled breathlessly, as she darted along behind them. Seaton turned in surprise and saw her face was streaked with tears. "Let them go!"

At that moment the howler troop split; two clustering blurs of brownish-black fur sped through the high branches in separate directions, a smaller party of younger monkeys made for the higher trees, while the main party, slowed by their young, cut back towards the river. Seaton, running closely behind the leading Okaina, followed them instinctively as they backtracked, while the rest sprinted after the breakaways. They all kept up their fearful racket, now rendered even more confusing as the two parties diverged.

He arrived in a small clearing to find the three leading Okaina prowling restlessly beneath a large hardwood, from which a huge branch had long ago crashed to the ground, dragging with it most of the surrounding trees' superstructure. A family group of the howlers, shrieking and grimacing, were prowling the topmost branches. The closest communicating tree was back the way they had come, and the Okaina were at pains to yell up from this point and keep the monkeys at bay. Only one of men carried a bow and he unloosed two arrows in quick succession, finding a target with only one. The howler, a young female, screamed and clung with all her strength to the branch upon which she had taken sanctuary, wrapping her tail around it for added tenure. She started to shake piteously but, from the Okaina's expression, it was clear that, even once dead, the likelihood of her falling to earth was remote. A hunter turned to Seaton and pointed insistently at his Winchester. He let loose a gabble of urgent words, while his colleagues, cupping their hands, kept up the barrage of shrieks and whoops and provocations to pen the howlers back.

Seaton's Okaina vocabulary failed him, so he glanced over his right shoulder for Callard. Then, seeing no one, and with the Okaina becoming more and more voluble, he unslung the Winchester, took quick aim on the canopy and fired three shots. Two full grown monkeys crashed out of the tree, and the Okaina rushed over to them with cries of approval, one of them delivering a final blow to each head with his chunto wood club.

"Why did you do that? You didn't have to do that," Hestia materialised beside him, staring into his face with a terrible and judgmental earnestness. Callard brought up the rear, and not far behind him came the other Okaina party, bearing the body of a young dead male howler, sizeable but nothing like the bounty that Seaton has shot from the skies. "It's like killing a child!"

"It's nothing of the sort!" Seaton felt the anger rising in him, partly because he had been coerced into the shots that had brought this judgement upon him, and partly because he had now been set alongside Cotterill as some mindless slaughterer of wildlife. "These people have to eat."

"They would have eaten something else," she sniffed.

Seaton waved at the party behind her, carrying the

252

young dead male, and eying the other catch with some envy. "I hardly think so." He even sounded like Brandon Cotterill; it really was too much. He turned to Callard. "I want none of this. Present it to them or the chief, or whatever is necessary."

Callard stared at him and it took Seaton a moment to remember the man's limited English. "Give the monkeys to the Maloka, from me." he repeated.

The party returned to the settlements immediately, in high spirits, apart from Hestia, who refused to share a canoe with the bodies and sat subdued in the last dugout, pulling on a lock of her hair, and sniffing ostentatiously. Seaton, she ignored. Much as she ignored the triumphal procession to the Maloka with the bodies of the monkeys, their presentation to the group and immediate butchery.

She avoided the dancing ground where, in one corner, the Okaina put up a green wood straddle and set a slow fire to smoke the corpse of one of the larger females and the young male. It was a long and not especially efficient process, crude and gruesome to western eyes, and only serving to preserve the meat for a few days at best, but it was a lingering formality of victory and the Okaina took to it with particular relish.

For the day after the hunt, Hestia hardly spoke to anybody, and never to Seaton. The Captain found it all too exasperating. Here they were, two Britons in the middle of thousands of square miles of wilderness, and the woman was indulging in some minor domestic tantrum, simply because her wishes had not been complied with. At least, it gave him some time to himself, he concluded, though the awkwardness around the Tambo was not conducive to a healthy recovery of spirits. Surely she couldn't sustain this ridiculous posture for long; she'd have to come to her senses soon.

While Hestia took pains to display a marked froideur

to Seaton, others were considering him in an entirely different light. The following afternoon, Callard appeared on the veranda in a state of some agitation. The Okaina were holding a tribal council, he reported, with Seaton as its subject. The Captain blanched at the news, and set down the book he was reading, Cotterill's much-thumbed though abandoned The Sea-Wolf. Councils were normally called to settle domestic disputes or declare wars. All males who had reached maturity sat around the tobacco pot and debated with endless speeches. The proposer or complainant of the grievance in question would perorate, often for hours, and would then smear some of the black tobacco liquid from the tobacco pot onto his tongue with a stick, replace the stick in the pot and pass it on. Those who agreed with him would also take a drink; those in opposition would pass it untouched, but only after a lengthy exposition of all their points of opposition. After everybody had had his full and often repetitive say, there was a ballot. The chief had the deciding vote, in the event that one was required. In this fashion a tobacco palaver could easily take all night.

"What are they talking about?" Seaton tried to keep the apprehension out of his voice. His military training had kicked in at once and he swiftly rehearsed the firing positions from the Tambo, the dispositions and temperaments of the Cholos that remained with him, and their chances of making their way down to the river and seizing a dugout to flee in.

"They wish to give you a woman. They say your house is incomplete." Callard replied. "The chief has many slaves and widows in his family." He added reasonably.

"That's utterly ludicrous!" What more could this continent throw at him? He saw Callard looking at him in his perplexed manner and rephrased the sentiment. "This is madness. Loco. Not right."

Callard nodded vigorously as he caught on. "Some women have told their men this. A child has seen you bathing. He called you an eifoke."

Eifoke was the Okaina word for a turkey buzzard. Nonetheless, Seaton hoped the unflattering and rather obscene comparison might put a stop to the trade. However, the feelings of the slave or the widow would not count for a great deal, where the tribe's generosity was involved.

Hestia came bustling out of the open specimen room door, "What's that?"

Seaton felt genuinely relieved to see he had her concerned attention, even though the cause was a regrettable one. He explained before Callard attempted to. "There's a difficulty. It sounds like the Okaina wish to give me a wife."

She turned from him to Callard as if for confirmation of this outlandish proposal, but returned immediately to Seaton. She stared at him uncomprehendingly, pulling a strand of hair out of her face, trying to gauge the effect on him of this news. "That's ridiculous."

"I've just said the very same thing," he smiled at her, in what he hoped was a placatory way, though his mind was still racing on how he might extricate himself from the Okaina's intended largesse.

The girl sat down beside him, shaking her head in what appeared to be a blend of bewilderment and quiet distress. Seaton looked across to Callard but there was no more information forthcoming. Suddenly Hestia gripped his arm fiercely and exclaimed, "You don't need a woman!" She looked at him imploringly, as if trying to prevail upon his better nature. "You've got me!"

West Sussex

Despite the doctor's misgivings, there was quite a turnout for the Reverend Attwater's sale of works cum fete. A throng from neighbouring farms and villages had arrived, in their better clothes, along with holidaying schoolchildren with long suffering parents, grateful for the distraction; persons of social consequence who suspected their absence might be ascribed to uncharitable motives; the full complement of the various church committees, except where age or infirmity or, more usually, both together prohibited attendance; and a few diehard enthusiasts genuinely seduced by the allure of hoop-la, tombola and the teas traditionally provided, at cost, by Larry Poulter and his wife. Foster found a space to park behind the Tun and Pipe and walked with Seaton over to the village hall, on their way towards the vicarage gardens, which were bearing the brunt of the carnival activity. From where they were, Seaton could see a small and cluttered encampment there, with a higgledy-piggledy arrangement of tents, still with military emblems stencilled to the lower skirts, pegged into the hallowed turf. He suspected the Reverend Attwater would be paying as much attention to the effects of the tent pegs as he would to the activities of his parishioners. Whatever moneys were raised that day, it would be at no small personal cost to him, when the divots came up.

Seaton and Foster threaded their way through the crowd bustling in and out of the hall; some of the farming men amongst them cast furtive and wistful glances across to the Tun and Pipe, which remained resolutely closed, for another half hour.

"What's in there?" Seaton looked, rather apprehensively, over the shoulders of those making their way into the hall.

"Local produce, art and the Scouts' display," replied

Foster, promptly. He'd been comprehensively briefed that morning by Mrs Simmons who had been co-opted onto the fete committee, and was now floating around the vicarage gardens in her new and fashionable hat, admired, modelled and, after some rather heated discussion, accepted as a gift during her last trip with Foster to Bognor.

Seaton evaded an early acquaintance with the art and local produce, eased his way through the crowd and stepped out purposefully for the vicarage. Foster marched alongside him, to conclude his reconnaissance reports. "Mrs Simmons says the hoop-la is all the stuff they lost their nerve on at the sale of work. And some of the jam's been about a bit." He thought for a moment. "All in a good cause, though. And the tea's not bad, of course."

They skirted the hoop-la, where an intense young man was directing ranging shots at an extravagant lamp-base in the form of a Spanish galleon in full sail. His younger brother watched him scornfully, jingling his pennies in his hand and waiting to deploy his superior skills in securing the prize. A solid woman in a floral dress stood beside the stall, a dozen hoops arrayed on a sturdy forearm, and gave the boy a dour nod of encouragement. She assessed Seaton and Foster as potential customers but then forbore to say anything, perhaps lacking the descriptive power to entice.

Foster slowed a little, and began tentatively, "Well, if there's nothing further for the moment, Captain..."

Seaton waved him off in a cheerful manner, determined that his disquiet should remain, as ever, a closely guarded secret. Yet, standing alone outside the Poulter's tea tent, he glanced discreetly about him and felt himself to be under scrutiny. Even allowing for some side effect to the comforting patina that Dr Richardson's chloral spread over the day, he knew this was not some

257

displaced anxiety. He had a natural aptitude for sensing when he was under surveillance, whether through thicket, lace curtains, field glasses or averted gazes. This sense had been trained and honed over years of military service, and was refusing to sink into desuetude even now. He knew himself to be a focal point of village gossip and malicious preoccupation, but beyond the clumsily disguised attention this would entail at any social gathering, he felt a more directed observation upon him. As ever, he would give no indication of his heightened awareness, but raised his straw hat to someone he thought he might have known from a local race day and turned to make a casual sweep of the gardens.

Enid Attwater sped out of the Poulter's tea tent, holding a plate piled high with chocolate éclairs, and rushed over to him; she had on the floral dress from the day he had given her a lift back from her sun struck excursion towards Wittering, although Seaton would never have noticed and she was determined not to alert him to that, not even through some amusing and self-disparaging remark. Instead, in a breathless manner redolent of that previous occasion, she managed to manoeuvre herself to the front of him, place her free hand on his arm and talk to him while walking backwards, smiling nervously and matching his every step, as she were a beginner in an esoteric dance class. He stopped as smoothly as he could, to spare her any further effort.

"Hello, Enid." He raised his hat, yet again, and smiled down at her. "Off to feed the five thousand?"

"Look, I'm so sorry for all my flustering, the other day." She pulled an unclipped strand of hair off her face with her free hand. "You must think me dreadfully rude or batty or something. But sometimes I just have to get away. And I can't have been thinking about the sun and the time and all that kind of thing." She gave a short, exasperated gasp, verging on a sob, and pressed on as if, in her haste, she could outrun any difficult ramifications of a decision she had just made. "You see, I don't have many friends here. No, that's not quite right. I just haven't made any. I just don't feel I'm a natural part of all this. To tell the absolute truth, if there is one, I don't think I fit in at all." She laughed a little too brightly. "The vicar's wife! Can you imagine?" She compressed her lips, slowed her breathing and then, peering into his eyes, she spoke with a soft intensity, "I think you can imagine. All too well, can't you? Not being part of it. Not being understood. Not being left alone. All that fuss about your drawings and the poor girl with the crocodiles!" She shook her head in perplexity. "You can't stop them. And they're all around you. What on earth can you do?"

"Hand round the éclairs?" Seaton felt for Enid, for her sense of displacement and her emergent and rather desperate discomposure. He was beginning to realise he genuinely liked the woman, but he really couldn't afford to be drawn into any personal confidences.

She looked down at the éclairs as if she had only just noticed them. "These? Some boys came up on the 32 bus from Selsea. They made some raucous remarks during the Scouts' gymnastics display." She heaved a deep sigh. "Duncan promised the Scouts these, if they refrained from any retaliation."

Seaton looked dubiously at the pile of sticky cakes; the Highleigh Scouts, many of whom were choristers, were a rough lot at best, barely constrained by Baden Powell's precepts of cleanliness and honesty. "Do you think it'll work?"

She considered this for a moment. "Only if it makes them too sick to fight," she concluded, and then looked earnestly up at him for one final time. "We don't think

259

like them, do we? Not in any way."

With this, she scurried away on her husband's mission of appeasement. Seaton looked around at the stalls of produce on sale, the hoop-la and the tombola, with the locals filing past it all, as if observing the obsequies at some charitable catafalque. He saw Sam Faring's wife solemnly rooting through bric-a-brac in search of some unwittingly donated valuable. At another stall, a basket-weaving matron held her peace while two other ladies of similar age subjected her craft to all kinds of tests of strength, in a disinterested manner. Everything was progressing in its normal fashion and at its normal pace.

Still, the sense of being targeted by some observer remained with him. Someone was approaching from behind and he turned to prepare himself, but it was only Sam Faring, smiling in his quietly affable manner and holding out his hand.

"Afternoon, Captain," said the farmer. "Very impressed with that drawing of yours. As a sportsman, I suppose, mainly. No judge of art, of course."

"They have an amazing eye for fish," replied the Captain, happy to land on field craft as a conversational topic. "Spot them through the surface, and then hit them just like that."

"Wouldn't do round here, would it?" Sam laughed. "Though I know a few as would try." He delivered what he thought was the good news. "It was sold, the moment they opened up, I reckon. Quite a price, too. Guineas. I wanted it myself, but I was too late. Little 'sold' star stuck up on it when I got there. Had to settle for some cows by the verger's wife. Just to show willing. Think I'd have enough cows by now, wouldn't you?"

Seaton laughed along with him, then bid him a good afternoon and walked back towards the village hall, while he digested the unpalatable but inevitable fact of the sale. He wondered who owned the drawing now, and found it mattered to him more than he had anticipated, possibly because the motive for the purchase remained unclear. Was it a charitable impulse or some mischievous pleasure in his current notoriety? He wished he'd thought things through more clearly, though it would have been impossible to refuse the doctor's request that he donate something. Still, he rather regretted he had and then, in order to dispel such maundering, decided to go to the exhibition and see if he could find out who now had it. Better to be in the know than in the fog of war. Back to the fog again. He was aware that his inclinations towards mysteries and unknowns veered from Keats to Clausewitz at the first scent of danger, and that the soldier was prepared to supplant the artist at a moment's notice. On such occasions, this military minded pragmatism was in some ways reassuring, even though for a long while he despaired of it as a natural brake on any instinctual artistic capabilities. Now, he had no predisposition either way.

He entered the village hall, and saw the vicar hovering around the Scouts' display at the far end, making placatory gestures. The display comprised largely of sheep shanks, bowlines, hitches and other knots in white lanyard stuck on gray card, their names painstakingly picked out in china clay beneath. A selection of campfire kit, Scout manuals and even a bone-handled sheath knife were arrayed on a trestle table, flanked by flags, and patrol pennants. The Scouts chewing on their chocolate éclairs were staring neutrally at the cleric, as he issued his blandishments and ultimatums.

In the middle of the hall there was an earnest extravaganza of needle work, crochet, quilting and macramé and raffia mats. It looked like nobody ever spent an idle hour in Highleigh and its environs, at least not amongst the Reverend Attwater's congregation. A few items were on sale, but the great majority appeared in the hall for purely educational and display purposes. Judging from the expression of wary pride on the faces of the women curating each section, this was more in the nature of a tournament than a sale for charity. Jams might be commoditised, baskets even, but macramé was not going to stoop to commercial considerations. This held true, but for different reasons, for Clover's small exposition of calligraphy. Some fine examples on beautiful silk paper of Chinese writing offset by delicate pen studies of lotus and bamboo were set against the robust simplicity of the mediaeval yeomen script, so beloved of her father, stamped into rag paper with biblical texts and appropriate etchings. The Lion of Judah featured again, heavily, as did Clover Maitland who was upon him the moment she sighted him.

"I thought you might not come," she said, smiling in relief. "Not after all their stupidity with the little Indian girls. And it's such a wonderful drawing."

"Felt I ought to make the effort," he replied, looking around discreetly and trying to locate the exhibition. He returned to Clover's display. "You've done very well, as usual."

"Just the formal stuff," admitted Clover. "I do have freer work, but you know." This thought seemed to spur her on. "Captain, certain matters came up at tea, delicate matters, matters of personal history. I just thought, if you ever need a quiet talk, with a friend, we have so much in common that…."

What was it that so attracted women to the undisclosed, thought Seaton? Could they sense it? Like leopards with blood? Within ten minutes, both Enid and

Clover had homed in, unerringly, on matters he wished to remain forever private. Both were inducing him to offer them up to their tactful attention. Both were in search of some common and secret ground, over which they could declare some compassionate dominion.

"My childhood was supposed to be free of inhibitions. I was taught the artist had no place for them. But sometimes one pays a price, I suppose. Perhaps an artist has a different sort of innocence. Anyway, I thought we might exchange…. It can wear you down, over time, I find…" Clover was stuttering to a halt.

He spotted the exhibition of local art over her shoulder, and then returned his polite attention to her. She too was troubled, he realised with a weary familiarity; perhaps that was what sent women like Enid and Clover out to search for the perfect receptacle for their self-reflective sympathies. He smiled at her as kindly as he might, suggested tea at Laurel House at some unspecified point in the future and excused himself.

The various works of local art had been hung on the far walls, in all too considered a manner, the result of long discussion and many personal preferences. It was not an inspiring sight, a pot pourri of tenuous landscapes, still lives from kitchenware to favourite figurines, startling portraits and scenes from popular imagination. They came in all shapes and sizes; some were framed, some pinned and curling in the hot afternoon. All flouted the laws of perspective and proportion to some degree; many strived to compensate with enthusiasm and bravura, some with the eccentricity of subject matter, some with surprising combinations of colour. Others offered no compensation, but appeared in stolid defiance and baleful contradiction of balance, tone, representation or colour. Amongst a cluster of these recalcitrants was his sketch of the Okaina fishers, neatly framed in a light wood, and with a paper star affixed to it. He hurried towards it.

He was aware of the doctor standing to one side, one hand in his pocket, the other cradling a glass of something, talking to somebody in the relaxed manner of a Bond Street gallery owner. There was a flurry of movement from behind him and, suddenly, there in front of Seaton was Dr Houghton-Copley, cool and neat in a light-grey, lawn suit with a creamy soft shirt and dark blue silk tie, one hand held aloft in some kind of welcome. He retained the ubiquitous blue leather portfolio under his arm.

"My dear Captain! Come to see how your progeny is faring? Well, it's sold, sir. To a mystery buyer." He noticed the shadow pass across Seaton's face. "Oh, not me. Malheureusement." He turned to admire the drawing. "Such restrained violence. All that passion so taut beneath the surface. So artfully concealed."

"I hardly expected to see you here," Seaton responded stiffly.

"Duncan brought me down to inaugurate proceedings, but when I saw the scale of the event, I declined." He leaned in conspiratorially. "So much better for a local man to introduce these things, don't you think? I believe there's a magistrate who leapt at the chance."

Seaton could see the doctor was coming over, so he spoke quietly and with a spare intensity. "I believe you have some papers belonging to me."

"Indeed I do," agreed the diplomatist cordially, and he reached into the portfolio. Then to Seaton's astonishment, he produced a mint copy of his own hardbound monograph, published at Northmore's expense for the RGS. "And I wish you to sign it for me. It's a masterpiece."

"Great success, your picture," Dr Richardson told Seaton as he joined them. "Not a contrary word out of any of them. They've hidden their disappointment admirably."

"Disappointment?" Houghton-Copley was dramatic in his perplexity. Seaton thought he was talking a shade louder than the situation merited, or than his own, finely attuned bearing would normally have permitted.

"Oh, after all the twaddle that's been going round, they were expecting something far more exotic." Richardson smiled sympathetically at Seaton. Mankind was behaving true to form, but at least his foreknowledge could give him some satisfaction, and the Captain some protection. "Savage fornication at the very least."

"Well, if that's what you're after," replied Houghton-Copley gaily, as he waved Seaton's monograph in the air, "it's all in here."

He leafed through the little book. "The vocabularies of the indigents are particularly impressive. Such meticulous attention to detail. Listen to this." He put on his gold spectacles and started to read in a loud, sonorous voice. "Anus – sirafo; Belly –ero; clitoris," At this, he gave Seaton an appreciative twinkle. "- hito; Hair (pubic) – hueke; Penis – hechina; pudenda –jana; semen – uke; testicles –hinyero; tongue –hufe; vagina –berirafo." He turned to the doctor. "You see, the Captain is nothing if not thorough!"

"That's just a fraction..." Seaton protested. He was acutely aware of the crowd of Highleigh folk hovering within earshot and that, as a result of the diplomatist's projected delivery, some were paying close attention, the merits of the various arts and crafts for the moment forgotten. He saw Dr Richardson looking quizzically at him, working hard to contain his amusement

"Oh, it's comprehensive, alright," allowed Houghton-Copley. "Captain Seaton certainly knows his subject. And such a handy collection of phrases, too. For scientific purposes of course." He turned the pages avidly and returned to his loud conjugation. "Listen. 'You are pretty.', 'I want you.', 'Are you a virgin?', 'Go and wash.', 'Hold me.', 'Lie down.', 'Turn over', 'I will punish you', 'Do you like it?'" He took off his spectacles with a flourish and proclaimed, "What a boon to future anthropologists, seeking intercourse with the local population."

The Captain felt his temples throbbing as the hubbub increased around him. Dr Richardson was smiling broadly now, as the diplomatist shut the book with dramatic finality and handed it to Seaton, with an earnest, "You will sign my copy, won't you? It really is one of a kind."

"Will you excuse us a moment, Doctor?" asked Seaton urgently, and Richardson threw up his hand in easy acquiescence and went off in search of a refill for his glass. Seaton immediately took the Houghton-Copley by the elbow, and was pleased to note how he flinched at the physicality. He drew the man through the dispersing Highleigh folk and off to one side, where he fixed him with a stony stare. "I want my papers back. Now."

Houghton-Copley extricated himself gently from Seaton's grip, but seemed otherwise unaffected "Come to Chichester tomorrow." He adjusted the set of his sleeve and then gave Seaton an incongruously broad grin. "I will give you lunch in the Cathedral. We can exchange confidences, and material too if you wish. Everything is in Chichester, my dear fellow. So you must come there. You'll find me a more than sympathetic host"

"And you will return my papers?" Seaton persisted.

"We'll sort it all out tomorrow," Houghton-Copley assured him as he shook Seaton warmly by the hand. "Now I simply must dash."

Foster and Mrs Simmons watched the diplomatist make his way out of the hall and over to the Episcopal

Rolls. The chauffeur opened the door for him and Houghton-Copley paused to give a courtly wave in the general direction of the Highleigh event, before suddenly plunging himself into the shaded interior of the car.

"Been up to his old tricks again," said Foster, grimly. "Machinations and all kinds of dirty talk."

"He reminds me of my Uncle Alan, when we were kids," replied Mrs Simmons. "Used to sit you on his knee and keep you there a little longer than was necessary." She laughed fondly at Foster's indignant expression. "Anyway, he's long dead now."

Foster watched the Episcopal Rolls turning sedately past the village hall to start the short journey back to Chichester. Houghton-Copley's motionless figure was just discernible through the rear side window. "This one isn't, though. He's here and he's causing trouble."

North-west Amazon

Seaton sat in the specimen room, the contents of his portfolio spread out on the work table. He was grouping them, by subject, by medium, and by quality, pulling out particular favourites and debating whether to discard what he regarded as mistakes or mediocre works. All in all, it was a respectable body of work, some of it accomplished.

His more personal pieces he had removed to a trunk in his room, locked and lodged beneath his bed, on the grounds that works with such emotional content had no place in the log of an expedition, and moreover that an expedition could have no call on the personal investigations of an artist, once he had discharged his obligations to the projects at hand. He'd locked them away, both to ensure their privacy and, in some measure, to limit the introspective attention he would give them. He could not look at them in the same dispassionate light that he viewed the landscapes, studies and botanical drawings he had, now, arranged in so conscientious a fashion. The others reflected his fever and, in that, were facets of the same disquieting unknown, and something to be approached with caution or late night abandon, when somehow he found the resolve to bring them out and search for their meaning and, with equal or more pressing urgency, their provenance.

What had drawn him to snatch studies of fecund Indian women? Why all that time capturing, discreetly, the curve of Hestia's collar bone, and the lacy detail on her undergarment? What had produced, beyond normal observation, the intense scribblings of frightened birds breaking cover from the entanglement or oily insects skulking in shadows? The portraits in death of Cotterill's jaguar, fly-encrusted in the dust, the charred and childlike corpses of the monkeys smoking on the griddle, what was in him that answered their dark and urgent call?

His fever was creeping back upon him, he knew, although he had to recognise some private turmoil could be as responsible as any bug or mosquito. Whatever brought him to this vertiginous, annihilating darkness, he felt increasingly incapable of dealing with it. He had always thought of his temperament as being easy-going, slow to anger and stoic when required, a blend of calm, curiosity and competence. He could no longer rely on that; something was dislodging all those assumptions and, with them, his appreciation of his own identity. Whether it was the jungle, his failing constitution or the behaviour of those around him, (he refused to single out Hestia overtly), he could not safely establish, and he knew that loss of perspective was, in itself, significant. This conscious lack of self-determination was occupying his every thought, and the dense heat of oblivion was closing in around him.

Hestia turned up out of nowhere and changed it all again. She arrived with Callard, breathless and almost too excited to talk and ran up and down the veranda, calling his name. On finding him tidying away his papers in the specimen room, she pulled at his arm, laughing at her own impatience but determined that he should accompany her nevertheless. The froideur of the last few days had simply disappeared, without trace.

"I've got something for you!" she cried. "Something nobody else has ever seen!"

He followed her unsteadily, as she took his hand and walked him down towards the Maloka, past the dancing ground, along the track meandering in its own deceptive way to the plantations, and suddenly veered off towards the river. She kept up a continuous commentary, about how she and Callard had been following the water course and had just stumbled upon it. How it was so hidden from anyone's view that she had tied her handkerchief to the thicket, so she might recognise the entrance on their return. How he simply wouldn't believe it. How she simply couldn't describe it. How she was so delighted to have found it, and she was giving it to him, because of all the things he'd done for her, the way he'd looked after her, which she really did appreciate, even if sometimes she didn't show it, because he would agree life had been difficult for her, recently anyway, and anyway that was all in the past.

She lead him down a narrow track which would have taken them to the river had it not suddenly veered away in a looping bend, made all the more difficult to negotiate by sharp spined palms striking out through a profusion of well established lianas. At the apex of this bend, they found her handkerchief, hanging on an elaborate climber, billowing occasionally as a breeze played upon it from behind a seemingly impenetrable wall of thicket. She grinned delightedly to him and pointed to the ground. At the base of the wall of shrub a barely discernable entrance had been stamped into the coarse grass and the mud, with overlapping tracks. Something two or three toed, in all probability, thought Seaton, though the spoor was far from clear; he thought it must be tapir, and small beasts at that.

"Ready?" asked Hestia, and with all the flourish of a pantomime magician, she took his hand and stepped through the wall of liana, pulling him behind her and into paradise.

The track cut down sharply to the centre of a tiny gulf, enclosed by high trees, and these covered with a curtain of the most beautiful orchids Seaton had ever seen. They hung down thirty feet and more, a cascade of coral, peach and varied pinks, the petals soft and welcoming, and the stamens with anthers in dark fiery red. It was as if they were standing inside some fantastically strewn bales of silk satin, dousing them in gentle, rosy-pink light. Even at this time of day, the fragrance enveloped them.

Hestia pulled a bloom off its stem and gave it to him; the flower folded coyly in on itself, yet revealed enough of its depths to enchant. He inhaled the scent, and let his fingers explore it, while his eyes devoured the flecks and patterns that made up is colour ways. It had a subtle waxiness across its outer petals, a brushed velvet touch to the under leaves, and a palate of colour that he knew would defy him. He stood in silent exploration of this wonderful thing, while she nodded to him in unspoken accord. Finally, she could keep silent not a minute longer.

"Callard's never seen one! And we showed one of the plantation women and they didn't know it either," she said. "I think it's unknown, and I want it to be called after you. Because it's private and," she shrugged awkwardly, "special."

Seaton had never found himself in an occasion of such a simple approbation of beauty, and also of such unconditional generosity, however sentimental it might seem to some. The screams of men and horses, the explosions, the ricochets, the filth and the madness of war, the private turmoil of wounds and guilt were all undone by this young woman's gift of a delicate and sensual flower, given to him because he was special. To have such a quality ascribed to him, in so truly enchanting a fashion was beyond contemplation. He shook his head feebly, as he grappled for the words.

"Well, do you like it?" she demanded with fond exasperation. "Say something!"

"I'm overwhelmed," he said, thickly. "It's beautiful." He waved a hand to indicate the canyon of coral orchids, the hazy atmosphere and their situation amongst it. "It's the most beautiful thing that's happened to me."

She hugged him fiercely, trapping his hands between them, and pressing even tighter against him, in automatic reaction to this obstacle. He could feel her body hard against his, the soft contours of her breasts, till she stepped back, laughing happily. Then, she dragged a strand of the flowers from the wall of blooms and waggled them at him, "What other woman would find this for you, eh?"

West Sussex

A silvery light from the three-quarter moon filtered through a gap at the side of the thick vicarage curtains and threw a pale aura around the head of the Reverend Attwater, who was sound asleep. He lay on his back, head pressed into a deep lace-trimmed, duck-down pillow, his small hands clutching at the top of the coverlet, as he rumbled stertorously. In sleep, he didn't much resemble

271

his outward, kindly self, his affable countenance being usurped by the expression of an exhausted and accordingly petulant child. He was not an exacting man, albeit rather fastidious in his routines and comforts, but in repose his face developed a somewhat querulous cast. Enid had noted the transition early in their marriage, and was grateful for its reversal in the morning.

Enid was not asleep; she knew wouldn't sleep for some hours yet, if at all. Finally, when she could remain alone with her thoughts no longer, she sat up in bed and rearranged her rucked-up nightdress, so it was both comfortable and, above all, decorous, against the remote possibility that Duncan misunderstood her advances. Then she shook her husband's shoulder, gently at first, and then a little more insistently. "Duncan, I've got to talk to you."

He lifted one hand from the coverlet and made a small gesture with it, as if making a desultory attempt to baptise a baby. "Later," he murmured. "Talk later."

"I can't bear it anymore," she said to him, sincerely, genuinely and without rancour. She looked down on his inert form, framed in silvery light and washed-out vicarage lace. "I'm sorry, but I really can't bear it any more."

Duncan turned on his side, with a small grunt of satisfaction, and pulled the coverlet up to his ear; he pursed his lips a little and snored in a gentle and serene fashion. Enid sank back into her pillows. She would not sigh. She would not cry. She folded her arms, waited for sleep and watched the moonlight wash into the room, to be rendered pale and insipid by the furnishings of the Church's appointed servant.

Chapter Ten

West Sussex

"I have waited long years for this moment, Captain. Does that sound melodramatic? I do hope so."

Houghton-Copley and Ainsley Seaton were seated in a private room within the Cathedral confines, facing each other across a round table which had been sumptuously and intricately appointed with the Cathedral Sevres, complemented by its finest silver and crystal, all set out on snow white damask. The warm summer sun, diffused by the ancient glass in the arched windows, cast whorls of golden light upon the polished wooden floor. A retainer, almost as ancient as the windows, wheeled away the trolley from which he had served them poached salmon, with mayonnaise, asparagus and new potatoes. He positioned the trolley beside the thick oaken door and then left, closing the door behind him. Houghton-Copley poured them both a glass of fine Meursault and continued his opening remarks.

"I think I shall need to explain myself." Seaton raised an eyebrow to this. "By which I mean that, if you are to understand the true purpose of our business here today, you will need a greater understanding of my personal history."

The Captain took in the room again, the panelled walls, the indifferent portraits in oils, dark and anonymous, the heavy mahogany cupboard, the side table upon which rested his hat and gloves. There was no sign of his papers anywhere.

"I've spent my professional and, indeed, my entire adult life in or close to centres of absolute power." The diplomatist surveyed his salmon with complacent approval. "I have been party to the secret mechanisms of what passes itself off as the natural order of things. From

273

your limited exposure, I'm sure you will accept such power relies on confidences, discretions and exclusions to sustain its primacy over those who are deemed to remain 'not in the know'. In return, it conveys upon its confidantes a protected status outside the ostensible workings of society."

"That, of course, is pleasant enough. Although, not without its price. One develops a taste for, let's us call it, privileged access to matters not commonly or generally known. Do I say 'a taste'? Perhaps I mean 'a hunger'. For I confess to deriving enormous personal satisfaction from being privy to the secret considerations of the powerful. I must stress that however esoteric, exotic or even illicit these matters appear to be, my interest is purely academic; in these realms, ethical considerations would be both pedestrian and redundant. Yet, unlike any academic, I have no desire to publish; I am simply content to know." He threw Seaton the familiar avuncular beam, peering over his spectacles and appearing in this action to have aged about twenty years. "One of my little foibles."

"Uncertainties, mysteries and doubts, is that it?" Seaton queried, with barely suppressed disbelief. The man operated in the shadows, that much was clear, but glossing his murky operations as some genial exercise in academic curiosity was all too absurd. "I would have thought a diplomatist had to be more level-headed."

"Oh, spare us the tubercular midget, Captain." Houghton-Copley bristled with an uncharacteristic irritation at the association, and Seaton saw, at once, the man was talking with a level of seriousness he had not witnessed before. "The confidential matters I deal with are not some paltry obscurantism. The fate of governments rest upon their outcomes; innumerable lives; financial interests on a worldwide scale; the future

274

wellbeing of nations."

"Surely, as a churchman, your first duty of care would be to their souls?"

"Perhaps I'm here to help you with yours." The rebuke was sharp and immediate, but when Seaton looked up from the table, where he had been searching for some inkling of how he might withstand the difficulties of the coming hour, he met with only an amiable smile and further exposition.

"As you know, I was tasked some time ago to sift through outrages perpetrated on Anglican and other protestant missions in Bolivia, Brazil, Columbia, and northernmost Peru. There was some talk of ethical horse trading with the Scarlet Woman. We would turn a blind eye. Rome would back-pedal in Kowloon." He shook his head fondly, "All nonsense, of course. But there's nothing like a bishop after lunch for bravado." He replaced his whimsical smile with a new air of narrative purpose. "So I journeyed to Bolivia, largely foregoing Colombia, and finally to Manaos. What a penance that was! What a penchant for dissembling that unhappy continent breeds! Still, I instigated the usual enquiries. I trawled diligently through depositions from survivors, reports bribed from policemen and the military, snippets garnered from hearsay amongst the planters and the rubber depots, riverboat gossip and travellers' tales. But it was you who finally seduced me in the matter."

"Me! Why on earth me?"

"You might call it a blinding coincidence, Captain. Although I choose to see in it, the unmistakeable hand of God, or fate or what have you, in this case operating through my analytical capabilities. You see, the true art of the intelligencer is the adroit collating of information; the collection is mere mechanics, the purview, in the main, of the seedy and the resentful. One looks for connections, one weighs the significance of patterns, one adjudges the significance of random associations. Analytical science or mystic art, I'm never quite sure which. I know it to be both a compulsion and a gift." He smiled with a quiet complacency. "It is my genius, Captain. I say that without any false modesty. And the proof of it is your presence here, today."

"I'm here because you made off with certain papers that belong to me," Seaton reminded him, but he himself could hear the element of bluster in his voice, amplified by his disquiet at the man's undoubted grip on the situation.

The diplomatist ignored this and returned to his peroration. "I had before me a hundred or so cases of such outrages, missions destroyed, pastors mutilated and murdered. All the grisly banality of sectarian and racial violence. But on only one occasion did they coincide with other significant, if circumlocutory, factors. Only once, did a survivor pop up in the custody of an expedition led by a man I knew to engage in projects of a similarly discretionary nature to my own. Moreover, this survivor was to be placed in the personal charge of a man destined to be one of our most renowned war heroes. It intrigues, sir, it intrigues, does it not?"

He topped up their glasses. Seaton noticed the churchman's plate was already empty, the cutlery neatly positioned, awaiting the return of the ancient retainer. He addressed himself to his own, despite a diminishing appetite, and determined to tread carefully with the wine, notwithstanding the dryness in his mouth.

"I stayed on in Manaos, a small thorn in the sides of the Scarlet Woman's myrmidons, ostensibly to consolidate and corroborate my report on the region. I suppose I was, in part, interested to see if anything of a strategic nature could be connected to the Northmore expedition. But in all truth, I was more intrigued by other matters concerning your exploits in the deep forest. As to my primary purpose, I could see there was nothing tangible to be achieved. Was the Pope to be rendered shamefaced by a bevy of senile old gasbags in gaiters, wittering on about the uncorroborated demise of a few Baptists and some other unaffiliated apostates?" Houghton-Copley smiled into his Meursault, took a graceful sip and swallowed. "Hardly be Pope if he was, would he? No, it was the folklore attached to your sojourn beside the Kahuanari that captivated me. I fancy they were singing about you all the way down to the Amazon itself. It really was quite remarkable."

Seaton found himself in strategic dilemma. He had intended to mount an immediate fontal assault, in the name of social decorum, to demand the other return his property immediately and respect his privacy from hereon. He had forced himself to sit out the man's fanciful conversational gambits, in the hope of discovering his true purposes, and the extent of his engagement with past events. However, with every passing moment he was losing the initiative, and his ability to personify some innocent and justly affronted protest at Houghton-Copley's duplicity was waning. More than that, he was becoming aware that the man had an almost preternatural familiarity with events he simply cannot have known about. He felt in the grip of an eerie fascination, like a man who has stepped on a mine but has yet to trigger the detonation.

Houghton-Copley seemed in expansive mood. "Stories travel vast distances in that forest, Captain Seaton. Events become narratives which are, in turn, converted into myths. And they roam far and wide. Year upon year, ever further. Myths and monsters in the guise of spells, chants, games and dances. Long ago and far away is always with us. You, yourself, have seen the dances. Well, years later I heard the chants."

"Were you aware..?" The diplomatist began eagerly, but then pulled himself up. "No, of course you can't be, forgive me. But, following your departure from the region, there were reports of local Indians refusing to wear European dresses handed out to them by mission fathers. Women and girls, normally either docile or appreciative in the matter, refused point blank to wear them. The missionaries would insist. They would refuse. In some cases, they would disappear to the forest immediately. The reason? They believed them to be sacrificial garments. Blood rites were spoken of. Propitiations by white men. Violations. Deaths by strangulation and drowning." He smiled broadly. "Quite magnificent, don't you think?"

Seaton put down his knife and fork. There would be no occasion for protest from now on; it was now a matter of simple denial, maintained as quietly and as staunchly as it could be. "I cannot connect the Northmore expedition with foolishness of that sort."

Houghton-Copley held up a hand to beseech his continued attention. "Then I heard about the strangling games enacted at the Gomes station. One Dr Bryan, pastor and medical man there, barely a hundred miles down the Kahuanari from your expedition site, reported the Witoto acting out the strangulation of a white woman, in this case a young man attired for the purpose in a mission dress, taken temporarily from one of their own. There is much singing about lewd matters, common enough in such rites, I believe, and then the boy is strangled, in pantomime, and thrown into the river. As a bride, mark you," he waved a fork excitedly in the air, "for the caimans."

"No explanations forthcoming, of course. But, any

allusion to the violent death of white woman, I felt, had to be germane. Especially one broadcast so widely and for so long. Of course, I'd heard there'd been the tragedy at the end of your expedition, itself shrouded in secrecy. I knew you to be removed suddenly, extremely unwell and, indeed, fortunate to survive the journey down river. And I was piqued, Captain, beyond any previous fascination, I can quite assure you."

"So, I did nothing but report inconclusively to their lordships and return to this country to continue my researches. My own private researches." Houghton-Copley moved across to a bell rope hanging beside the windows and gave it one firm tug. "I read all the published accounts of the Northmore expedition, down to every claw mark and beetle dropping of Munby's exhaustive notes. Northmore's grandiose pontifications. Cotterill's roustabouts on the chase. And that's when I discovered your delightful vocabularies. Piquant! At last, I thought, something to get one's teeth into. But slim pickings, really. The terminology of savage fornication. A few choice lines of dialogue for scenes as yet unstaged. Wouldn't do at all."

The ancient retainer arrived at the door again, this time carrying Houghton-Copley's blue leather portfolio. The churchman took it from him and closed the door in his face. "We have a fruit salad awaiting us. It'll keep." He said by way of a hurried explanation.

He strode over to the table, piled up all the Cathedral Sevres, crystal, silver, even the cut flower centrepiece to one side and started to pull out drawing after drawing and laying them in front of Seaton. "But then I talked to the old booby himself, and he led me onto these."

The first scattering were studies of Indian woman, two straining to lift a pumpkin, the sinews in their thighs

279

taut, their backs arched, one with her sex in careless display, then others, less dynamic but equally intimate, bathing by the river, nursing infants, twisting the cassava squeezer, dancing singly and in line, slumped across hammocks, bending over fires and cookpots. "Such glowering physicality! Such a sensuality of line!" cried Houghton-Copley. "My dear Captain, you were simply besieged by the erotic!"

Seaton pushed them around, trying to recall their inception, for the most part receiving mere glimmerings of association, but behind them was a presentiment of something he had yet to recognise. Houghton-Copley produced another sheaf with a flourish. "Then there's this marvellous detailing. Look at this wonderful hair, matted with sweat into the nape of... an Okaina girl, I presume? And this breast barely glimpsed through the armpit of a woman. What was she wielding? A machete?"

"A hoe, very probably," Seaton's reply was toneless. "Or their rough equivalent, at least."

"Now, this is delightful." The diplomatist was holding it at arm's length, and peering at it over his glasses. "A collar bone and the barest intimation of breasts, with that patina of heat and moisture upon them and only just contained by with some lace trimmed garment." He turned the drawing around so that the Captain could see it. "Some European item, wouldn't you say? And hardly a mission handout. Such fine lacework, and captured so meticulously. Perhaps not entirely fashionable, but definitely lingerie, rather than a mere nether garment." He favoured Seaton with a winsome smile. "Am I to deduce Miss Williams, here?" He shuffled through several others as if in a series. "This ear must be hers, surely, with a little earring like that. And this stretched cambric across a ribcage, with the curve of the hip beneath. And these haunches sitting so daintily on

280

that bench, with her canvas bag so neatly beside her. All snatched from life, in secret, eh Captain? Such a roving eye!" He returned to the colour sketch of the lace-fringed décolleté. "But this I think is my favourite of this series."

"I drew everything around me," Seaton took the drawing from him and studied it, or rather affected to study it. He could smell the straw and honey scent coming off her, sense the ever-present movement of hand to hair, plucking, teasing and rearranging, then pulling at the straps of her camisole, smoothing it around her ribs or adjusting it above the jut of her breasts, against the humidity of the day, and then flapping with distracted irritation at the ever-present flies; she had been so animated that day. After the tobacco palaver, when she'd heard the Okaina's proposal for his bride-to-be. The life was gone from the line, but it hovered around the assembly. She had groaned and chattered and laughed and disapproved and scorned, all by way of disguising her jealousy. Yes, at the heart of it, the woman in her had already staked some atavistic claim for precedence. Her rising voice, her rising chest had let him know directly.

He realised the diplomatist had stopped talking. The man was standing back and looking at him expectantly and holding a final cluster of drawings to his waistcoat. "And so to our crowning glory," he breathed excitedly and dealt them out across the table, as if they were playing some eccentric game of baccarat. "Your floral interiors, I like to call them. Bromeliads. Epidendras, Cuscia. So intimate, so lovingly precise and all so remarkably human. Take this one," He snatched it up and stared fondly at it. "I'm no expert but I looked it up in every reference I could find in the Botanical Society's library." He noticed Seaton's start of surprise." Oh, there's none like me when I'm on a scent, Captain. No detail too small, no nook too obscure, I will search everywhere. But, as I said, I drew blank with this. I call it the flower vagina. Almost human; such subtle colouring, such shading. A medical man would call it a remarkable coincidence. But more than that, though, Captain? From the life? From memory? From wild surmise?"

Even as Seaton struggled for breath, he attempted to give no indication of the new tightness in his chest. He took the drawing from Houghton-Copley and attempted to give the appearance of an unemotional appraisal. He couldn't quite recall the making of it. It may possibly have been some exercise between his growing apprehension of the reproductive imperative of nature and his fascination with the exotic, flooding in unbidden about him. A nocturnal study, to articulate in some form the preoccupations his own nature was imposing on him. He could not recall its making, but he knew it to be a precursor. Harbinger or handmaiden, it accompanied a darker representation still.

Houghton-Copley put his hand inside his coat and drew out a wallet; Seaton was in some measure surprised to see that, far from being his characteristic cornflower blue, it was a deep burnished mahogany colour. The churchman opened it carefully and extracted a sheet of ragged paper folded in half. This, in turn, he opened with great delicacy and held out to the Captain. He introduced it with a quiet confidence. "And then there is this, Captain Seaton. Loose-leafed in your journal. Of which we shall speak more anon. Although I must congratulate you, straight away, on such exquisitely tormented prose." He gave one of his airy waves, unnoticed by the Captain who stared motionless at the small sheet of paper before him. "Such evocations of hunger and desire. Such a relentless need, amongst the implacable confusion of nature. Baudelaire, Rimbaud, they pale before you. Who'd have thought it?"

He set the sheet in Seaton's hands, leaned in upon him, paused and then announced with firm conviction, "This is for me your finest work. In the whole canon of your truly intimate studies. The sensuality is overwhelming. Such concision. Such power in so few lines. The dashes of colour, just enough to stabilise the essential symmetry. The textures, from sponge to satin. The implicit warmth. The moist, salty landscape of passion." He tapped the tiny coloured sketch and affected a sincerely puzzled expression "Did you not say that the Okaina depilated? Well, these delicious tufts are blonde, are they not?"

North-west Amazon

It was as though he was seeing them for the first time. Recognition vied with fascination as he turned over each sketch and held it up to the pallid glow of the kerosene lamp. The open trunk lay beside the bed, where Seaton had dragged it out. He sat on the bed itself, pulling out papers from it and sifting through them, not quite accepting what he was looking at, though, with some discomfort, he found himself anticipating the shamefaced treasures at the bottom of them all.

Outside, the Okaina were dancing. They had been dancing for hours now and, if their preparations and number were anything to go by, they could well be dancing for days. The perpetual rhythms of their drums and the mesmeric repetitions of their sonorous chanting forged one preternatural cadence. At first, it had reminded him of the ceaseless churning of the huge engines on the steamer carrying his regiment to South Africa; the hypnotic regularity of directed power that vibrated though the decks with their own insuperable sense of purpose. Here, with the flutes and pan pipes that laced in and out of the tempo, and the occasional hoarse cries that counterpointed it, there was something about the incessant drumbeat that held a primal imperative over his consciousness.

The moon was full, while bonfires and innumerable torches lit up the treeline and the Maloka in fine relief from ground up, so that the night blended from silver into old gold. Through this precious mist, the drums and chanting bewailed the eternal struggle of man. It may have been a celebration, he didn't know, but it sounded fatalistic, melancholy and somewhat ghoulish. He had retired to his room, bidding Hestia goodnight, and turned to his private collection for some kind of balance to the brooding power of the music, the painted, circling bodies and the stamping feet in the forest

His heart was palpitating in a cadence not dissimilar to the complex pounding of the Okaina drums, and beneath their singing, he could track the sibilance venturing to take over the hearing in his left ear. When he had sat back on the bed from dragging out the trunk, he had felt the blackness sweep though his brain and had willed himself to sit upright till it passed. He was determined not to succumb tonight. Once he had finished reviewing these personal works, he would dose himself with Warburg's tincture, the bottle of which stood on the small chest of drawers on the opposite wall.

His focus was swimming slightly as he scanned the drawings in his hands. They were attempts to capture the radiance of the orchid Hestia had found for him. Seaton's orchid, she liked to call it, or *orchis seatonis*, which she pronounced with Munby's clipped Lancastrian gravitas, the likeness captured to perfection. The likeness of the orchid itself had somehow escaped Seaton. Each time he managed to construct the right balance of light descriptive line with intricate blends and combinations of soft shades and colours, he found some other primordial configuration taking possession. In the early stages this had manifested itself as a delicate usurpation of the soft pinks by the flush of skin tones and textures, till the inner petals palpated with arousal. As things progressed, the outlines themselves changed, the stamens distended, the petals and leaves stretched out in yearning and welcome, until finally what he saw within and beneath each writhing composition, was the open mouthed wonder of the human vulva.

These he discarded soon after their production and moved onto settings with the blooms in more modest if still feminine surroundings, as if by this change of composition, he could ameliorate the seductive power of the plant. He drew out sketches of *orchis seatonis* nestling in tresses above the collar bone of an unknown woman, then welling up from her cleavage, then a wreath of blooms encircling an anonymous breast, the stamens subtly echoing the swollen nipple and, finally, a coy rendition of a solitary bloom emerging snugly from between pale white thighs, its complimentary colours and soft outline fusing with the host body, a fig leaf that served to accentuate rather than conceal.

After that, he had dispensed with the flower altogether, and produced some reverently traced studies of the genital flower of a not so anonymous but still innocent woman. When he looked at these, he felt a sense of rapture rather than sensual release. Even though they remained necessarily concealed, he could not think of them as erotic or, and he felt a griping nausea over the word, pornographic. Nothing was further from the truth. They formed the initial workings towards a paean, an approach to understanding the final and intimate beauty.

Nonetheless he felt ill at ease, embarrassed by his preoccupations here. Indeed, he had tucked these explicit pictures away in a journal he'd brought along for more

285

general observations, but which had only just turned to. He was a soldier, not a monk. An artist, not an aesthete. He was a man and had done what other men described as manly things. Why then, this sense of unease and incipient shame, now he was moving towards a finer and closer understanding of the elements comprising and provoking true and vibrant sensuality? He was immersed yet again in this debate when, amongst the ceaseless percussion of the Okaina, he detected another more staccato rhythm, that of somebody drumming on his screen door and, pulling himself from his deliberations, he found it to be Hestia.

"Can I come in?" There was urgency in her voice.

"Give me a moment," he called back, looking round at the drawings on his bed and at his feet. He scrabbled to pull them into some order, so he could throw them into the trunk and conceal it beneath the bed, without making such a galumphing noise that would alert her to his activities.

She was already in the room before he was half way there, and found him, flustered, leaning over the box, trying to secrete his work without actually damaging it. She sat down heavily on the bed beside him, and picked up the one drawing he had overlooked.

"I got a bit scared!" she smiled brightly, and then looked down at the drawing in her hand, "What's this? Your orchid?"

He tried to keep his movements calm and steady, and looked down over shoulder, his mind running through an endless sequence of unsatisfactory explanations, each more transparent than the last. To his partial relief, she was holding one of the earlier orchid colour sketches, where the distortions were still minor, though for him, the carnal echoes were all too visible. Hestia studied it closely before speaking. "I think you've done better ones." She handed it back to him and leaned over the trunk, her eyes alight with curiosity. "Have you got more in there?"

Seaton took the drawing, slipped it in with the others and shut down the trunk lid firmly. "These are my rejects. Far too embarrassing to show anybody."

"Oh, come on!" she laughed lightly. "They can't be all that bad!"

"Worse," he replied, forcing a casual grin, as he slid the trunk back under his bed. "If I thought you'd like them I'd show you, but they're best forgotten, I'm afraid."

Hestia sat on her hands, scuffed her toe on the floor in front of her, and showed no signs of moving. "It's all that, going on, just over the way. Doesn't feel right."

"We're quite safe," reassured Seaton. "If that's what's worrying you. They're not remotely interested in us."

"Not anymore," she gave him a significant smile.

Callard had averted the gift of a woman to Seaton by advising the chief, through a man in the tobacco palaver, which was then in its tenth hour, that Hestia, though young and not active in the kitchens or in the field, was in fact Seaton's wife. This had caused some comment and some hilarity. What kind of man took a useless girl into his household? An eifoke, of course, said the father of the child who'd witnessed Seaton bathing. One of the women asked another how they could be certain she was useless, when she might be a witch. This possibility was discounted, due to the apparent low status of Hestia within the white company, which was out of keeping with the natural status of the shaman in any tribe.

The chief, not wishing to see an issue he had advocated before the tobacco palaver fail in such short order, suggested Seaton might enjoy a supplementary wife, for plantation and cooking chores, while his white wife continued to do for him whatever it was she actually did. Callard deflected this with a reference to Hestia's jealousy and primacy as first wife. This domestic situation was clearly familiar to the chief, for having congratulated the palaver on their generosity of spirit, and regretting the impossibility of acting upon it, he drew proceedings to a halt.

So, Seaton and Hestia were married in the eyes of the Okaina, and the Captain could remain safely unattached. When they had first learned of Callard's diplomatic coup, Hestia found it intensely amusing and asked the Captain if he intended to give her charge of all the household accounts. He was rather put out by his summary conjugal status, particularly at the thought of what capital Cotterill and Munby would make out of it at his expense, on their eventual return. He only hoped it wouldn't be bruited further than the Igara Parana, then realised he was sounding like some old West Sussex aunt, all decorum and half closed curtains. Some men had been made Gods by the indigents amongst whom they had lived, some crowned kings and some elected holy men. He had been married. At first, Hestia received some reproachful looks from some of the elder women when she passed them working in the plantations, singing her songs and swinging her arms, but soon her marital derelictions were relegated into the all-encompassing mystery of the white men, and thereafter ignored.

Okaina man and wife, they sat side by side on the bed, listening to the celebrations outside maintain their momentum. Seaton looked down at his hands, and waited for his own internalised gyrations to settle down. Hestia, perhaps relinquishing any hope of her equilibrium outlasting the intoxication crashing about them from the

Maloka, shivered and stood up. She paced up and down the room, arms folded, striving to ignore that which would not be ignored, then with a kind of desperate jollity she rounded on him, "Well, if you're not going to show me your stupid pictures, what are we going to do? I'm not going back to my room. You can't leave me on my own with this going on! It's not fair."

He stood up and looked through the screens covering his window. The pulse beating in his throat resonated with the liquid bass of the Okaina's great hardwood drum, and in their common vibration a natural synergy was disclosed to him. Out there was life, healthier, more vital and, above all, more natural than anything mulching and festering in his introspections, it was magical and uplifting, if only he would allow his sensibilities to appreciate it. There was a dance outside, both exotic and familial, and beyond that a glorious profusion of night blooms in all their glory.

"Show me your rotten old pictures. Go on," she wheedled, although he could sense this request was made out of dissatisfaction with the present arrangement rather than any real desire to pry. Prying would be a suitable alternative though, if she were afforded no other entertainment.

Seaton remembered Munby talking of how some orchids were pollinated only by night, how they intensified their fragrance to attract the pollinators and how, from this, the legend arose that they opened their petals to the moonlight. There was a full moon tonight, perhaps not altogether coincidentally, given the Okaina's meticulous preparation for their ritual celebration. It was moonlight that owned this night, not shadows and threats. "Why don't you go and put your shoes on?" he suggested in a tone which, though cheerful, brooked no argument. "We can take a little walk."

"You're being silly," she scoffed nervously. "We can't go out there."

His mind was made up to 'go out there'. With that, came a fresh resolve to prevail over the darkness and the fever that threatened to envelope him. "Why not? It's a lovely night. We shall see some wonderful things."

She looked out through the screens towards the haze of the bonfires and torches, and the trees luminescent in the moonlight; he could see she was affected by the uncommon beauty of the night, but not yet won over.

While she peered outside, he pulled a jacket on, slipping his pistol unobtrusively into the pocket, talking to her all the while, "I'm not talking about the dance, Hestia. Though, God knows, that'll be a sight to see." He moved over towards her. "I'm talking about some of the orchids. There are stories that their leaves open at night. And because they're pollinated by moths and night-fliers, their fragrance is at its strongest now. The Okaina believe they're in touch with the spirits."

She chewed ruminatively at the inside of her cheek, peering out between the screens and then turning back to him, still unsure but now intrigued and, he sensed, willing to be excited by the prospect.

"Moonlight, orchids in full bloom, legends and magic, heady perfumes on the night air," he laughed. "Where's the romance in you? Thought you girls were all for that sort of thing."

"Do you think your orchid will be open now?" She was smiling, rather proprietarily, at the thought.

"How else are we going to find out?" He shrugged and looked at her.

"I won't be a moment," she said, and dashed from the room. "Wait there, won't you?"

Seaton breathed out slowly and relaxed against the chest of drawers. They were moving away from the trunk beneath his bed, and out towards the healthier concupiscence of orchid and moth. He took a swig of the Warburg's tincture to tide him over and stepped out onto the veranda. Hestia was out of her room in seconds, her canvas shoes laced, pinning up her hair, a hairclip between her teeth as she talked, "I bet they are, orchis seatonis. I bet they're down there behaving disgracefully!"

When they arrived at the dancing ground, Seaton was taken aback by the number of people involved. Many must have walked in from homes in the forest that were days away. A large group of spectators spread along the outer wall of the Maloka, watching the two long concentric circles of dancers. The outer, a broken circle, was made up of men, in their wild adornments of feathers and beads. Each man held a jingling dance-pole, with which he beat the ground as he stamped out the measure. The poles were decorated with calabashes full of seeds that rattled and jangled along with the flutes and pipes. Within the outer, broken circle was a smaller circle of the women, which progressed in the opposite direction. The women, naked and painted in variations of scarlet, white, purple and black, were lit up by the flames of the bonfire and the flickering torches; the patterns on their skin, which he himself had replicated, were now cast into glistening costume. A few wore beaded corsets for the occasion but, to Seaton, nothing matched the splendour of the multicoloured mazes the women had applied to their limbs and torsos.

The tall white feathers fixed to the men's heads and shoulders lashed silver white in the moonlight and their bodies, picked out in white and black pointillism, brought a lunar, cooler dynamism to the warm, fecund, earth tones of the women. The flames, smoke and embers mingled with the swathes of moonlight and the earth shook with the beat of the drums and the stamping of the

Okaina's feet, as the song progressed. They were singing a refrain, started by the women and answered by the men, something to do with the chief's manioc and his wife's cassava squeezer, which played out its mild eroticism in endless calls and responses. At some appropriate point, one of the men would produce a call from their exceptional repertoire of bird and animal imitations, which echoed with the roundelay off the trees surrounding the settlement, and spread out into the darker recesses of the forest, where even the moonlight and the aerial fire embers could not permeate.

The whole earth seemed alive and interconnected. When Seaton felt Hestia's hand slip into his own and squeeze it, it seemed purely an extension of the intermingling to which they were witness. He turned to her and saw she was looking up to him with a broad grin. "Hear that?" she asked, "They're singing about you, now."

He listened to the refrain and, sure enough, the word 'eifoke' was being repeated and played with. The women added something about 'ei hidobe' and this was taken up with great relish, the sentiment being investigated, repeated, conjectured upon, advanced and then toyed with again. Always the words 'eifoke', 'ei' and 'hidobe' swapping between the circles as the great drums pounded on. Hestia was seized by a fit of the giggles and started to swing his hand with hers, as though to pump herself back to good behaviour.

"What are they saying now?" What on earth could be that funny? Perhaps some further indelicate description of himself, now to be enjoyed by Hestia.

"I'm your little monkey wife!" she gasped with delight, and then translated each phrase quickly and approximately, as the Indians circled and sang "The turkey buzzard he has married. He has married a

'Hidobe' – little monkey. 'Ei' is wife. What will she feed him? Which tree will they live in? Will their children have... fur or feathers?"

Not for one moment did the Okaina look at the subjects of their refrain. Yet there was an implicit welcome in everything they were doing, in the gentle mockery and the mild, almost disinterested censure. They were folding this strange, white couple into their tribal community by their very inclusion in the song, and that must be enough.

"Wonder what they'll make of us wandering off to the river," said Seaton. The Okaina refrained from any amatory activity inside the Maloka, preferring the discretion of the forest, and he felt a regrettably staid impulse to withdraw his hand from Hestia's. Any hesitancy on his part was robustly overwhelmed on her part, as she gripped his hand tighter than ever, held it down to her side and laughed at him.

"Not going to stop for a lot of village gossip, are we?" she said and, turning from the dance, she set off for the waterside beyond the plantations, pulling him along after her. "Come on, I want to smell those flowers!"

They ran, she lightly and he breathlessly, down towards the treeline surrounding the plantations. Seaton was beginning to regret he hadn't brought a lantern. He hoped the narrow paths they were about to plunge into would be aligned to allow a modicum of moonlight. He didn't want either of them breaking an ankle or stirring up a sleeping peccary or any of the numberless dangers that awaited the unwary jungle traveller at night.

The perpetual drumming accompanied them, not seeming to fade with distance, and the moonlight, freed from the haze of wood-smoke and resinous torches, cast an eerie clarity on the forest around him. His eyes were drawn to the details of the fibres in the lianas, the patterns on the tree bark, the veins of the leaves, even the scuff marks in the path beneath him, and he knew, with the return of this meticulous detail, that he had not outrun the bout that awaited him. As his awareness leapfrogged, the dank and torpid smell of the forest rose up to meet him. Sight, sound, smell; that only left touch and taste, until he felt the hot, insistent clamminess of Hestia's hand, each beat of her pulse resounding through the primeval comfort of her sweat mingling with his. With his free hand, he tapped at the side pocket of his jacket for the Warburg's and founded only the lumpen mass of his pistol. The dancing might mask the sibilance in his ears, the moonlight offset the impending darkness, but the overload was waiting for him, unless somehow he could manage, through skill or willpower, to outflank it.

In the meantime, there was Hestia's carefree laughter and the orchids. She stopped and turned to him, as the treeline loomed over them, to announce carelessly, "I'm old enough to marry, you know." She watched him catching his breath before adding, "Mr Kettering said he'd wait for me. And that was two years ago."

Seaton felt a spasm of irritation, whether with her, Mr Kettering or himself he wasn't at all clear. He drew in a lungful of warm night air and waited for his heartbeat to settle, before replying, "I hope he's a patient man."

"Who?" She looked perplexed, as she wiped her forehead with the back of her hand; the other hand still had firm hold of Seaton's.

"Kettering," replied Seaton, finding himself strangely agitated. "Two years is a long time out here. How patient was he about his player piano?"

"Not very," said Hestia, and then she brought her concentration fully onto the conversation. "Why should I worry, anyway? He was only a boy."

She looked hard at him, as if he had missed

something he was supposed to understand, and that it was a disappointment to her. He smiled sheepishly, thinking she had sensed the stirrings of some ridiculous and juvenile jealousy in him. Whether that was the case or not, she appeared to take his smile as some kind of apology, and with her normal mercurial change of mood, jumped up at him, kissed him clumsily on the cheek and called out, "Come on, Captain! You're supposed to show me your orchids!"

With that, she set off at the canter again, and they plunged into the tracks beyond the plantation, that led in tortuous disarray down to the river, where the forest and the night engulfed them.

West Sussex

"What is your business with me? I can be no part of your," Seaton struggled to find a suitable word to reflect his distaste, but had to settle for the prosaic, "diplomatic procedures, clearly."

He had waited for the ancient retainer to restore the lunch table to its working glory, remove the debris of the poached salmon and leave them with a large crystal bowl of fruit salad, a Queen Ann creamer brimming with double cream, and a glass of Muscat apiece. The old man had taken forever, which is what Seaton thought the diplomatist had intended when he had suddenly gone to the bell pull to summon him. Anything to unnerve and destabilise. The diplomatist, for his part, had sat upright and stared at the Captain with an unwavering serenity, as the old man retrieved the used crockery and reset the table, moving the piles of drawings as discreetly as he might. Only once the man finally had shut the door behind him, did Houghton-Copley address himself to the Captain's protestation.

"We have no business together at all, Captain. Not

in any formal sense." He sat up suddenly, brushed at his lap with his napkin, folded it and placed it in front of him, beside his untouched fruit salad, and then sat back in his chair. "In fact, you might say I am here in a private capacity. A very private capacity indeed. We are dealing with very personal matters here, are we not? An affair with fatal consequences."

Seaton gripped the table and breathed deeply; the old ferric tang dispelled in an instant, he was pleased to note. He wasn't quite finished yet; he would not simply fragment under this man's disturbed and disturbing attentions, though his disorientation was debilitating, he had to admit. The years of private reckoning had taken their toll and now, with Houghton-Copley's manipulations compounded by Dr Richardson's chloral, he was forcibly reminded of the exhaustion and the struggle he had undergone during the last thrashings of his fever, before Munby and Hestia Williams had dragged him to the surface. Once again, he resolved to hold on. Whether he would prevail was now of no consequence, he had to find out what he was involved in.

"Get on with it." He looked Houghton-Copley directly in the eye. "Whatever you have in mind, just get on with it. And be damned."

Houghton-Copley's eyes widened at this. Indeed, his whole demeanour changed to that of a deeply wounded man, determined to maintain his composure. "Captain, you misjudge me dreadfully. Do you think me vulgar enough to affect some kind of public disclosure?" He stood and paced about the table rubbing his hands in some agitation. "Nothing could be further from my mind, I assure you. You might deem it a matter of Christian charity." He gave the phrase great emphasis. Then, he stopped pacing, dropped his hands to his sides, turned to the Captain and said with commanding simplicity, "I wish to see you at peace with yourself. To free you from your terrible isolation. Can you not envisage what a blessing it would be, to break out of that wretched cocoon of yours?" He shook his head in sad appreciation, "How unhealthy it must be for you in there. How lonely it must have been for you, in sole charge of that devastating memory, and how mortifying to stay so alone."

He pulled his chair up beside Seaton's, sat upon it and laid a hand upon the Captain's arm. "Well, now you have me to share your travail, and you'll soon see how quickly your heavy chains will drop from you. Once you have unburdened yourself, the truth can no longer afflict you, my friend." He nodded earnestly. "I am your friend. Who else do you know who has taken such a close interest in your suffering? Treat me as your confessor if you will, but assuredly as your friend. Simply, tell me what happened to you. Everything that happened to you, back then."

Seaton stared at the drawings, the orchid pudenda uppermost on the heap. The sunlight through the leaded windows picked out the highlights he had so delicately traced in the golden tufts fringing the delicate folds of pink, peach, coral and warm grey. How could he put any of this into words? How could it possibly travel from tantalisation intimation, the first tingling approaches of some primal tsunami in which love took on a rapacity beyond all civilised constraint, to the coarsest interchange of some prurient social transaction? How could he place that most fragile flower in the churchman's porcine grasp?

"I shall come and see you tomorrow. At Highleigh. We can go through it all together. The incident." Houghton-Copley moistened his lips and proceeded with assurance and purpose. "We can review the past, to expunge it. Excise the demons. Put everything in context. We shall look at your drawings with our greater understanding. We might read your journal, together. I've left it in Duncan's vicarage, for safe keeping." He broke off with a mischievous and self-reproachful moue, "Wicked, I know, but irresistible at the time." Before gathering himself to assure the Captain, "I'll pick it up on my way."

He walked over to the mahogany cupboard and opened it. It appeared to contain a variety of administrative articles, among them box files, folders, envelopes and letter presses, from which he selected a large cardboard folder. He measured it by eye and returned to the table with it. Then he gathered up the drawings, placed them carefully in the folder and handed it to the Captain, together with a twinkle that was disconcerting in its apparent sincerity. "Here, Captain, as a gesture of my good faith. I shall return your journal, the last of your property, once you have relieved yourself of your story. I shall retain a private edition. Unsigned." He tapped his heart. "Locked in here, for no other man's eyes. And you shall be free."

"I really can't begin to understand you," replied Seaton. With a firm grip on the folder, he stood up and went to retrieve his hat and gloves from the table by the door. "Let alone accommodate you in what you ask."

"You can and you will, Captain." The diplomatist smiled broadly as he accompanied Seaton to the door. "Think of it. An hour or two's gentle reminiscence, in an entirely sympathetic ear, I assure you, and then the whole thing thrown behind you. For good and all. It'll be such a weight off your mind, believe me."

He watched the Captain walk off down the corridor with that subtly lopsided gait of his, disappearing into pools of darkness and emerging into swathes of sunlight, as he passed by the arched windows, looking out onto the cathedral grounds. "I shall be with you by noon!" the diplomatist called brightly, but insistently.

The Captain gave no evidence of hearing him, but even the pigeons outside had gone up at the noise.

~~~~~

Dr Richardson had to concede that things may have passed off better had he not allowed himself to be inveigled inside the Tun and Pipe for a glass of cider. He had been on his way to the village hall where the fete reconciliations were taking place. It was a hot day and Larry Poulter was sitting at one of the two outside bench tables, with Sam Faring, and both had cooling drafts of cider in front of them. Faring's wife was a staunch support of his practice, and Larry Poulter's would one day, no doubt, have to be, so the doctor accepted the invitation and all three men trooped inside. One thing led to another, two of Faring's acquaintances turned up from Wittering, amusing chaps it must be said, and so it was some time later that he made his way over to the village hall. By now, he had a slight headache impinging on his sense of general wellbeing, and no inkling that his wife had taken it upon herself to help out with the arts and crafts committee, by checking their totals, and comparing them with Enid Attwater's overall fete accounts. Both factors, he later felt, had proved disastrous.

Enid was sitting at the table lately at the disposal of the Scouts, now piled high with notebooks, envelopes with banknotes and teetering piles of coins. She was checking the piles of coins against totals already inscribed by her husband, who was fretting above her. "It's almost all coins, this year," he sighed. "We'll have to get a boy to carry it all to the bank."

"Too many ha'pennies by half!" Clover called over from where she and Ursula were painstaking dismantling her display, interleafing each item between plain sheets of paper and setting them inside one of her larger presses, itself decorated with Chinese motifs. "Tight-fisted, the lot of them."

Ursula, in a Chinese print trouser suit and wide-brimmed straw hat, was gingerly rubbing some fingerprints off one of the Judaic texts with an India rubber. She gave an angry toss of her head, her hat stabilising itself like a billowing sail. "This looks like chocolate. Some ghastly child's been wiping his paws all over it."

The Reverend Attwater chose that moment to walk across to the art and crafts committee, seated up on the small stage in a circle of chairs, exchanging envelopes and accounts, with Nancy Richardson presiding. "Ladies, dear ladies!" he called. "And how are we getting along?"

"There was some confusion," announced Nancy. "But we are all resolved now, I believe."

What the rest of her circle thought remained unclear, for at that moment, Dr Richardson entered the hall, hands in his pockets and whistling "Lilibullero", and walked with steadfast purpose down to the far wall where Captain Seaton's drawing hung. Having satisfied himself it was still there, he turned to the general company, whilst pulling his wallet from an inside pocket, and announced genially, "Afternoon all. Come to settle up. Two guineas, I believe."

"Colin!" Nancy's voice cut across the hall, querulous, commanding and just a touch uncertain. His heart sunk nonetheless and he turned to face the judgement of the court. He had bought Seaton's Okaina fishers both on impulse and on principle. The impulsive element arose from a sudden desire to support the man in his vulnerable stance before the shallow and vacillating good opinion of Highleigh society. The principle was his ensuing wish to show them he was a freethinking man above their petty scandalmongering, even if it meant investing two hard-earned guineas. He had elected to forget that in order to demonstrate his principles to Highleigh he had also to demonstrate them to his wife. Now, he was reminded.

"What on earth are you doing?" She had not moved from the stage, but stood amongst the art and crafts

300

committee, her hands clasped before her, awaiting his abject supplication.

"I've just bought the Captain's picture," he attempted. "Nice piece of work. Good cause. Go rather nicely in…"

"Don't be ridiculous," she cut him off. "Withdraw your offer at once."

He chose to ignore the peremptory tone she was using to him in front of the same public he had intended to confound with his independent principles, but chose a more strategic objection, "Well, I can hardly leave the vicar in the lurch now, can I?"

"Sam Faring was showing an interest in it," an arts and crafts committee stalwart informed Nancy, disparagingly.

"I dare say," Nancy replied bleakly, and then her fury got the better of her. "It's outrageous."

Clover put down her portfolio and walked across to the stage. "What's wrong with it? It's a wonderful piece of observation."

Nancy gave the arts and crafts committee her long-suffering look, before snapping back, "All very well for some of us to vaunt our bohemian inclinations to the heavens. But there is no place in decent society for nature run riot. However clever you might think it."

Ursula pulled at Clover's sleeve, with a stage-whispered, "Don't tangle with decent society, Clovy. You might catch something."

"Highleigh is not the jungle, Miss Maitland." Though incensed by Ursula's intervention, Nancy refused steadfastly to acknowledge her. "We cannot have perverse carnality of this sort."

"It's a hunting scene!" protested the doctor. "Every drawing room in the area is dripping with them." The neatness of the observation empowered him to continue, "It is very much to my taste, as a countryman. I should like it in my surgery. And I intend to buy it."

"I am accustomed to your throwing your money away on drink," Nancy replied with some asperity, "but I will not permit you to purchase that deviant monstrosity, simply to spite me."

Dr Richardson weighed the meaning of what she had exposed to their neighbours. His mouth opened and closed. He needed to consider his position here, but nothing quite made sense, precisely when he needed it to.

"It's the children, isn't it?" Clover cried in amazement. "The drawings of the children. You haven't even seen them, and you've stirred up all this scandal."

"I have stirred up nothing," replied Nancy icily. "But I'm happy to say I know what behaviour is suitable and what is not."

"It was a generous donation," The Reverend Attwater offered in mediation. "If perhaps not altogether suitable."

"Suitable!" Enid blazed at the table, surprising them all; Dr Richardson began to think this wasn't going to be quite the one-sided massacre he had anticipated. Enid turned hotly on her husband. "What do you know about art?" She pointed at the remnants of the art exhibition, hanging limply on the wall, waiting to be reclaimed by their creators. "Loopy cows and badly drawn apples? Is that your art, Duncan?" She shook with a sudden irritation. "Art is not suitable. Don't you know that?"

Attwater looked across at the village paintings. He did not feel qualified to judge, it was true, but he would not have them denigrated. "People put a lot of effort into it, Enid."

"Effort isn't talent, vicar." Ursula pointed out sweetly, and Enid gave her a short grateful glance.

"Art is not suitable. Art is not nice," Enid continued. "Art is about truth and feelings and…" She caught her husband's embarrassed smile and Nancy Richardson's unwavering and condemnatory stare, shook her head and pushed her hair back off her face. "This is going nowhere. I'm reconciled here. All the totals are correct, now. I'm going to organise your dinner."

With that, she stood up, gave the doctor, Clover and Ursula a nod of hard-pressed solidarity and hurried away out of the hall. The arts and crafts committee sat with their hands in their laps, their matronly bosoms heaving. Clover and Ursula returned to packing up their display and Nancy returned to the attack. She addressed her husband, directly and with great emphasis. "Colin, you may not care about discrediting yourself in front of our friends and neighbours, but I will not have that picture in my house. The associations are too shameful." She stamped her foot "The man's a disgrace! Can't you see that?"

Richardson had the sour taste of old cider rising up in his throat. He felt the pain behind his eyes coalesce into one white vortex of blinding light. The true and severe nature of the situation had dawned upon him, and with that realisation, he saw, with utter clarity the full, blinkered injustice of his wife's position. He also saw he had chosen her arena and her audience with her customary acuity. She was surrounded by the like-minded, endorsing and commiserating with her outrage. He flapped a tentative arm to dispel the waves of disapproval beamed at him. "The man painted savages in a jungle. He painted them well. He's been somewhere exotic and kept his eyes open, and brought us back the news. What possible disgrace is there in that? He's a member of the RGS. A war hero. A bloody hero!"

"Come, come," the vicar interrupted hoarsely. "I'm sure nobody meant to suggest…"

Nancy stepped down off the stage and walked towards her husband; she could see he was floundering. He, in turn, was reminded of long-gone classroom terrors, but tried to hold his ground with a shaky simulation of open affability.

"That man's behaviour in that jungle was shameful and unforgiveable. Just like yours is now A little less cider and a little more thought, and you would not have placed yourself in this invidious position," Nancy said with quiet intensity. "I can only apologise to our friends," here she turned to offer those present an icy and formal smile, "for your boorish and intemperate conduct."

Dr Richardson appealed silently to Clover and Ursula for support. Clover smiled apologetically, biting her lip. Ursula threw her a questioning glance which Clover returned with a barely discernible shrug, and he knew he was on his own. This was, after all, a domestic matter albeit a very public one. The better bred would consider it their duty to disregard it.

"Well?" inquired Nancy icily as she waited for his apology.

"I'll be in my surgery," was all he could manage. He stared evenly at her, praying for the strength and courage to confront her with all her shortcomings, but then walked stiffly past them all, one hand in his pocket, the other swinging in what he hoped resembled an insouciant manner. As he closed the door behind him, he knew he was slinking away, abandoning the Okaina to an indeterminate future on the wall of the village hall and yielding the high ground, once more, to a wife for whom it had no value, and who probably despised him for it. He couldn't, for the life of him, think of what else he could do.

Chapter Eleven

West Sussex

Seaton walked across the dunes, oblivious of the damage he was doing to his brushed calfskin shoes. He held his jacket over one shoulder, his tie was now loosened and he had left his hat in the car. He took deep slow drafts of salt air in through his nostrils, breathing out through his mouth. He was trying to affect some freshness of spirit, some clarity of thought, but as the waves glittered and the gulls called from on high, all he felt was weary and rather soiled, the stiff onshore breeze notwithstanding.

He had come here often as a boy, newly liberated from yet another school term, free to roam this vast concourse of sand, coarse grass and ever-evolving shallows. It was forever windy and the tide seemed forever ebbing away, but in the salt lagoons and the vast sand-swept perspectives there was a sense of peace, and of expansive freedom, on a scale unknown in the corridors and classrooms of school, or the cluttered orientalism of home.

He had spent long hours, then, pottering about and not thinking, but just feeling the powerful oxygenised rythms of the coast sweep him up and carry him along with them, uninflected, unnoticed and yet a small cogent part of the whole. Someone would be waiting up on Coastguard Lane, rarely his mother, to take him home for tea, his skin chapped by the sun and the wind, his lips cracked, his heart opened by the limitless horizons, and with that little tremor of disappointment and regret that came from knowing he was going back to Laurel House, where he was to be limited, once again, by the ambitions of others.

Watching some oystercatchers, busily investigating pools dimpling in the wind, carefree and driven only by their own circumstance, he felt the familiar boyhood constriction hovering around him. The foreknowledge, shameful in its preordained collusion, that someone else's purposes were yet again coming to Laurel House to coerce him, to command his present and shape his future, a future now valueless because so much beyond his own control or even caprice.

Today, at least, it was Foster waiting for him in Coastguards Lane. His journey home would be in the company of a witting, if powerless, companion. He had told his old sergeant there was to be an interview tomorrow lunchtime that would have far-reaching consequences. That, in all likelihood, the household would not be the same again, but that he wanted Foster and Mrs Simmons to be certain he would ensure their interests and wellbeing would be in no way affected by the upheaval his meeting with Houghton-Copley would activate.

The diplomatist's professed Christian concern had not convinced him in the slightest, but whatever the true nature of his involvement, and however distasteful that might prove to be, Seaton was determined now to present Houghton-Copley with a precise and frank disclosure of the events that seemed to fascinate him, if for no other reason than to protect the past from the man's sinister and persistent intrusion. No lawyer could exercise sufficient control on such personal and intangible matters, and flight was inconceivable. He would face the music of his own making. There was, he hoped, a certain redeeming dignity in that, although it meant an unsettled future for those close to him.

Foster had said they been through uncertain times before, on a daily basis on the Western Front, with many more tangible threats and dangers than he felt the diplomatist could have in his wake the following day. He, for one, was content to see what was what, day by day, and take his chances as they came. He would be with the Captain, come what may, and he was sure that nothing could match what they had survived in Passchendaele. He also felt, sure as eggs were eggs, that nothing could happen that the Captain couldn't get on top off, and he himself wouldn't be selling himself lightly, for that matter. As for Mrs Simmons, he was emphatic on the point; she would no more consider her interests before the Captain's than run off with Houghton-Copley to some hotel in Paris. They had a quiet and somewhat obligatory laugh at that, but the man's commitment and support were clear. It saddened Seaton, privately, that such strength of decent feeling would, in the end, be outflanked by the forces of precedent, history and the manipulative skills of the powerful.

He turned his back on the sea and walked back to where he knew Foster would have parked the Bentley. There was nothing to be achieved on the dunes. After a thirty-year absence it seemed he had lost the knack of appropriating some sense of opportunity from the ozone and, unlike his boyhood self, he had some dispositions to make, before he was taken up and swept away by the inescapable commitments of the morrow.

~~~~~

Dr Richardson stared stonily at his apple trees. He had not affected his garden duster and secateurs and he had no intention of attempting any maintenance work in the orchard, spurious or no. The damn things could rot or flourish; they were as irrelevant in his life as he was. He simply wanted to stay out of the house, facing away from where he knew Nancy would be primly organising his household, and for a moment, if not a minute, feel what it might be like never to have married her, never to have felt her presence in his life. He had at one time, years ago, idly daydreamed of life as a widower, but even then he knew he'd been with her too long for him to ever erase her wholly from his consciousness. Her absence would haunt him as much as her presence diminished his life. That was

307

the icy truth behind the words "till death do us part". You both had to die, to be free of each other.

He sighed heavily, and sunk his hands in his trouser pockets. He had gone as far in life, professionally, personally and above all in his free spirit, as he was ever going to go. Now, if he examined his world with some measure of equanimity, he could see he had neither expectations nor consolations, and that he could anticipate none. He and Nancy would passively torment each other to the grave.

He thought about how he had abandoned the Captain's drawing of the fishermen; the damned vicar was happy enough to take his money for it, before Nancy had put his foot down, yet they'd both cringed at the first sign of a scene. Very much the dominant species, Nancy. Her blind, aggravated certainty clearing all before it. The overwhelming might of the intractably ignorant, he muttered to himself, but then gave up even his resentment as a bad job. He was weak and she was brutally strong in her own way. He supposed they were both deeply and, perhaps, equally unhappy. Nothing he could do. Perhaps, now, he might learn not to care so damn much about it.

He heard her call out to him, in that rare tractable tone she used when things had gone too far, when emotions had swirled a little too near the surface, and the equilibrium of their world was in danger of becoming disturbed, maybe even irrevocably. It was an artificially warm tone of voice, yet welcome for all that, and with a winningly tentative tremor to it. Don't destroy what certainties we have, the timbre seemed to be saying. They're all I have and my hold on them is fragile. He listened to the unspoken dependence and his eyes brimmed at her vulnerability and his anguished complicity. Before he could make out her words, he knew he was going to give in again, for the sake of a greater continuity.

"It's a lovely evening," she called pleasantly. "I've set you out some sherry and biscuits on the terrace."

"Thank you," he called over his shoulder, in a voice thick with unshed tears.

She didn't chide him for his lack of courtesy, for presenting his back and averting his gaze into the mouldering apple trees. Instead, she offered, "You could watch the sunset and relax. You work too hard, you know."

"I'll do just that," he managed a casual grin as he turned. He walked back to sit in the garden chair she'd set out for him, every muscle straining to simulate relaxed disregard and good humour.

She returned his smile for as long as they could both bear it, and then darted inside to busy herself with Maeve in the kitchen, while the doctor dutifully relaxed, holding his sherry and waiting for the sun to go down.

North-west Amazon

Seaton's lungs were straining to cope, his heart hammered in his ribs, and the muscles in his legs complained stridently at this sudden burst of activity after so long a period of desuetude. His eyes, narrowed against the darkness, darted about him for imminent dangers and he was convinced the tunnels were closing in on them. Hestia had let go of his hand and was now streaking along in front, darting and dodging in and out of pools of moonlight and the black tendrils of the night forest.

Their footfalls reverberated around the narrow tracks while the beating drums and chanting of the Okaina pursued them round every corner. Hestia flew ahead like the White Rabbit and, in the chase, the mood of the evening seemed subtly to change. They were descending into the mysterious at breakneck speed, thrusting themselves down into a primordial territory, both actual and personal, probing ever deeper towards some exotic epiphany

Suddenly she was upon the place, snatching up the handkerchief she had left tied there and waving it at him, with little skips of triumph. As he reached her, she nodded encouragingly at him, "Smell them? Can you ..?"

Where they stood the track was filled with the scent of orchids permeating through the thicket between them and the tiny playa. The soft fragrance hung on the night air and absorbed the rumble of the Okaina carnival and the thumping of his heart. Hestia took his hand. "Ready?" she said.

"I'd better go first." The soldier in Seaton, alert to the perfect lay of the ground for an ambush, reasserted his position. He set her to his left side, leaving him free access to the revolver in his pocket, and then took her hand. "Here we go, then," he smiled.

With that prosaic observation, they ducked in through the thicket and into a better world. Just as the fragrance of the orchids was all pervasive, the moonlight was all encompassing. The moon picked out the treeline on the opposite bank as brightly as any magnesium flare. It transformed the flow of the Kahuanari into a glittering mosaic of blacks and silvers, diamond hard against the murk beneath. It drenched the cascades of orchids surrounding the playa, softening their coral, pink and flesh tones into a delicate melange, whilst accentuating the form and detail of every petal, stamen, anther and leaf, as if each flower were the ornate work of some Moorish master craftsman. The sound of the Okaina's dance washed along the moonlit waters and into their private gulf, amplified across the river surface so that the tribe might have been but a few meters away. The music intermingled with the exotic perfume of orchis *seatonis* blooms, as they sent out soft, insistent messages to lovers somewhere abroad in the night skies

"Isn't it wonderful?" Hestia looked up at him, her eyes brimming with excitement, and seemed to be searching in his for some response as yet unknown to him. His heart opened to the night. It was everything he had painted, everything he had scratched towards, now made real and offering itself up to him as the one true reality. It was life as it is meant to be lived, and this was the girl that had brought him to it.

"It's quite magical," he smiled down at her and spoke with feeling. "Thank you. Thank you, so much. You have brought enchantment into my life."

She gave him a small complaisant smile, brought her hands up to rest lightly on his waist, and tilted her head to one side, before replying, "You're welcome, Captain. I think enchantment suits you."

He looked around at the river, the orchids and the sky above. He looked down to the girl who had delivered him into this enchantment. He heard the rites of the Okaina proclaiming their vitality across the flow of a great river. He felt he was present in his own life at last. What he had taken as the debilitating ravages of fever had, in fact, led him to an acute appreciation of the present moment. He was here, he was alive and he was in his proper place amongst the pure, uninflected purposes of nature.

He put his hands on her shoulders, feeling their warmth beneath his palms, and with one sure movement pulled the straps of her camisole over them and down to her elbows. Her breasts were exactly as he had drawn them, the tension, the pale, soft colours, the contrast between curve and the firm lines of the nipples, voluptuous confirmation of his inner vision. They rose and fell with her breath, they had weight and shape; they, like life, were fulsome and demanding. No mystery now, but the wondrous immediacy of beauty and sensation. He moved one hand round to the nape of her neck, holding her face up towards him and cupped her breast with the other. The skin was warm and firm and pulsed with life, as did the mysterious protrusion of the nipple into the palm of his hand. He could feel her heart hammering through to him, joining the Okaina's celebration, as it floated in across the silver and black waters.

The instant he had uncovered her, her expression had changed rapidly from wistful engagement to puzzlement to disbelief and finally to outright shock. There was a moment of stricken discomfiture between them, as the proprieties fought to regain control over this solecism from the world of the nether gods. He waited for her to join him in this joyous liberation from the button boot world. She should be truly at home here, he thought. In fact, she should be better acquainted with it than he was. She, who had taken them through the miraculous gateway of the orchids. He felt a new surge of gratitude towards her, for bringing him to this home and was taken unawares when she tried to dart back from him, both angry and embarrassed. "Don't!" she yelled and it was more petulant than pleading.

"It's alright," he soothed. "It's just as it's meant to be. We've come so far, Hestia. Don't draw back now."

She pushed angrily at him, trying to pull her clothing about her to cover herself. She seemed in a fury, a rage fuelled by some perceived affront to her innocence. He could see her inexperience was holding the two of them back. Nature was innocent, but it was hungry and vital. Innocence was a guileless celebration of all opportunities, not repudiation, repression and censure. He was finally learning that, and he had to take her, his beloved, with him. She had dropped out of the raw rhythm of life about them and must be gathered back in, before the magic was lost to her. He couldn't allow her to smother her own joy.

"Leave me alone!" she insisted, slapping at his nearest

312

hand.

He moved forward quickly to placate her, kissing her neck, calling her his "hidobe" and burying his head in her hair. She pushed fearfully against him, and her struggle ignited the darkness within him. The susurrus in his ears raged like a cataract; the smell of the orchids entwined with the musky odours of her own sweat and fear, redolent of their first meeting beneath the trees at the burned-out mission, and filled his nostrils. He could see her in minute detail, the striation in the muscles, the tiny light follicles on her goosepimpled skin, the pucker of her nipples, the trails of sweat and saliva veering across her torso, the frayed seams of her torn shift, sending their own tiny fibres up into the moonlight.

He pressed her into the cascade of orchids, pulling up her dress and feeling the tendons flexing in her thighs as she strained against him, lashing her head this way and that to avoid his kisses. The skin of her thighs were as smooth as the stems of palm fronds and a light coating of sap guided his hand ever upward.

The orchids were smothering him, in fragrance, in sensual hunger and in the blind imperative of generation. The drums in his heart pounded along with hers, her cries harmonised with the wild Okaina songs, his muscles tautened and hers relaxed, as he bent her back amongst the aerial roots, pulling apart her thighs to receive him. He felt her teeth sink into his shoulder, as he tore at the encumbrances between his worshipping hands and her most precious flower, and exalted. He felt the savage litany of the Okaina flow through his veins and into her, and basked in the accordant warmth of the forest emanating from her body through the mulch between them. As he pressed himself ardently, devotedly, upon her, he knew the majesty of the moment had taken them up, bathed in moonlight and drowned in the smell of the orchids.

Whether she was calling out or singing, it made no difference; she was part of the savage music of the forest. They were finally playing their part in the riot of nature, following an older authority.

He pulled her head to him be with her at the budding of this rapture, and saw her face, filled with fear, disappointment and misery, and knew he could not permit that centipede to invade their flower. He could not accept the pain and the horror that convulsed her as she shuddered against him. If only he could take them to their natural fusion, she would be safe and at peace. She would understand the gift both she and the forest had bestowed upon them.

He relaxed his grip on her, stroking her cheek, and tried to whisper his fond assurances, but she used this hesitancy to break free. In her haste and anger, she floundered from the orchid cascades into a cluster of Huaco palms beside the tiny playa. The razor-sharp leaves cut at her naked legs, lacerating them through a skirt already torn and sundered, but she was oblivious to any further pain. Regaining her balance, she turned to him and stood her ground on the narrow beach. The river waters lapped round her feet; dark shapes were assembling amongst the dazzling glitter behind her. She was a vengeful hobgoblin now, scratched and bleeding, her fists balled in fury, and she screeched out her revulsion. "You monster! You animal! You vile…thing!"

He ran towards her, desperate to bring her back to their understanding, their unique affinity in the midst of this enchanted night. "It's not like that! It's not like that!" he implored, scrabbling to catch hold of her as she twisted and turned to be free of him. He could not lose her affection now, he had to make things right between them; the schism was unbearable.

She backed into the river, her head jutted forward in

314

defiance, her right arm outstretched as she pointed at him and screamed at him again, "Don't touch me! Don't you touch me!"

She was stumbling backwards into waters that swirled ever stronger, under the assertive call of the powerful currents in mid-stream. He waded in towards her, keeping his feet with difficulty, their salvation now the sole purpose of his being. He moaned in wretchedness and dismay, and stretched his own hand out, thinking to pull her back to the shore and true reconciliation. She spat at him, her eyes full of enraged repudiation, clouded intermittently by hollow despondency, at a world capable of dragging her so far from grace.

"I love you! I love you!" He pleaded with her as he struggled on into the current, to bring her safely home, but she retreated and receded, as the surface of the river shone diamond bright below him. The moon bore down, the drums beat on and the waters churned, as suddenly he stopped and gazed, horror struck, about him. Regardless of his piercing need, she was no longer there.

For that instant, there was no past, no future, just the pure, unwavering reality of the present and, as he opened himself to that unrestricted immediacy, the present devoured him, down to the tiniest vibrating elements of his being; mind, body and what passed for a soul. One moment he was present, and the next, he too had disappeared.

West Sussex

Mrs Simmons set the finishing touches to the Captain's dinner tray and looked over at Foster, sitting pensive and still at the kitchen table. He was poking at the table surface with an aimless forefinger, focusing on places a long way away.

"Why's everyone so down in the dumps?" she said, managing to sound more exasperated than concerned.

"Should have seen him on the dunes," Foster replied tonelessly. "Like a man who's seen his own ghost."

"One of his glooms," she tried to rally him. "You said so yourself."

"I've been with him in all sorts, pet," Foster gave her a smile he clearly didn't feel quite up to. "Places you'd never want to see. Hopeless places. Horrible. Frightening." He made a gesture to assure her, unbidden, that he would not trouble her with any detailed reminiscence. "Always kept going, carried you with him, went on to the end. Always got you out safe." He shook his head. "There's something about him now. Like he's not going to defend himself. Like he's given it up as a bad job."

"What on earth does that church man want?" Mrs Simmons pulled the chops from the griddle; she turned to appeal to Foster in pained bewilderment, "I mean what can the Captain have possibly done, to bring that kind of man here?"

"Nothing. He's done nothing." He looked up at her with a determination that bordered on defiance. "Except mind his own business. Pay his own way. And look after you and me."

She brought the tray over to him and he stood up to take it in. For a moment they shared an intimate and commiserating silence, before she said, "Well, he's not going under while we're here, is he?"

He looked around quickly to make sure the scullery maid was out of the kitchen, then to Mrs Simmons' great surprise, he broke his own golden rule and kissed her warmly on the cheek. "No, pet, he's not!" he said, and then he picked up the tray and set off for the gallery.

North-west Amazon

In the midst of endless, shapeless, amniotic nullity there was noise; he didn't listen, but the noise persisted.

Without his collusion, it developed in him an atavistic awareness of the presence of others. Footsteps, that was it. The sound of footsteps. Shod footsteps, at that. And voices, not just singly but in simultaneous conversations. A radical departure from the void. The limbo outside his small circle of pain was peopled again.

As the unknown arrivals, with their heavy boots and their vibrant tones, reconstructed his external geography, setting a world without limit in place around him, something synergistic was taking place within him. He could feel air on his skin; indeed, he could feel his skin. If he came back in deeper from that, towards the void, he could feel pain and stiffness, and heat and nausea as orientation flooded in. The voices had called him out from the void, whether he wanted to return or not. It seemed he was powerless to resist them. So, he calmed his breathing and listened.

They were on the veranda. Good God, he knew what the veranda was, where it was, how he had spent his time on it and with whom, but he would forget about whom, he would just listen to the voices.

"He's pinned these up everywhere," said a young male voice, which he somehow knew to be American, hiding its anxiety under a jocular tone. "Naked women and flowers. Tambo 2. Specimen room. And the Okaina say he got married. What in Sam Hill has he been up to?"

"No, no. Callard's explained all that. A pretence to confound some native initiative he believed to be indecent." The responding voice was deep and travelled and so, so familiar, that it might have been his own. "Seaton's not that kind of chap at all. Very correct. I assure, you."

"I'd hardly call these drawings correct."

"He's an artist," A flatter and equally familiar voice joined them. "With a raging brain fever. And the Okaina have been pumping him full of Christ knows what to cure

317

it. He's been out of his mind, if he's been conscious at all."

"He's a gentleman," the deeper voice said with conviction. "And that is why we shall destroy those. One doesn't confront a sick a man with the state of his bedding. Or does one, Mr Cotterill?"

"You're right. I'm sorry," Cotterill sounded abashed. "I guess the girl's getting to me. Do you think he knows about that?"

"It's unlikely."

"Nothing in his journal about it?" asked the flat voice.

"His journal is even more highly charged than the drawings," replied the deeper voice, sadly. Then it coughed. "Ravings mainly. Of an indecent nature. Nothing to tell us anything, there."

"Jesus. We'll have to tell him about her when Munby pulls him round."

"If Munby manages to pull him round," corrected the flat voice. "Let me tell you, Munby's not counting his chickens there. He should be showing some signs of life by now."

Did he know about the girl? The girl was his universe. Her desolation, the heartbreaking confusion of their lost innocence, their irrevocable separation, that was his Calvary. He had lost her. And she was lost to him. There was only her terror and her reproach, misbegotten by overpowering love. He cried out in his anguish and his grief.

Not a lifetime after that, the remnants of the Northmore expedition filed into his room. In their separate fashions, they cosseted and fussed over him. Cotterill even held his hand, perhaps by way of restitution for earlier unworthy insinuations. When Munby thought he was strong enough, they told him that Hestia was dead. The Okaina had found signs of what had happened to her, in a playa beyond the plantations, not far from the track where they had discovered him, unconscious and exposed, some undefined period after their dance had ceased. They had searched for her, but had only found remnants of clothing which they had left on the veranda for him, saying that as it was his wife's property, it should remain with him. From the tracks and these blood-stained scraps of fabric, they could tell she had been attacked by caimans. Seized as she rested by the bank. Dragged violently beneath the waters. Torn and devoured by ancient beasts. The discards fought over by shoals of barbarous fish, unheeded fleshy shreds drifting down to the bottom feeders. They hadn't gone as far as to say that. Neither had Northmore nor Munby nor Cotterill. But he could sense, in microscopic detail, how the forest had reclaimed her as its own.

The Okaina had sent their shaman to him, and their wise women, and tried with herbs and ancient remedies to keep him out of the ground. They weren't sure how long he had been lingering; Callard and the cook thought two weeks at least, but it might very well have been more.

The expedition had returned to attend him in his extremis, entirely by chance. Their business had been unsuccessful and required them to return, in some haste, to where they could make a report. As soon as he was fit to travel, they would set off on the long and perilous journey out of Eden, and back to safer climes.

He understood the words, the facts and even the intentions. The purpose and the ultimate point of it eluded him, as did the nullity from which he had been reluctantly withdrawn.

West Sussex

Seaton finished his dinner at his desk in the gallery, mainly in deference to the efforts of Mrs Simmons and Foster, who had added a glass of hock to the tray, in a personal attempt to dispel the melancholy atmosphere Houghton-Copley had engendered. He lit a cigarette, fished a small brass key from the depths of a desk drawer and went over to the free-standing cabinet, containing all his wartime effects, the orders, medals and citations, arranged around the prosaic means of their generation, his service revolver. Foster who had insisted on this display and had commissioned its design and its construction, had forborne to include the brass combined trench-knife and knuckleduster, the nailed club and, above all, the Mill's bombs which, for practical purposes, had superseded the revolver in almost every one of the actions deemed worth of recognition. Foster liked things to be done properly and with tactful acceptance of the delicate sensibilities of the civilian world when it came to the mechanics of slaughter, much as the war memorial committees felt throughout the land, when they busied themselves with their commemorations. He had supervised the joinery, the selection of the satins and plushes in which to mount the orders, the printing of the labels, and even ordered small bags of preservative crystals to ensure the documents did not fade or curl. Foster had worked hard to preserve these glittering testimonials to fortitude, valour and survival. He could not, or would not, see the terrible inversion of all his Captain's hopes that the objects signified.

For Seaton, volunteering for active service was entirely a matter of restitution. After years buried in the country, the passing days taken up with a disinclined recuperation and latterly, at Northmore's pressing, the RGS monograph, the war came as a welcome opportunity for reparation, and he seized upon it. Those who saw him at the time, believed him to be the very embodiment of a patriotic veteran, determined to put his experience under fire to good effect for King and Country. However, at first, he was applauded but not accommodated. His age and his health proved obstacles for a time, the Hussars trying to deflect him first into recruitment and then, after interminable interventions by perplexed but well-placed friends, into Intelligence. Neither, of course, would serve his purpose.

It was Hestia, as always. He needed to put things right between them. His loss and his contrition, made all the more unbearable, appropriately, by their secrecy, might be mitigated and, at least in temporal terms, put to rest by a relatively purposeful death, if that could be achieved. He accepted that, in some measure, his suffering had not been adjudged complete; the fever had not been permitted to take him, and any act of self destruction would be an evasion of what he owed to her, the full acknowledgement of her passing and its manner, the awful misconnection, the reconstitution of love into the desperation of need. He believed, or rather he wanted to believe, that a determined attempt to die in the cause of some greater movement of history would demonstrate to her the true subordination of his own will, and that an arbitrary and untimely death would provide some recompense for her own.

He'd got in through the Artists' Rifles, a number of whose stalwarts he'd known socially over the years. This proved simpler than he had expected. He simply turned up and announced himself at the Depot in Duke's Road, enjoyed a clamorous and affecting reunion and, following some bureaucratic gymnastics characteristic of the regiment, was duly sent across to France, as an OCTU instructor. From their training centre at St. Omer, the Artists provided a considerable percentage of young officers to front line regiments. They also valued initiative, intelligence and drive, so Seaton had every hope he could slip away from the classroom and into action, without the stultifying opposition to such maverick behaviour prevalent in most other regiments. His courses were supposed to cover orienteering and firearms drill at close quarters. Most of the "Embryos" in his classes were more up to date on these matters than he was, but an astute Major pressed him on his raiding experiences in the Cape, and from then on he was fledged. For six weeks he taught the requirements of command in flexible assaults, and in two months he was seconded to a line regiment, to put them into practice.

From the early days of opportunistic forays, and sporadic reconnaissance, trench raiding had become an acknowledged discipline and one that Seaton, with his jungle awareness and complete disregard for his own outcome, was destined to excel. The labyrinths of enemy firing and communications trenches were a mouldering equivalent of the enclosed jungle tracks of years before, beside the Kahuanari. If anything, Hun trenches held less of a threat for him, the enemy presence being assured and the upshot almost inevitable.

Despite the element of surprise and the other covert advantages of night work, casualties were continuous, and as the size of the raiding parties increased, so did the dangers. The likelihood of an overall success became less and less, and there were fiascos where the body count surprised even those poor souls habituated to the arbitrary death of those around them, and their own inevitable demise. Yet, Seaton's star continued to rise. As the war went on, and the raiders became subsumed under the general direction of the High Command, their objectives changed with the day; prisoners, destruction of firing points, disruptions and feints, probes prior to an attack or diversions from one, intelligence on repairs to the wire,

Hun numbers, unit identification, even the snatching of prototype weapons; but it was all the same to Seaton. He wanted to get the job done and die in the attempt; unfortunately, he didn't seem to be able to do both.

He did seem to be able, without any effort on his own part, to gather quite a reputation for himself as the "Artist" marauder. This came with a degree of dash and notoriety, the Artists' Rifles having their own lines of communication within their surviving graduates spread through the Army groups, and occasioned his services being requested on many different sectors. His activities had none of the dash and flash of the RFC, bumping about upstairs, dropping bombs and fuel oil across the lines, but they attracted their own amount of unaccountable élan.

To Seaton, there was nothing remotely charismatic about creeping into a sleeping army to snatch or slaughter its outlying pickets, steal their secrets or memorise dispositions that would be changed before sunrise. Crouching in the dark, face blackened with burnt cork, his cap comforter pulled down over his head, wearing a ragged brown sweater from the Army and Navy and other ranks' webbing, puttees and trousers, he felt and looked more like a housebreaker than a holder of the King's commission. His nine man bombing party; a sergeant, two bomb throwers, two carriers, two bayonet and hatchet men to defend the team and two replacements to keep the assault going when casualties occurred, looked as disreputable as he did. Bags of bombs over their shoulders, clubs and knives stuck in their belts, everyone would have a last gasper, with an optional silent prayer, before he led them out. Then, with his own canvas sack of bombs and a trench cosh to supplement his revolver, he would clamber out of his trench, and creep across no man's land, hoping any preparatory artillery barrage had destroyed the enemy firing points and discouraged any diligent sentry duty. If they made it across without coming under fire, directed or random, Seaton and his men would knife any man they found still to be on watch, then slip down in to the Hun trenches and run along the muddy duckboards, the throwers lobbing their Mill's bombs into the dugouts, with the hatchet men following close behind to hack down any Hun staggering into the main thoroughfare, in a stunned attempt to escape the carnage.

Once they'd achieve their objectives, or lost a critical number of raiding party members, or it was clear that their luck had just plain run out, they'd scramble away over the parapet and scurry back to their own lines, dragging any wounded with half a chance or more, and whatever they'd managed to loot, be it schnapps, luger pistols, or documents and maps (the latter at a higher premium of course, but not necessarily to the bombers).

While the survivors collapsed into their own dugouts to wait for the customary, reviving tot of SRD rum and the extraordinary experience of finding themselves still alive in a new dawn, Seaton would retire to his, to light up a Gold Flake, and write up his report. When all had settled around him, he'd pull from his inside pocket a small oilskin pouch containing a scrap of material, discoloured and stained, and edged with curled lace, the parting gift from the Okaina in memory of his wife that never was. In the darkness, as his men struggled to sleep around him, he would hold this relic of Hestia's camisole to him and feel the tears welling up inside, and he would have to apologise to her once again. He was not dead yet.

For their own sardonic purposes, the Gods were not disposed to extinguish a life held so cheaply. After three years of active service, Seaton found himself still very much alive, despite his best efforts, and with the further and compromising burden of other men's lives resting on his decisions and his composure under fire. In large part his survival, and the majority of his citations and mentions in despatches, was the result of his having to shepherd his men through the danger he had flung himself into. For the rest, it was attributed, widely, to the inexplicable workings of fortune. As one old sergeant had told a new arrival to the firing trench, fresh out of Blighty, "Captain Seaton's got the luck of the devil. So you stick close, my lad."

The boy had stuck close, but had died within the week anyway, clubbed down one night outside the wire by an incoming Hun patrol, which Seaton had seen off with his remaining bombs. The old sergeant had died in the interchange too, making way for Foster, who stayed by him for the last two years of the carnage, and who was now enquiring whether the chops had been to his liking, and if he wished for some coffee?

Foster saw that Seaton was on the point of opening up the trophy cabinet, and joined him with an avuncular smile of quiet pride. "If I might say so, sir," he began, "Whatever Dr Houghton-Copley's on about, he'll never be able to touch what's in there."

He tapped the glass with his forefinger. "Men did great things then, sir. Maybe not for much, but they did them anyway." He collected the tray and then paused, to repeat his quiet assertion, another defiant gesture against the atmosphere he felt the diplomatist had introduced to the house. "They stood their ground, and did them anyway."

"Carry on, Sergeant," said Seaton, without emphasis, as Foster left the room. Then he unlocked the valorous past.

Flanders

Once again, they were trapped in an impossible position, under insuperable forces, in broad daylight and all for King and Country. Seaton, his sergeant, Foster,

Privates Musgrove and Kirvan, together with the corpses of Privates Ellis and Collins, were pinned down in a shell hole which was filling rapidly with water, and fast turning into a whirlpool of evil smelling liquid mud. At the far side of the hole was a leg. Seaton focused on the leg, collecting his wits as the world fragmented around them. How long the leg had been there, he had no way of knowing. Its provenance and history were certainly not of any tactical interest; shell holes appeared and disappeared under a bombardment at an alarming and unpredictable rate, and this one could go any minute. Furthermore, it was impossible to know whether it was a German or British leg. The boot, which might have assisted identification, had been blown into whatever dimension shreds of flesh, globules of brain and fragments of ordnance were all dispatched to, in the unholy destruction wrought by the artillery, trench mortars and MG08 machineguns the Hun had trained particularly upon them.

The leg had one advantage over him. It was not to be remotely affected by the complete negation of nature around them, as any recognisable feature of life, any logic, any design, intention or hope was obliterated by the impeccable workings of technology, chemistry and brute system. In its disembodied and disinterested situation, the leg had evolved into a state of grace above, or perhaps beyond, the tumultuous annihilation that mankind were calling down upon themselves. It stood or, rather, it lay apart.

Kirvan had taken machine gun rounds in his stomach and thighs and was screaming consistently, as the blood welled up about him and merged with the mud. Foster had shoved a haversack, Kirvan's rifle and his own rolled-up greatcoat beneath the writhing man, to try and keep him from drowning before them, like so many had before. Musgrove, face down on the Hun-side slope, appeared to be weeping as he hugged his rifle and kicked down steadily into the mud, as if treading water, to maintain his position.

Privates Ellis and Collins were slowly disappearing into the deep slime at the bottom of the hole. In the full fury of the assault, they'd alerted Seaton to this current sanctuary by being blown into it by some HE; this accomplished, they lay beneath the feet of the survivors, being swallowed up by the respite they had never had the chance to appreciate.

"Different story last night, sir," Foster called over.

Seaton and his unit, as the battalion's trench raiding specialists, had reconnoitred this sector the previous night, avoiding any contact with the enemy, and Seaton had sent in his report, following all the normal procedures. They had been incorporated into today's attack, because of Command's optimistic conviction that their prior knowledge of the state and disposition of Hun wire defences would prove invaluable during the assault. Quite what they could add to his own full report and the aerial photographs brought back by the RE8's, and quite how they could communicate this to the accompanying waves of PBI, through 550 rounds per minute enfilading fire, Command had not sought to clarify and Seaton had not sought to enquire. As the world was turned inside out around him, men eviscerated and vaporised, the air turned into fire, the earth into water, and every natural law was flouted or distorted, he found it easiest to stick to operational procedure rather than enquire about strategic matters. Nothing made sense; he could not trust even his own direct observation. He had a suspicion that he hadn't registered the full extent of nature's implosion around him; that in some sense he was a habitué, in collusion with the obliteration of all human values.

It had been that way with a simple physical thing like his sense of smell. When he first arrived at the lines, those years ago, the first thing that had affected him was not the scale of the slaughter, he had not quite appreciated that then and his previous battle experiences had inured him to the early signs, but the overpowering smell. It was a complete repudiation of steady and entropic mulch of decay and rebirth that so characterised the deep forests of the Amazon, it was not even related to the smoggy, murky atmospheres of an industrialised and civilised Europe.

The stench of putrefaction, as thousands of corpses rotted in plain air or in shallow graves, blended with that of the living, unwashed and fearful, their feet particularly malodorous, with their overflowing latrines, their cooking, their stale cigarette smoke. This in turn merged with the rotting sandbags, and stagnant mud within the trenches and the searing smells of creosol and chloride of lime, there to stave off disease for those destined to be shot down on the morrow. Beneath it all, the constant presence of cordite and the lingering smell of poison gas. The first day amongst it, he thought he would not be able to breathe for the cloying stench of it all; now, like the blood, flesh and brains of other men spraying the mud around him, it had ceased to impress itself upon him. It had, to all intents and purposes, disappeared, along with most of his ethical perspectives. Yet, Hestia remained, and the job to be done; his compact with her was the only decency left to him.

On that thought, there was a sudden deluge of mortar fire, churning up the exposed ground around them; mud, red hot metal splinters and screams flew up into the air. The impacts were regular and ranged and rolled away from them, a creeping barrage back towards their own lines. This was followed by a concentrated outburst of MG08 fire from a position both new and disconcertingly near. Seaton shot a look over to Foster, cradling Kirvan's head in his lap, trying patiently to quiet his shrieks, like a nursemaid with a fractious baby. "They're coming over at us!" he alerted the man.

Foster looked round at the shattered remnants of their patrol and shrugged his shoulders, as if to say there was not a great deal any of them could do about that, but both men knew they would certainly try. At that point, three frantic young men, Lancastrians all, dived in over them, from the Hun's direction, and lay trembling and breathless, on top of Privates Ellis and Collins. The least shocked, noticed Seaton after a moment and attempted a jerky salute, "They're coming back, sir! They're coming back!" he screamed, his eyes wide and hardly focused.

"Who are? Who do you mean, man?" Seaton put all his officer caste into the peremptory tone, to counter the rising panic in the young soldier.

"Huns, sir!" the man sharpened up. "There's none left of us."

Musgrove pushed himself up towards the rim of the shell hole, scooped the smallest depression out with his hand and cautiously raised his eye to it. He jerked his head back down immediately as the area around it erupted, and machine gun rounds spattered them all with detritus. He slithered back down to safety, in front of the amazed Lancastrians. "There's a new nest, sir," he reported. "Two guns, I think, light."

Seaton crouched down by Private Collins, pushing two of the Lancastrians off him, and relieved him of his bomb bag. Ellis was wearing a canvas, ten pocketed grenade-carrier, and Seaton stripped him quickly of it, before pulling it over his own tunic. Checking swiftly, he saw Ellis hadn't managed to dispose of a single bomb, before the HE had sent him to his rest. He called across to Musgrove. "Where, exactly?"

"Pretty much directly ahead, sir. Ten yards, fifteen." He saw the Captain's eyes narrow. The details had to be right. The details could kill you. "Fifteen, for safety, sir."

Foster laughed outright at the expression, and Seaton had to smile to himself. "Well done, Musgrove. Don't want to run out of ground out there, do we?"

Foster set Kirvan down to meet his Maker as best he might, and they handed out the bombs between them, the Lancastrians clipping them to their webbing, Musgrove and Foster favouring two open bags cross-slung and under each arm. The Lancastrians, having arrived in some comparative safety after who knows what torments above, showed little inclination to leave it, and stared glumly at the Captain, as they all bunched together at the bottom of the Hun-side slope.

"We have to put the guns out," Seaton said to them all. "Or we'll never get home."

Foster clapped one of the new men on the arm. "We can be on them in seconds, my lad. Couple of bombs each, then I'll race you back, if you like."

This fetched a wry grin from the boy. There was a moment of nose wiping and preliminary spitting, a gathering of breath and a repression of thought, as Seaton led them back up to the rim.

"You know the drill," he said tersely. "All out together. Two yards apart, and don't stop for anything. Straight at them. Ready?" They nodded. "Fuses done?" They primed the bombs in their hands, and nodded again. "Right, come on."

Once out of the hole, he was impervious to what was flying at or around him. He just saw the crouched shapes of the gunners ahead, the spattering muzzles and the smoke belching around them. The wire glittered diamond hard below him, the mud churned and tugged at his feet, the rumble and clatter of the guns merged with the drumbeats of the Okaina as they chanted, the cordite and the forest mulch fused, and he ran on, throwing his bombs in quiet earnest, assuming that his men would be behind him, where it would be safer, and waiting for the impact to herald his departure.

Three weeks later he was informed that he had been cited for a Distinguished Service Order, for rallying troops and securing a position under heavy fire with 'contempt for personal danger'. As a captain, any act of outstanding bravery in combat would normally have warranted a Military Cross, and the DSO signified to those around him just how close he'd come to winning the Victoria Cross itself. Close but sadly not close enough, seemed to be the feeling on all sides, though for different reasons. Seaton returned to his dank, cramped hidey hole, while men snored and the rats foraged. In his daily litany, he took out Hestia's scrap of lace and cambric and wondered what he'd have to do to get his final just reward.

West Sussex

Seaton removed the medal from its presentation case, paying scant attention to the white enamelled cross with its gold edging and the Imperial crown surrounded by laurel leaves, the red and blue ribbon, with its plain gold bar also bearing the Imperial crown. He pulled out the blue plush bed it rested on and took from underneath it, his scrap of Hestia's camisole. Replacing the medal carefully, he took the fabric and his revolver and set them to one side, before locking the cabinet again and covering it with its appointed protective cloth. Foster wouldn't remove this until Seaton gave his permission, usually prior to entertaining some guests, so his modification to the display would remain unnoticed until much later. He walked out of the French windows and into the balmy night, to bring Hestia's remnant and his revolver into the summer house, where he would leave them for the night.

He would meet Houghton-Copley there, fully resolved not to duck the diplomatist's questions any more. He'd try and put Hestia's history into balance with him. Maybe if he were plain spoken and entirely truthful, he could provide the man with an account that, in its completeness, would remove any opportunity for further misrepresentation, and provide an epitaph without salaciousness, for her at least. He'd shoot himself afterwards. The summer house could be more easily cleaned, or burned down for that matter. He had no desire to cause Mrs Simmons or Foster any unnecessary inconvenience.

He looked up into the clear midsummer night sky and thought for a moment of Hestia, her frail beauty, the love she couldn't find within, and the peace he hoped to be able to restore to her in the morning. He stood motionless on the lawn for some time. This would be their last night together, after all, and he could afford to indulge himself a little moonlit sentimentality. Then he went back inside and made his way up to bed, leaving Foster to lock up.

~~~~~

On her way back from the bathroom, in her silver satin pyjamas and a cloud of musk and almonds, Ursula saw Clover's bedroom was still empty and dark. She adjusted the towel wrapped around her head, and checked if her friend was in her own room instead, to find she wasn't. This was unusual. Clover usually locked up while Ursula finished her bath, and then came up to her bedroom, lit her perfumed candles, slipped into her peignoir and hovered about to see what might or might not transpire. She never remained downstairs for longer than it took Ursula to complete her toilet, and Ursula had taken her time that evening. After all the mayhem and recriminations in the village hall, she could feel her skin drying out and her hair splitting, and had taken measures accordingly.

Enid's little outburst on art had, she knew, left them both unsettled. This was partly because they felt its subject was rather more in their province than hers, partly because such a passionate deviation from social protocols had shaken even their professed bohemianism, but essentially because Enid's suddenly declared emotional turmoil had stirred up related feelings in them both, on matters that were better left undisturbed.

"Clovy?" She could feel a growing tetchiness overtaking the languor from her bath. She didn't care for routine, obviously, but she didn't like to be unsettled either. Not twice in one day. Where was the girl?

There was no answer, which made things worse. One of life's certainties was that Clover would respond immediately when called, regardless of what she was doing or, indeed, who was calling her. Clover's whole nature was one of concerned response and Ursula's tetchiness dissipated into a sudden apprehension. She could feel it creeping up from her stomach and gathering itself to become full-blown alarm, and so decided on immediate action.

She took three or four tentative steps down the tiny stairway and peered over the hand-carved banister and into the main room. There was only one light on, set on the hexagonal table beside the massive fireplace, and Sir Austin Maitland's farm implements loomed distorted and sinister on the wall. It was more by the sound of her suppressed sobs, that she located Clover. Sat on the sofa, clutching some drawings in a disconcerting echo of Dr Richardson's deflation in the village hall, the girl rocked to and fro in voiceless keening. Slowly, as Ursula's eyes became used to the dimness of the light, she could see her friend's crumpled face, the tears running down her cheeks from eyes shut tight in her extremis. Occasionally her mouth would open but, apart from some half-formed groan, she forbore to let anything out and continued rocking forwards and backwards, clinging onto the drawings, almost as if protecting a baby.

Something built of their long association, and an exact understanding of the leeways and tantrums they normally granted each other in the pursuit of a reasonably happy coexistence, held her back from any dramatic intervention. She could see from Clover's relentless swaying and her inconsolable expression, that this was not time for one of their parlour games. So she walked quietly into the room, sat beside her friend, looked closely at her and in as soft a voice as possible, interrupted her silent threnody. "Clovy, angel, it's me. What is it? What can I do?"

Clover burst into sobs at this, and kept on rocking; Ursula put a hand on her shoulder, and let it ride upon her friend's wracked form. Clover whimpered and rocked and eventually hiccoughed out between sobs, "We don't get over it, do we? Ever. It's our history. Done. Forever." She focused with a sudden icy fury. "Bloody man! Bloody, bloody man!"

Ursula used this final desolate outburst to wrap an arm about her friend and slowly coax her to a stop. "He's dead," she spoke softly, but her eyes were narrowed in anger at what the great man was accomplishing from the grave. "He's bloody dead and he can't touch you now."

Clover looked down at the drawings she had crumpled to her chest and Ursula could make out they were studies of her, as a girl, with the unmistakably deft and intrusive lines of her father. Clover appeared as an altar girl, a water-nymph, a child priestess and a naked handmaiden carrying a bowl of blossoms. They were worth a fortune, no doubt, but were suffering under Clover's grip. Ursula tried to disengage them from her, to take them to a place of safety until she could regain some sense of their value, but Clover held them fast.

"Enid was right. Art isn't suitable, is it? Or nice. Art is never nice." She frowned at the sadness of this. "Art is touching, and fondling and keeping secrets and giving our bodies to the Lord. Each time, I stood in that barn I was terrified. Waiting for the next pose. The next investigation. He wrote it all down. Very scientific. All those sketches of my bottom and everywhere. And I was terrified that I'd let him down in some way, even when I did everything he asked." She stared at Ursula, and spoke with a terrible sincerity. "I did everything, Ursula, everything he told me. Even when he asked me to make things up for myself. I did that too, because he told me to." Then, she spasmed with tears, "I was a good girl. I was always a very good girl."

"You mustn't torment yourself like this, Clovy. He was a monster. You were a little girl. What chance did you have?" soothed Ursula.

"It's not just that. I could bear all that," Clover moaned out her distress again. "It's you. What he did to you. Because you're my friend, my only friend. He must have known you wouldn't tell. And yet you had to come back to that, every holiday. Back to that! I'm so ashamed I can't bear it."

Clover scrunched at the drawings in her hands, sniffing and shaking her head, searching for some respite from this seemingly endless misery, and Ursula knew, at that moment, that she couldn't go on with this any more. Not as it was. She pulled the towel off her head, finger combed her hair, took a deep breath and then took Clover's hands in hers. "He never did anything to me Clovy. Just a few sketches in my drawers. He never came near me."

Clover searched her face in complete bewilderment. "But you said…"

"No, I didn't." Now it was all coming out, Ursula felt a weight lifting off her, a relaxation, even a youthful simplicity regaining her mind. "You said. I just let you think that."

"But why?" Clover started to shake her head wildly, from side to side this time. As if to shake some sense into it. "Why would you do that?"

The outstanding questions were a block to any release, Ursula could see that. She had to give up everything. For all the transcendent liberation of the truth, the tears came anyway, and she finished her explanation in heavy sobs. "Because I had nowhere to go, and no money and not much else really. Can't paint and draw like you. Can't do the letters and the designs, or anything, and I thought you might get tired of it all and you might throw me out after...a while...and I'm so sorry, Clovy."

They snivelled side by side for a while, before Clover straightened up. "He didn't touch you? Never?"

"Never." Ursula pulled a handkerchief from her pocket which Clover absently appropriated and blew her nose heavily. Ursula wiped her own nose with her towel.

"And I've been wearing all that itchy Wicca stuff," Clover realised. "And drinking that awful stinky tea." Ursula nodded shamefacedly. "For years."

They both looked at each other, puffy-faced and dishevelled, and from somewhere in their schooldays, a snigger began, first as little snort of derision and then flowering into full-blown peal of raucous laughter. Clover stood up and dumped the drawings behind the sofa. "I'm going to have a gin!" she announced with some force.

"No!" cried Ursula, as she stood up with her. "Irish coffee!"

"With cream!" hurrahed Clover.

"We'll be up all night!" Ursula yelled happily, and she dashed off to the little kitchen to light the kettle and look out the whiskey they hid from old Mrs Jennings.

~~~~~

The Reverend Attwater sat at his desk, holding his glass of warm milk, and watched his wife talking to him. He saw her lips moving, saw her slight but somehow determined figure standing in the doorway in her nightdress, but he was finding it difficult to make out the meaning of her words. He frowned slightly in concentration and nodded repeatedly at her, as if encouraging her to continue while he struggled to understand.

She was leaving. He could not make her happy but that was not his fault, they were simply unsuited to each other by virtue of age, temperament and outlook. He felt a deal of responsibility for her happiness and tried to declare it, but she bid him to be quiet because she needed to make things quite plain to him, before she finished her packing. They had entered into a marriage that both had seen as offering some security, some comfort and a fair interchange of personal support. There was, however, a great deal more to a real marriage and he had to acknowledge that. He had married enough people. Young people in the main. He knew what the marriage contract essentially entailed. Spiritual, mental and physical union.

The Reverend Attwater suddenly felt very tired and, in his hand, he could feel his milk cooling; he wanted to sleep, perhaps for a very long time. He was quite thankful when his wife turned to leave, but then she came back again.

He must not blame himself. She was as responsible for this misalliance as he was. Although, when her father had proposed the match, it was as much out of family considerations as any affection for him personally that she had not made her misgivings felt. She had been as untrue to him as she had been to herself and she wanted to apologise to him for that. But she could no longer maintain such an inappropriate relationship. It was draining the life from her. A life she had a right to as much as any other human being. She needed to feel alive. She needed to feel she belonged somewhere and that place would never be here.

She would always remember his kindness. And then, at last, she closed the study door behind her. The Reverend Attwater stared at his milk, the skin forming on the top which he always found faintly repellent. He had two pressing problems to resolve. Firstly, where would he tell the congregation that Enid had gone? She hadn't been forthcoming with that information. And secondly, where would he sleep tonight, if she were packing away her things in the bedroom?

He would resolve the second problem by continuing to sit at his desk and possibly moving over to the armchair if his joints stiffened, as they usually did after any extended period of paperwork. The first problem he'd have to leave to Divine disposition. He hoped the Almighty made his purposes clear soon.

Chapter Twelve

West Sussex

It was shaping up for a glorious day. Dr Lambert Houghton-Copley was awake bright and early, breakfasted by eight and busy in the dean's office by five minutes past. Over the years and across the world, he had found a pre-emptive stance with bureaucracy to be an indispensable means in gaining his own ends, with the minimum amount of insistence. Interrupting a junior canon in his first cup of tea of the day, he required that all expenses incurred within cathedral grounds be forwarded to the Chancellor's office of Lambeth Palace for settlement, in due course, and that his luggage be taken to Chichester station and put upon the eight o'clock train for London that evening. He would be going straight to the station from Highleigh, and had no wish to further inconvenience the Chapter, or indeed himself, by returning to the cathedral prior to his departure.

He was inconvenienced in the matter of transport, however. Jealous eyes had been fixed on his retention of the Episcopal Rolls during his, to some minds, lengthy sojourn at Chichester, and a good deal of exasperated debate had taken place in the Close about his entitlement and his effrontery in that matter. When the diplomatist made to requisition the car one final time, for his day's activity in Highleigh, he was met by an apologetic yet firm rebuff. The car was required at midday by the dean, who was entertaining a very important personage, and had, he suggested, privy claim on his own conveyance.

Houghton-Copley had bartered in Shanghai and Manaos, and finessed in the capitals of Europe, yet he was unable to make any headway here; veiled threats and allusions to greater powers fell on deaf ears of a junior canon more terrified of his dean than the Synod and very probably the Almighty Himself. Houghton-Copley was made of sterner stuff than to acknowledge his reversal but, with both his reputation and his collection to consider, was moved to more indirect efforts. He commandeered the office telephone, called Captain Seaton's number and talked to Foster. He would be arriving at the Reverend Attwater's vicarage shortly before noon and would be in need of transportation up to Laurel House, and back to Chichester later in the day. There had been an administrative failure, here he glared at the junior canon, at the cathedral and his car was unavailable after midday. Unforgivably, it would have to return for some function immediately he had alighted. Would Foster ask the good Captain if he might oblige him? Foster was gone a moment and then returned to say he would be pleased to attend on Dr Houghton-Copley at the vicarage at noon.

The diplomatist replaced the receiver and, with an icy glance, dared the junior canon to deprive him of use of the car before midday. The junior canon's reserves of courage were quite used up and he simply nodded glumly. He would spend the morning in silent prayer that the car returned in time, and that nobody questioned him about its whereabouts.

Houghton-Copley bustled along the corridors, humming quietly to himself, running through the business of the day, and the long years of patient, in the main, investigation and research that had led up to it. A steady and persistent construction of surmises, associations, hunches, coincidences, deductions and informed conjecture, shored up by correlations, corroborations and authentication, soon to be confirmed by the Curiosity, himself. He felt a glow of quiet pride in a job well done and promised himself, this time, to take pains to savour the moment fully and immerse himself thoroughly in the intoxicatingly full-blooded experiences he was vicariously to undergo. He knew he would discard the matter soon enough, no longer a novelty, its originality tarnished by familiarity. The very fact that he knew all about it meant it was no longer a curiosity to him, merely an oddment. It was invariably the same cycle, the exhilarating rapacity of the hunt followed by disaffected torpor after the kill and then, the restless quest for fresh experience.

For the nonce, though, Captain Seaton's secret remained to be teased out. It was still tantalizing, provocative and enticing. He checked himself in the ancient and partially opaque mirror in his room, the dark blue, three-piece suit and university tie, the sizeable, antique pearl pin. Rather fine, he thought. He appreciated his formal but slightly raffish aspect, the perfect blend of confessor and boulevardier. It should bring the Captain along nicely.

He sat at the tiny escritoire he had insisted be installed in his room, for his confidential correspondence, and despatched his daily missive to his Grace. The old man liked to have a stream of correspondence from him; it gave him the impression of having eyes and ears everywhere, along with a few aperçus with which to surprise his guests at dinner. Houghton-Copley always took trouble over these missives. They contributed greatly to his intellectual and somewhat acerbic reputation within his Grace's inner circle. He brought an exciting whiff of Realpolitik to the palace, tempered by a vaunted expertise in the Classics, and his letters brought a daily reflection of how an exceptional mind was employing itself, diligently, to the Church's welfare. They were, thus, one of the chief means by which he earned his daily bread and ensured a great deal of travel, in appropriately elevated conditions, upon private enquiries pertaining to the interests of the Church Militant in general, and the Archbishop's office in particular. It pleased the diplomatist to note that, as a result of his patronage, the Archbishop was the chief sponsor of his private research projects, of which Seaton, he thought, might prove the apogee for quite some time at least.

Today, Houghton-Copley admonished some factions within the Church for ignoring the parlous state of the world economy, and insisted on a more rigorous attitude to the financial self-sufficiency of churches abroad. With incompetence, unworldliness and penury abounding, it was time for those at the centre to consolidate and sustain their interests; the future of the Church lay in it keeping a tight, centralist hold on the purse strings. The Vatican allowed for some regional independence of budgets and priorities, but the bulk of the assets remained lodged with, or mortgaged by, Rome. In order to give unto Caesar, one first had to retain something to give, and bank it correctly. He hoped a strong central discipline would be maintained, to ensure those in spiritual need could always count on the Church's true ministrations.

He sealed the letter, feeling rather proud of his restrained and simple peroration, and rang for the servant allocated to him by the cathedral. When the old man arrived, he sent him off for a half-bottle of champagne or a whole one if none was available. He had to sustain the inner man; the Church would be powerless without its vigilant policy makers.

For an hour he smoked and drank and looked idly out of his window onto the grass below, before summoning the old man again, in order to supervise the packing of his clothes and effects, and their transportation to the dean's office. Then, leaving his luggage in a pristine pile in the personal care of the junior canon, to whom he also entrusted his sealed correspondence with the Archbishop, he sauntered out towards the Episcopal Rolls, and what he knew would be a most entertaining day.

~~~~~

Enid Attwater dragged her two old leather suitcases, scuffed and jam-packed, the locks twisting in protest, down the hall and stood panting by the vicarage front door. She adjusted her hat, took her raincoat and overcoat from the coat-rack and folded them over her arm. Then, she rehearsed lifting the suitcases and managed to teeter around the hall with them, before setting them down, heavily. It was going to be touch and go getting anywhere near a bus stop, but freedom was never lightly won.

She put the raincoat on, reasoning that she was going to be boiling anyway, lugging all her stuff down to the Selsea Road, and then tied her overcoat to the smaller, just, of the two cases, with kitchen string.

There, she was ready. Before she opened the front door, she turned back and for one final time breathed in the muffled atmosphere of the vicarage. The aged wood, the steady ticking of the clock in Duncan's study. The overriding sense of emptiness and timeless disapproval. Now she was leaving, it seemed bigger than she remembered. The walls no longer encroached. It was large and musty and empty of more than just people.

She'd heard Duncan moving off to the church well before parish communion, and could hear the organ now, presumably some impromptu rehearsal with his choristers, his usual pretext for remaining out of sight. Only today, she quite valued his discretion, whatever it was born of. Mrs Gibson was equally absent. Normally Enid ran into her at all hours of the day, and had to endure the woman's silent irritation as she 'got in the way, again', but that morning she'd had the kitchen to herself and the complete run of upstairs while she finalised her packing. She was certain, though, that as she closed the front gate behind her, there'd be a twitch of a curtain somewhere as Mrs Gibson saw her off the premises.

She opened the front door and lugged the cases

through before closing it, locking it and posting her key through the letter box; whether Mrs Gibson was haunting the place or not she had to leave everything tided behind her. Then she picked up her bags again and moved out into the wide world. Now, she really would have to think on her feet, all the way down to the Selsea Road. She only hoped she wouldn't topple over with the weight of her possessions; she had tried to leave so much behind.

She left the gate open. Mrs Gibson could always close it, if she had a mind to.

Then, as she moved out onto the open road, she saw Larry Poulter adjusting the vegetable display on the tables outside his store, and a thought struck her. It was an idea for which she alone was responsible, the success of which only she would have to account for. It was her first example of thinking on her feet, and it didn't seem so bad at that. In fact, she thought it was a corker

On the way over to the shop it felt like one of her ankles might snap with the strain at any moment, or an arm pop out of its socket, but she kept up a determined and cheery smile, for her own sake as much as for the unseen Mrs Gibson's, and drew her shoulders back as much as the dead weight of the luggage would allow.

Poulter watched her coming from afar, with a kind of eerie fascination. The vicar's wife, flushed and brave-faced, was bearing down on him in full flight, carrying what appeared to be half her household contents. He would have gone to her assistance, but couldn't quite decide whether that might be demonstrating too much involvement in village affairs, and by the time he had discounted any real danger in it, she was upon him.

"You're laden down there, Mrs Attwater," he wiped his hands on his apron and shifted Enid's cases to one side of the doorway, lest they trip and injure an incoming customer.

"Mr Poulter, I wonder if I might ask you a favour."
Enid's shyness was swept aside by her inspiration, and by
the growing and uplifting realisation that she would never
again have to concern herself with the proprieties of
Highleigh society. "If you have a delivery to make today,
could you possibly deposit me by a bus stop on your way?"
She noticed a slight stiffening beneath his attentive
manner, and hastened to reassure him, "Not right now. I
can wait. All day if need be." She shared her planned
itinerary with him, if he was to be part of it, he had a right
to know. "I'm going to Chichester Station. So, I can get a
33 if you're going Wittering way, or a 32 if you're going
near the Selsea Road."

Larry Poulter smiled uncertainly and glanced back
into the back of the shop, where his wife Ruth was
replenishing stock; in truth, he was looking for instructions.
Was he to be somehow implicated in what could become a
major event in village life? Could they afford the
repercussions? He could barely make his wife out in the
shadows, and so called out tentatively, "Ruth?"

Ruth, a dark and intense woman, bustled out of the
gloom with a glass of cold lemonade, a strange light in her
eyes, and, for her, a surprising amount to say for herself.
"Here you go, dear. Far too hot to be dragging those cases
around." She handed the glass to Enid, and gave her
husband an old-fashioned look. "Bus stop indeed!
Whatever next? You'll take Mrs Attwater to Chichester
Station. You can pick up some cooking oil while you're up
there. We're short."

They weren't, and Larry Poulter knew it, but for that
moment he saw his wife in a light that was both old and
new. Old, in that he remembered the carefree girl she'd
been when he'd first joined the railways, and new because
he thought she'd forgotten all about it. He gave her a
private grin, quickly took off his apron and went looking

for the keys of his little delivery van.

"I couldn't possibly put you out!" cried Enid. This had gone further than she'd anticipated.

"Poulter likes a drive," replied Ruth, ushering Enid further into the shop. "Now you sit down and I'll cut you a little ham and some bread for the journey. Shameful what they charge on the trains nowadays."

~~~~~

Sam Faring and Foster stood in the cool stillness of the empty lounge bar at the Tun and Pipe, and looked through the ancient window. Through the yellowed swirls of the antique leaded panes, they could see Larry Poulter loading Enid and her luggage into his delivery van. Both men held a half of bitter; it was early in the drinking day. They silently toasted her departure.

"Always thought she was a good woman going to waste," said Sam.

"Not any more, by the looks of things," replied Foster, and he led them outside to their customary table, with a commanding view of the vicarage, the village hall, Poulter's store and the central machinations of Highleigh's social life.

They passed an agreeable hour, talking about the new Southdown bus services, ferrying people down to both Wittering and Selsea now, damn near every hour till mid-evening, and how they would have to adjust their business plan, to avoid direct competition with them. They deliberated over which vehicles they'd need to run a truly luxurious service, for the better class of tripper, the relative merits of shuttling and day trips, and many other thorny commercial challenges that the Faring and Foster Bus Company would have to meet when the great day came. Sam Faring toyed with the idea of day trips and mystery tours with luncheons thrown in; he suggested Foster might like to co-opt Mrs Simmons for this. Foster thought she'd rather drive the coach than cook for a load of townies out for a paddle and touch of the sun. Everything was, as ever, left pleasantly unresolved when the Episcopal Rolls pulled up outside the vicarage.

"That'll be your man, then," noted Sam, as the chauffeur went round to the rear door and opened it to allow the diplomatist to step out into the warm sunshine; the driver, perhaps mindful of the valedictory nature of this commission, taking a shade longer than was strictly necessary.

"We'll let him settle," replied Foster, picking up their two empty half pint glasses and ducking back in to the cool, dark interior of the lounge bar with them. "You've time for one more, no doubt?"

No sooner had he crossed the threshold than the pot-man took the glasses from him and went to see to their replenishment; Foster returned to his seat and he and his friend settled back to enjoy the show. They watched the diplomatist acknowledge the chauffeur's final salute with a nod that verged on outright disdain, and then walk swiftly down the vicarage path, while the Episcopal Rolls moved smoothly away, back to its official and prior engagements in Chichester.

Houghton-Copley pushed at the vicarage door but found it locked. He then rang the bell, and waited. After a while, he essayed the door knocker, at first with a peremptory single knock and then, as time progressed, with more vexed sequences. He looked about him angrily and gave an exasperated shake of the head, as if even the garden were conspiring against him in rustic noncompliance. From where Foster and Faring sat, they could see Mrs Gibson venture out of the side door, wiping her hands on a kitchen cloth, and steal up the side of the house, with a censorious expression set on her face, to peer round the corner at whoever was responsible for the

347

brouhaha.

"Probably thinks Enid's come back," said Foster, interpreting this roundabout manoeuvre.

"Damn me, you're right!" replied the farmer, recognising the truth in an instant. "Devious old baggage."

At the sight of Dr Houghton-Copley, tapping his foot in barely restrained fury and seizing the knocker again, Mrs Gibson jumped back as if she'd been stung by hornets, fled back round the house and disappeared inside. Within seconds the front door was opened, and she stood in the entrance hall, eyes downcast in a fair representation of docility and contrition, as the diplomatist berated her, before forcing his way inside. The door was closed carefully behind him.

"Not a lot for him in there," observed Sam. "He's missed Enid. And the Reverend's got the choir at it again."

"Entertain himself, easy. Man of his capabilities," said Foster, taking the glasses of beer from the pot-man's tray and handing him some change. "We'll leave him to it for a bit, shall we?"

~~~~~

Back at Laurel House, Ainsley Seaton sat on the terrace outside the gallery and sipped at his late-morning tea; Oolong in the family Spode, one of the smaller graces of life, understated, delicate and yet so rich an experience. The letters had all been written and sealed and left on the writing desk, where Foster would collect them later that afternoon, as in the normal course of events. Instructions, bequests, sincere thanks, apologies for inconveniences caused, good wishes, cancellations of subscriptions, final settlements of account, a life tidied away he hoped, leaving no impediment behind.

He looked out on the geometrically precise beds with their profusion of summer flowers; the uniform blooms in waves of gorgeous and complementary colours; the trimmed borders; the regular configurations of shrubs and rose standards; the meticulously planned sweep of lawns, bisected in subtle harmonies by the narrow, weedless paths and shaded by trees whose shape and context were preordained a century before. The garden presented nature on its best behaviour, domesticated, refined and set within a broader simulacrum, that most expansive of fictions, the English countryside, conjured from scrub and meadow in the days of Capability Brown.

He felt a profound debt of gratitude to the prospects of these gardens, though he knew them to be completely bogus. They constituted his daily protection from the riot of the deep forest, with all the voracious and secret purposes of brute generation, and the dislocating memories of devastation, mud, slime, fungus and rot amid the bedlam of the Flanders bombardments. Nature unbounded and nature perverted, the English garden denied them both.

He was in his summer gardening clothes, a pair of ageing but well-pressed cricket trousers, an open white linen shirt and his canvas shoes, having decided to meet Houghton-Copley as a man interrupted in his own home. If such informality proved beyond him at the last, there was a serviceable, striped blazer hanging in the summer house, with a silk scarf in the Artists' colours stuffed into the pocket, which he could pull on while Foster led the interloper across the lawns.

He was wandering across the lawns himself now, with an entirely different purpose in mind, holding the cardboard folder the diplomatist had given him yesterday. He made his way behind the rhododendrons that masked the larger shed and the compost heaps, enjoying the acrid warmth of the grass clippings that hung in the air. There was a brazier on the far side of the shed, old, rusted and set on flagstones and he put the folder down beside it, and unknotted its ties.

Seaton crumpled his physical studies of the Okaina women and laid them at the bottom of the battered cylinder, taking care they should not fall through the larger holes left there by earlier conflagrations. He rummaged in his trouser pockets for his matches, struck one and held it to the underside of the Okaina women with the pumpkin. In such an enclosed but ventilated place on such a warm day, the combustion was instant.

Then, one by one, he fed his encomia to the great love of his life into the fire, where they flared into flame, glowed vibrant and alive for a precious moment before fading and dimming into light ash. He had not been able to protect their intimacy from prying eyes before, but he would ensure their privacy, in death. He looks fondly down at each little sheet as it fed the flames and returned to its inspiration, leaving the barest, wavering afterglow on his retina as it transcended.

~~~~~

Houghton-Copley sent Mrs Gibson off about her business and walked through into Enid's drawing room. He noticed that a number of books were missing from the shelves and, for a moment, his heart skipped a beat. He'd slipped Seaton's journal behind her tiny library, in a moment of caprice, partly to enjoy its proximity to a young lady fumbling her way into ever deeper fictional waters and also to entertain the delicious possibility of her finding and reading it. She would remain discreet, he had no doubt of that, miserably and doggedly discreet, but she would have eaten of the Tree of Knowledge. What a marvellous loss of innocence that would have been, and in so incongruous a setting that it was almost too much to hope for. However, the small red-leather journal remained in place, its ribbon double knotted about it, exactly as he'd left it, thrust behind some volumes of Bernard Shaw. She'd never got round to Shaw, that much was clear. Probably a blessing all round.

He enjoyed a little chuckle as he weighed the journal in his hand. It was all going so well and, although he had often thought about this day, to his great delight, it was all still new to him. An experience so prefigured, was still fresh. He felt like a schoolboy on his first trip to the circus, assured of excitement, colour and spectacle. He had so constructed the situation as to be both schoolboy and ring master. Who could ask for more?

He heard the clasp of the vicarage gate clatter shut, followed by heavy steps on the gravel path outside. Pulling back the curtains, he saw Seaton's man, in his driver's jacket, making his way up to the front door. He looked across at the carriage clock on the mantel; nicely punctual, he thought, early, if anything. He had made quite the required impression on the Captain, clearly, to occasion so scrupulous an accommodation. He had the initiative now.

The man disappeared from his view and, seconds later, there was a thunderous assault on the door knocker. Mrs Gibson appeared, tremulous, from the kitchen but he waved her back in, as he walked past her, journal in hand, to open the door.

"Dr Houghton-Copley?" Foster asked, respectfully.

~~~~~

Seaton washed his hands carefully, changed his shirt which had attracted a small amount of detritus from the funerary rites, and pocketed three cartridges for his pistol from the locked metal cabinet inset into his bedroom cupboard.

Before despatching Foster to collect the churchman, he'd arranged for Mrs Simmons to lay out a cold collation in the dining room. Her waste of effort embarrassed him somewhat, but better that than causing her further distress through an early intercession. He would not be giving Houghton-Copley lunch. He would give him an

351

unabridged and frank account of his time with Hestia beside the Kahuanari, and then have Foster drive him back to Chichester directly. He would suggest Mrs Simmons went as far as the village with them, giving her some small commission at Mr Poulter's; stomach powders he thought, something he could require fresh and with an unstated imperative. He knew from experience that Foster would return to pick her up and return to Laurel House by a scenic and entertaining route. That would give him more than enough time to set his notes about the house, requesting them to call for Dr Richardson, but on no account to enter the summer house.

He had about half an hour before the man was expected, so he allowed himself a scotch and soda and then went over to the summer house, to arrange some chairs on the veranda, and load the pistol.

She was waiting for him, of course, mud-streaked and naked. Knees still drawn up under her chin, her arms clasped tightly around them. Her wide, green eyes observed him carefully from under the wild tangle of her hair, as he crossed to take up the first of the wicker chairs. As he leaned in close by, a little shudder ran through her body, causing a tension in her haunches and a flexing of her feet, before she settled back into the shadows.

"Not long, now," he assured her gently, as he carried the chair out into the sunlight. He thought he heard her sigh, although he didn't dare intrude upon her privacy with more than a glance. She seemed to him more pensive than on previous occasions. Perhaps it was the welcome finality of events to come that was softening his appreciation. "It will be alright. I shall tell him the entire truth. I shall not cheat you on that. But perhaps you would prefer not to be present once he's left."

She looked up at him in mute reproach and, for a moment, his own eyes swum with tears, not at the thought of what would follow the churchman's departure, but at the thought of what violent transformation she had already been party to.

"It's all I can do," he told her, softly. "God knows, it's all I can do."

He took out Hestia's scrap of fabric and examined it anew. It looked somehow insubstantial in the bright summer light, almost on the point of disintegration, with all the dilapidated fragility of some disputed Holy relic. Still, it was his only tangible connection to a future lost at the outset, so long ago. The drawings of her that he had just burned, evoked her better, but this was hers and of her; it embodied her on her terms, and he had to respect that.

It was all that remained to him of the moment of their separation, a moment still veiled from his conscious memory, reduced to the glittering empty waters of the Kahuanari, this fabric being presented so much after the event that, in itself, it stood for a desperate retracing of steps, a craving to remember, rather than a memory itself. To his great regret, he hadn't been able to freeze himself in time along with it. He hadn't been permitted that infinite stasis during the war, after so many supplications. He had grown older, like everybody else, to discover that ordinary life becomes plainer and plainer with every day. Patterns form. Cycles appear. Perspectives establish themselves. Everything repeats. Nothing surprises. And, along with everybody else, you are left with an uncluttered view of your own mortality, your own uninflected futility. Except, he truly couldn't be like everybody else. He was an unfinished article, and this scrap of stained, lace-fringed cambric marked the precise moment of his arrested development. He turned to hold it up to Hestia, to show her he still kept up the observances, but her corner was empty now, and soaked in shadow.

Now, his nemesis was coming to finish things off. To

help him, indirectly, become the complete item. He didn't know what possessed the man, although he felt it was something inherently distasteful, and he didn't really care. The fixated collection of mean details, the collusion of the powerful, the intrusions, deceptions and the sheer perversity of the man's obsessions were of no consequence now. The diplomatist was coming to call it a day. To bring a sense of ending. Better the truth than a Hun bayonet, he thought. At least he'd be able to make his peace with the truth.

~~~~~

Dr Richardson came out of his gate, bag in hand, just in time to see Houghton-Copley pass by in Seaton's Bentley. Mastering his surprise, he raised his hat, but the churchman seemed absorbed in some contemplation and didn't respond. This was all the same to the doctor, though he was puzzled to find the man back in the parish. He and the Captain were apparently seeing quite a lot of each other, and the doctor didn't for one moment believe the Captain would find it a diverting experience. What's more, with the Captain in his customary retiring frame of mind, coupled with the effects of the chloral, the doctor couldn't see how their meetings would afford Houghton-Copley anything in the way of entertainment either. He, for his part, had at least provided some solace to the Captain in such trying social circumstances. The chloral should see him through. Houghton-Copley would require more stringent clinical measures. He smiled to himself at this. Then, wishing the church dandy well of it and the Captain his continuing composure, he despatched the business from his mind and set off for the village and old Mrs Etheridge's swollen ankles. Mrs Etheridge was aunt to one of his surviving Indian army majors, and so was deserving of special attention, that constituency being both loyal and regular in settling its accounts.

Ainsley Seaton sat back in one of the wicker chairs, his scotch and soda depleted and replenished, and a pack of cigarettes brought over from the gallery. He permitted himself an interim glance at his pocket watch. "Not long to go now," he told Hestia, but for the moment she appeared to have gone. It was just past noon.

He had run through the familiar wartime sequence of emotions, where foreboding blended into apprehension which then displaced itself in impatience, to be superseded by an ever more sincere stoicism, underscored by steely purpose. This sequencing had been repeated and honed to perfection over years in the trenches, prior to every patrol, attack or engagement, and he found its resurgence now somehow reassuring. Then Houghton-Copley appeared abruptly on the terrace outside the gallery, accompanied by Foster who, as previously arranged with the Captain, pointed the diplomatist in the right direction and then retired inside.

Houghton-Copley smiled genially around him, and then called out across the lawn. "Well, here we are at last. And what an auspicious day."

The Captain stood up and walked out onto the lawn, shielding his eyes from the dazzling light, to call back, "I thought we might talk out here." It was a non-negotiable statement, and the churchman merely waved his assent and made towards him.

The diplomatist hurried along the path with his peculiarly precise steps, waving a small red-leather-bound book in the air. "I have here the last of your mementoes. And I'm expecting great things!"

He nodded briefly at the summer house to convey in a gesture his approval of its design, its setting, its comfort and shade, the garden chairs set out on its veranda, and the decanter of scotch with attendant soda bottle on the garden table between them. "How agreeable," he confirmed, with another smile.

Around them bees were busying themselves amongst the dahlias; finches and great tits bustled to and fro in the shrubbery. A light breeze rustled the higher branches of laurel and oak tree alike and, away over the fields, young crows were calling for food to unheeding parents.

"If you wish some kind of exposition from me, doctor, I shall require an explanation of your own peculiar interest in the matter," Seaton began as they settled into the chairs. "You cannot expect me to confide in someone whose purposes remain unknown to me." He held up a hand before the other could reply, to add the caveat, "If this is to be a frank discussion, can we dispense with any further allusions to Christian charity on your part?"

The diplomatist waved a hand in an accommodating gesture, "If you prefer it, Captain. I'm certainly not here in any Lay capacity."

Seaton poured a generous measure of whisky into Houghton-Copley's glass and, to his silent supervision, added a splash of soda. "We may confine ourselves to the truth, then?"

"I'll go first, shall I?" said Houghton-Copley brightly, to Seaton's partially disguised surprise. "I shall be as frank with you as I would wish you to be with me. The last of my Christian homilies, I assure you. I shall expose the entirety of my purpose to you directly." He sat back, sipped at his scotch and soda, found it entirely to his satisfaction and continued. "My calling is but a means to an end. It affords me the opportunities and the wherewithal for more personal, more keenly valued pursuits. For men of my education, intellect and background, some personal preoccupation is essential to counterbalance the heavy burden of public obligation. I have neither family nor country seat; I find the idea of either nauseatingly banal. The thought of breeding is simply too pedestrian." He gave Seaton a shrewd look. "I can see you have eschewed it yourself, possibly from other motivations, but you have yet to replace it, I believe, with anything other than stasis and desolation."

The Captain stiffened. If a personal testament were expected of him, he would require some measure of courteous attention, if not respect. "Your remarks are both personal and offensive."

"Yes, indeed," agreed the diplomatist, "and profoundly necessary, if we are to understand each other. I repeat, men in my position, and very possibly our position, have grander passions to contend with and to channel. Our interests are as arcane and as vital as our other engagements in life. Some men collect works of art; paintings, bronzes, porcelain. All very worthy in its way, but somewhat limited in ambition, don't you think? Such wonders are merely decorative, after all. Some become obsessive with historical artefacts. I know a peer who would do murder for Drake's drum. Others collect buildings or swathes of country, though it has always seemed an arid pleasure to me. Men like Northmore collect species, pinned to cards, displayed in cases, ever more difficult to locate and entrap and thus ever more ennobling to display. Men like you seem to collect medals, and wounds."

The Captain interrupted brusquely, "So, which particular hobby-horse is yours?"

"I collect Curiosities," replied Houghton-Copley, simply and affably. "Grand Curiosities, it goes without saying. Furthermore, Captain Seaton, I believe you to be one of the finest flowerings of the species. And so close to home! There's something subtly and delectably deviant about the South Coast. It must be the sea air, the chalk

357

and slate in the blood. Curiosities spring from the loam, you know, or are drawn to it, as by osmosis." He wagged a finger to avert some spirited interjection that Seaton had no thought of making. "Take Ned Warren and his piffling Uranians down at Lewes. Do you know him? Bostonian. Rich as Croesus and one of the pederasts of the age. Founded a colony of fellow aesthetes in Lewes House, in which he reigns in venomous and misogynous splendour, and from where he travels the continent, collecting antiquities, boys, social diseases and other objets trouvés. He once commissioned a Rodin and had the genitalia enlarged, on the golden ratio no doubt. I was quite taken with him for a while." He seemed lost in fond thought for a moment and then, "Such a marvellous specimen of refinement and decay. Quite the Curiosity, but not in your class, I fancy! His passion for the unnatural verges on the vulgar; nothing for you or me there."

Seaton began to protest at any complicity this sinister man might propose between them, but Houghton-Copley had already moved on. An avid collector's quests, chance discoveries and successful acquisitions brooked no interference. "Then there's that sanctimonious old pervert, Austin Maitland. I must admit I was very nearly diverted by him. Particularly after our entertaining tea at the Old Forge." He shook his head in admiration. "The delicious effrontery of the man. All that muscular Christianity and that oh so bruised, if equally muscular, daughter of his. Imagine, twenty years ago, I was actually posting him the alibis and protocols for his divinely inspired acts of criminal congress!"

"You cannot know that!" Seaton burst out at last. He would not permit Clover Maitland to become enmeshed in his own extremis, not by even the subtlest of associations.

"Oh, but one can suppose, can one not?" Houghton-Copley was entirely undaunted by the Captain's anger. "Most of the pleasure is in the supposition. Let us leave corroboration to policemen and other lesser beings." He thought for a moment. "You know, now I think about it, I'm sure I referenced Leda and the Swan for him. Never seen a Maitland version, though. Have you? He clearly preferred to remain Old Testament." He looked across to Seaton. "Not unlike yourself. The very stuff of Genesis, your story, isn't it? Only, you seem to have departed from Eden, tout seul."

"I will not continue with this," Seaton stood up and looked around him in some exasperation, tinged with bewilderment. The neat rows of dahlias, gorgeous in the sunlight, filled his gaze with colour. "Not like this. The things you wish me to talk of are too important to me. These are things I have lived with for years. Things that never leave me. They have changed me beyond measure. Separated me from any life I might have…" He rounded on the diplomatist, "Your intrusion into my life has been unwarranted and deeply disturbing. I have agreed to meet you, to make an end to it. A decent end. And now you reduce everything to facetious remarks about Curiosities and Genesis." He moved from the shady confines of the veranda to the chimerical freedom of the sun-drenched garden, but somehow the feeling of constraint persisted. "If you came here looking for prurient disclosures like some libidinous old …" He drew up and completed the analogy precisely, but with no great satisfaction, "I'm sure there are many private booksellers who could furnish you with that sort of material. Indeed, I would not be surprised if many of them were familiar to you!"

Houghton-Copley clapped his hands and a beam of appreciation lit up his face. He squinted into the sun towards the Captain, who now paced the lawn at the foot of the summer house veranda. "Well said, my dear chap!" he cried. "Entirely erroneous of course, but straight from the heart." He leaned over and patted Seaton's chair. "Do come back and sit down. I'm getting a headache watching you prowl up and down like that."

Seaton stepped back into the shade of the veranda but did not as yet sit down. Ludicrous though it was that this rather portly and somewhat effete man, in his ridiculously refined tailoring, should engender the primitive impulses of fight or flight, Seaton felt those atavistic urges quarrelling within. He followed the path nearest to him, that of well-bred if disdainful objection, "I shall not confide in someone for whom I am plainly some perverse form of entertainment."

"Nor would I expect you to. Good God, man, not after all you've been through." Houghton-Coley gave Seaton a look of such sudden, compassionate identification that, to his surprise, the Captain found himself taking his seat again, albeit in a state of dazed consternation, both at the diplomatist's apparent concern and his own unexpected sensitivity to it. Over the years he had suppressed all thoughts of compassion; he had no right to it, no right even to need or require it. Compassion was the just desert of others. To glimpse it now, even as a mere possibility, became a deeply disquieting experience. The availability of uninflected kindness and understanding, even from such a sullied source as the diplomatist, had upset the simulation of natural balance he had nurtured over the years. He was all at sea.

He wondered if somehow Hestia had conspired to wash away the protective layers of his self-denial, and leave him more prone to the insidious effects of other people's charity, their pity or their distressing concern. To register his need for human kindness seemed an act of betrayal, and yet his rejection of such humanity was, in some way, a dereliction of his duty towards her too. He had to feel his way carefully here, he knew, but where to?

He moved a hand out for his glass of whisky and soda. Houghton-Copley reached it first and handed it up to him, almost sacramentally. "I have given you the best and the worst of me, Captain." He spoke softly. "In the Cathedral, I told you I wanted to assuage your suffering, to free you from your own guilt and, I suspect, your self-contempt. And that is noble and Christian and true in its way. And today I have confessed to you of my appetites for the powerful and the arcane. I've confessed to the sensuous pleasure I derive through indulging my ego, as smutty Mr Freud would have it, in pursuing privy knowledge of the unthinkable." He watched Seaton struggling to digest this, and summarised rather brusquely; he had a point to make, after all. "I enjoy watching other people break through society's boundaries, Captain Seaton. Perhaps because I lack the courage or the energy myself. I am fascinated by those who will not recognise civilisation's taboos and proscriptions. That may be unhealthy to you, but it is what I am and I have confessed it to you. You know who I am. You know both sides of what I am. I have hidden nothing from you. Can you say you are any better than me? Can you not meet me now in honest disclosure?"

"You stalked me!" objected the Captain. "Hunted me down, and cornered me!"

"Agreed," replied the diplomatist hotly, "And now I wish to entrap you in a huge net of understanding and clarity. Could there be a worse fate than that?" He looked at the Captain with what was intended to seem a good-natured and affected severity, while he ran though his own performance so far. This was all going rather well, he concluded. If he pulled it off, he would have created the first father confessor self-acknowledged to be actively seeped in sin. The satyr as saint. Now, that was a Curiosity to beat the band. He might use him again.

He watched the Captain's face as the man sought to adjust his assessment of the situation, his prejudices to date, along with the bona fides of the man he had believed to be his persecutor. You can trust me because you despise me, the churchman urged silently. Because you know that, at heart, I am as enmired in sin as you are. Come on, man. Let it go.

"I will tell you what I can," replied the Captain, quietly. "Though I am not in the least interested in your opinions on the matter, whatever they may be." The diplomatist smiled patiently at this, so Seaton reiterated, "I await neither your absolution nor your censure. Nor will I discuss the matter with you. I will tell you what happened and nothing more."

"That is all I could ask for, Captain. I simply wish to know how it was. Oh, you might amplify your emotions. Describe your experience. Put flesh on the bones, so to speak." The diplomatist shrugged as if this was a matter of course, and then waved the man on, "Please, favour me with your most sensitive recollection, in the greatest detail you can recall."

"The matter is quite simple, Dr Houghton-Copley," Seaton sounded suddenly weary. His eyes scouted out some other landscape, well beyond the churchman's view. "It has none of the complications you wish to ascribe to it. I went into the deep forest. I became overwhelmed by fever and by the rapacity of the forces of nature in there. I felt out of place and out of my depth. I lost my bearings, as a soldier, as an artist, as a man. And I became perpetrator of the tragic violation of an innocent, if anybody can remain an innocent in the midst of the jungle's infernal and primordial procedures. So far from grace, and regulation."

"How on earth did it come to such a pass?" Houghton-Copley took care not to appear precipitate. He could feel the harrying hounds tugging on their leashes and yearned to give them their head. However, he steeled himself to dismantle, circumspectly, the dam on the Captain's flow of reminiscence. "Everyone is prone to jungle fever. And the most heated disorientations of spirit. It's an inevitability for expedition in those climes." He introduced her name with great care. "But this Mission girl, Hestia, how did she manage to intrude upon your purposes? And to such a remarkable extent?"

"I thought I was in love," Seaton said quietly. Daisies bobbed in the sunlight, little pinpricks of light in his swimming vision. He corrected himself. Precision and honesty were paramount here. The exequies had begun. "No, I was in love."

"Of course you were," Houghton-Copley insisted. "Nobody ever thinks they are in love."

There was something in the pained assurance of his tone that prompted Seaton to ask, in some surprise, "Were you ever in love?"

"Not directly," replied the churchman. He smiled and spread his hands in acknowledgement of this gap in his experience. "But I have some hopes of Hestia." He leaned forward with a knowing smile, "Was she pretty, amusing, gamine?"

"You've seen the drawings," replied Seaton. "I imagine you've already drawn your own conclusions." Then his face betrayed a fraction of the pain that coursed through him. "She was lovely. Luminous with life. Her smile lit us all up. Her every movement had a capricious beauty to it." He stumbled on the inadequacy of his descriptions.

"And you captured her in such detail," encouraged Houghton-Copley. "We might revisit those drawings, shall we? You have yet to tell me which ones were truly studies from life."

The Captain indicated the rhododendron bushes, still flowering at the bottom of the garden's main aspect, "I've just burned them. In a brazier. Behind the rhododendrons."

This time the diplomatist rose to his feet, flushed with anger and frustration. "But those were things of beauty! You really had no right to deprive..."

Seaton gave him a pained smile. "Oh, I can see it all quite clearly enough. I have no need to refresh my memory, I can assure you. It never leaves me."

The diplomatist sat back down heavily, but was not to be so easily mollified. "I must insist we inspect the ashes. In case something has escaped this act of wanton destruction." He felt for some uncomfortable object beneath him, and brightened as he brought up Seaton's little red-leather journal. "Still, we have this, yet."

He found his hand held in an iron grip and his eyes held by an equally unyielding stare, while the Captain removed the leather journal from the churchman's numbing fingers and tossed it inside the dark well of the summer house. Seaton's voice was cold and precise. "We will have no need of that. Simply scribbled reminders of an ugly past. If you wish my story, you must take it from me directly."

"The past is never ugly," quibbled the diplomatist as he rubbed the circulation back into his fingers "It is simply behind us. But we may dispense with the record if you wish. And if you are prepared to supplant it."

Mrs Simmons appeared on the terrace. She stood there, a silent sentinel testifying to the lunch awaiting them both. She would not approach; she simply waited till she had caught Seaton's eye, then turned and went back into the house. The Captain stood up. "Perhaps we might walk," he said.

"I'm hardly dressed for a ramble." Houghton-Copley looked dubiously at his highly polished shoes.

"Just around the rhododendron garden," suggested Seaton. He wanted to be away from the everyday comforts of Laurel House. What he was about to reflect upon, for the first time in public, was far from everyday. "The season has passed now, of course. And the display is almost over. But a couple of the azaleas don't appear to know it."

Together they walked along the path that bisected the lawn and into the labyrinth formed by the rhododendrons and azaleas, that Foster had so patiently tended over the years. There were still complimentary swathes of colour washing over their darkening leaves, where the blossoms had once burst out into miraculous profusion, but in the main the blooms were dying or dead. The petals, dry and fading into the most subtly coloured decay, formed a crisp carpet beneath their feet as the larger shrubs loomed over them. A summer breeze set some of the top leaves trembling and sent small clouds of confetti-like petals adrift in the sunlight, to fall into the shadows and the dark foliage beneath. Houghton-Copley kept pace with the Seaton, and kept his counsel; as the plants engulfed them, the Captain drew his most private past out of the darkness.

"I was not prepared for the jungle. Not with everything I had previously experienced as a soldier or with anything I surmised might befall me as an artist. Nature hems you in. Forces itself upon you. Magnificent and terrible. The trees, the wildlife, the insects. You don't have a space that is your own. Or any timescale that is human to relate to. You share everything with the forces of nature. The cycles of life and death and regeneration. My painting came alive. I came alive, in ways I could never have foreseen."

"Primal and spiritual and doomed." The diplomatist essayed a sympathetic smile, but Seaton simply pressed on.

"I caught a fever. Northmore had to move on. And I was left alone with Hestia. You can't get more alone than the middle of the Amazon, I can assure you. My life changed there and then. To be so close to such a thing of beauty. Oh, not in the classical sense, perhaps. More of a sprite than a goddess. But even amongst the untrammelled freedom of the Okaina and the riot of nature, her carefree nature transfixed me. Nobody was as free as she. Or made me feel as free as she did."

"You'll be composing Arcadian lyrics, soon," chafed Houghton-Copley. He felt the need to move on himself, and reach the finale of the Captain's and Hestia's isolation. "What happened with the crocodiles?"

"There weren't any," snapped Seaton, weary of them, and then he amended, "The caimans may have taken her at the end, but they will not be in my story."

The diplomatist gave a gesture of compliance with both hands, but stopped walking. The Captain nodded in unspoken acquiescence and went on to the heart of the matter.

"We were down by the river. By a cascade of orchids. My orchids." He interrupted himself, to credit their true provenance, "She'd found a completely new strain, which she named after me. It was a small bond between us."

"Ah!" Houghton-Copley clapped his hands lightly together. "The orchid you set between the thighs of the..."

"The orchids were beautiful, too. Enchanting. And she wanted me to be remembered for them." He breathed out heavily, the memory weighing upon him. "The Okaina were holding one of their festivals. The night was full of their drums, and their dancing and moonlight. And the smell of the orchids."

"You were there amongst the orchids, and you took

her."

"She teased me about marriage to another man. She kissed me. She told me I deserved some enchantment. I held her."

"You lifted her dress?" Houghton-Copley produced a worldly smile.

Seaton ignored this and shook his head to clear the vision away. "I held her. I kissed her. I told her I loved her. She knew that, anyway. I put my hands upon her."

"She was a beautiful child," Houghton-Copley enticed the man towards his own, private enchantment.

"She was a woman. Old enough to marry." Seaton disabused him at once, but the churchman discarded his chagrin. He was cavalier in matters of arousal. "She was older than me in many things."

They stood there for a while without speaking. The Captain in silent contemplation, and Houghton-Copley in patient anticipation. He had the hunter's instinct for pacing his approach, for giving the quarry time and space enough to deliver itself. Eventually the Captain confessed.

"I pressed myself upon her in the orchids."

"You put your hands on her?" Houghton-Copley repeated Seaton's earlier words, as if for clarification, and the Captain sighed and nodded. The diplomatist's heart soared, and he sought to press his advantage. "You diddled her first, then?"

"What?" the Captain could not quite believe what he was hearing. He returned to his embrace with Hestia which, even with its dénouement, felt somehow less shameful in its guilty actuality than in this, its exhumation.

"You pressed down on her. Thrust your hand up her skirts. Those naked young limbs, that delicious little nether mouth, you've seen it, you've drawn it, you put your hands upon it." The churchman closed his eyes for a moment, drawing up every simulation of memory that he could; it was important that no detail be overlooked. "And there it was, partially hidden, moist and salty amongst the orchids, waiting for your probing fingers, your tongue, your membrum virile." He broke off for a delighted observation, "Oh, it might very well be something of Pierre Louÿs." Then, sharper, "Did you finger her, man? Rub her off? To make her ready?"

Seaton was still beside the river, trying to summon up the physicality of Hestia's body against his, the last tangible proofs of her existence and her overwhelming attraction. Yet the precious and, oh so fleeting, contacts with the slick smoothness of her skin, the firm contours of her body, hovered just out of recall. Only a tactile intimation remained, to torment him. He brought himself back, with some regret, to try and make sense of the churchman's wretched encroachments. "Did I what?"

Houghton-Copley seemed to retain his composure with effort. He breathed out deeply, then pulled his shoulders back and spoke slowly and deliberately to the Captain, as if to a not very bright child, "Tell me what you did, exactly as you did it. Did she start easy and turn coy? Was she naturally wanton? Was she somehow experienced? Or was she completely unaware of her erotic attractions? Did she cry out in alarm? In delight?" The pace of his questioning picked up, punctuated with little stabs of a pudgy forefinger. "Did you have to force her legs apart? Did she fight you? Did you subdue her with a blow? Hold her down as you tore her clothes away? Were her breasts as you have drawn them? Was she tidy or protrusive, down there?" He snorted with exasperation. "Speak to me!"

Seaton stared, silently. He could barely make out what words the man was saying, let alone absorb their purpose or their cataclysmic impropriety. "This is no way to conduct..." he stuttered.

368

Standing tall, Houghton-Copley thrust an accusatory finger at him, and the pathways between the rhododendrons resounded with High Church incantation. "Truth can be the only way to put your burden down, Captain. How soon did you penetrate her? Was she ready? She must have been tight. Did she bleed?"

Seaton, dumbfounded, summoned up the energy to reason with the man. "I tried to make her see the sense of it, the rightness of it, the naturalness of our appetites; I tried to make love to her. I wanted to be one with her. Don't you understand?" Seaton's face contorted with misery, "I loved her. I was a new man that night. I owed her everything. I wanted to make her happy."

"So you clutched her to you and mounted her like a beast!" Houghton-Copley clenched his fists and gave a low roar of triumph, surprisingly deep and bearlike for a man of his frame. "Oh Captain, what a deliverance! Priapus reigns supreme!" He put his hand on the Captain's elbow now, eager for more, for the possibilities of further secret pleasures and perspectives. "You must tell me, can such an experience stale? Does it survive the horrors of war and the vagaries of peace? Is it a vivid daily recollection or some tarnished memento in the corner of your life?"

"My life ended at that moment," replied the Captain, disentangling himself from the diplomatist's grasp, "It never leaves me."

"But, do you never feel drawn to rekindle the intensity?" Houghton-Copley persisted. "Surely, once that rare, delicious fruit is tasted... Surely, you have been tempted? Your senses must cry out to renew the experience!"

Seaton wheeled away in disgust, but the diplomatist was still rehearsing the experience in his mind, locking in all its ramifications, "Little salty, sweat-soaked slut. Sperm-soaked in all probability, am I right? Smeared and scratched and wild with the pain and the passion of it. Have to kill her, wouldn't you? Couldn't bring a thing like that back to civilisation."

Seaton turned back so suddenly that Houghton-Copley flinched and stepped back into an azalea; a blackbird, disturbed in some purpose beneath, flew up between them, leaving in its wake a cascade of dying blossom, once mauve and now the corroded brown of old, dried blood.

The Captain looked at the diplomatist in wonder, "You have no humanity in you at all, have you?"

"Murder is acceptable, but erotic pleasure a little too strong, eh?" Houghton-Copley's patrician affront was somewhat diminished by a slight cracking in his voice.

"She's lost to you. Utterly lost. Cut off from your understanding." Seaton bent his mind to fathom this complete disconnection. It baffled him. "What are you trying to make of her, with all this?"

There was a cough from behind them. Seaton turned to find Foster, in his usual stance of the attentive pugilist. Foster ignored Houghton-Copley and addressed himself directly to the Captain, "Perhaps you better leave this to me, sir."

"Captain, are we to be private, here?" Houghton-Copley's remonstration had a wary tone to it.

Still the steward did not acknowledge him. Instead, he walked carefully along the path, before stopping and pointing at the base of a large azalea, to say, "Gentleman'd break his neck easy, if he fell heavily over them roots."

"I dare say, Foster," replied Seaton absently, "I dare say."

"Oh, come now!" protested the diplomatist, his eyes expanding yet further in his apprehension. "Am I to follow Hestia? Will you despatch two of us?"

"No trouble at all, sir," said Foster calmly, shifting his balance expertly, prior to taking hold of the churchman. "Bit of a dab hand, as you know."

"You cannot! You must not!" His voice broke as Houghton-Copley beseeched them both. "Let me alone!"

Seaton looked from his sergeant to the fearful face of the churchman. The sergeant poised to seize the diplomat; Houghton-Copley sagged against the shrub, panting like an over-exercised mastiff. After a while the Captain turned to Foster, "We won't be needing you, Foster. We're almost finished here."

"Right you are, sir," Foster paused imperceptibly. "If you're sure you can manage?"

Seaton seemed not to register Houghton-Copley's uneasy and dishevelled appearance, nor his steward's hesitant withdrawal. He simply took up his narrative again. Once more he tried, patiently, to determine precisely what had happened to him in an episode every second of which was imprinted on his mind.

"I think everything must have become too real for her. Too immediate. Too grown-up, perhaps. I don't know. I tried to explain. But it was all too real. She pushed me off. Ran from me. She went into the river. I tried to bring her to me. Not for..." He waved a hand, as if unwilling to return to physical matters already exposed at some length, "but to bring her to safety. Some secure place where I might lead her back to love me."

Houghton-Copley readjusted his necktie. He eyed Foster, who had moved back along the path during the Captain's haunted remembrances, assured himself of the sergeant's safe distance, and then returned to the Captain, under the irresistible compulsion to hear the end of the story that had so nearly killed him.

"She wouldn't come back. I went out to help her. But she wouldn't have me near her. She was fearful and angry.

None of the things I wanted for her. And then she was gone, and I couldn't find her. Not anywhere in that infernal night. With the noise and the river and the damn Okaina dancing on. She'd left us all behind." He drew himself up and looked at the diplomatist directly. "I touched her, intimately. And I tried to enter her. But the truth is, I have not been afforded even that questionable consolation. Our love, my love, is as unconsummated as it is unrequited."

Seaton looked down, and then about him. He seemed at some loss as to what to do with his hands. Finally, he returned his attention to the diplomatist. "Now, if you would care to refresh yourself, Foster will show you to our guest's bathroom, and then take you back to Chichester."

Houghton-Copley looked doubtfully at the driver, stationed, relaxed yet fully attentive, a discreet distance away. "Am I to arrive in one piece?"

"His driving is impeccable," Seaton replied, and seeing the misgivings still registering in the churchman's eyes, he added quietly, "You have my word."

Houghton-Copley gave a little starting motion, part way between a wave of the hand and a court bow, then turned and left the Captain to his deliberations amongst the moulting azaleas.

~~~~~

Foster accompanied the diplomatist into the house and entrusted him to Mrs Simmons, who with the most gracious enquiries after his wellbeing which were ably, if monosyllabically, fended by Houghton-Copley, accompanied him to a bathroom, and returned on the instant with fresh towels. While Doctor Houghton-Copley restored himself to his comforts, he confronted his face in the small mirror, and awarded himself a tired and consoling smile.

Nothing for you here, he thought, except violence and misunderstanding, the brute essentials of the countryside. Such a waste: not of his time, the hunt had had more than its share of diversions and amusements, but of opportunity. Seaton's experience had been something exceptional, he was sure of that, but he would never get close enough to be able to enjoy it with him. The man simply would permit himself any of the gratification natural to the act, let alone be willing to share it.

He dried his hands on a soft towel, smelling beguilingly of lavender, and suddenly wished for his rooms in Oxford, the solace and reliability of his books and opinions, and the more generous reminiscences of those who had stepped outside civilisation's boundaries, and were prepared to tell the tale.

He noticed with relief, and a touch of pride, that his hands had stopped shaking. He could congratulate himself too on the creation of the satyr-cum-saint. He would certainly seek further employment for him, if circumstances permitted, which he rather thought they would.

He looked out of the window and down onto the delightful garden. He would find the Simmons woman and have her pour him a substantial brandy. Then he would wait for the chauffeur in the vestibule. He saw Captain Seaton step out from the rhododendron garden and walk purposefully back over to the summer house. He hoped the Captain would stay there; he felt no need to speak to him again before his departure.

~~~~~

Seaton entered the summer house and crossed rapidly to the pile of picnic rugs in the corner, under which he had secreted his Service revolver. He needed to feel the cold weight of it. Where Houghton-Copley had raised up a fug of innuendo and uncharted moral confusion, he could impose, upon himself at least, a final

373

clarity.

He stretched further under the rugs, sawing his hand this way and that. Then he stood back up with a terrible presentiment and hurled the pile across the room. The pistol was gone.

"Mrs Simmons has it now, sir," said Foster, standing in the summer house doorway. He picked up the picnic rugs and started to fold them back into some sort of order. "Though you be doing us both a service, if you didn't require its return for the moment."

"Popping up all over the place today, aren't you, Sergeant?" Seaton observed drily as he straightened up, and stood back to let the man work. "Am I to have no peace in my own home?"

"Decided I'd hold myself available, sir." replied Foster. "I thought it might be on the side of a challenging day. And that you might be in need of a little extra attention."

Foster began to restack the garden chairs at the far side of the room. Hestia had made no reappearance and Foster's presence in her accustomed corner seemed to bring some of the daylight with it. Seaton watched the calm, matter-of-fact way that the steward occupied himself, the careful manner in which he avoided eye contact and kept his physical presence as unobtrusive as possible. Yet, the Captain could feel that the man was operating under great strain. God knows, he had seen this profession of indomitable assurance often enough, in the middle of terrible and calamitous events, and had often survived them thanks to the man's selfless control. Now, however, the Sergeant had been brought to this same extremis through no engagement or volition of his own. Foster had more than earned the right to his confidence, even a partial one.

Without knowing quite how he would resolve it, he

began. "This must all seem very peculiar to you, Sergeant. And I think perhaps I owe you an explanation."

His sergeant interrupted him immediately "Don't reckon many secrets withstand more than a few hours of a Hun barrage, sir. Hear all sorts, don't you? Men screaming for their mothers, their wives, lovers. For dogs, even. For God, and all. Making their final amends. Their goodbyes and their sorrys. Confessing their sins. Giving up where they wandered from the path. All kinds of paths, at that. Lot of desperate misery there is, under a bombardment. And it all has to go somewhere. Up in the air is favourite, to my way of thinking."

"We went through a lot of those," said Seaton, reading slowly and with increasing understanding between Foster's carefully lettered lines. He would be following the man's lead in all this; he owed him that, too.

"Yelled along with the best of them," smiled Foster, as he stepped back from the neatly stacked chairs. "Well, you do, sir, don't you? When you're being shook to pieces and the earth won't swallow you up, who wouldn't?" He frowned, and then picked his way forward again, an old trench raider looking to bring them both safely home, "Thing is, when it's all done and dusted, I reckon the least said, the better."

With the summer house interior restored to some order, Seaton could see his little red-leather journal was now lying on top of a chair stack, where Foster had chosen to leave it. He went across and picked it up, wiping the dust from its covers. It was a replica of a reality he could no longer fully recall. "Some things aren't that easily left behind, perhaps," he suggested.

Foster looked hard at him, "Begging your pardon, sir, that's not right. The way I see it, anybody who's been through the horrors we've been through…well, we've all suffered enough."

375

There was a moment of quiet between them; a moment in which a compact was offered. Too much suffering had gone into the construction of history, and too much pain was involved in ensuring it overshadowed each waking day. It was time for the present, such as it was, to take precedence. Seaton nodded. "You'd better convey His Highness back to the stews of Chichester," he said. "And ask Mrs Simmons to put a plate together with whatever can be salvaged from lunch for me, will you?"

"On my way, sir," and Foster. As he walked back across the lawn towards the terrace, Seaton thought he could hear him whistling; quietly, aimlessly even, but nonetheless Foster was whistling.

~~~~~

Twenty or so minutes later, Doctor Houghton-Copley sat in the back seat of Seaton's Bentley, hands folded in his lap, and stared listlessly out at the hedgerows rushing past, with their sporadic tangles of flesh-bloomed dogwood flowers, and colourful outcrops of foxgloves and red flowering nettles. Occasionally a song thrush would go up, disturbed in its worm hunt, as Foster guided the motorcar swiftly and surely through the country lanes, up across to the Wittering Road, from whence he'd drive them into Chichester. Not more than two hours previously, Enid Attwater had taken this road, chauffeured in her turn by Larry Poulter, and in an altogether different frame of mind.

Foster surveyed the diplomatist in his rear-view mirror; the man seemed tranquil enough. Foster assumed this cool resilience was the prerogative of the diplomatic corps, which he fancied was something like the officer class, only with more dissembling.

"I've been with the Captain a long time, sir," Foster began, "Long enough to know he's an honourable gentleman."

"Yes, yes," Houghton-Copley breathed heavily, "A prince amongst men, no doubt."

"Someone like me, though, sir," Foster continued carefully, "has nothing much to lose, really. Oh, I was glad to get out of Flanders alive, I will say. And I take some pleasures in life. But it's the Captain who's been responsible for all of that, largely. And I wouldn't miss nary a one, if I thought it would be to his better advantage. I wouldn't hesitate, sir, if you take my meaning."

Houghton-Copley sat upright and adjusted the set of his jacket fussily, "I have many vices, Foster. But petty vindictiveness is not one of them. Your threats are entirely unnecessary."

Foster smiled politely into the mirror. "Better safe than sorry, sir, eh?"

~~~~~

He'd taken his journal out to the summer house, as the dusk closed around him, lit a garden lantern and sat back down on the veranda. His fingers were trembling as he untied the double bow, another of Houghton-Copley's affectations, no doubt, and unwound the doubled up ribbon, but he pressed on in quiet determination. He needed to see what he recognised, confront what he recoiled from and try to piece together what he had been, and what had happened to the man he had lost.

What began as formal, stilted notes slowly unravelled into exclamations, harsh observations, infinitesimal doodles or graphic reductions of reproduction in all its forms. Even these erratic attempts at comprehension and record descended into a pained screed of terrifying need. Love, savagery and beauty possessed him; he visited them from every angle, and finally discovered their fusion in Hestia. She was blonde and darkling, green-eyed and a child of the forest. She matched his own oscillation, and belonged with him like no other. He extolled her in intimate detail; he rehearsed their sexual explosions; he debated every possible combination of experience and every orgasmic outcome. He abandoned words and took to strident diagrams, hacking into the pages in his hunger. He shrieked with anger at the delay in their consummation. Nature would not be mocked, it would despoil.

He moaned aloud. This was madness. Unconstrained need, contrived in some distorted human form. Who on earth had he been, what had he become and how ever had he come to that? He stared at the marks his predecessor had made; he could make them out but he could never comprehend them.

He sat quite still, with the innermost torments of another man in his hands. He knew from all the years he had housed the poor creature, whose anguish scrambled across these pages, that he could not outrun what he had done. The past led in judgement to the present and so predetermined the future. There was no variance to this, no room for accident, bewilderment, reversal; nothing escaped the recrimination of continuity. Yet, he wondered whether a man might not be defined by his present actions, rather than by what had gone before. Did he truly have to stay with a man he couldn't abide?

He heard a sigh and a shuffle behind him in the dark, and knew she'd returned. He peered back into the darkness within the summer house, found her crouching in her corner and stared deep into the wide green eyes that threw their question deep into his heart.

"I wasn't that man, then," he told her and, at last, he believed it. "And I am not that man now."

The moths buffeted the garden lantern and something scampered through the shrubbery at the foot of the garden. Hestia breathed slowly and easily, watching and waiting as the night acted out its dramas and necessities around them.

"If, in all honesty, we cannot recognise our past," he asked her, softly, "don't we have the right to leave that past behind?"

She released an arm from around her knees, to pull an errant strand of hair from across her face, and then she faded away.

Epilogue

West Sussex

"All things bright and beautiful,
All creatures great and small,
All things wise and wonderful,
The Lord God made them all."

The Reverend Attwater's congregation sung out lustily; this one was a firm favourite. The church was full again, another packed out Sunday Holy Communion, though on this occasion, his sermon would be one skimmed together from old notes. It wouldn't matter, however; the parish was in attendance to show its communality, not its intellectual capabilities.

"Each little flower that opens,
Each little bird that sings,
He made their glowing colours,
He made their tiny wings."

Reverend Attwater, hands clasped in front of him, surveyed his flock with an air of general abstraction. He looked more puzzled than woebegone, as some might have expected, and he was, incontestably, very well turned out. This was due, in the main, to his vestments being regularly laundered and pressed by various leading committee members; Mrs Gibson's muted objections notwithstanding.

Mrs Attwater's absence was less remarked upon than Dr Richardson's now customary Sunday appearances, at his wife's side. Following their much reported exchange in the village hall, they had withdrawn somewhat from village life and, it seemed, had been thrown more upon their own resources. He carried her hymnal and sat impassively by

380

her, while she, veiled and gloved, fixed her eyes on some point in the middle distance directly ahead of her. She would nod to polite enquiry, but otherwise kept her peace. Some of the uninformed wondered what she had done to drag her heathen husband back to Sunday observance, but the village, for the most part, left them to their own sheltered devices. Dr Richardson's practice was opening up to more and more of them, and they did not wish to cause any needless injury or offence.

> *"The purple-headed mountain,*
> *The river running by,*
> *The sunset, and the morning*
> *That brightens up the sky."*

Whatever had prevailed on Dr Richardson, had failed with Captain Seaton's steward Foster, who maintained his habitual picket in the Bentley, parked beside the Tun and Pipe, a newspaper on his lap as he fretted at the crossword. Mrs Simmons was in her usual place, however, side by side with her good friend, Mrs Peters, both ladies meticulously turned out and a charming sight as they shared a hymnal.

Captain Seaton stood in place across the aisle from them, with Clover and Ursula in the pew behind him. The two young women were singing along with schoolgirl enthusiasm, rather than religious conviction, but the Captain kept a steady head and his eyes upon the vicar, who appeared to be searching, though without urgency, for something or somebody amongst them. Seaton had reclaimed a light cream, linen suit from some lavender packed recess in his wardrobe, which, with his Hussars' tie and rose-gold cufflinks, gave him an elegant and somewhat aristocratic air. He had politely resisted a lunch invitation from Clover, but was going to entertain Dr Richardson later. The doctor had taken to long afternoon walks on

Sunday, and would drop in to Laurel House on his way home, for a game of billiards and a glass of something equally restorative.

There was a sudden and astonishing effusion of light somewhere up to Seaton's right, and he looked up quickly towards one of the church's modest but vibrant stained-glass windows. The sun had set it alight, and its classic biblical hues cast themselves down upon him and those singing around him, drenching them in refracted colour. He steeled himself for some vertiginous development but, as so much more often now, nothing further occurred. The orchids, bromeliads and philodendrons remained in their place in the plans chest in his gallery, a muted record of what was truly past.

> *"All things bright and beautiful,*
> *All creatures great and small,*
> *All things wise and wonderful:*
> *The Lord God made them all."*

All around them, Highleigh was in high summer. Under a cloudless sky of dazzling blue, honeysuckle was blooming in the hedges, alongside the shepherd's rose, and thriving fragrantly on cottage walls. The elders were in full fig and hawthorns blossomed amongst the roadside profusion of foxgloves. Bugle covered the woodland floors in misty blue swathes, while the yellow pimpernel pinpricked their shadiest corners and poppies bobbed radiantly amongst the hayfields

The swifts darted and soared, the earthworms burrowed below, and the caterpillars worked diligently everywhere they might, under the industrious attention of blue tits and finches, who had new families to feed. Foraging bumble bees crested the thermals, and stoats, hunting in families, trained their young to pull down baby rabbits. Brooking neither variation nor interruption, the course of nature moved immutably on.

Author's Note

I have long been fascinated by the strains and dislocations experienced by explorers, artists, pioneers and other compulsives who have crossed the line of accepted behaviour and moved off into unknown territory. Whether driven by adrenalin, ambition, addiction or evasion, they seem to confront the same essential human conundrum.

Once you've truly crossed the line, you place yourself in an unprecedented perspective that must change both you and the world you believe you have left behind. It is difficult and often impossible to come back with any consistent sense of self and place.

To palliate this displacement, the explorer, artist, pioneer or compulsive has to press on ever deeper into uncharted and often hostile territory. This blind affirmation of purpose can only be illusory, of course, and is full of danger. Suddenly discovering yourself so very far from home with only your transitory 'self' to refer to, can lead you to act in ways you would never have seen yourself countenancing before.

This too has to be accommodated or normalised. It keeps doubt and disorientation at bay and often seems the only way to sustain any sense of identity and the possibility of a safe final destination.

This cycle of dislocation, denial and dysfunction took me to the London Library.

I was looking for adventure in 'Topography' when I came upon *The North-west Amazons - Notes of some months spent amongst Cannibal Tribes* by Thomas Whiffen: Constable and Company, 1915. I sat in the reading room, perusing the contents, the plates and some highly charged tribal vocabularies in the appendices, and was at once transported.

A few weeks later, Ainsley Seaton appeared in his

gallery in Highleigh, West Sussex, with grave matters on his mind.

From then on it was as much an expedition as an act of fiction. I set off with John Hemming's magisterial and comprehensive *Tree of Rivers. The Story of the Amazon*, Thames & Hudson, 2008, and Gordon MaCreagh's honest and often absurdist account of his 1923 Amazon expedition *White Waters and Black*, University of Chicago, 2001. I read about Baptist missionaries, Victorian botanists and Edwardian intelligencers, all braving hazards beyond the terrain. I read about trench raiding and the relentless horrors of the Western Front, talked to friends in the Artists Rifles and read Barry Gregory's *A History of The Artists Rifles* 1859 - 1947, Pen and Sword, 2006. I read Fiona Macarthy's superlative biography *Eric Gill*, Faber and Faber, 1989.

I read widely and often off the beaten track, discovering much of the dark processes of empires and their offices, the labyrinthine realpolitik of religious institutions, with equally global ambitions, and the shadowy motivations behind seemingly homespun pioneers in arts and crafts. And all this through investigating the quest for personal redemption for those who have gone too far out to return safely.

I found so many willing guides and experienced explorers along the way. I'm indebted to Douglas. J. Hill, regimental historian to the 14th Hussars who amplified their campaign in the Boer War for me, and to Alan Lambert, a private authority on public vehicles and bus routes in West Sussex throughout the period of Seaton's later life there, and who even accommodated me with the timetables and stations visited of trains from Chichester to London in 1925. Tabitha Cadbury, Valeria Biffi and the Cambridge Museum of Archaeology and Anthropology were equally generous with time and expertise.

I was blessed with the finest of fellow expedition members; the late and exemplary Gillon Aitken who agreed to represent me and novelist Andrew Barrow who introduced us. Both were staunch and active supporters of Seaton from the first, reading chapter by chapter as produced. I owe them and Andrew Kidd, my editor, a debt of gratitude that cannot be repaid. Along with the anonymous reader at Penguin Viking whose detailed and glowing report gave me the persistence of a deep forest man trying to cut his way back to the river, space and daylight.

Thanks too, to Stuart Leasor for steering Seaton's Orchid into publication and Graham Wood for his gifted design. Both are old friends whose expertise finally brought this venture into home port.

About the Author

Chips Hardy was born in West London and educated at Latymer Upper and Downing College, Cambridge. He has written successfully for television, theatre, film and publication, alongside a career as a Global Creative Director. Paradox, dysfunction and the quest for redemption are ever-present themes in his work, culminating in the award-winning hit BBC1 and FX drama series "Taboo", which he co-created, wrote and produced with his son, Tom Hardy.

Taboo went on to earn him the Writers Guild of Great Britain award for best long form TV drama. Work with comedian Dave Allen won him a British Comedy Award. His darkly comic play on disability and dislocation – Blue On Blue – has been revived to support disabled ex-service personnel. An earlier novel, "Each Day A Small Victory", plotting the unyielding quest for survival amongst the wildlife inhabitants of an English country lay-by, was published in English and Polish.

An inveterate traveller, Hardy has survived machetes in Guadalupe, bombs in Gaza, local hospitality up the Orinoco and all manner of dangerous social transactions across four continents.

He lives in Richmond-On-Thames with his wife, Ann.

Also by Chips Hardy

TABOO

A TV Drama series in 8 episodes
BBC1 and FX (2016)
TABOO follows James Keziah Delaney's return to London from Africa in 1814. When his father's legacy leaves James a poisoned chalice, with enemies lurking in every dark corner, he navigates increasingly complex territories to avoid his own death sentence. Encircled by conspiracy, murder, and betrayal, a dark family mystery unfolds in a combustible tale of love and treachery.

Dark, brooding and consistently brilliant.
The Observer

Taboo is a work of Wicker Man genius. Taboo might be full of grime and torment but it's also dry-witted, shot through with sharp and knowing one-liners.
The Guardian

The best thing on television…Taboo has a strong plot at its dark heart. You want to know what will happen next, which is refreshing.
The Sunday Times

A swaggering brute of a costume drama.
Daily Telegraph

One of the most extraordinary, subversive, dramas British television has ever produced.
Daily Mail

Taboo takes the grim and distant world of 19th century London to extremes of darkness and wonder…. If Charles

Dickens had been a TV scriptwriter, then he might have come up with something like this.
Daily Express

Dark, compelling and often haunting... one of the more unique and thoughtful offerings of the new year.
Los Angeles Times

If you like your historical fiction grim and your cobblestones dirt-caked, if you don't mind looking into some of humanity's bleaker facets, this one's for you.
Boston Globe

It is filled with darkness, danger and mystery, and has a level of quality and import not often seen in television miniseries.
San Francisco Chronicle

There's an almost hallucinatory strangeness to Taboo. It's a heady brew of gothic melodrama, revenge western and Greek tragedy which both nods to the colonial corruption of Joseph Conrad's Heart of Darkness and appears to answer the question: what would happen if you combined the works of H Rider Haggard, Charles Dickens and Lord Byron, threw in a bit of commerce and some philosophy, and gave the whole thing a 21st-century twist?
The I

This is what TV is supposed to be, a visceral experience that leaves you desperate for the next episode. Taboo has been one of the finest dramas on British Television in decades.
The London Economic

Dark, dirty brute offers compelling drama.
The Australian

"Taboo" is a period drama that relishes its cutting and incendiary dialogue as much as the crudest details. Taboo" is a delicious tale of retribution ….an addictive, slow-burn story, and a damn entertaining journey.
Indiewire

This is prestige television covered in grime and soot... Taboo is less about sprinting to the next fight scene, plot twist or mysterious nudge, and more invested in luxuriating in disgusting, filthy beauty.
Nerdist

BLUE ON BLUE

A three act play on dysfunction and disability.
501 Latchmere Theatre 2007
Tristan Bates Theatre, Covent Garden 2016

Moss, a middle-aged, ex-professional soldier, was badly wounded in a friendly fire incident in the last Gulf War. He's lost both legs. Carver, his highly strung nephew, is a failed burglar on probation has been badly wounded by other matters. Carver shares Moss's Council flat in London where they maintain an intricate and dysfunctional intimacy. When MARTA, a young and lively welfare home help arrives, her caring upsets this delicate balance and things spiral way out of control.

A visceral, poignant and darkly funny play…this witty and moving drama examines the subtleties and vagaries of self-harm and co-dependency. It tackles important questions that are all too easily shied away from.
Broadway World

The play is fundamentally about mental health in a domestic drama setting, but happens to have a character who's a double amputee and wheelchair user. It's not about Moss 'disability, but his relationship with his nephew Carver, who is struggling to build a normal life as a self harmer with OCD. This little, well-made play with great performances is the sort of theatre that truly works towards championing diversity.
The play's the thing

A tightly written, fast-paced play, metaphorically illustrating the much wider issue of the treatment and perception of mental and physical disabilities.
A Younger Theatre

In the heart of London's theatre vortex, the Tristan Bates Theatre is the ideal home for Chips Hardy's painful and witty dark comedy Blue on Blue. This production magnifies the difficulties that can arise when an outsider with good intentions ignites a volatile situation. Looking at the battles of daily human experience this fast paced, smart-mouthed script has been exquisitely produced to create an unforgettable piece of theatre.
Everything Theatre

EACH DAY A SMALL VICTORY
With Illustrations by Oscar Grillo
Can of Worms Press, 2007

Each Day a Small Victory contains dateline dispatches from what to passing motorists is a lay-by on an English country road but to the indigenous inhabitants is more like a war zone. It records life as it is survived, with all the drama, beleaguered optimism, muttered jokes and clenched terror that inform the survival and otherwise of its wide cast of characters. Most of them looking over their shoulders. All of them on borrowed time. It's a struggle constructed of hope, chaos, violence and all kinds of surprises. Some of them pleasant. Most of them lethal.

'Pulp Fiction meets Wind in the Willows'
Jake Arnott, author of The Long Firm

'The memorable feat of a quirky and engaging imagination.'
Sir Roy Strong

Hardy has created hard-edged drama and raucous comedy by dealing with animals as they really are: naked and feral, consumed by an unending struggle for survival.
Suzanne Munshower, The Guardian

'Highly original and beautifully written ... Each Day A Small Victory is not just a rich, sensuous, deeply humorous animal story - it is also a brilliant celebration of life, death and the whole damn thing.'
Andrew Barrow, Country Life Magazine

The anti-hero of the book, Max, is a stoat whose only aim in life is to find his next meal, while avoiding becoming someone else's. In that sense, it's the most honest animal story I've ever come across, and it's a great read. Chips clearly knows his countryside very well indeed - there is plenty of detail about the various animal characters and their habits.

Sporting Shooter Magazine

Printed in Great Britain
by Amazon